JUNGLE STREET

Danny Flaherty's family moves to a new neighborhood, so he's out of the Shining Sinners, and looking to get in with the Golden Dragons. Getting into a new gang means an initiation, and Danny's ready for whatever they've got in mind. Mike Reilly, the Prez of the Dragons, first asks Danny to infiltrate a neighboring gang. Easy. Then he's asked to participate in a robbery. Not so easy. He has to hit the owner on the head with a bottle, and now the guy's in a coma. Could be worse. But the final initiation is the tricky one—Danny's got to make it with three Dragon debs in front of the whole gang. And that's how he meets Lisa, Reilly's girl. It's all been kicks up till now. But Danny has big plans, and nobody is going to stop him from taking what he wants.

RUNNING WITH THE BARONS

Marty Capuano might be short but he was a big man in his Lower East Side gang. Now his family is living in Jenkinsville, Ohio, and he feels like he's been banished to Nowheresville. So he goes looking for a new gang and finds the Dragons. Marty is the best there is with a blade, and he makes pretty short work of the Dragon's pres. Now he's sitting on top again, with the former pres's deb, Jojo, and the fear and respect of the whole gang. But this is only the beginning. There's a snooty chick named Jill who snubbed him when he first hit town, and she's got to be brought down a notch … and there's the bartender who wouldn't serve him a beer … Marty still has a lot of folks to get even with, and he's only just started.

Jungle Street

Running with the Barons

ROBERT SILVERBERG

Stark House Press • Eureka California

JUNGLE STREET / RUNNING WITH THE BARONS

Published by Stark House Press
1315 H Street
Eureka, CA 95501, USA
griffinskye3@sbcglobal.net
www.starkhousepress.com

ISBN: 979-8-88601-083-1

Cover design by Jeff Vorzimmer, ¡caliente!design, Austin, Texas
Text design by Mark Shepard, shepgraphics.com
Proofreading by Bill Kelly
Cover art by James Meese

PUBLISHER'S NOTE
This is a work of fiction. Names, characters, places and incidents are
either the products of the author's imagination or used fictionally, and
any resemblance to actual persons, living or dead, events or locales, is
entirely coincidental.

First Stark House Press Edition: May 2024

INTRODUCTION

Street gangs have been with us at least since the early nineteenth century, but the genre of street-gang fiction reached its acme in the middle 1950s, with the advent of MANHUNT magazine, which featured kid-gang stories in nearly every issue. and of Evan Hunter's novel THE BLACKBOARD JUNGLE of 1954 (movie version, 1955), which brought street gangs into the main stream of American popular fiction. It became a stylized art form with its own lingo, its own narrative tropes, its own typical characters.

I am anything but a kid-gang warrior myself, but as a professional writer in that era I could easily adapt to any sort of fictional genre, and writing about gangs was no more difficult for me than it was, as a science-fiction writer, to produce stories about alien intelligences or malevolent robots. Although I never wrote for MANHUNT, I was a prolific contributor to several of its competitors, magazines like TRAPPED, GUILTY, SUSPECT, and WEB, filling their pages with grim tales of the brutal lives of young inner-city hoodlums. When I began writing paperback novels of crime and erotic action later in the 1950s, I used many of my kid-gang stories as the nucleus for longer work. JUNGLE STREET and RUNNING WITH THE BARONS are two of those, returning to print now after more than sixty years.

—Robert Silverberg
June, 2023

Jungle Street

ROBERT SILVERBERG

CHAPTER ONE

I walked down the streets, just getting the feel of the neighborhood, getting to know how it looked and smelled. It didn't take me long to find out that this was a hell of a lot like the neighborhood I had just moved out of, except that this was Golden Dragon turf down here and I had been living in Shining Sinner turf. Otherwise everything was the same, just that now I was a hundred blocks further south from where I had lived before.

Over on the left side of the avenue was the housing project—dozens of tall reddish buildings, each of them fifteen or twenty stories high, all alike. We couldn't get into the housing project where we lived uptown, because my old man made too much dough. You couldn't get an apartment in that project if you made more than $5000, and he was pulling down $5350.

That was a screw. The government always screws you. They build these houses for us, and then for three hundred fifty lousy bucks we had to go on living in a pigsty on Columbus Avenue until he could get to the top of the list waiting for an apartment down here.

We had three rooms up there. For five of us. One room was the kitchen, and one room was my folks' bedroom. The third room was around the size of a closet, and I had to live in it with my kid brother and my kid sister. My kid brother, he's almost twelve, and he's a brat. My sister, she's no kid, really, she's a year and a half younger than I am, which makes her fifteen when you figure that I'm sixteen and a half. My parents kept shaking their heads because my sis and I had to share a room. She's always been well developed for her age. I used to try to give her some privacy, but I couldn't help seeing her getting dressed and undressed all the time. She has big round, knockers, pink and close together. And a cute little fanny with dimples in it. They say it ain't right for a guy to be interested in his own sister, and I guess it isn't. But some of those nights when Sis waved her fanny around our room, it was all I could do to keep from crawling into bed with her and taking a ride.

Well, I didn't. It wouldn't be right or something. Sis slept in the same bed with my kid brother Ray, and I slept by myself. But Ray was growing up fast himself. He and Sis couldn't go on sleeping together or there'd be trouble. So there was talk in the family of putting Ray in my bed and putting me on a cot in the kitchen. Man, I didn't go for that idea. So I was glad when we got the letter telling us we could move to the housing project downtown.

Of course, that meant I had to pull out of my gang, the Shining

Sinners. It meant breaking up with my deb Flora. That hurt. Flora was okay. She was tall, as tall as I am, which means five feet seven and a half. And she really filled out her sweater. Like I mean, she had a pair you couldn't get your hands all the way around. But she wasn't a cow. Her boobs were firm and tight, and when she was naked they stood up by themselves instead of dangling and dropping the way some girls' do when they're that size

I remember my last night with Flora. I hadn't broken the news to her yet. We were in Central Park that night, up in the thick woods south of Lenox Avenue, where at night you can sit on a blanket and do whatever you want and never get seen by anybody. We had a couple of cans of beer and the blanket, and we were stretched out in the dark. The moon was out, but the trees above us kept more than just a trickle of light from coming down on us. It was a hot summer night, maybe eighty-five degrees.

Tomorrow morning I was leaving for the new housing project. So this was the night I had to let Flora know. I figured I'd save it for the end, so it wouldn't louse up our evening. We drank our beer and then we stretched out and necked for a while, and I unzipped her jeans and got my hand inside, on her thighs. She wasn't wearing any panties, and the skin was cool and smooth at first, though it soon got warm. She turned around to face me, and we kissed, my tongue going deep into her mouth, and her hands doing exciting things to me.

We stayed like that for a long while. Then I used my free hand to unbutton her blouse and get her bra unhooked. The cups dropped off, and I got my hand on the merchandise. Flora had some pair! Big tight boobs that you loved to squeeze. I was squeezing them now, and her nipples were getting stiff and beginning to stand up like little soldiers. She was panting and rubbing her legs together, crossing them to imprison my other hand, and then I was getting the fever too, and I let go of her and got the clothes all off her, tossing them in a heap. Her body was very white in the moonlight, except for the reddish-brown tips of her breasts and the dark triangle where her legs joined her body. I flopped down on top of her and she wriggled her hips and I was inside, and she was moving and so was I, ever so slow at first then picking up the speed until we were going at it like wildcats, really pounding away, and she was making little noises and scratching at my back and I was way up there, until all of a sudden she started to move five times as fast as before and I held tight to her and felt the thrill as we made it together, real good.

And then I started thinking right away, what a lousy shaft it was to have to give all this up. But I had to. I told myself I'd find another piece as good as Flora soon enough. I just had to get myself established in the Golden Dragons down in my new territory, and then I'd pick out a woman and everything would be okay.

We got our clothes on again, just in case somebody came along and wanted to make trouble, and we were lying there puffing on butts. I was leaning up against a tree and Flora was stretched out with her head on my chest, and I had my hand in her blouse playing with her stiff little nipples, and as I stretched my hand over one entire big breast I decided that the time had come to give her the bad news.

I said, "We've had it, kid."

"I don't dig you, Danny."

"I mean to say we just blew the last chorus."

"You giving me the dump, Danny? Ain't I good enough for you, man?"

"You're plenty good. But I've got to cut out. We're moving tomorrow."

"Moving?"

"My old man got us a place in a housing project all the way downtown. Down in the Golden Dragon turf."

"And you're gonna go with them?"

"I got to, Flora. Hell, I can't stay here. I can't live in Central Park."

She was silent for a long time, I guess getting used to the idea that everything was finished between us. She didn't try to argue any more. After maybe five minutes, she turned around and said, "We better make this last night a good one, huh, Danny?"

"Yeah," I said.

We did. She began to touch me, and we went at it again, and it was better this time than the first. Then we rested for an hour or so, and did it again. Man, was that ever a sweet night! We sure finished things up the right way. I took Flora back to her place, and we stood in the hallway kissing, and I felt her up a little, taking one last good squeeze of her boobs, and then we said goodbye and I went back to Columbus Avenue for my last night in the old dump. I felt kind of let down, now that I was leaving the old turf. You get used to a place, no matter how much it stinks, no matter how much you hate it.

It was half past eleven when I came in. My folks, they were asleep, and everything was packed and the house looked empty. I went into my room. Sis and Ray were asleep. It was such a hot night that they had thrown the cover off and both of them were just wearing underpants. If my Ma had known, she'd have whipped them, because we were supposed to wear pajamas all the time so we'd be decent. I stood there, looking at them asleep, Ray curled up in a little ball and Sis next to him, lying on her side with her breasts going up and down with each breath. Tomorrow night, I told myself, I'd have a bedroom all my own, practically. Just Ray in it with me. And Sis would have her room, too. She could sleep naked if she liked, and no sweat.

A hell of a good-looking kid, my sister. The last couple of years she was like a stranger to me, though. I didn't know much about her, and she didn't talk much to me. Or mix with my gang friends. I didn't even know whether she'd ever been laid or not. Of course, she was fifteen, and in our neighborhood it's a safe bet to figure that no girl gets to that age without being laid. But I kept seeing her as my kid sister with the runny nose, and I couldn't imagine her in bed with a guy. For all I knew, one of my pals had been banging her for years, but I couldn't guess anybody likely. A damn good-looking girl, she was. I took another look at the big round globes of her breasts. Almost as big as Flora's. And a nice little behind, too. I shook my head, telling myself I oughtn't look at my own sister that way, and got into bed.

Hell, it wasn't *my* fault I had to sleep in the same room as her. Not my fault she was lying there wearing only a pair of panties. I knew of plenty of other guys who fooled around with their sisters. And one guy who actually knocked his own sister up. The family hushed the story, and gave the kid out for adoption, but I heard about it from somebody in the gang anyway.

This was the last night we'd all be stuck in the same bedroom. It was better that we were moving. I don't mind breaking laws, but I didn't want to get in trouble with my own sister.

… The next day we moved. And so now we were in the housing project downtown. I walked around the streets, getting the feel of the neighborhood. I looked at the big tall buildings, all alike. Pretty dull jazz. The streets were baking and frying in the July heat. Little shimmering heat-waves came up from the hot sidewalk. The neighborhood people sat around on benches in front of the project buildings, fanning themselves, sipping Cokes, rocking carriages.

And over on the other side of the street was Flopsville. Blocks and blocks and blocks of cheap dingy rooming houses, hock shops, bars, dumps. In a few years they were going to rip all that crap away and put up another housing project over there too. The way I figured, inside of twenty years there wouldn't be a single goddamn thing in New York except big housing projects.

I shrugged and crossed the street. Anything to get away from the sameness of the project buildings.

I kept looking around. I knew what I was looking for, too. I wanted to find the home of the Golden Dragons. I wanted to get into the gang, to start moving before I went crazy with boredom.

This was the third day in the new neighborhood for us. I was taking things slow. The first two days, I kept myself busy helping my folks get moved in. Arranging the furniture, unpacking things. Today they didn't need me. So I could go out and look around.

It was hotter than the back door of hell. It was at least 90 degrees, maybe 95, and not a breath of wind. Hot air lay all over the city like a heavy blanket. I was wearing a striped polo shirt and a pair of jeans. I had my switchblade in my hip pocket, and I kept my hand in my pocket over the blade, so it wouldn't lump up big and be visible through the tight jeans.

I was glad we had made the big move in the summertime. That way I had a couple of months to get settled down before the school semester began. By the time September rolled around, I would be in good with the Golden Dragons, a member in full standing.

I didn't want to go into a new high school cold, a stranger, a guy who just shows up one morning and says he goes to school here. A guy can get slashed up that way. But if I was a full member of the Dragons, I wouldn't have any troubles. I could just move right in.

I thought about school.

What a stinking crock that was! Seven lousy months, that was all I had to go until I turned seventeen and could quit. I was itching to get the hell out. No more high school for me the day I turned seventeen. No more sitting around in battered old desks listening to some potbellied coot telling us about Julius Caesar. I'd get myself a good job with some garage, make myself fifty-sixty-seventy bucks a week, and really live it up.

A guy can have a lot of fun at night if he makes that kind of money. I was tired of living on nickels.

I walked around the corner. There were some tall buildings in this block, and they gave some shade. Not much, but some. The streets were dusty. Shopkeepers stood in front of their doors, waiting for customers. One old geezer looked at me as I came along and he sort of went pale and looked away in a hurry. I could practically read his mind. He was thinking, *There's a new one. A new delinquent to terrorize the neighborhood.*

I smiled at him, like to tell him I wouldn't make any trouble for anybody unless they made it for me first. But he ducked into his store. I kept walking.

The more I thought about things, the gladder I was that my folks had moved down here. The Shining Sinners had been a good gang, all right. And Flora a hell of a great piece of tail to pal around with. But I'd find somebody as good as Flora down here. And everybody all over the city had heard of the Golden Dragons. The Dragons were a mixed gang, Irish and Negro, and they had a great rep as a bunch of boppers and stompers. Over across the other side of the neighborhood down here was the turf of the Red Eagles, a Puerto Rican-Italian bunch.

The Dragons and the Eagles had some rumbles last year that got into the papers. Those Dragons really had lots of guts.

They were for me, man. I like action. I kept my eyes open for the Golden Dragons. They were the sort of gang I wanted to be with. And I figured I was the sort of guy the Dragons could use.

I walked on, down to the next corner. And there they were, sitting in a little dump of a candy store. I could tell right away that they were the Golden Dragons. I stood outside, looking through the spotted window. They had a gang look about them. They kept their eyes wide, didn't say much, moved all together in a unit. You can spot a gang, if you've been around them much. They aren't just a bunch of different guys taking up space in a candy store. They're a—well, they're a gang. I can't put it into words. But you can feel that they're together.

I walked in.

There was lots of conversation going on, but the second I stepped inside the place all the talking stopped. Fifteen pairs of eyes were fastened on me. When a teenager who nobody's ever seen before walks into a candy store in gang turf, he gets a looking-over. And if anybody challenges his right to be there, he damn well better be prepared to show them why, or else.

I knew that right from this second on I was going to be watched very closely by the Golden Dragons. And the first wrong step I took was very likely to put me in a back alley somewhere, with a new mouth carved where my throat used to be.

I moved in very carefully, not wanting to look pushy but not giving an inch either. I sat down at an empty spot along the counter. The soda jerk looked at me. He was a skinny baldheaded creep with a nose about half a yard long. You could see that he was scared stiff of having the gang kids hang out at his place, but that he knew there wasn't a goddamn thing he could do about it so he might as well make the best of the situation.

He said in a thin, high-sounding little voice, "Yes, please? What's yours?"

"Make it a black-and-white, Dad."

"One black-and-white. Okay. Okay."

He opened his canisters and dished up the black-and-white double quick. He put it down in front of me.

"Thirty cents," he said.

I gave him the money and picked up my spoon. I sat real quiet, itching where I felt all the eyes on me. Lots of eyes. Cold, hard eyes. I spooned the ice cream. Real casual-like, without getting fidgety. The place was quiet. Quiet like a cemetery.

When I finished the ice cream I swung around on the stool, got off it, walked over to the booths where the Golden Dragons were sitting. The Dragons were packed in, four to a booth. I didn't see any debs with them. In a way I was glad. If they had their debs, they might feel like showing off by trumping me before I could say anything. This way I had a chance to get somewhere.

I kept my face hard and my hand in my pocket, over the knife.

I said, "I'm looking for the Prez."

"The Prez of what, daddy-o?" came the slow, sleepy voice of a big colored fellow with a wide purple scar slashing across his cheekbone.

"The Prez of the Golden Dragons," I said.

"Who they, daddy-o?"

Everybody at the four booths laughed it up. I knew that gang laugh. It isn't a pretty sound when a whole gang laughs the same way.

When the fun died down I said casually, "Any of you characters ever hear of a gang called the Shining Sinners? Their turf's uptown."

"Yeah," said a thinnish redheaded fellow with freckles. He smiled nastily. "I heard of the Shining Sinners, man. They're a bunch of faggots."

I kept my temper. This was all part of the routine. If I jumped at the redhead now, I'd get stomped to a pulp by the whole gang.

I said in an even voice, "You got a knife that's ready to back that opinion up Freckleface?"

"I'm ready any time, creep."

"In here or outside?" I said, my hand moving around in my pocket to let him know I had a blade in there.

"In Macy's window, if you like," he said. He stood up. He was just about my height, maybe half an inch taller. "The Shining Sinners are a bunch of faggish faggots," he repeated loudly. "If you don't agree, well, man, you can just go and shove it."

I slipped my knife out of my pocket and let some of the black butt stick up out of my fist. I had my finger on the switch, and all I had to do was press it and that deadly steel would come whipping out.

"This is what I'm gonna shove," I said. "Right into your lousy gut, man."

For half a second it looked like we were going to have a stand right there in the middle of the candy store. I glanced into a cracked mirror over the booth and caught sight of the soda jerk standing back of me behind his counter, practically having apoplexy.

A gang doesn't like to do any fighting in its candy store. But I wasn't part of the gang yet, so I didn't care where we had our stand.

Except there wasn't any fight. Just as things got ready to explode, somebody nodded and two of the Dragons slid out from their seats. They got between me and the red head with the freckles.

The guy standing closest to me, a brawny-looking Irishman with a blonde crewcut, said in a tight whisper, "Put the knife back in your pocket, fella. There ain't gonna be any fights in here. You can't take us all on."

"I ain't lookin' to cut anybody up," I said. "I just want to talk to the Prez about getting into the Dragons. I didn't ask this crapperoo over here to give me a rough time about the Sinners."

"You from uptown?"

"I'm shifting my turf," I said. "My old man got into the housing project. I want in."

Crewcut nodded slowly. "Okay. We read you, daddy-o. You got your message across. Come on outside in back and we can talk about it a little."

I took a long, slow look at him. I didn't want to get led into any traps.

But the way he looked, I figured he was on the level. I had scored my point. I had taken the first step toward getting into the Golden Dragons!

CHAPTER TWO

Four of them led me through a door in the back of the candy store, through a little dark corridor. There were two of them in front of me and two of them behind me, and if they wanted to jump me this was their chance. But they didn't. We came out into a narrow alley bordered on all sides by the backs of buildings.

I had the knife put away in my pocket again, but I kept my hand on the butt, just in case they wanted to make trouble. But I didn't read them for a fight just now. They wanted to sound me out, was all.

I looked them over. The freckle-faced redhead who had spoken up was there, and the blonde guy with the crewcut, and the scarfaced colored fellow, and a flatnosed greasy-haired guy who hadn't said anything inside.

Blonde crewcut came forward and gave me the eye. "What's your name?" he asked after a moment.

"Danny Flaherty," I said.

"I'm Mike Reilly. I'm Prez of the Dragons." Reilly introduced the others. The redhead with the freckles was Jimmy Niles, who was called Jimmy Nails. The scarface colored lad was Mack Brown. The flatnosed one was Johnny Slash, real name Johnny O'Brien. Together, the four of them made up the War Council of the Golden Dragons.

They looked me over. Johnny Slash ran a hand through his greasy hair and said, "So you were a Shining Sinner, you say huh?"

"Yeah."

"Prove it, man."

That was easy enough. I rolled up my polo shirt and gave them a look at the letters of scar tissue carved on the skin of my belly. The letters S. S, for *Shining Sinners*. I said, "Like, take a look at these, huh?"

"Who put them there?" Mack Brown asked in his slow drawl. He was a big ox of a guy, six foot two or three and shoulders about as wide. But he looked fast.

"I put them there," I said.

"Do all the Shining Sinners carve themselves up?" Jimmy Nails wanted to know.

I shook my head. "I did it for a gag."

"Where's the Sinner turf?" Mike Reilly asked me.

I told him, giving him the boundaries block by block and alleyway by alleyway. Then I named every man in the gang, by his real name and by his nickname if he had one. That seemed to satisfy them that I was what I said I was. They didn't know whether I was faking them or not, of course, but the way I reeled the names off must have sounded okay to them.

"And now you want in with the Golden Dragons, huh?" Jimmy Nails said.

I nodded.

"How old are you?"

"Be seventeen in seven months," I said.

"Gonna quit school?" Reilly asked.

"You bet."

"Then what?"

I shrugged. "Nothing much. Hang around for a while. Get me a job and live it up a little."

"You ever kill a man?" Brown asked.

"No," I said, because it was the truth and they'd know it if I tried to fake. "But I've cut plenty of guys up, though."

"Would you cool anyone off if you had to do it?" Mack persisted.

I nodded slowly. "Sure," I said. "I'd do it if I had to, yeah."

"We ain't got room for chickens in the Dragons," Johnny Slash said. "You got that, man?"

"I got it. I ain't no chicken."

"Suppose your sister got felt up by a Spic. What would you do?" Jimmy Nails asked.

"How do you know I got a sister?" I threw back at him.

"That don't matter. If you had a sister and she got felt up by a Spic, what would you do?"

I shrugged. "I'd go after him and carve him, guess. Unless she was the one who started up with him. I wouldn't carve him then. But I'd beat the hell out of *her*."

"Do you have a sister?" Johnny Slash asked.

"Yeah," I said.

"How old?"

I didn't like the looks on their faces. "Fifteen," I said. "But she don't run with the gangs. She goes her own way, and won't change."

Mike Reilly grinned. "Is she stacked, man?"

"She looks okay. You looking for some tail?"

"You offering her?" Reilly asked.

"Not on your sweet butt. I'm just telling you right at the start that she won't go for any of you."

"She still got her cherry?" Jimmy Nails asked.

"How the hell do I know?" I answered. "Look, is she the one who wants to be a Dragon, or—"

"Okay," Mike Reilly said, "We're getting off the track. Why do you want to be a Dragon, Flaherty?"

"I want to be with it, man. I'm gonna be living in your turf from here on. I don't go for moping around alone. I want to be on the inside."

"Okay," Mike Reilly told me. "Go over there and wait while we discuss you."

I walked away and leaned against the wall while they had a huddle about me. I wasn't worried or surprised by what was going on. It works the same way in any gang that's worth a damn. You can't just walk in and ask to be accepted. They won't bow down and tell you you're in. You've got to go through the tests first. You've got to prove that you've got what it takes to be a Golden Dragon, or a Shining Sinner, or a Count or an Assassin or whatever gang you're trying to get taken by.

I didn't even try to hear what they were saying. I just waited, with my hands in my pockets.

A couple of minutes later, they called me over. Mike Reilly said. "We've decided to put you on probation, like, man."

"How long?"

"One month." he said. "Maybe less if everything turns out right. We want to see how you work out. You work out okay, you'll be one of us, you'll be a Dragon. If not, you pack up and scoot."

"I'm with you," I said.

"Right, man. We got a few things we want you to do. Just to show us if you got guts. We ain't got room for no chickens in this organization."

My face tightened up "How many times I gotta tell you?" I said, "I ain't no chicken."

"Telling us don't do no good," Mack Brown drawled. "You gotta show us."

"Okay," I said. "Any way you like."

"Come on," Reilly said. "We'll fill you in on what we want you to do."

They led me out into the street in front of the candy store and told me what my first test was to be. I was going to have to go across into Eagle turf, on the other side of the avenue, and have myself a soda in the candy store where the Red Eagles hung out.

It was risky, but not really dangerous if I kept my head. None of the Eagles knew who I was. That was the thing on my side. If a full-fledged Dragon that everybody knew walked in there he'd get his guts carved up sure as anything. But a stranger could work the caper with no sweat if he didn't go asking for trouble. At least, a white stranger could. If some colored boy went into that store, he'd get his head handed to him. I might get by.

The whole idea of sending me in there was to see if I kept my head in a tight jam. If I funked up, it would prove that I wasn't worth belonging in the Dragons.

I wasn't worried.

I said, "When you want me to pull the caper?"

"Any time you feel like it, man," Reilly said.

"It's getting close to lunchtime," I said. "I figure I'll go get some food in me first. That okay with you?"

"We ain't rushing you, man," Johnny Slash said. "Take all the time you want. Take a year."

"I'll see you later," I said.

I left the Dragons' candy store and walked back up the street toward the housing project for lunch. It was just around twelve o'clock. The sun was big and hot. It looked like it took up around half the sky. There weren't any clouds and no breeze at all. Breathing the air was like breathing engine fumes.

I was busy thinking about the candy store bit I had to pull later when I noticed a cop car pull up at the curb just ahead of me. There were two cops in it. I didn't pay them any attention, just kept on walking. The only way to treat the fuzz is to ignore them.

But as I walked past, one of the cops stuck his head out the window and said, "Hey, kid. Get in here."

I stopped short and a muscle went ping in my cheek. "What the hell for? I ain't done nothing!"

His face got ugly. It was a lean, long, dark-complexioned face. His nose had been broken and hadn't been fixed too well, because it skewed toward the side a little.

"We just wanta talk to you," he said. "Get in the car. You ain't under arrest."

I didn't like getting rides with the fuzz. I said, "Talk to me out here."

"Listen, kiddo, get yourself in the car, or you *will* be in trouble."

I still held back a second or two. Then I figured it was safer to do as they said than to disobey them. When a kid who looks like a gang kid disobeys a cop, about anything at all, he can wind up with a bullet in his back. The cops don't like to fool around with our kind. If some had their way, they'd shoot us on sight.

Of course, I was worried about the switch I was carrying. If they searched me, I'd be in hot water. And I'd lose a damned fine piece of steel. I had to take my chances on that, and hope they wouldn't look.

I got into the car, in the back seat.

The cop who had called to me swiveled around to look at me. "I'm Sergeant Spinelli," he said. "It's my job to keep an eye on all the kids around here. You're a new one, aren't you?"

"Yeah."

"What's your name?"

"Danny Flaherty."

Spinelli gave me a smile that was supposed to be a friendly one, I guess. I figured he was trying psychology on me, trying to make me think he was like a big brother to all us kids.

"How old are you, Danny?"

"Sixteen and a half."

He nodded toward the project. "You live there?"

"Yeah."

"Just moved in?"

"Yeah," I said.

"Where'd you live before?

"Uptown, East Side."

He smiled again, and the smile was just as phony as the last one. "You look like a sensible fellow, Danny. I just want to give you a little warning. There's a lot of rough gang stuff in this neighborhood. If you want to play it smart, don't get yourself mixed up in it, hear me? Keep your nose clean."

"I ain't done nothing, Officer Spinelli," I said like I was a choirboy out for a noonday stroll.

"Nothing yet. But I see a lot of you kids move in this area and get right going with the gang. There was a gang where you came from, huh?"

"I suppose."

"You didn't run with them?"

"Not me, Officer."

The other cop jabbed him. "The kid's snowing you, Lou. He's a juvie from the word go."

"Shut up," Spinelli said quietly. He turned back to me. "Take my advice, Danny. Stay clear of those kids. They're heading straight for Nowheresville. There's no percentage in gang stuff. Understand me?"

"Sure, Officer."

"I try to talk to each new kid who moves in around here. Take a tip from me, and play it the smart way. That way you'll live longer and be happier."

For a moment he didn't say anything more, and neither did I. I figured that was my cue to get moving.

"That all you wanted with me, Officer?"

"That's all."

"Well, thanks for talking to me, Officer Spinelli. Can I go now?"

"Sure, Danny. You can go. Take it slow."

"So long, Officer."

I got out of the cop car. They drove away, rounding the corner. I was so sore I was boiling all over. I had to spit. The mushy mouthed bastard, trying to give me a sticky little sermon! Calling me Danny and smiling and telling me to stick to the straight and narrow! And squelching his buddy about me being a gang kid.

It was a damn good thing Officer Spinelli hadn't looked in my pockets. If he'd found the switchblade, he would have changed his opinion of me.

Well, to hell with him, I thought. Him and his greasy smile and his broken nose. Looking out for each new kid in the neighborhood, calling him into the car for a little conference. I bet he felt like a great big daddy, handing out that spiel about keeping away from the rough, tough, mean gang kids.

To hell with him.

I wasn't going to play it the gutless way.

Not me, man!

I was going to be a Dragon!

I walked quickly up the block and into the housing project. There was a sort of a lawn. and a curving walkway that led up to the lobby of the house. I walked in, and went to the elevator on the left. We lived on the twelfth floor. I pushed the button. The elevator light went on. The elevator register said the car was in the basement, but on its way up. A second later, the door was rolling back and I got in.

There was a girl in the elevator.

She had been down in the basement, doing her family laundry. The cleaned clothes were in a little basket at her feet. She was maybe sixteen or so. Clean, well-scrubbed. She was wearing a white blouse open at the collar and a pair of green slacks. Not jeans, but green slacks.

And she was built.

The blouse was a little big on her, but even so I could see the way her breasts rose steeply under it. I stripped the blouse and bra off in my mind and saw those nice little, round little, big little boobs.

The slacks were pretty tight. Tight enough to tell me that she had a flat belly and wide hips and a behind that curved out just far enough, but not too far.

The face was good, too. Very white skin, black hair, dark eyes. Flashing eyes. Full lips. The only thing that was missing to make her beautiful was a smile. She was scowling at me.

I looked her over from top to toe as I walked into the elevator. I pushed my button and then I turned around, leaning against the wall and looking at her.

"Hi," I said.

No answer. Not even a smile.

"I'm Danny Flaherty. Twelfth floor. We just moved in here."

She looked at me like I was a toad with purple warts. I saw her tongue flick out and moisten her lips.

"It don't cost nothing to be friendly," I said. "Can't you smile?"

"Please," she said, in a ritzy way. "I'm not supposed to talk to strange boys."

"How in hell's name are they gonna *stop* being strange if you never talk to them?"

She almost smiled at that. But she was afraid of me, I knew. I could see by the way color came to her cheeks and her breasts moved up and down under the white blouse that she was scared, that she was thinking maybe I was going to rape her right here in the elevator. The car stopped, suddenly, at the ninth floor. The door opened.

She bent down and picked up her basket of laundry. The seat of her slacks went tight as she bent, showing me the outlines of her buttocks. I hadn't had a girl in three days, not since that last big night with Flora. And this girl had class. A figure. A face.

"So long," I said.

She walked out of the car without a word. The door rolled shut.

Damn bitch! I thought. *Stuck up bitch!*

Probably thought she was too good to speak to me. Too good to talk to juvenile riffraff like me. And scared witless too. I figured for sure she was a virgin. Sixteen, maybe, and saving it for her husband. Went to high school and belonged to Arista and got good marks, and was thinking about getting a scholarship to some college.

She wasn't a Flora. She was a girl from an entirely different world from me, the world of ordinary people. I hated her. I wanted her. She was too proud to talk to me. I made a vow. I didn't even know her name or anything else about her except that she lived on the ninth floor, but I made up my mind that I was going to have her one of these days, before too long. I'd peel her stark naked and get on top of her and give her something she wouldn't forget too soon.

I hate it when someone treats me like dirt.

I want to get even.

I filed her away in my mind. A moment later, the elevator stopped at my floor. I got out, walked down the hall to our apartment, rang the bell. I never remembered to take my key with me.

My sister answered the door. She was dressed in a pair of shorts and a polo shirt. I could see right away that she didn't have a bra on underneath because I could see the dark circles of her nipples. Hell of a thing when your own sister dresses like that.

I nodded to her and came in. "Lunch ready?"

"Five minutes," she said.

My mother was in the kitchen, getting things fixed up. My mother is a thin woman with a tired face. She's had a rough life, and I sometimes feel sorry for her. Altogether she's had five kids. But the oldest, my brother Ronnie, he got killed in Korea. And there was a girl named Carol who died when she was a baby. I was the third. She's had a hard time with my old man, too. He works hard, but he drinks hard too, and doesn't spend much time with her.

My kid brother Ray was reading a book. He's the studious type.

I called my sister aside, while I was waiting for lunch to get ready. We went into her room.

I said, "Don't you own any brassieres?"

"Christ, Danny, are you gonna get on my neck too?"

"I don't want people to get the wrong ideas about you, Sis. You oughta wear a bra."

"It's hot weather."

"Put one on anyway."

She made a face at me. Then she peeled her polo shirt off, turning slowly to give me a view of her full heavy breasts, and got a bra from her dresser. She put it on, pulled the polo shirt back on, and stuck her tongue out at me.

"That better?"

"It's okay."

"You got any other orders, boss?"

I said, annoyed, "Listen, Sis, this is just as tough a neighborhood as the one we came from. You walk around like that outside, some guy's gonna toss you on your rear in an alley and give you the works."

"I can take care of myself," she said.

I shrugged. "Okay. I ain't no preacher. I called you in here to ask you a favor."

"What kind of favor?"

"There's a girl in this house, she lives on the ninth floor. She's around as old as you are, maybe a little older. I want to find out what her name is."

"So ask her."

"I did. She gave me the high hat."

My sister smiled. "What's it worth to me to find out for you?"

"You bitch. Two bits?"

"Fifty."

"For fifty I'll find out myself."

"Okay," she said. "Two bits. You interested in her, Danny?"

"I might be. She's a looker." I described her and Sis promised to find out who she was. A picture drifted into my mind of the unknown girl, naked and whimpering, trying to hide her breasts with her hands while I grabbed hold of her and took her.

Funny thing. Telling my own sister to dress more decent, and at the same time dreaming of taking some girl on the ninth floor. What the hell. It's a lousy world. You protect what you own, and you grab what you can.

"Lunch's on," my mother called.

I went into the kitchen.

CHAPTER THREE

I ate lunch quickly, without saying anything to anybody, without hardly ever noticing what was on the plate. My mother didn't make any remarks. She was used to me not talking much at the kitchen table. Hell, what was I supposed to talk about? Gang gossip? The girl I had laid the other week? Like, there just wasn't much for me to say to my mother, so I didn't say anything.

Sis didn't talk either, just forked the grub into her mouth. My mother and my kid brother jabbered a blue streak at each other. The kid was twelve, and that's the age when they do a lot of talking.

He was skinny, squeaky-voiced. Nothing much to him. Spent all his time reading books. We didn't get along too good, my brother and me. He thought I was a dope, and I guess I had to admit he was right, but you don't like your own kid brother to tell you that you're uneducated. Even if you are.

When I was through eating, I got up and carried my dishes over to the sink, and said, "I'm going out, Ma."

"Where are you going?"

"Just out."

"Don't forget to come home for dinner? Hear? Your father doesn't like to be kept waiting."

I nodded and headed for the door without saying anything else. I knew my mother would only start bugging me about getting a summer job, if I stuck around the apartment any longer. She wanted me to contribute to the family's support, but I wasn't interested in any summer job. The time to get jobs was after I quit high school, not on my vacation time. And anyway, I had someplace to go.

On the way down in the elevator, I kept hoping that the car would stop at nine and that girl would get on again. This time I'd make sure she wouldn't high-hat me. But no such luck. I went straight down without a stop.

The turf of the Red Eagles began four long blocks from where I was. I walked west toward the boundary, taking my own sweet time about getting there. The day was turning still hotter as the afternoon moved along. By this time it was probably close to 100 degrees, I kept my hand in my pocket, on the butt of my blade,

I crossed one street, another, another. Now I was on the final block of the turf of the Golden Dragons. The final "safe" block. Up ahead of me was the big avenue that served as the boundary line. Across it was the territory of the gang that I was already starting to think of as The Enemy, even though I wasn't a Dragon yet.

I crossed the avenue.

I felt a little queasy in the stomach, not much. The queasiness of caution, not fear. There wasn't much to be afraid of. This was enemy turf, but unless the Eagles happened to be in a really rough mood they would most likely leave me pretty much alone.

Sometimes a gang will just go out roaming and stomping for the pure hell of it, beating up any Negro or Puerto Rican or Irishman or Italian they happen to find in their turf. But you couldn't tell I was Irish just by looking at me. I knew that if I didn't make any trouble, the Eagles wouldn't bother me any. And if they *did* bother me all the same, well, I had to be ready to take care of myself.

That was what the Golden Dragons wanted to see. How well I took care of myself when unexpected trouble turned up.

I kept walking.

The Dragons had given me the address of the candy store where the Eagles usually hung out. It was about two and a half blocks inside Eagle turf. I walked along through the hot streets until I came to it. Two Puerto Ricans were standing out in front, talking rapidly to each other in Spanish. They were lookouts, posted to keep watch in case a raiding party from an enemy gang came along. I walked in between them, and saw them give me the eye.

Play it cool, Danny-boy, I told myself.

Inside, the place was pretty much like the Golden Dragon hangout. There was a long counter, a magazine rack, booths, a jukebox—the usual candy store arrangement. About nine or ten of the Eagles were standing around the juke, snapping their fingers in rhythm to the song that was playing. There were a few debs, a couple of trim little Puerto Rican chicks wearing flashy jackets. I saw everybody giving me the eye in a cautious way.

I sat down at the soda counter.

Play it cool, Danny-boy.

The soda jerk looked at me. He was fat and bald. Like Officer Spinelli, someone had broken his nose once, but the soda jerk's nose wasn't just crooked; it had been smeared all over his face. He was sweating in the heat, and his double chin looked shiny. He didn't seem happy about having me come into his store. He seemed to know that there might be some trouble on account of it.

"Yeah?" he asked.

"Gimme an egg cream."

He nodded and started to fix it up. I could practically feel the eyes crawling over my back. The Eagles were busy wondering who I was, how come I had walked right into their turf, right into their hangout itself.

The counterman put my soda in front of him. I paid him and started to drink it down. I tell you truly. I wasn't very hungry just then. But I made sure, to swallow down every drop.

The Red Eagles still hadn't made a move. The place was very still. They were biding their time, wondering, measuring me.

The first sign of fear and I was cooked, I knew. I got up slowly, walked over to the newsstand, glanced at the magazines for a moment and picked one out. I looked through it. It was a girlie magazine, all full of pinup pictures. Some of those girls had real big knobs. They were photographed with their boobs practically exploding out of the page in three dimensions. Looking at them, I remembered. I needed a woman. I wasn't used to going without one this long. I told myself that as soon as I was set with the Golden Dragons, I was going to look around and find myself some cooperative chick with boobs as big as those on the girls in the mag.

I put the magazine back on the rack. I hoped my face still looked calm. I wasn't afraid inside. I'm not chicken, remember. But just then I felt a little nervous. You get the difference? Not scared, not yellow, not chick-chick. Just not really loose, either.

I walked out of the store. The two Puerto Ricans were still on guard out front. They looked at me peculiarly, but didn't say anything to me. They exchanged a couple of words in Spanish. I don't understand Spanish.

I started to walk back the way I came, knowing that trouble was about to start. I went four steps.

Then one of the Puerto Ricans said quietly, "Hey there, man. You."

I turned "You talking to me?"

"Yeah. Where you from, man?"

I pointed. "Avenue B."

"That's Dragon turf."

"I don't know any Dragon stuff, man," I said calmly. "I'm new around here. I was thirsty and I came in for a soda, is all. You got any objections to that?"

I turned again and started to walk away. Not fast, just relaxed-like. I didn't look back. I didn't need to. I knew what was happening. The Eagles were having a quick conference. They were deciding whether they wanted to make trouble for me or not. Maybe I was a new member of the Dragons, they were saying. And if I was, I had just insulted the Eagles by marching boldly into their home territory. Turf has to be guarded. You can't let the enemy go trampling all over your territory unchecked.

I kept on walking.

I got to the corner, crossed it, started toward the next block. My throat was kind of dry. I had fulfilled the first step in my Golden Dragon initiation. But I wasn't home free yet. Golden Dragon turf was still a block and a half away. Were the Eagles going to let me get away with it?

For just a second I thought they were. Then I heard the footsteps and looked around and saw four Eagles coming after me, half a block away. I guess they had ended their conference in a hurry.

I can run pretty damn fast when I have to. I turned face-front and ran. I looked back once, a quarter of a block down, and saw that I was beating them; they wouldn't be able to catch me before I reached Dragon turf, and if they wanted to cross the boundary to get me they might be buying more trouble than I was worth.

But I didn't want to win a leg-race. Being able to run away isn't anything to be proud of. I wanted to build up my rep down here. I wanted to show the Golden Dragons that I wasn't chicken.

So when I reached the next corner, the block before the boundary, I swung around and ducked north, into a quiet little sleepy side street. The Eagles went steaming right past, all but one of them. He had seen me turn; the others hadn't. He came up my street.

He was an Italian, with black duck-tail hair and big muscles bulging under his T-shirt. He was maybe six feet tall, a two-hundred-pounder. Built solid. He was holding a switchblade in his hand, all of it hidden except the rim of the butt. He came charging up the block like a runaway tank. I waited where I was until he was practically on top of me. Then I stepped out of hiding.

Half a second after he saw me, the big guy was thumbing the button on his switch. But I was way, way ahead of him, and he never got a chance to cut me up. I brought my fist down hard on his wrist. At the same time I pulled my knee up and gave it to him. He spun around and howled like a girl, big as he was. The knife dropped from his hand. He reached for it, quick, cat-fast for all his size, but I was faster. I picked up my foot and stomped down on his fingers, feeling them roll under my heel. He let out another yell, louder than the first one.

Quick-like, I snatched up the knife. Now I had a switchblade in both hands—my own in my right hand, his in my left. He stood there, a couple of feet away, with a stupid expression on his face. He flexed his bent and bloody fingers a little and didn't know what to do. He was big and strong, but not very smart.

"Come on," I said. "Walk with me."

"What—"

"Skip the conversation. Just walk."

I walked him up the block and around the corner, and down to the avenue that separated Dragon turf from Red Eagle turf. He was sore as hell, cursing me out in Italian, but he wasn't going to try anything barehand against a guy who had two knives.

Suddenly I saw the other three Eagles, the ones I had lost, coming up toward me from a block to the south. I decided not to hang around for further fun and games. I didn't want to push my luck too far. Leaving my prisoner where he was, I broke into a sprint and got across the avenue just as the light turned red. A bunch of cars came swooping down behind me, cutting off the four Eagles, who were stranded on the far side.

They didn't come after me now, even when the traffic let up. They knew how fast I could run. I would be in the heart of the Golden Dragons turf inside of two seconds, and that would leave them cut off.

I felt pretty good about things.

I thumbed my nose at the four Eagles. Then I sprinted for the Dragon candy store. Up the block, around the corner, turn to the left.

The whole bunch of them were there when I walked in. I was sweating and puffing from all the running I had done. I went straight to the booths in the back, where the Dragons were clustered.

"I just been over in Eagle territory," I said.

"That so?" Mike Reilly challenged. "Tell us what the soda jerk looks like, then."

"Big fat slob with a flattened-out nose. Double chin. Bald head. You want more?"

The Dragons looked at each other. I saw them nodding, saw them nudging each other. I could bet they were thinking. *This guy's okay.*

I gave them a little more. For good measure, I described half a dozen of the Eagles. Then I told them about the four guys who had chased me back to Dragon turf, how I had outrun them and led them up the wrong street.

"I had a little stand with one of them who I couldn't shake," I said. "A big guy, lots of muscles. Ducktail haircut. He didn't do so good. I stomped on his hand and took his blade away."

It was my big moment. I put the extra blade down on the tabletop in front of Mike Reilly. That really gassed them. I could see their eyes light up.

"Satisfied?" I asked.

Reilly looked up. "You did okay, Flaherty. But you're not a Golden Dragon yet. You still have a long way to go, man."

I was sore as hell about that, but I kept my objections to myself. The way I figured it, I'd done plenty, going into Eagle turf and right into their goddamn hangout, and then grabbing a blade away from one of their toughest studs. But I kept my mouth shut. Anything the Dragons wanted me to do by way of initiation, I was going to do without complaining about it.

Reilly got up. "Come on out into the back alley with us, Flaherty. We'll talk over what you're going to do next, man."

The other three members of the War Council got up too, and we all went out into the back alley where the private conferences were held. Jimmy Nails, Mack Brown, Johnny Slash, Mike Reilly, and me.

"Okay," I said, when we were out there. "Where do I go from here?"

In a quiet voice, Mack Brown said, "We're figuring on pulling a burglary bit tomorrow night, Flaherty. We could use some loose cash. You feel like coming along with us?"

"You don't have to," Jimmy Nails said.

I knew that I *did* have to, no matter what. I was free to back out, but if I did I'd also be backing clear out of the Golden Dragons at the same time.

So I said, "I'm with you. Tell me more."

"It's a grocery store," Reilly said. "It stays open till midnight. The idea is, we bust in at midnight and grab the day's take just as the grocer's closing up."

"How many of us?" I asked.

"Me, you, and Johnny Slash," Reilly said. "Old Mack here, he organized the thing, but turns out he's gonna be busy tomorrow night somewhere else. So it's just the three of us."

"We figure it'll be worth four or five bills," Johnny Slash said. "Not bad for a night's haul."

I nodded. "Sounds good."

"You ever do any of this stuff uptown?" Reilly asked me.

"A little," I said.

"Ever get caught?"

"Nope."

They explained the setup to me. The way it was going to work, I was going to walk into the store just before closing time and get into a discussion with the grocer. About anything. The weather, the baseball standings. Meanwhile, Johnny Slash would stay lookout in front. Reilly would climb around the back of the place, through a staircase that led down through the building to the first floor. The light switch was in the back. Reilly would push his way through the back door and knock off the switch.

The second the lights were out in the store, I was supposed to pick up a big bottle of juice and clobber the grocer with it. Then Reilly and I would clean out the cash register and beat it.

Everything had to work out split-second. If I chickened, the whole thing would fall apart. But I wasn't going to chicken.

"You got the idea?" Reilly asked.

"Yeah."

"Okay, Flaherty. We'll see you tomorrow night. Come around to the candy store about ten or eleven o'clock. You can take off, man."

"I figured I'd hang out here for the rest of the afternoon," I said.

"You take off, man," Reilly repeated. "You do your hanging around here when you're a member of the Dragons, not before."

I wanted to answer him back, but I figured that wouldn't be smart. So I turned and walked away, up the street, across to the project.

It was only the middle of the afternoon, not even three o'clock yet. I didn't know what to do with myself. The Dragons had brushed me off till tomorrow night. I had loads of time to kill and nobody to kill it with. Uptown, there were all my old pals. But down here there was nobody but a bunch of strangers called the Golden Dragons, and I wasn't one of them yet.

I walked over and sat down on a little bench in front of one of the project buildings, and wondered what the hell I was going to do with myself between here and the time of that grocery store job tomorrow night.

Time was going to pass awful slow till then.

I thought about that chick on the ninth floor. This was as good a time as any to start making up to her. But I couldn't just go around ringing doorbells on the ninth floor until I found the right apartment.

No, I needed an angle. And while I was sitting there wondering what to do, my angel came dropping down from heaven like a miracle.

My sister came walking up from the supermarket, with a bundle of groceries in her arms.

And with her was the girl from the ninth floor.

Sis saw me and called. "Danny! Danny, come help me with the groceries." She gave me a wink.

I got up, went over to her, took the package from her. At the same time, I took another look at the chick with her. Still wearing the tight slacks, the open-collared shirt. My mouth watered for her.

Sis said, "Elaine, I want you to meet my brother. Elaine Halperin, this is my brother Danny." Sis said to me, "Elaine lives in our building, on the ninth floor. She's in the same grade I'm going to be in when school starts."

Elaine looked at me in a frosty sort of way. "I've already met your brother."

"But we weren't introduced," I said. "Now I'm not a strange boy. I'm a neighbor."

We went into the house, started toward the elevator, got in. As we rode upstairs, Sis told me of how she had met Elaine in the grocery store, recognized her as a neighbor, and started talking. When the elevator reached nine, Elaine got out. She gave my sister a polite sort of smile and gave me a kind of a nod.

I could tell she didn't like me. She knew right off that I was a gang boy, and she was a little annoyed at herself for having let my sister befriend her.

The elevator door closed. Sis said, "Okay, big shot. You owe me two bits. I got you her name and an introduction and everything."

"Here. Take the groceries and I'll give you your dough."

"You don't sound grateful."

"What do you want me to do? Kiss your boots?" I took a quarter out of my pocket and handed it over.

Sis took it. Then she said, "Danny, you aren't going to get anywhere with that girl."

"She tell you so?"

"Not in that many words. But she isn't the type who'd fall for you. She's an honor student at school. She won't let you get near her."

"Let me worry about that," I said. I held the door open for her, but didn't get out of the elevator myself. It was too early to come home.

I rode downstairs and went back to the bench I had been sitting on. Well, I knew the girl's name now. That was a step in the right direction. But Sis was right—I wasn't going to get anything from Elaine Halperin. Not unless I took it from her.

Well, maybe I would.

Meantime I needed a woman, quick. Needed one so bad I could taste it. I thought of getting on the subway and going uptown to find Flora. But that wouldn't work. By this time Flora would be shacked up with somebody else. I'd be buying trouble if I tried to get anything from her now.

I got off the bench and started strolling. Uptown, I would know what to do. Any time you were hot, you went over to 110th Street, down to the basement. Rose, the janitor's daughter, would always be there when you rang the bell. Rose wasn't all right in the head. You'd ring at the door and she'd come to answer it, and maybe she'd be wearing a slip or maybe just a blouse and nothing below the waist. And you said, "Rose, how about a good time?" and she said, "Sure, come on in."

Rose was around twenty-five or twenty-six. She hadn't ever been married. She had had a bad case of acne and her face was all scarred, but below the neck she was beautiful. And she'd go down for anybody, any time, and not charge for it. So you'd walk in and she'd be taking off her clothes the next minute, and giggling a little. The bed was never made in her room. She'd lie down on it and open up and you did anything you wanted to her. She didn't care. I remember one guy who said he went in there and did it to her with an ear of corn, and she liked it.

Of course, you had to be careful not to get caught by her father. The janitor would catch you and throw you out, and then he'd whip Rose. I remember when I was a kid, eleven or twelve, I stood by the window on the street level, looking in, and there was Rose stark naked lying on her belly and her big plump buttocks were sticking up, and her father had his belt off and was coming down, *whack! whack!* and her backside shook every time he hit her. A regular free show, it was.

Having somebody like Rose in the neighborhood was handy when a guy had just broken up with his deb or something like that. And she was fun in other ways. Like when we'd get her to come over to the clubhouse and take us all on. It didn't bother her to get laid twenty, thirty, forty times in one day. She just lay back and giggle while it was going on.

A regular sex machine, that's what.

Well, maybe there was someone like her down here, only I didn't know where. It was too late to make any trips anywhere today. But I figured that maybe tomorrow I'd go up to the old neighborhood and pay Rose a visit. Quiet-like, without meeting any of my old friends, because I didn't want them to know that I had to go five miles uptown to get a piece when I needed it. And that I had to stoop to laying someone like Rose.

I felt pretty disgusted. But I knew things would change once I was in the Dragons.

I walked around a little while, and then I went back to the house for supper.

CHAPTER FOUR

It was sort of a dull evening. We sat around watching television and drinking beer. The heat was awful. We kept the windows wide open, but it didn't do much good. All of us sat around in underwear, it was so hot. My father had a lot of beer to drink, and after a while he got so stewed he even offered some to Ray. But the kid didn't take it. That's the sort he is.

Sis was sitting there in her bra and underwear too, and when she got up to go to the john I caught myself looking at her backside, at the two round cheeks wigwagging back and forth under her panties. I started to sweat a little. I was glad we weren't all sleeping in the same room anymore. I was so hard up I might even go after her.

I made up my mind. *Tomorrow I pay Rose a visit. For sure. Hell of a thing when you can't take your eyes off your own sister.*

Funny thing was, I didn't even know what would happen if I tried anything with Sis. Some girls I knew didn't mind having their brothers fool around with them. But others got sore as hell. I wondered about Sis. I didn't really know what kind of a girl she was, didn't know if she'd scream and yell or if she'd cooperate. She liked to show her body off, but maybe that was just to tease people. She never talked about getting laid or anything.

I took myself a nice cold shower and went to bed early. The next morning, after breakfast, I told my mother I was going to be out all day and wouldn't be around for lunch. She didn't even ask me where I was going. I was glad about that. If I told her I was going back to the old turf, she might get annoyed. She wouldn't figure I was going back there for Rose, because she didn't know about Rose. She'd just be afraid I was going to get involved in a gang fight or something like that.

I started to walk toward the subway. I had gone around half a block when I ran into Officer Spinelli in his car. The cop was driving around the neighborhood looking for trouble. He stuck an arm out the window of his car to wave at me, and said, "How's it going, Danny?"

"No gripes," I said, shrugging, as he slowed down and stopped at the curb next to me.

"You met any of the gang kids yet?"

"I been keeping to myself, Officer. Trying to find me a girl, that's what I been doing. You know where I could find me a nice piece around here?"

He gave me the big hah-hah. "You look like you don't need any help, Danny."

"Haven't had much luck yet."

"You just keep your eyes open. Something nice'll turn up." Then he gave me some more crap about staying out of gang stuff, turned on the smile, and drove away. I hissed a curse after him. Why did the bastard have to keep on bugging me? Why the big brother act? Seemed that I couldn't take two steps in the street without having that damn cop car pulling up next to me.

I kept going toward the subway. It was only ten in the morning, and the heat hadn't really been turned on yet. The temperature was maybe 75 or 80, which was practically like the North Pole after some of the heat we'd been getting.

Another half a day, I thought, and then I'd be pulling the job with Reilly and Johnny Slash. Before long, I'd be allowed to come and be welcome at the Dragons' hangout in the candy store, and also in their clubhouse. The day before, Reilly had been hinting a little that maybe I wouldn't have to go through a full month's probation before I got admitted to the gang. Maybe just a couple more capers would get me in in good standing. I could see that they were really stoned by the way I brought back that big muscle-bound Eagle's switchblade, even though they tried to look cool about it.

Man, I felt ten feet tall right then. I was going out to teach these downtown birds a thing or two about the kind of cat I was.

Right at the start they'd been putting me down. But already they were changing their minds about me. The grocery store bit was going to change them a lot faster. And whatever stunt they had after that. Once I got into the Dragons, I was going to go to town. I wouldn't be satisfied until I was top man in that outfit.

And I had the guts to get there too. The Golden Dragons were a pretty cool bunch, all right, but I was a hell of a lot cooler. They were just starting to find that out. Before I was through, I'd make good and sure they all knew it goddamn well.

I paid my fifteen cents and got on a subway train. I still wasn't used to these downtown trains. Uptown, we didn't travel around much. Maybe down to Times Square for a movie sometimes, but never all the goddamn way down to where I was living now. I managed, though. I went uptown and took the shuttle train at Grand Central and got on another train and then another one, and by twenty minutes to eleven I was out in the open again and back in Shining Sinner turf.

It felt funny to be back home. To see Central Park and Cathedral Parkway and the big church, and all the rest of the home turf. It was a quiet morning up there, I walked quickly up to 110th and Columbus, to Rose's place. I looked in the basement window and didn't see anybody. Hell of a thing if nobody was home. It was just Rose and her old man, the janitor, living there, anyway. If I didn't find Rose, I told myself I'd go hunt up Flora. I wasn't going back downtown till I got what I wanted.

I went into the building, down the basement stairs, past the washing machines and the storage rooms. I knew the route well. The first time I was here, I was thirteen years old. Seven Up brought me. He was fifteen, already in the Shining Sinners, and he figured it was time I got myself laid. So he took me and introduced me to Rose. Rose didn't give a damn how old anybody was. So I unbuttoned my trousers and got on top of her and found out how good it was to make it with a woman instead of locking yourself in the bathroom.

That was three and a half years ago. Six months later I was in the Shining Sinners as a junior. And now I was coming back to pay Rose another visit.

I rang the doorbell.

I waited maybe half a minute. Then, just as I was about to go away disappointed, the door opened.

Rose.

"Hi," she said. "You visiting me?"

"Hello, Rose. Remember me?"

"No."

Not much in the brains department, was Rose. "My name's Danny," I said. "I used to come here every now and then. Why don't you invite me in?"

"Sure. Come in."

I stepped over the threshold. Rose was dressed the way Rose always dresses. I mean, she was wearing a sort of a nightgown thing, pink and transparent. It came down to around the middle of her legs. It was all torn and tattered, and one big breast was sticking right through one of the holes. Rose was a tall girl, taller than I am. With her acne-scarred face and her stupid eyes, she didn't look like much except below the neck. There she had plenty. Big heavy breasts and round belly and nice plump cheeks in back.

She just stood there dumbly, not knowing what to say. Rose wasn't long on conversation.

I said, "Your father home?"

"He's fixing somebody's toilet."

"You want to have some fun, Rose?"

"Sure." She giggled. "I like to have fun. What kind of fun you like?"

"This kind," I said. I pulled her toward me and put my hand over the bare breast that was sticking out of her gown. It was big and firm and warm, and the nipple was set in a dark circle the size of a silver dollar.

I played with the nipple for a moment, and Rose started to shiver.

"You're nice," she said.

She had the mind of an eight-year-old, the body of a twenty-year-old. Sleeping with her always made me a little ashamed of myself, I got to admit. But what can you do, when you need it bad and you don't have a regular piece of your own?

We went inside, into Rose's bedroom. It was a mess, like always. I picked up the hem of her nightgown and lifted it over her head. She stood there naked, this big heavy girl, with her breasts shaking a little and the nipples standing up stiff. I walked over to her and put one hand on each breast, squeezing them. Then I moved to her side, running one hand down her back to her buttocks and bringing the other one down her front until it hovered over her midsection. I touched her, and she shivered. She started to pant. She started to pull me toward the unmade bed.

I didn't undress. I wanted to be ready for a quick getaway in case her father came back. I got down on top of her, and she started to moan and make little slobbering noises. A strong odor of sweat came up to me, and a different odor, the Rose-smell, the smell of a bitch who's always in heat.

She reared upward and received me.

With Rose you didn't need to worry about fine points. You just went ahead and banged away, because she enjoyed it all the time. I looked down at her and saw her drooling and singing to herself. Her breasts were jiggling beneath me. Her hips kept moving, faster and faster, heating me up, and I held back a minute, making it last longer because it's sweeter that way, and then I figured what the hell and started to move fast myself, and it was all over.

I settled down onto Rose's big warm soft body and caught my breath for a couple of minutes. Then I pulled myself free of her and got up.

"You gonna go?" she asked.

"Yep."

"Stay here. Let's play some more. That was fun."

"I'll come back some other time," I said. I wanted to clear out fast. I had gotten what I came for, and now she just disgusted me. She lay there with her legs drawn up into the air, her breasts moving fast.

"You were nice," she said. "What's your name? I forgot it already."

"Danny."

"Danny. Come back tomorrow, Danny?"

"Sure, Rose. Sure. If I'm around, I'll stop in and pay you a visit."

I ducked into her john and cleaned myself up. When I came out, Rose was still on the bed, waiting for me in case I felt like taking another ride. I didn't. I went to the door instead, and left.

I felt loose, now. Even when it's with a dog like Rose, you feel good all over after you've made it. But I didn't plan on paying many more visits to Rose. A guy who has to go to Rose for his loving isn't worth much. She's good for a trip now and then, but not as a regular thing.

I looked around the street. This was Shining Sinners turf, and though they were my best friends I didn't want to run into any of them now. But I hadn't gone half a block when I walked smack into Bonzo.

He yelled out to me, and then I had to stop and say hello to him. Bonzo was one of the old-time Shining Sinners. He'd been in the gang long before me. I guess he was maybe nineteen or twenty.

"Payin' a visit, huh?" he said.

"Figured I'd come uptown," I told him. "We forgot to take some laundry out of the store."

"How's it going with you down there?"

"Not bad. I'm in the Golden Dragons."

He looked impressed. "Good going. That's a fast-moving bunch."

"Don't I know it, man."

"Come on," Bonzo said. "Walk me over to Rose's place."

"What does anyone go to Rose for?"

I grinned at him. "You have a fight with Louise or something?"

"Louise is having her monthly. And old Rose is fun just for a change."

"Yeah," I said.

"You got yourself a piece downtown already?"

"Sure," I lied.

"You don't waste no time."

"What about Flora?"

"She don't waste no time either. She's making it with Billy Floyd now."

I shrugged. Billy Floyd was a new man in the gang. Big and strong like an ox. He'd always been interested in Flora, and I guess he'd just moved right in on her when I gave her up. "Send her my best," I said.

"Will do. You wanna come to Rose with me?"

I shook my head, "I don't need that kinda stuff," I said. "See you around, Bonzo."

"Yeah. See you."

He went his way, I went mine. I felt kind of sentimental about the old bunch all of a sudden. But then I realized I was out of things. Way out. I wasn't part of the gang anymore. My chick was making it with somebody else. I was just an ancient has-been who used to be a member. Nobody gets forgotten by a gang quicker than somebody who moves away.

I got into the subway and went back downtown. I stopped off at a pizza stand for lunch, then went over to a schoolyard and got into a basketball game. Hell of a note when you've got to go around to schoolyards to kill time. I played all afternoon. The kids in the yard were creeps, mostly. Coolies who didn't join the gangs. They tried to get friendly, but I kept my distance. Pretty soon I'd be a Golden Dragon and wouldn't need to play games with their kind.

Then I went looking for Elaine Halperin. Didn't find her. Right then, I didn't care. Rose had taken care of me for now, and it wouldn't be for another couple days that I'd get the itch real bad. But my mind was still made up. One of these days I was going to tear into that Halperin bitch. I'd break her cherry for her.

At last the afternoon was over. It seemed to go on forever. I kept waiting for night to come. I went upstairs, had supper.

That night I left the apartment around eight o'clock. I told my folks I was going to a movie and wouldn't be back till late. I used my brains and remembered to take my house key. My folks didn't squawk. They were used to me coming and going as I pleased.

I hung around in front of the house for a while, trying to pick up a chick. No luck. Two broads came by, wearing tight polo shirts and blue jeans that were like a second skin. They were the sort who hung out with gang kids. I could tell that by the way they walked and moved their hips. You could see that they put out just by looking at them.

I whistled, but they just kept on going. Anything that was worthwhile in this neighborhood was out trying to catch one of the

Golden Dragons. They weren't interested in a guy who didn't belong to the gang. I let it pass. Pretty soon I'd belong to the gang, and then I was goddamn well going to get mine from these broads and all the rest like them. Five times over, and then some.

Around half past nine I figured it was time to amble over to the Dragon hangout. I got to the candy store in a couple of minutes and went in.

There were half a dozen of the Dragons there. Mike Reilly, Johnny Slash, and four others who I didn't know by name yet. I walked right up to them like I was one of the regulars. Johnny Slash and Reilly were sitting together by themselves in a booth, and I sat down with them.

"What's swinging, man?" Reilly asked.

"Nothing much. Hot night."

"You can say that again," Johnny Slash said.

"But don't bother," Reilly added.

"You all set?" Johnny Slash asked me.

I shrugged. "Sure I'm set. What did you think?"

"Just asking, man."

"Well, I'm just answering," I told him. The soda jerk came over and took my order. Malted.

Johnny Slash said, more to Reilly than to me, "Man let's go out and get some beer We can use that ID card I'm carrying."

"Cool it," Reilly said to him. "You don't want no beer tonight, man."

"It's hot, Mike."

"Beer louses up your reflexes. We want to be sharp, man. We can save the drinking for tomorrow."

Johnny Slash looked at me. I shook my head. "Mike's right," I told him. "We got to move fast."

"Yeah," Johnny Slash agreed.

We killed a couple of hours in the candy store. One by one, the other Dragons left to go over to the clubhouse and meet their debs. There was just the three of us left. We didn't talk much. I was still a stranger, so far as they were concerned, and they weren't gonna let me forget it. They asked me a couple questions about the Shining Sinners, how big a gang we were, how we did things, but otherwise they didn't take much notice of me.

Then it was around half past eleven. Reilly said, "Let's get going."

"Yeah," Johnny Slash said.

We got up. I felt cool, real loose. The grocery store was about two blocks from the candy store. It was a nice dark night, not much of a moon. People were sitting around with their windows wide open, trying to get some fresh air. As we walked, we joked and whistled. Mike Reilly nudged me and said, "Take a look at that, man." I looked across the street, one of those old buildings full of little apartments. Up on the second floor, lights were on and a window was open and a girl was walking around stark naked. You see everything in New York. Man, was she built! She was maybe sixteen or seventeen, and she had two ripe knobs in front of her and a cute little backside. She was a blonde, all over. She had just taken a shower or something, and she was walking around her bedroom hanging things up, and we stood there for a couple of minutes watching the way her boobs jingled when she walked. Then she caught sight of us watching her. She turned the prettiest shade of pink and ran over to the window and pulled down the blind. We laughed and kept on going, looking at other windows on the way but not finding anything interesting in them.

"Here we are," Reilly whispered, as we crossed the block where the grocery store was.

Before we did anything, we walked all around the block, separately, our hands in our pockets, looking for fuzz. When we had circled the block completely, we met on the corner and compared notes. None of us had seen anything. There was no cop on patrol.

"Okay," Reilly whispered to us. "I'm going to get started climbing. You got a watch, Flaherty?"

"Yeah."

"What time you got?"

I told him. He made me set my watch to the same time as his. Then he said, "Give me five minutes and then go into the store, Flaherty. Be ready when the lights go out. You miss your cue and we're all screwed."

"Don't you worry none, man," I told him. "I'll be ready."

He nodded and started to walk off.

The job was under way.

CHAPTER FIVE

I counted off the minutes, slow and easy. Reilly had gone into an apartment building that had its front around the corner. It was a big building with a bunch of stores running all along its ground floor, and you could get into the stores from a kind of corridor that ran down through the whole length of the building in back. Usually the back doors were always kept locked by the owners of the stores, but this night was a miserable hot night, a real muggy sweaty one, and if you kept those back doors open you got a pretty good draft through the store, enough to let you breathe a little.

That was what Mike Reilly was counting on, that the back door of the grocery store would be unlocked and ajar. If he couldn't get in from the back I would have to pull the caper all by myself.

Johnny Slash posted himself in front of the door to be our lookout. He leaned against a lamppost and put his hands in his pockets. We had already arranged what kind of whistle he would give if he saw trouble coming.

Then I walked past the store and took a look in. There were no customers inside. Just the proprietor, a middle-aged little guy sitting behind the counter reading a newspaper. He was bald and meek-looking. I went in quietly.

He looked up, put the paper down. He seemed to tense up just at the sight of a teenager coming into his store this late at night.

He said, "Yes? Can I help you?"

I gave him an easy smile, so he wouldn't get scared and maybe mess things up. "I want two quarts of cold beer," I said. "Make it Ballantine."

He folded his paper up nervously, got up, went to a freezer compartment in the back of the store. I stood still, listening, thinking maybe I could hear Reilly moving around in the passageway behind the store. Not a sound. I looked around for something to hit the old man with. There were some nice big bottles of apple juice on the counter, wide bottles with narrow necks that I could get my hand around good and tight. Those would do.

He came back, carrying two quarts of beer. He looked very pale and tired. I felt a little sorry for him. But what the hell. We could use the money. And I had to prove I was tough enough to belong to the Golden Dragons. I couldn't worry too much about him.

He put the beer down on the counter and said, "Is there anything else?"

"No, that's all."

Suddenly he looked at me real close, his bloodshot eyes drawing up in a squint. "I got to ask you to prove your age. I can't sell you this stuff if you're under eighteen. That's the law, and I didn't make the law."

"I'm nineteen, mister," I told him. There was still no sign of Reilly. Not a sound. I started to get a little edgy. Something was wrong. Maybe the door was locked. Maybe I was going to have to do the job all by myself.

"I'm sure you're old enough," he was saying to me. "Believe me, I want to make the sale. But first I got to see your ID card. A cop comes around and sees you leaving with beer this hour of the night and ask questions, I can get into all kinds troubles, you know."

I nodded. "But you ought to take my word for it, mister. Don't I have an honest face? Do you think I'd lie to you about my age?"

"I'd ask the same of anybody. You got to show me the card. If you've got one, what are you afraid of? And if you don't have one, I'll have to ask you please to go away and forget about buying this beer."

"Okay, okay," I said, sighing. Where the hell was Reilly, I wondered? "Just hold your horses, mister. I'll show you my goddamn ID if you're gonna insist about it."

"I did not make the law," he said.

I slowly took my wallet out of my pocket and began to flip through it for the ID card that wasn't there. I kept up a running mumble with myself while I looked, telling myself I was sure I had seen it in here just yesterday, and where the deuce could it have gone?

Sweat dripped coldly down my back. I couldn't keep on stalling forever. Pretty soon a cop would come by, or some other customer, or something, and the caper would be dead.

I was just about coming to the back of my wallet. The grocery store man, positive now that I was under age, was starting to get up steam to tell me to leave. I was wondering what I could possibly use now to stall a little longer.

Then I heard noise from the back of the store.

Someone was trying to push the back door open. But it was locked! Reilly wasn't able to get in! I was all alone and on my own.

Hearing the sounds of someone banging on the metal door, the old man swung nervously around. I bit my lip tensely. This was it. It was all up to me.

"Who's there?" he called out. "Who's banging on the door out there?"

He started toward the door in back. I looked behind me, saw the street was empty out in front. I put a handkerchief around my hand, picked up one of the big apple juice bottles by its narrow neck, leaned across the counter, and smacked the bottle down hard on the back of the old man's bald skull.

There was an ugly loud *thunk* of a sound and the bottle seemed to sink into his head. He dropped without a groan, just folding up and falling.

I knew I had to move fast, now. I ran around behind the counter and pushed the NO SALE key on the cash register. The register popped open and there was all that lovely money poking me in the face. I grabbed it up quickly, tens, fives, ones. I left the change where it was—no use bothering with chicken feed—and jammed the bills into my pockets. The whole thing took maybe half a minute. My fingers were shaking a little as I scooped the bills out of the compartments and pushed them into my jeans.

I ran to the front door, slowed myself down, and stepped out into the street, closing the door behind me.

There was nobody outside but Johnny Slash. He was still leaning with his hands in his pockets, waiting. He looked at me, puzzled.

"Where's Reilly?" he said.

"He couldn't get into the store. The door was locked. Come on, let's beat it."

"But Reilly—"

"He can take care of himself. I've got the dough. Come on!"

Johnny Slash and I started to move off. A moment later, I heard footsteps behind me, coming up fast. I turned. It was Reilly, coming around the corner at a fast trot. He looked boiling mad.

"The son of a bitch had his door locked," Reilly said.

"I know." I patted my bulging pockets. "I conked the old geezer myself when I heard you banging, and I've got the dough. Let's take off."

I could see by the look they both gave me that I had stoned them again. They glanced at each other. They looked impressed.

Then we nodded and broke and scattered, off into the dark night. I felt real big, man. I tell you, I felt fifteen feet high. Real big.

I went loping off down the streets, hoping I wouldn't get lost in a neighborhood I didn't know very well yet. The arrangement was that we would split up after the robbery and then light out for the Dragons' clubhouse. I had never been there, but Reilly had given me the address. He told me to take my time getting there, since it would be locked up until he or Johnny Slash reached it.

I doubled around a couple of times, feeling twitchy with all that cash on me. If a cop came across me now, I'd be as good as cooked. But I kept close to the buildings, in the darkness, and turned corners carefully. Nobody bothered me, and by half past I was at the address Reilly had given me earlier.

The Dragons' clubhouse was a basement apartment, three or four blocks from the grocery store. I went into the building at the side entrance and found myself in a dark courtyard. I crossed the courtyard, went down a couple of steps, and turned left. There was a door. I knocked.

"Who's there?"

"Flaherty."

The door opened slowly. Johnny Slash looked out at me, then opened the door wider, letting me in. He and Reilly had both beaten me to the clubhouse.

I walked in. The place looked okay, a lot better than the Shining Sinners' clubhouse had looked. The way this clubhouse deal works, one of the alumni of the gang, somebody over twenty-one, signs the lease for a basement apartment in a tenement somewhere. Then he steps out of the picture. The gang pays the rent every month—thirty or forty bucks, usually—and the landlord doesn't mind, because the landlords of the buildings in a gang area don't mind anything that goes on in their buildings.

The Golden Dragons' clubhouse was a four-room place. There was a kitchen, a living room, and a couple of other rooms which were probably equipped with beds. Mike Reilly went into the kitchen and opened the refrigerator and came out with three bottles of beer. We went into the living room. The furniture was old and looked like it came from the Salvation Army. The springs of the sofa were showing.

"Okay," Reilly said, handing the beers around. "Let's see the haul."

I began dragging crumpled-up bills out of my pockets and dumping them on the floor. I kept on pulling them out until there was a whole carpet of money around me. Then I turned my pockets inside-out to show that I wasn't pulling a sneak with some of the dough.

Johnny Slash got down on his knees and started unfolding the bills and arranging them in stacks. A stack of tens, a stack of fives, a big stack of ones. It took him five minutes. Then he started to count them. Reilly and I watched as each stack got counted. Reilly scribbled the totals down on a piece of paper.

"Three hundred forty-nine bucks," Reilly said. "Hey, that ain't bad. That ain't bad at all."

"Coulda been a lot worse," Johnny Slash said.

I put in quietly, "What happens to the money, now?"

"We divide it," Reilly said. "We got rules in the constitution about that. One fifth of the proceeds of any job like this goes into the club treasury to pay expenses. Like I mean, the rent. The rest gets divided equally among the members. The guys who actually did the job don't get any more than the rest of the gang. Share and share alike, that's how we work it."

I didn't say anything. Johnny Slash said it for me. "Mike, I think we oughta vote Flaherty here a full share of the loot, even if he ain't a Dragon yet. He's the guy who did the job, after all."

"But he's still on probation," Reilly said. "The constitution says we gotta divide among all the members. That don't include him."

"But how can you cut the guy who did the job out of a share of the take?" Johnny Slash asked.

I didn't butt in. I wanted my share of the money, sure, but I wanted to be a Dragon harder. There'd be plenty of time later to get my share of the dough. I didn't want to be figured as a grabber.

Reilly said, "We'll let the gang decide tomorrow. I ain't gonna go against the constitution on my own say-so. Even though I think we oughta cut Flaherty in. Let's figure out the arithmetic."

The three of us sat down and worked things out. The club treasury's share of the take was seventy bucks. That left two hundred seventy-nine crackers to be divided up. Not counting me, there were fifteen members of the Golden Dragons. Fifteen into two hundred seventy-nine came out to $18.60 apiece. Counting me in as the sixteenth, the share would only be $17.50. So it would cost everybody in the Dragons better than a buck to count me in.

I wondered if they'd do it. Even though I had been the one who got the money for them. It isn't easy to take a buck out of your own pocket just because another guy might be entitled to it.

But I didn't raise a fuss. I finished my beer and said, "It's getting late. I'm gonna shove for home."

"Okay," Reilly said "See you at the candy store tomorrow, huh?"

"Yeah," I said.

I walked out. His words were echoing in my ears. He was inviting me! I figured that meant I was as good as in. It took guts to pull a job like that all by myself. They were impressed. I figured they would decide maybe that my probation was over, that they could take me in as a full-fledged member of the gang instead of holding me dangling for a month.

It was half past one or so when I got back to the housing project. Everything was very quiet. I rode upstairs, let myself in, tiptoed to my room. My kid brother Ray was fast asleep. I got undressed, jumped into bed. But it was a long time before I fell asleep. I kept going over the robbery in my mind. Part of me felt sorry for that poor grocer. But the rest of me didn't care much. A guy who has three hundred fifty bucks in his cash register at the end of a day doesn't need much pity. Even figuring that only forty or fifty bucks of that was profit, that still comes out to a couple of hundred bucks a week he was making. He could spare some of it. And he had helped to make me a Dragon.

The next morning, I couldn't hardly wait to get over to the candy store. I was sure they were going to tell me that my probation was over, that after last night's job I was in, I was a Dragon.

But maybe not. Maybe they'd let me sweat a little while more before making me a member.

I got to the candy store at ten o'clock in the morning. More than a dozen guys were there already. They looked at me in a way that told me that they already knew about what had happened last night.

I wasn't sure where I stood with them when I walked in. Reilly said hello. Then he said, "We're gonna vote on admitting you to membership, Flaherty."

"I'm glad to hear that."

"First we gotta discuss you, though. Go on through and wait in the backyard."

I shrugged and went out the back way, into the courtyard. I sat down against the wall of one of the buildings, and waited for the time to go by. Ten minutes passed. Fifteen. Twenty.

Then I saw the door opening. The officers of the gang were coming into the courtyard. Mike Reilly, Jimmy Nails, Johnny Slash, Mack Brown.

I stood up.

"Give him the dough," Reilly said.

Johnny Slash fished into his pocket. He took out a ten, a five, two singles, and some small change. A total of $17.50. One full share of the haul. He handed it to me.

"Here," he said. "The members voted to cut you in equal with them. That's your share."

I looked at the dough in my hand. "Does that mean I'm gonna become a member of the gang, or is it just a payoff for good work?"

Reilly said, "We voted to end your probation, Flaherty."

"Great!"

"But you ain't a member yet. First there's the initiation. You got to pass that before you can be a member."

"Any time you say."

"We say tonight," Reilly said. "Come to the clubhouse at eight. If everything goes okay, you'll be sworn into the gang tonight."

I grinned. "Be seeing you, then. Tonight at eight."

I left the candy store. The gang didn't want me around until tonight. So I had another long day to use up. But this was the last one I'd have to kill by myself. By tomorrow, I'd be a member of the gang. I'd be on the inside instead of just a stranger.

I wandered around for a while, then went up to the house to see about lunch. Lunch wasn't ready. My mother had bought the morning paper, though, and I picked it up and leafed through it.

I was looking for something particular.

I found it.

It was on page three, a story of the grocery store robbery. I read it through quickly. It said that the police had found the unconscious grocer at two in the morning. His wife was worried when he didn't come home at the usual time, and called the cops, who went over to the store to investigate. They found the grocer out like a light and the cash register empty. No clues. The take was estimated at "three to four hundred dollars," which was close enough.

As for the grocer, he was in the hospital with a possible skull fracture. They listed him as in critical condition, and at press time he hadn't recovered consciousness.

The article didn't say anything about possible suspects. I turned to another page, read a couple of stories, put the paper down. Too bad about the grocer, I thought. But most likely he'd pull through. He'd survive and say that his attacker was a teenager, but he couldn't go any further than that. I don't look out of the ordinary. I don't have freckles or buck teeth or a big nose or anything else that might catch the attention. Besides, he probably wouldn't identify me, because he would want to go on doing business in this neighborhood and he would know what would happen to him if the gang kids found out he'd informed the cops. So I was safe. The case would just go down in the police records as another unsolved juvenile robbery. There weren't enough cops to go around to track down every grocery store robber.

I had lunch. Then I hung around the house for a while, not doing anything particular.

I wondered about the initiation. Some gang initiations could be rough. When I got into the Shining Sinners, I didn't have to do much. Just put out lighted matches with my bare hands and drink a quart of beer chug-a-lug and do a couple of other things like that. But I knew gangs where they made the new man run a gantlet socking him with cartridge belts as he ran. And other gangs where they made you spend a night on a roof naked in the wintertime. It all depended on the mood the gang was in when they dreamed up the initiation.

Well, I was ready for anything they could throw at me. I'd show them I wasn't chicken.

After supper that night, I told my parents I was going out. They didn't argue. I walked over to the clubhouse, getting there just around eight. I went down into the courtyard, into the basement, knocked on the door. I heard plenty of noise coming from behind that door. Like a real big party was going on.

The door opened.

"Enter," Jimmy Nails said.

I stepped in.

The place was jammed. All of the Golden Dragons were there, fifteen of them. Five colored fellows and the rest Irish. And there were a lot of girls, too. It was the first time I saw the Dragons debs. There were maybe a dozen of them—two or three of the guys didn't seem to have girls tonight and most of them were lookers.

Jimmy Nails said to me, "I'm in charge of your initiation. Come on out here with me."

He led me into the middle of the floor and introduced me to everybody as a would-be Golden Dragon. I looked around, nodding at them all.

Jimmy Nails said, "Your initiation will be in three parts. You must pass all three parts in order to become a member of this club. First you must drink the sacred drink. Blindfold him."

I let Mack Brown tie a handkerchief over my eyes. Someone else put a glass into my hand.

Jimmy Nails said, "Now you must drain the sacred glass in one gulp."

For a fraction of a second I was worried. That glass could contain anything from horse piss to iodine. And I once heard of a case where a gang was initiating a guy they really hated, and gave him a glass of sulphuric acid to drink. Burned his guts out.

But the whole point of the initiation was to see whether I was chicken or not. So without stopping to think about anything, I put the glass to my lips, tilted my head back, and gulped it down.

Whoo-ee!

It was like drinking a bolt of lightning. Later I found out what was in the glass. It was a mixture of cheap whiskey, tabasco sauce, beer, salt, mercurochrome, and vinegar. It went down fast, and I felt it bounce. But I kept control. My throat was burning, but I didn't cough, didn't even say a word. They took the blindfold off me.

"How do you feel?" Jimmy Nails asked,

"Fine," I said. "What do I get for a chaser?"

"Nothing. You have passed the first ordeal. Now for the second."

I waited. Johnny Slash came toward me. He drew out his switchblade knife and held it, unopened, in front of my face. I stared at it, but I didn't move.

He flicked the switch.

The blade shot out. I forced myself not to blink. The distance had been figured to a T. The point of the blade was about half an inch from my eyeball. I stood very still while Johnny began to pass the knife in slow circles in front of my eyes. A sneeze by either of us and I'd be blind. He kept going back and forth for maybe a minute. The minute seemed like two days. Then he pulled the knife back from my eyes. I felt sweat dripping down. This knife stunt was worked other ways, too. Sometimes the guy being initiated had to strip naked and stand perfectly still while the knife was passed between his legs. That was tough, especially when there were a dozen girls watching.

But they didn't try that one on me. Johnny put his knife away.

Jimmy Nails said, "You have passed the second ordeal. But the third and hardest is still ahead of you. You can back out now if you want to."

"I'll take my chances."

"Okay," Jimmy Nails said. "Mack, get the hat. Johnny, hand out the pieces of paper."

I stood against the wall, wondering what the hell was coming next. The drink they had given me still tingled in my belly. I told myself I was ready for anything they could think up.

Anything.

CHAPTER SIX

I began to get the idea of the final ordeal when each of the debs in the room took a piece of paper and wrote her name on it. Mack Brown went around with the hat, and each girl dropped her slip of paper in.

Jimmy Nails said to me, "Anybody who wants to be a member of the Golden Dragons, he's gotta be a he-man. We don't have no room for fairies here. You get what I'm saying, man?"

"Keep talking," I said.

"You gotta prove it to us. So you take this hat and pick three names outa it. Then you're gonna make it with those three girls."

"One right after another?"

"That's the idea," he said. "You figure you're up to it? Maybe you wanta chicken out?"

"I'm not chickening," I told him.

"There's just one thing more you oughta know The action gets performed right here. In front of all of us. *Now* you wanta back out?"

I was quiet for a minute. Hell, laying three girls in a row isn't the easiest thing in the world to do. And doing it in front of a mixed audience was a bitch of a job. But we had done plenty of fooling around in the Shining Sinners. Orgies, the newspapers would call them. Ten or twelve couples all naked, doing it at the same time. That wasn't quite the same thing as what I was asked to do here. But other times we had screwing exhibitions, and me and Flora had had our turn at them while the rest of the gang and the debs stood around and watched and made bets and all. So I wasn't embarrassed by the idea, if you get me. Just a little worried. I wanted everything to work out right.

"What if I don't pass?" I asked.

"Then we beat the crap outa you and throw you the hell outa here," Jimmy Nails said.

I nodded. "Okay. Gimme the hat."

Mack Brown came over to me and held the hat out. It was a floppy cloth hat, and the slips of paper were folded up in the bottom of it.

"Close your eyes and pick one," he said.

I reached into the hat. My fingers closed on one of the slips. I pulled it out and opened my eyes.

"Read the name," Mack Brown commanded.

I unfolded the slip of paper. "It says Lisa."

"Lucky bastard," somebody muttered. I looked around, Jimmy Nails pointed at one of the debs and said, "There she is over there."

She was grinning at me. I felt excited, all right. Of all the girls in the room, she was easily the best looker. She was a lean blonde with soft golden hair dropping down to her shoulders. Her breasts stuck out in front of her like a pair of grapefruits. Laying her wouldn't be a task, it would be a party!

Mike Reilly said, "Lisa's my deb, Flaherty. There are guys in this room who'd gladly sell their sisters to get a turn in bed with her. And you walk right in and grab one off like that."

"I didn't ask for it," I said. "But I'm sure not complainin'."

"Pick another name," Mack Brown said.

I closed my eyes and fished in the hat again. I saw the setup. Each of the debs had to take part in this, whether she wanted to or not. And it was just chance that I'd pick the deb belonging to some particular gang member. They were all willing to risk having somebody else lay their deb once, for the sake of the amusement.

I pulled out the second name and unfolded the paper.

"Joanne," I read.

Jimmy Nails pointed her out to me. She was the deb of a fellow named Smokey. Joanne was a redhead, kind of skinny, with a turned-up nose and Irish eyes. She wasn't much on looks at all, especially after Lisa. But hell, that was just the breaks. She looked up at me kind of shyly, but she seemed interested. Her regular steady, Smokey, was a chubby kid with a kind of piggish look about him, and maybe she figured I'd give her some fun Smokey hadn't.

"Go on," Mack Brown said. "Now the last one."

I reached in. I spent a long time stirring around the papers. Joanne and Lisa were relaxed, but the other ten debs all looked kind of nervous. Maybe some of them weren't happy about the chance of getting picked.

"Lora," I read out.

All of a sudden a girl was on her feet, shouting. She was a tall girl, taller than me, and really stacked. She was wearing a black pullover and her big breasts were bouncing around in it as she got to her feet. She wasn't pretty: her nose was flat, her skin lousy. But she sure had a body. And now she was fighting mad.

"No, goddamn it! I ain't laying for some new guy in front of everybody!" she was yelling.

Johnny Slash took a step toward her, and I realized she was his deb.

"Shut your mouth, you bitch!" he said quietly.

"No! I won't do it! I'm your deb, I ain't gonna get into no circus act!"

"We all agreed," Johnny Slash told her. "It's for the initiation. Everybody had the same chance of getting picked, Lora."

"I don't give a crap! I ain't the kind of girl who does—"

Whack!

Johnny's arm blurred and his hand went across her mouth in a tremendous backhand slap. Her head went cracking back and I thought it would come off altogether. She staggered a couple of steps, almost fell. When she took her hand away from her mouth, I saw that her lip was bleeding. She had gone very pale. Nobody in the room was speaking.

Johnny came toward her again. His face was frozen in anger. He started to lift his hand, and she cowered, ready to block the blow, but instead of slapping her he brought his hand down fast and rammed her in the belly. She doubled up in pain.

Johnny said coldly, "You bitch, you don't get any fancy ideas around here, get me?"

She didn't answer. She was just whimpering.

Out came Johnny's knife. He flicked out the blade and stood over her and said, "One squawk outa you and I'll cut your fat tits off. You gonna cooperate or am I gonna have to—"

"No, Johnny! I'll do it!"

"Damn right you will," he said. The knife went back into his pocket. He looked up at Jimmy Nails. "Sorry," he said. "She's still kinda new around here. She gotta be taught her place."

Nobody said anything. A couple of debs looked annoyed at what had happened. But one rule around a gang is that the deb is her stud's property. When a caper is planned, the deb don't raise objections. Once she hooks up with a gang kid, she does what he wants. And if he wants her to strip down and lay publicly for a stranger, she does it—or else.

"We'll continue," Jimmy Nails said. "Bring in the mat."

Two of the Golden Dragons went into one of the bedrooms and returned with a mattress that they dumped down in the middle of the floor. I stood to one side, trying to look cool and collected.

Jimmy Nails said, "It's half past eight now. You got exactly one hour to make it with all three of those girls. Pick any order you like. Okay, start."

I looked over the three girls. Lisa, Joanne, Lora. Lisa was easily the prettiest. By miles. Joanne was skinny and plain, while Lora was so big she was practically sloppy. The temptation to start off with Lisa was big. But I'm not that dumb. The trick was to save the prettiest for last, when I'd need stimulation. Start with the worst, then take the next worst, finally Lisa when I'd be pooped out and needing some extra incentive.

"Lora first," I said.

She came forward. Her lip was still bleeding, and she looked angry and vicious. She was doing this only because she was scared not to, but she didn't want to do it, that was for sure.

In a low voice she said, "What do ya want me to do?"

"Strip," I said.

She hesitated. In the corner of the room, Johnny Slash cracked his knuckles loudly. He took his knife out of his pocket and began playing catch with it.

Lora started to strip. She pulled her black jersey up over her head and dropped it to one side. She didn't have any bra on underneath, and her big breasts swung from side to side. They were the biggest I'd ever seen. Huge. They had little dimples in them, they were so big. They started right below her collarbone and must have gone a foot down her chest, as well as sticking out a foot.

She stood there with those enormous boobs sticking out, and every eye in the room fastened right on her. She was sweating, and blushing all over. Her hands went to her belt. She opened it, unzipped, pulled her jeans off. The jeans were tight, and it was a struggle getting them over her hips. They came, finally. She had black panties on underneath them, and she rolled them off and stood naked in the middle of the room. I could see she was embarrassed by it. She was huge, monstrous, her thighs big and thick like lampposts. Johnny Slash sure liked his women big. I figured this one for close to two hundred pounds. And not ugly, either.

I began to undress. I didn't mind peeling in front of the mob. I'm built well, so what the hell do I have to be ashamed of? I took my shirt off, my pants, my briefs. Just looking at Lora's body, those big breasts, that king-size backside, made me hot. I saw the other girls looking at me. Maybe they were wishing I had picked their names instead of Lora's. I don't know.

Lora just stood there like a statue.

"Lie down," I said.

She got down on the mattress. I got down on top of her, and it was like stretching out on foam rubber, she was that soft. But she didn't make a move. I saw her game now. She would do what Johnny Slash ordered, but she was damned if she would cooperate with me. Anything I did, I'd be doing *to* her, not *with* her.

Well, to hell with her. I didn't need her to cooperate. I could manage all right by myself.

Jimmy Nails hadn't said I had to *satisfy* the three girls. Just to make 'em. That was okay.

It was the damndest thing. I've laid girls who went half out of their minds when I touched them, and I've laid girls who were being half-raped and fought me all the way. But I hadn't ever laid a girl like this, who just stayed there without moving, without doing a thing.

For a moment I figured I'd just move fast and get it over with and get off her and to hell with the bitch. But something in me felt bad about doing it this way. With her like a dead lump of lard.

I said to her, "I know you don't wanta do this, but you might as well enjoy it as long as you are doing, it."

"Go to hell," she said quietly.

A hell of a conversation for two people who are on a mattress with their bodies joined already. I felt a sudden flare of anger. I tightened on her breasts, feeling my fingers sink deep into their spongy fatness, and I lowered my head to her shoulder and took a bite out of her, and I drove myself deep into her …

And she came alive.

Despite herself, it took hold of her, and she started to pant and shake and arch her back, and then the big ripples started going through her, and I knew she was out of control, running wild, and I kept rocking back and forth above her until I felt the shivers running through my own body, and inside my head I heard three quick claps of thunder and I let out my breath in a long slow sigh and it was over.

I looked down at Lora. She opened her eyes now for the first time since I had bitten her. She looked kind of dazed and shaken up.

"You bastard," she whispered, but I knew she didn't mean it. "How'd you do that to me?"

"A trick I learned in Afghanistan," I said. I slipped free of her and stood up. She scrambled heavily to her feet and began to get back into her clothes. I was breathing hard, feeling a little surprised myself at what had happened. I took a quick look at Johnny Slash. He didn't look too happy about the way I'd made his deb perform like a goddamn trained seal on the floor.

Jimmy Nails said, "That took ten minutes. You want to take a breather?"

"Yeah," I said. "I'll take five or ten."

I put my pants back on. I didn't feel much like standing around in the raw between bouts. I sat down and caught my breath. I was sweaty and sort of tired. Two more rounds still ahead of me. And it would get harder and harder and harder all the time.

I let nine or ten minutes go by. Then I stood up and said, "Okay, I'm ready."

"Which girl next?" Jimmy Nails asked.

"Joanne," I said.

Joanne came forward. She was very nervous, I could tell. Close up, I saw that she couldn't have been much more than fourteen or fifteen at the absolute tops. A skinny little slip of a girl who probably hadn't reached her full growth yet. What the hell. I wouldn't complain.

I told her to strip, and she peeled quickly, with a bit of embarrassment. When she was naked, I could see that she couldn't be past fourteen. That cat Smokey was a goddamn cradle-robber. Joanne's breasts weren't much more than little bumps, and her hips were narrow.

She was scared. But willing.

I got down next to her on the mattress. She was on the bony side, and I was wondering if I could turn myself on at all for this frail chick.

But then at last I was ready. I turned, getting on her, grabbing her to me. We moved slowly at first, then faster, and I felt the tingling begin and knew that this was going to be a fast one for me, and I tried to heat her up, doing everything I could for her, only nothing seemed to get through to her. She was trying hard, but I couldn't stay with her, and after maybe five minutes it was over for me. But Joanne wouldn't give up. She kept on pistoning her narrow hips, and it was starting to hurt me, and I tried to give her what she wanted, but nothing was happening, and finally she slowed down and released me.

"Sorry," I said.

She smiled. A sad little-girl smile. "Wasn't your fault. I'm like that all the time."

Then I stepped back, feeling really winded this time. My heart was pounding away like crazy. Jimmy Nails told me that half an hour was gone. That wasn't bad. Two thirds of the assignment done in half an hour. And the best-looking female left for last.

"I'll take ten this time," I said.

I went into the john and washed some of the sweat off me. I was dripping wet. I felt pretty beat, too. The weather was hot, and I was worried about passing this damn initiation. Even with Lisa still ahead of me. What if I flubbed it? Would they really kick me out on my butt, or would they let me get by anyway? I wondered.

I came out of the john. Somebody offered me a can of beer and I took it and drank about half of it. Then I turned, looking for Lisa. She was sitting on the couch, and when I looked at her her face put on an interesting smile. Christ, she was beautiful. Sleek and smooth and soft and satiny, and a mischievous look in her eyes.

"Come on," I said to her.

She rose and came over to me. "Do you want me to undress?" she asked.

"I'll undress you," I said.

I felt a throb of excitement as I put my hands on the front of her sweater. I let them rest on her breasts for a moment, just taking a first feel to sample what was ahead of me. The sweater was silky to the touch. I knew her skin would be, too. I pulled the sweater over her head. She was about five six or so, a tall girl. I took the sweater off her and unhooked her bra, bringing it forward off her breasts.

She was *built*.

Her breasts rose high and firm, and they were pale white, sort of creamy color with a glow of their own. The nipples were small and pinkish-red, and they sat near the top of the curve, looking up at me. My hands shook a little as I put them on those two round ripe boobs of hers.

This was plenty of woman, all right. Mike Reilly had himself quite a piece.

I opened her jeans and got them off, and her panties, and she stood there naked with her golden hair down around her shoulders, and the tips of her breasts inches from me, and her body all pink and white and creamy and wonderful. I took her shoulders, ran my hands down her back to her buttocks. The skin was like satin.

We lay down together on the mattress. Our lips came together, and her tongue touched mine. For I don't know how many minutes we kissed, and I forgot all about the audience, forgot all about the initiation.

Then she drew me down on top of her.

And nothing happened.

Nothing at all.

I don't know if it was because I was tired from Lora and Joanne, or if I was just flustered because this girl was such a dream. But the way I was, I might have been ninety years old. I was lying naked next to the most beautiful girl I'd ever seen, and I couldn't do a goddamn solitary thing.

For a couple of minutes we tried to get somewhere. No go. People were muttering things behind me. I felt my face going red. Was I going to foul up, now? Time was running out on me. I didn't have more than five or six minutes left, I bet. And the way things looked, I wasn't going to be worth a damn for a lot longer than that.

I looked at Lisa. She still had that same strange smile on her face. And I knew I was in her power. I couldn't do a thing unless she would help me.

She smiled.

Then her hands started to rove over me.

I relaxed, knowing she was helping me, hoping everything would be all right. Her fingers wandered magically. I began to breathe harder. I had my hands on her breasts, and the nipples were stiff against my palms, and I was looking into her eyes and seeing strange flecks of gold there, and our bodies were very close and yet still I was helpless, but the excitement was growing in me, growing by the minute as she used all of her skill, and then we were kissing, her tongue like a hot dart in my mouth.

And it began to happen.

I don't know the exact moment. One moment I was helpless, and the next I was on fire, burning up in the flame of her body, entering her, and she was moving, doing things with the muscles inside her, and when I opened my eyes for a moment I saw her with her eyes closed and still smiling, and then her fingers were raking lines down my back and she was starting to moan, and I was carried away with her as sounds started to come out of her throat and mine, and it was like this was the first time I had ever done it with a girl, and the world was full of light and I felt the shudder of delight and rockets going off inside my head, and Lisa was stiff against me, her whole body shaking with pounding delight, and I felt it flowing through me like an electric current, and it was *oh* and *oh* and *oh* again, the current flowing through both of us, jolt after jolt, after jolt, and we were way up, far out, and then it was ending, hard as we tried to hang onto it, it was ending, and down we came out of the stratosphere and it was all over, and I gasped for breath and pillowed down between Lisa's wonderful breasts and shook with exhaustion.

I was beat.

But I had passed the test.

CHAPTER SEVEN

Ten minutes later, I had my clothes back on and I was drinking from a glass of half-and-half that somebody had put in my hand. It was good stuff, a mix of muscatel and bourbon bought out of the club treasury.

One thing was sure.

I was in.

They gave me the oath, which I can't repeat here because it can't be printed. And then they told me I was a full-fledged member of the Golden Dragons. The words were music to my ears. Now, all I needed was a deb, and I'd be set up.

I knew who I wanted for my deb, too. The only minor hitch was that she was Lisa, and she belonged to the Prez of the Golden Dragons, Mike Reilly himself. I was asking for plenty of trouble if I tried to take the Prez' deb away from him. But I didn't give a damn. The little taste I had had of Lisa's body convinced me that I had to have her again. Sooner or later, there was going to have to be a showdown between me and Mike Reilly for her.

But not yet. I couldn't move too fast. I was still new around here. I couldn't go challenging the top man, because he'd be surrounded by loyal guys who might slit my guts if I made any move against him.

So that night I didn't have a deb. Not that I needed one, after my initiation. What I really needed was a good night's sleep. Later, though.

A Dragon named Coco came over to me, grinning and said, "Man, you really did okay out there."

"I was kinda worried for a while," I said.

"We initiated a guy same way last year," Coco told me. "He punked out. Couldn't make it with the second girl. Just sat there and cursed till his hour ran up."

"What happened to him?"

"We tossed him out," Coco said. "A guy gotta pass the initiation." He lowered his voice. "Tell me something, huh, man?"

"Sure,"

"That Lisa. What's it like, making it with her?"

"The most, man. Really the most."

"Jeez, you sure had it lucky. You know how long I been stiff for that one? Ever since the first day she come into this clubhouse. That was last year some time. But Reilly don't let nobody touch her. Except for initiations, and this was the first time anybody picked her name out."

I smiled to myself. So I was really a lucky, then, if I was the first guy in the gang outside of Reilly to get into the lovely Lisa. I wanted more of that stuff, too.

I spotted Lisa at the other end of the room, leaning against the wall and talking to Reilly. Even though she had her clothes on again, I kept seeing her naked, kept seeing the whiteness of her skin and the roundness of her breasts. I walked over to them and said hello. I gave Lisa the eye, and she smiled at me in her strange way. Then I caught Mike Reilly looking at me as if he was reading my mind.

He said, "Now that you're in the gang, Flaherty, we've got to find you a deb. I'll talk to a couple girls I know. They been thinking of joining the gang, anyway."

"They better be lookers," I said.

"If you don't like 'em, don't take 'em," he told me. He glanced at Lisa and added, "One thing I ought to tell you, though. Don't get any ideas about any of the girls who are Dragon debs already. We don't go for deb-stealing around here. The guys get rough with anyone who tries it."

"I wouldn't pull any crap like that, Mike. But let me tell you this. If you dropped dead tomorrow I wouldn't waste any time making a play for your chick here. She's really the most, I tell you truly."

"Don't I know it," Reilly said. "But you've had all you're gonna get, man. At least while I'm around." The conversation was getting sort of grim, so he laughed and poured some more half-and-half into my glass, and called over a couple more of the Golden Dragons so I could learn their names.

One tall drink of water name of Lookit said, "I hear you got an ace of a sister, Danny."

"Yeah."

"You gonna bring her down to the clubhouse now that you're a member?"

"I don't bring her nowhere. She goes where she pleases."

"I was just wondering," Lookit said. "My deb Lulu moved to Queens. I'm sorta looking around for a replacement. You got any objections if I try to get somewhere with your sister, man?"

I shrugged. "I don't own her. You get hold of her and see if she goes for you, is all. Maybe she will, maybe she won't."

"Just wanted to find out if you objected."

"I tell you, she does what she likes."

Lookit thanked me—I don't know for what—and moved away. I really didn't give a damn about what Sis did. She was old enough to look after herself. If she fell for this Lookit guy, that was her affair. He wasn't bad looking. A basketball player type, maybe six foot three. Hell, I figured Sis was probably out on her own somewhere, and it would be safer if she was here where I could keep half an eye on her.

The party went on for a couple hours that way. There was a lot of necking, and some of the couples slipped into the back rooms to make it with each other. Then around eleven o'clock the doorbell rang. Mike Reilly was all wrapped around Lisa and had his hand up her sweater, but he got free of her in half a second and went to answer it, along with Mack Brown. They opened it half an inch and looked out. I heard a voice out there. Then Reilly and Mack went into the hallway and were out there ten minutes.

When they came back, they were grinning. Reilly said in a loud voice, "We just had a visit from Joey and he had the goods. The club treasury laid out fifteen bucks for thirty joints. Anybody who wants, it's half a buck a blast."

Mack Brown held out his two big hands. In neat rows on his palms were a bunch of cigarettes, with dirty brown wrappers.

I knew what they were.

They weren't Luckies or Old Gold. Oh, no.

They were M, Big M. Maryjane. Mootah.

Reefers.

I turned to a guy named Zorro and said, "Who's this Joey cat who was out there?"

"The connection," Zorro said. "Comes around once a week or so, Especially after he hears there's been a job in the neighborhood on one of the stores."

"Only sells reefers?" I asked.

"Hell, no. He sells anything. Bennie, H, cocaine, if there's a kick in it he peddles it. But we don't use much of that stuff around here. Except Vince, he's the horsehead in the gang. The guy over there."

Vince was a small guy with half-closed eyes and a funny expression. He hadn't said much, and he didn't have a deb with him. Now he was grinning In a half-assed way, and I figured he'd just gone into the john and turned on.

Usually you don't get more than one or two heroin addicts in a gang. Horseheads aren't much fun. They're off in their own private worlds, they don't go for chicks much, they're lousy in a rumble. Me, I tried H once and it was a good kick, but I didn't go back to it again. I didn't want to get hooked. Once was enough to tell me what it was like, but I've seen too many poor bastards with the monkey on their backs.

Marijuana, now. That's a different thing.

I never knew a gang stud who didn't take a reefer now and then. It isn't all that dangerous. Oh, you can get hooked if you're dumb enough, or you can go on from M to rougher stuff. But the reefers aren't supposed to be habit-forming unless you start smoking them five or ten a day, and at half a buck a joint it's hard to get into that kind of habit.

I'd had plenty of reefers in my day. And now Mike Reilly and Mack Brown were going around peddling them to everybody in the room. They came to me.

Reilly said, "You go for this stuff?"

"Bet your sweet butt I do, man."

I dug into my jeans and found a half buck. I handed it to Reilly, and Mack Brown gave me one of the reefers. I studied the joint for a second. It was better workmanship than the stuff we got uptown. The paper it was wrapped in was cut even, and it wasn't as brown and flimsy as the uptown kind. And the ends of the joint had been tamped flat in a professional sort of way.

All around the room the Golden Dragons and their debs were lighting up. I struck a match and touched it to the end of the joint and took a long, deep drag.

A reefer burns fast. You gotta haul that smoke down into your lungs in a hurry. I dragged it way down; a couple more drags and I was at the bottom of the butt. I got rid of it and leaned back and waited for the kicks.

The first time you take M is always the best. You go way out of the universe, up into outer space where the stars go blink-blink-blink. The second time is almost as good. After that, it depends on how often you let yourself have a blast. I know guys who don't feel a thing, because they smoke M every day. But if you go a week or two between joints, they hit you real sweet.

I hadn't had one in maybe two and a half weeks. So this one took me hard. I went way up, out, up and, over. I was drifting in the middle of the air. I closed my eyes and saw Lisa, naked, drifting near me. I reached out and took her, and we started to make it, and there was no sweat, it just kept going on and on for maybe half an hour, the two of us drifting, in outer space and making it.

Then the kick started to wear off. I opened my eyes and there wasn't any Lisa, because she was across the room with Reilly. There was a sweet taste in the back of my mouth, and my eyes hurt a little, and I felt kind of low. Sometimes that happens, too. You go all the way up, and when you come down you come down *hard*. I looked around the room and saw the Dragons and their debs glowing and lit up on the M, and I wished like hell I had a deb too.

I got up and went down the hall to the john. I was in the crapper maybe five minutes, feeling sorry for myself because I didn't have a deb like Lisa. Then I opened the door and started to go out, and damn near walked into—who do you think?—Lisa.

She pushed me back into the john and got in there with me. I did the first thing that came to my mind. I put one hand on her breasts and pulled her tight for a kiss. But she went stiff and backed away from me.

"No, Danny. Don't."

"But I want you."

She shook her head. "That's what I got to talk about with you, Danny. You gotta forget about me."

"Look, I made it with you out On the floor, Lisa. You're the greatest. You're the hottest thing I ever saw."

"I'm Mike Reilly's deb."

"Junk him!"

She looked frightened. "He'll kill us both, Danny! He don't let nobody fool with me. I only came in here now because he's asleep." She was very close to me. "I had a good time out of you, Danny. If anything ever happens to Mike, I'll be your deb. That's a promise. But don't make trouble. As long as Mike's around, keep away. Find yourself some other girl. And don't try to jap him, either. Mike's got friends in this gang. You do anything to him, they'll get you."

"So I gotta forget about you?"

"Yeah," she said. "Please, Danny."

"Gimme a quick kiss. One last one."

She hung back for a second. Then she was in my arms, and my hands were grabbing her breasts and feeling their firmness through the sweater, and she had her belly against mine and her hips were going from side to side, and for half a minute I felt like dragging her to the floor.

Then I felt her going kind of stiff and cold, and pulling away from me. So I let go of her and went out of the bathroom, back up the hall.

Mike Reilly was still sacked out with a dreamy smile on his face. Everywhere else, Dragons and their debs were busy with each other, except for the loners, Vince the horsehead and Lookit and a guy named Sonny. Vince was sitting in a big arm chair with his eyes closed and a junkie grin on his face. Lookit and Sonny were mixing sneaky pete and cheap bourbon and were getting stoned as fast as they knew how. I went over to them and took the bottle away from them and poured myself a nice big one.

For maybe half an hour I guzzled with them. Then I started to get tired of drinking that junk. So I picked up and got out. It was after one in the morning, and a couple of Dragons had left already, and the ones who were still there were either stoned or busy with their debs. I wasn't either, and it hurt me to see Mike Reilly on the couch with his hand up the front of Lisa's sweater. So I picked up and cleared out of there.

The walk home loosened me up a little. It had been a pretty hectic night. There was that initiation, and the reefer, and all the drinks. Plenty for one night. Especially when you've had three girls, and one of them is something like Lisa that turns you all topsy-turvy inside.

As I walked home, I figured out what I wanted to do and where I wanted to head now that I was a full-fledged member of the Golden Dragons. For the next three or four weeks, I would play it cool and take things slow. I'd find myself a deb who would give me a good time, and I'd get to know the other guys in the gang. I'd make them see that I was an okay guy. I'd pick out a few friends and start building loyalties.

Then—maybe around September, if I felt strong enough in the gang by then I'd go to Mike Reilly and demand a new election of the gang leaders. With five or six guys backing me, he'd probably give in. If I won the election, fine. If I lost, I'd challenge Reilly to a hand-to-hand stand for the Prez job and for Lisa.

And I'd beat him.

Danny Flaherty, Prez of the Golden Dragons. It sounded nice. In the Shining Sinners, I was only the Number Two man, the War Councilor. But that was because the top man was a pal of mine, and I didn't want to jap him or push him out of his spot. Here it was different. I had nothing personal against Mike Reilly. I even liked the guy some. But he had Lisa, and I wanted Lisa, and so something had to give.

In the meanwhile, though, I'd have to play it slow. Find me a deb. Maybe go after that Elaine Halperin broad and try to get somewhere with her.

I was full of plans. Tired as I was, I took a long time falling asleep.

The next morning, after breakfast, I headed over to the candy store where the Golden Dragons hung out during the day. It was an okay feeling, knowing I could walk right into their place and belong there. Five or six guys were there when I showed up, and a couple of debs. Mike Reilly was sitting at a booth by himself, along with Lisa and another girl. He flicked a finger at me to call me over.

"What goes, Prez?"

"Got someone here I want you to meet. Vickey Monaghan, this is Danny Flaherty."

We looked each other over. Vickey was easy on the eyes. Nothing like Lisa, in fact not as pretty as a couple of the other Dragon debs, but plenty all right. She was a brunette with short hair and a good face. She was wearing a shirt with the tails out, and there were two nice big bumps sticking out under the skirt. She didn't look shy, either. She looked like a girl who liked to put out and wanted somebody who could give her a good rise.

I slid into the booth next to her, facing Reilly and Lisa. Vickey's blue-jeaned thighs were up against mine. She was warm and firm.

Reilly said, "Vickey used to be the deb of a cat name of Bebop. He got cooled off in April when we had the big rumble with the Red Eagles. Vickey quit the gang, sort of in mourning. But I talked her into coming around again to meet you."

"I didn't think I'd ever get over it when Bebop got it," Vickey said.

Her voice was deep and pleasant. "But it's been three months. I was sort of interested in getting back into the Dragons debs. Only none of the loose cats appealed to me. Till Mike talked me into coming down today."

Well, it was a pretty transparent move. Reilly was afraid I was getting interested in Lisa, so he dug up this pretty good chick to take my mind off her. I grinned across the table at Reilly and put my right hand down on the cap of Vickey's knee. She didn't take it off. After a moment I moved my hand up her jeans, putting it on her belly for a moment, then snaking the fingers forward on her legs. She clamped tight over my hand. So I knew I was in like Flynn with Vickey, just like that.

I said, "I didn't hear much about that rumble with the Eagles in April. What was it about?"

"They were claiming a block of our turf," Reilly said. "We showed them they were wrong."

"Big fight?"

"We killed two guys and sent one to the hospital with a cut throat. And they got one of our guys. The fuzz were all over the place for weeks after that. They're still all around."

"Hasn't been any action since, huh?"

Reilly shook his head. "Us and the Eagles both, we're layin' low. The cops get word of rumbles too fast. They bust 'em up. Anyway, it's too hot for a rumble now. We just been relaxin' this summer."

"Any of the fellows getting tired of playing it cool?" I asked.

"A couple," Reilly said. "But I'm keeping the lid on, just for now."

I nodded. That was interesting. No rumbles in three months. Probably that was causing some annoyance in the Golden Dragons' rank and file. Some of the guys must be bugged about no action. It gave me a selling point for when I challenged Reilly for the top. If I promised to get rid of Reilly because he played it too cool, it might get me some support. A gang needs action. You get bored hanging around candy stores and busting into a grocery store now and then. A good rumble keeps your blood moving in your veins.

I slipped my hand from Vickey's legs and around her shoulder, then under her arm to the side of her breast. She grinned and wiggled up closer to me. We sat around batting the breeze for a while in the candy store.

Then I got a surprise.

Lookit walked in.

With my sister.

Sis is a short girl, around five two, and Lookit was better than a foot taller than her. He had his arm around her and they looked real cozy.

Kemo whistled. "Hey, Lookit, who's the broad?"

Lookit grinned. "Ask Flaherty."

"Who is she, Danny?" Cannon called across three booths.

"My sister," I said.

There was a whole chorus of whistles. Sis seemed to be enjoying all the attention. It's hard to know what's on her mind, because she keeps a sort of mask over her face, not a real mask but like hiding her inner feelings with a funny smile. She came in and she and Lookit sat down at the booth next to ours. Lookit swung around and said. "Mike, I got a candidate for the Dragon debs."

"So I see." Reilly looked at me, then at Sis. "Looks like now we know why Flaherty's so ugly. His sister got all the looks in the family."

Everybody laughed. Me too. I didn't mind.

Lookit said, "She wants to join tonight."

"Okay. We'll take care of it."

I said to Reilly, "Is there an initiation for Dragons debs too?"

"There sure is, man."

"What's it like?"

He had a peculiar smile on his face. "You'll see tonight. It's different each time. We gotta meet and figure something good out."

I frowned at that. For all I knew, the initiation for Sis would consist of having her laid by every guy in the gang. I wouldn't put up with that. I was all mixed up for a moment. I knew Sis was big enough to take care of herself, but I couldn't help having all kinds of automatic big brother feelings about what other guys did to her. I told myself I was being silly, being half-assed about it.

But after a while I excused myself from Vickey and drew my sister aside.

"You serious about joining the gang?" I asked her.

"Why not? You the only one allowed to?"

"They aren't nice guys."

"They're your friends. And I'm tired of being a loner, Danny. I didn't belong to the gang uptown. But now I'm going to."

"You like this Lookit guy?"

"He's okay," Sis said. "I met him the day we moved in, and he tried to make a pass. I told him not yet, and he came back today. I like him."

"You prepared for the initiation?"

"I'll manage," Sis said.

I looked straight at her. "They can ask you to do anything. Anything at all."

"So?"

"Suppose they ask you to jump off the roof?"

"They won't ask me to do any crap like that."

I wet my lips. "Suppose you have to get laid, right in front of everybody?"

Sis' eyes twinkled. "I'll manage."

"You've done it already?"

"Plenty of times. Maybe fifty."

"Christ," I said. "You never told me."

"Did you ever ask me?"

"A guy don't ask his sister if she's had it."

"Well, I have. And you know who the first was? Your pal Seven Up, from the Shining Sinners. When I was thirteen. I thought he told you."

I was half annoyed and half tickled. For the first time, I felt that Sis was my kind of people. She wasn't a stranger to me anymore. She was going to be a Dragon deb.

I went back and sat down next to Vickey.

"You like me?" Vickey asked.

"Sure thing."

"You want me to be your deb, Danny?"

I put my arm around her and squeezed her breast. "That enough answer for you?"

"No," she said. "I want more than that."

"You'll get it," I told her. "Tonight, at the clubhouse."

CHAPTER EIGHT

After supper, Sis and I walked over to the Golden Dragons' clubhouse together. We didn't say much to each other. Sis seemed kind of nervous about the initiation. And so was I. I didn't want them to make her do anything that would hurt or embarrass her. But I guess I just didn't know my sister well, because there was nothing to worry about.

Maybe half the gang was in the clubhouse already. Sis went straight over to Lookit. Vickey hadn't gotten there yet, so I poured myself a drink of Thunderbird and sat down on the couch. People kept coming in. Vickey got there five minutes later and plopped down on the couch next to me. The whole gang was there, finally. Everybody with a deb except Sonny, who was still looking around, and Vince, who wasn't interested.

Jimmy Nails got up and said, "Tonight we got another special event here. A new deb is being initiated, recommended by our good pal Lookit. Her name is Sally Flaherty, and she's the sister of our newest member, Danny Flaherty." Jimmy looked like he was enjoying this. "Will Sally Flaherty step forward now, huh?"

Sis got off Lookit's lap and stepped out into the middle of the floor, right where I had stood the night before. She looked kind of tense.

Jimmy Nails said, "We got to initiate the debs properly because that's how we find out if they've got what it takes to be Golden Dragon debs. Sally Flaherty, are you willing to be initiated into this outfit?"

"Yeah," Sis said.

"Okay. Here's what you gotta do." He paused a second. I felt a butterfly in my stomach. If Ma only knew what was going on here, she'd be having conniption fits. This was sort of rugged for me, too. Because I was worried about Sis and what might happen to her. This was kind of a double initiation for me, in a way.

Jimmy Nails said, "We're gonna put a record on and you're gonna dance to it. All by yourself, in the middle of the floor. Every time I clap my hands, you gotta remove one article of clothing. If I clap my hands three times, that means you gotta take off three things. Got that?"

Jimmy Nails gave a signal and somebody put a record on and started the record player. It was one of the big hit tunes, a rock 'n roll number we all knew. Sis began dancing, making up the step, moving back and forth. The moving relaxed her, and she began to grin.

After the record had been playing maybe twenty seconds, Jimmy Nails clapped his hands together. Once. Sis didn't miss a beat. She unbuttoned her blouse and dropped it off and kept on dancing in her bra and jeans. Maybe ten seconds later, Jimmy Nails clapped again. Off came Sis' jeans. Now all she wore were socks and a bra and panties that were so transparent you could see the darkness at her thighs. The room was very quiet. The striptease routine had everybody wowed. Sis was a good dancer, and she was really getting a kick out of this. She didn't seem at all embarrassed. I felt sweat dripping down my back. I had seen Sis naked plenty of times, sure, but never anything as sexy as this. I knew it wasn't right, wasn't normal for me to get heated up by my own sister.

Jimmy Nails clapped again. Off came a sock.

Again.

Another sock.

The record was more than half over, spinning along toward the finish, and Sis still had her bra and panties on. The singer was in the final chorus now. Was he going to let the record finish without peeling Sis all the way?

That was the way it looked. Only with maybe five seconds left to the record, Jimmy grinned like a devil and clapped his hands.

Twice.

It sort of took Sis off balance. She had figured she was getting off easy. But when the two claps came, she shook her head and slowed down and unhooked her bra. It came off and her breasts thrust out, big and round and firm. Then she took the panties off. She was naked. She didn't look at me. Maybe she felt a little ashamed of being naked in front of her older brother. I don't know.

The record ended. Sis was all shiny with sweat from her dancing, and her breasts were going up and down fast. You can bet that every male eye in the room was watching the action with keen eager interest.

Sis said, "Can I get dressed now?"

"Not yet," Jimmy Nails told her. "There's still more to come." He looked around the room. "Everybody sit right where he is. Lisa and Judy, come here and help out in this one."

Lisa and Judy, who was a short thick-bodied blonde girl belonging to Kemo, came forward. Sis was still standing naked in the middle of the room, a puzzled expression on her pretty face.

Jimmy Nails said to her, "Lisa and Judy are gonna spin you around until you're dizzy. Then they'll let you go. The first guy you touch, you're gonna make it with, right here in front of everybody."

The same thing occurred to Sis and to me at the very same minute.

"What about my brother?" Sis asked.

"Does that include me?" I said at the same time.

Jimmy Nails grinned. "This ain't Sunday School, it's the Golden Dragons. Like, anything goes. If she touches you, Flaherty, you're elected. And that oughta be fun!"

The bastards! They had dreamed this up special for me as a kind of extra initiation stunt. They figured it would be a good gag if the new deb had to make it with her brother. But they had chickened out a little. There was only one chance out of sixteen that Sis would pick me. It didn't have to be that way. They could have ordered me to do it, and seen what would have happened.

A mattress was brought in. Lisa and Judy blindfolded Sis. Then they began to spin her. Round and round and round, with her breasts bouncing and her buttocks jiggling as she turned, round and round and round, first her front facing us, then her backside.

I was sweating.

I didn't know what the hell I would do if she touched me. Maybe I *couldn't* do it with her. I had thought of it plenty of times, sure, but doing it with your own sister, in public, that was a hell of a thing to ask a guy to do—

They let go of her.

She staggered crazily forward, dizzy.

She came plunging straight toward me.

I sat still. It would have been wrong if I had tried to get out of the way. Nobody was allowed to move. Sis took three wobbly steps forward.

This was it, I thought. One chance out of sixteen, and it was going to be me.

Then she fell.

She lost her balance and dropped to her knees, maybe a foot in front of me. She sat there on her knees and hands, with her breasts swaying from side to side. She tried to get up. She made it on the second try. I braced myself to catch her. But, dizzy as she was, she went lurching off on a diagonal.

She dropped into the lap of Johnny Slash.

I let out a sigh of relief. It seemed like everybody in the room had been thinking the same thing. Sis pulled her blindfold off in a hurry, and I heard her let out her breath as she found out that it hadn't been me she landed on.

Johnny Slash got up, grinning. His deb Lora didn't look so happy about things. Johnny led Sis out to the mattress in the middle of the room. He took his clothes off. He reached out for her, put his hands on her breasts.

I won't describe what happened next. All it was, was Johnny and Sis on the mattress with each other. But for me it took hours. It's a hell of a thing to watch your sister, giving an exhibition in front of a couple of dozen strangers. And Sis was good. She wasn't any scared virgin. She forgot all about the audience, and really cut loose with Johnny Slash.

Then it was over, and she was getting dressed again, and Jimmy Nails was welcoming her into the gang. Lookit was shaking hands with everybody, just like he had just got married. He was proud as punch. He shook Johnny Slash's hand extra hard. Funny deal, since Johnny Slash had banged her and Lookit himself hadn't. Not yet.

I got myself a drink, and one for Vickey, and we went over to say hello to Sis. Sis grinned up at me.

"That was a narrow escape, wasn't it?" she asked.

"You don't know how narrow. Another step and you would have landed in my lap."

"I thought I was heading away from you," she said. We looked at each other. I was still trying to get used to the idea of Sis being experienced. Being a gang girl. In my mind's eye was the picture of her with Johnny Slash. I wasn't going to forget that picture for a long time.

Then I turned away, back to Vickey. She was getting a little drunk, and she was very interested in me. I didn't feel too hot for her. I mean, she was okay, but the one I wanted was really Lisa. Well, Lisa wasn't available, so I was going to have to make do with what I could get, at least for the time being.

Somebody put a record on, and Vickey and I started to dance, slow and smooth, body tight up against body, and I danced her right out into the hall and into one of the bedrooms at the back end of the apartment. I had had enough of this public sexing for a while. I wanted some privacy, kind of for variety.

We danced into the room and I snapped on the lights and hooked the little hook that kept the door closed. It was a small room, maybe ten feet by twelve, and there wasn't anything in it except a mattress on the floor. I dropped down on the mattress and Vickey flopped down on top of me.

We rolled over, and I unbuttoned her blouse and opened her bra, and found the zipper of her jeans, and then all of a sudden she was naked. She had a nice compact little body, and her breasts stuck out high and firm. I put my hands around them. She gasped and whispered, "Squeeze them, Danny, squeeze them hard!"

I squeezed them.

The nipples turned hard as rock, and she started to writhe and pant, and she fumbled with my clothes and practically ripped them off me, and then she was scrambling all over me, and she was kissing and biting and nibbling and doing a million things, and then she said, "Hit me! Beat me, Danny! Spank me!"

I had known a couple of girls like this one before. The more you banged them around, the greater the kicks you gave them. So I pulled her across me and there were her nice tight pink buttocks sticking up, cute as anything, and I brought my hand up and slammed it down hard, and there was a loud sound of the slap and my hand bounced on the tight flesh and the skin went red and she let out a little sigh of pure pleasure.

So I kept at it, spanking her until her backside was fiery red, and each time I hit her she gasped some more, and then I turned her over and grabbed her breasts and squeezed them hard and bit her shoulder, and she kept on getting hotter and hotter till I thought she'd go up in smoke, and all of a sudden she reached down and took me and guided me to her and we were going up and down and really making it hot and heavy, her body arching up off the foul-smelling mattress and her legs scissored around my hips, and we kept on going, on until we thought we couldn't last any longer, and then went on still more, and then *boom* and we let it happen and then slumped down to get our breath and come back to the world.

For a long time we just held tight to each other. I was shot. This girlie did it the strenuous way. But she was hot as a firecracker. I could see that I was going to have plenty of fun with her until I could make my big play to take Lisa away from Reilly.

After a while somebody started banging on the door, so we got dressed.

"Yeah, hold your horses!" I called. We unhooked the door and came out. Cannon and Belle were out there to use the room. They were in such a hurry that Belle's blouse was open and her bra was hanging askew. Two nice pretty little knockers were showing, but I was so worn out from my torrid session with Vickey that I didn't much care. Belle and her stud rushed past us and into the bedroom to take care of their urgent business.

We started back toward the living room. Going past the bathroom, we noticed that the door was open and the light was on. We looked in. Vince was there. He had a piece of rubber tubing wrapped around his bare left arm to make the veins stick out, and in his right hand he was holding a spoon with white powder in it. He was cooking the powder with a match to make his fix. There was a hypodermic needle sitting on the sink. He didn't notice us. He had a dreamy smile on his face, like he was already feeling the effects of the fix he was going to take.

I felt a little sick, watching the horsehead preparing his fix. I closed the door so he'd be alone, and we went back into the main room.

It was pretty wild in there. Somebody had gone out for beer and wine, and there was plenty of both. Empty cans were everywhere. I looked around for my sister, and I saw her. She hadn't bothered to go into the back rooms. She had just pulled her jeans and panties down half way, and was sitting on Lookit's lap.

Kemo came over to me. "The connection was here a little while ago to sell Vince his fix. I bought a couple reefers. You want to go halfies with me?"

"How many you got?"

"Four. At half a buck each."

I gave him a dollar and took the joints from him. I handed one to Vickey, kept one myself. We lit up. The smoke went down, way down deep, and in a couple minutes I wasn't feeling any pain. Vickey and I just sprawled out on the floor and let the kicks take us.

I don't know how much time passed, but the next thing I knew the place was dark and I was sitting up looking at my watch and it said three o'clock. Which was three in the morning.

The party was over. Vince the junkie was snoring in one corner, and Judy and Kemo were at the other side, and Vickey was sacked out next to me. There were a couple other miscellaneous bodies flopped out here and there. Up on the couch, a girl was lying with her back towards me, and two pale buttocks were gleaming in the darkness, and I walked over and saw that it was my sister, and Lookit was draped next to her on the couch.

I had the taste of cotton in my mouth and my eyes hurt. I bent down and slapped Sis' butt. She woke up and looked over her shoulder at me.

"Whozat?"

"Danny. Get covered and let's go home."

"Must be late, huh?"

"Three in the morning. Come on."

She got up and collected her panties and jeans and slipped into them. We tiptoed out of the clubhouse and into the street.

"Jeez, that's the life," she said.

"Yeah. Ain't it."

"Did they give you a reefer, Danny?"

"Yeah. You?"

She nodded. "I never had one before. It's the most ain't it?"

"Just make sure you don't get any ideas," I told her. "If you want a little M now and then, that's okay. But stay off the H. You don't wanta end up a horsehead like Vince, you know."

"Ain't it time you stopped lecturing me, Danny? Jeez, I got enough brains to keep off heroin. You got the idea I'm still a little girl."

"Not after tonight I don't," I said with a laugh.

"You sore at me for all the things I did?"

"Me? No, kid. We only get one life. We oughta grab all the kicks we can."

"That's how I feel," she said. "I always thought you'd get sore at me if I tried to join the Shining Sinners. So I went with the gang guys on the sly. I figured I didn't give a damn anymore if you found out about me."

"You wanta be careful, though. I ain't lecturing, now. A guy can fool around and nothing much'll happen to him. But if you get yourself knocked up, Ma'll throw you out of the house."

"She thinks I'm a good girl," Sis said.

"Don't let her find out different."

We turned the corner. Our building of the housing project was right across the street. I was tired, but I was in a real good mood. For the first time, Sis and I were real good pals. We weren't snapping at each other. We were just walking along and talking nice and easy.

I got an idea.

How Sis could help me in something I wanted to do.

Something involving that Elaine Halperin poot.

I grinned. I filed it away in the back of my head. We crossed the street, went into the house, rode up in the elevator. At three in the morning, the whole world seemed to be asleep. We tiptoed into the house. Sis went into her bedroom, I went into mine. I got undressed fast. But when I wanted to go into the john, the door was locked, and Sis was taking a shower. All of a sudden she was Little Miss Modesty, locking the door that way. I almost laughed out loud, remembering some of the things she'd done earlier that night.

I found a newspaper in the kitchen and took it into my room to read while I was waiting for Sis to come out of the john. I looked at the sports pages first. Then I turned to the front of the paper.

There was a little article there about the grocery store holdup of two nights before. It seemed the grocery store man was still in the hospital. He had been in a coma since the robbery, not regaining consciousness. He had a fractured skull. The doctors weren't sure whether he was going to live or die.

I read the article over half a dozen times. I had to stop to remind myself that I was the guy who had put him in the hospital.

Maybe he would die. That would mean I had murdered him. I smiled, trying the idea on for size. One of the things that always had cheesed me a little was that I had no kills to my credit. I had been in plenty of rumbles, but somehow I had never cooled anyone.

Well, maybe now I'd have my first one. I couldn't feel very proud of skulling an old man, but at least I could say that I had scored. That was a big kick. What are we alive for, except to grab all the kicks we can?

Sex, that's a kick. Sure. A damn good one. A guy can't ever get enough of that.

Drinking, that's another kick. An okay kick. Marijuana. Sure, M is good too. If you don't let it get the upper hand with you.

Heroin, H, there was something to be said for that. I had tried it. But horse isn't such a good kick, because it takes more than it gives, and before long you use it and don't get any kick.

There were others.

Rape. That was a kick I had tried a couple of times. It makes you feel real big to grab a girl and rip her clothes off and take her. The way I figure it, you get kicks from what you do to other people. If you take something from a girl that she values, you've gained something. Or at least that's the way I look at it. I'm brainier than a lot of gang guys. I spend a lot of time thinking. Maybe I should have been a professor. And the way I thought it out, taking a girl's cherry is a hell of a gratifying thing.

And so was murder. That was one kick I hadn't experienced yet. Taking life—that's living big! Only I wasn't happy with doing it this long-drawn-out way. An old man slowly dying, there wasn't much kick in that. But sticking a knife into a guy, twisting upward—that must be something!

I wondered if the old guy would die. That would make me a murderer. But it would also make it impossible for the cops ever to pin anything on me, if he died without identifying me. Murder scot-free. I liked that idea.

Sis was finished with the shower. She came out, wrapped up tight in her bathrobe like a virgin who was afraid of showing anything to me. She said goodnight, and I went on into the john to wash up.

My mind was wound up and going, now. I kept thinking about good kicks to get. I kept coming back to the idea of rape. Yeah, man! But it had to be done just right. I didn't want to go to the pen for twenty years. There wasn't any kick in that. Not the slightest.

CHAPTER NINE

I saw the Elaine Halperin girl in the elevator the next day. She snooted me again. I said hello, and she only glared at me, and put herself as far away from me as she could be while still remaining in the same elevator car. I stared at her back and told myself I was going to make her feel sorry for her snotty ways. I was going to make her feel *very* sorry.

Later that day, when Sis and I were walking over to the candy store, I said, "I need your help in a little caper I want to pull."

"*My* help?"

"That's right."

"What's the deal?"

"The Elaine Halperin girl. I want to have some fun with her. Only she won't cooperate. I don't think she likes me, you know that?"

"She's afraid of you, Danny."

"Well, I'm gonna give her good reason to afraid of me. If you'll help."

Sis was suspicious. "What are you gonna do to her? Danny, don't hurt her. She ain't like us. You do something to her, it'll affect her for the rest of her life."

"Now who's lecturing who?" I snapped.

"Still and all, she's only a girl—"

"Older than you are."

"But—"

"Look, Sis, some of the things you did last night weren't exactly choirgirl stuff. Now I got a kick in mind for me. Are you gonna help me or do I have to get along without you, huh?"

I looked sharp at her, letting my words sink in. After a moment, she said. "Okay. What do you want me to do?"

"The Halperin girl goes down to the washing machine in the basement of our house every week to do her family's wash. Talk to her. Find out when she's going down. Tell her you want to do your wash the same time she does hers, just to be friendly neighbors and all that crap. Then let me know when laundry time comes."

"What then?"

"You leave the rest to me. Just get her down into that laundry room."

"And when you go to jail for rape, I go too because I helped decoy?" Sis asked.

"Not if you play it right. If the cops ask you what happened, you say a Puerto Rican came into the basement and grabbed the Halperin girl. She won't contradict you. She'll be too hysterical to see anything."

After a little more persuasion, I got Sis to agree to act as decoy for me. Then we spent the rest of the morning lounging around the candy store. Sis went back to the house in the afternoon, promising she'd hunt up the Halperin girl and have a chat with her. Somehow Elaine thought of me and my sister as two entirely different kinds of people. Sis was respectable in Elaine's eyes. Me, I was just riffraff, gang garbage, a juvenile delinquent.

Well, Elaine Halperin was in for a bit of a surprise about my sister.

That night at the clubhouse Sis said to me, "I talked to her. She takes her laundry down on Saturday mornings, usually."

"That's tomorrow."

"Yeah. I arranged to meet her down there around eleven in the morning. We're gonna discuss school. I asked her to tell me something about the subjects I oughta take when I go back to school in September."

"She think anything was fishy?"

"Nah," Sis said. "But— Danny—"

"Yeah—"

"Do you *hafta* do it?"

"You gonna be a pain in the rear about his. huh?"

"I just figured maybe I could talk you out of it. She's such a kid."

"She's sixteen, ain't she? Old enough to be made. If it's good enough for you, it's good enough for her."

Sis didn't give up. "Look, Danny, suppose she was me. I mean, suppose I was that kinda girl instead of a Dragon deb. And you were my big brother. How would you like it if some gang guy came along and—and raped me?"

"That's different," I said. "She *ain't* my sister."

"Supposing."

I shook my head. "That kinda crap don't work, Sis. I only worry about my own. I don't go around supposing. If some guy grabbed you in the basement and I found out, I'd knock his head off. But that don't have a damn thing to do with what *I* want to do. I see something I want. So I grab it. That's the way things happen in the jungle. And we live in a kind of jungle."

Sis still felt like arguing, but I shook her off. I knew my line of reasoning didn't stand up solidly. I just didn't *give* a damn. I wanted what I wanted, and to hell with supposing things were the other way round.

So the next day—Saturday—I hung around the house in the morning instead of going to the candy store. Around eleven, Sis got together the laundry bundle and went downstairs to the washing machine. I waited ten minutes. I felt the excitement starting to build up in me, the way it always did before a caper. I tingled all over inside. It was an excitement that kept rising and rising until the caper was at its peak. And then something like hitting the old grocer on the head would bring the bit to a boil, and I'd feel the kicks taking hold of me.

This was one kick I hadn't tried for a long while. I raped a girl in Central Park when I was fifteen. She was more than a girl, actually a married woman and pretty loaded with money, too. She was out walking this dog, this little pink poodle, and I came past and grabbed her and threw her down in the bushes where nobody could see us. I put one hand over her mouth and with the other hand I pulled up her skirt and ripped open her panties. Then I got on her and you know what? I think she actually enjoyed it. Yeah. Her eyes were all wide with fright, and then I started moving around and I saw her eyes change expression, like she was with it, and she sort of struggled to breathe and toward the end she was really cooperating. Meanwhile the pink poodle kept yapping at my heels. When I was through I got up and left her there in the bushes. I watched the papers the next day, but nobody said anything about it. That was a funny one. I bet her husband was some worn-out businessman and that was the first good time she had in ten years.

Then the next time I did it, it was on 109th Street and there was this teenage girl, a lot like Elaine Halperin. I dragged her off the street and into a basement and gave it to her there. She screamed and cried all the way through it, because she was a virgin. That one got into the papers the next day—no name, of course, just the address where it happened. But she was either mixed up or else afraid to tell the truth, because she told the cops a colored guy had raped her, and so of course I never got into any trouble for it.

Now I was pulling the caper again. And this would be the best of all.

I got into the elevator. It was empty. I pushed the button and rode down to the basement.

The basement of our building was a big, sprawling affair. I had already investigated it. There was the washing machine room, and there were a bunch of storage rooms, some of them in use and padlocked, others dark and empty. Right across the hall from the washing machine room there was one of the dark and empty ones.

I stepped into one of the empty storage rooms and fixed myself up. I had one of those rubber Halloween masks that fits over your entire head and gives you an ugly face. It's impossible to tell who's underneath it. Then I was wearing my black leather jacket, zipped up tight, and a pair of khaki pants instead of blue jeans. And I was wearing black leather gloves too. There wasn't any of my skin showing. I figured that Elaine would never be able to identify me. She wouldn't even be able to tell if I was white or black, let alone what I looked like.

I looked around carefully, making sure there was nobody coming. Then I tiptoed toward the washing machine room. Sis and I had already arranged a signal. If there was anybody using the washing machines besides her and Elaine, Sis would drop a sock in front of the doorway.

There wasn't anything lying there. I reached the door and peeked around.

Sis and Elaine were the only ones inside. They had already put their laundry in the machines, and were sitting around gabbing while the laundry got done. They were on a bench, Sis sitting sideways so she could see the door, Elaine sitting with her back to the door.

I went in.

Sis saw me, and reared back, looking startled, because I hadn't told her about the Halloween mask. Then she gasped and jumped up, pretending to be scared out of her wits, so later on Elaine wouldn't figure out that Sis had been part of the arrangement. I came up behind Elaine and grabbed her before she knew what was happening. I clapped one hand over her mouth, and with my other hand I grabbed her wrist and twisted her arm up behind her back. Then I used the twisted arm as leverage to get her up off the bench and march her right out of the room.

I had to push her. And drag her. But having the arm pinned behind her back made her less uncooperative. She kept trying to bite my hand, but couldn't get her teeth through the glove.

There was one stroke of luck I hadn't even counted on. For some reason Elaine was wearing a skirt instead of slacks or jeans. That made my job about fifty times easier.

I pushed Elaine across the hall and into the empty storage room. With my foot, I nudged the door closed, slamming it hard. Then I turned Elaine around.

She saw the mask. She was practically bug-eyed with fright.

I pushed her down. She landed hard, on her back, and her skirt went up around her knees, then higher, showing me thighs and a pair of white panties. Working with gloves wasn't so easy, but I had to do it that way. I put one hand in the neck of her blouse and ripped. Buttons popped. I grabbed the front of her bra and ripped again. The cups came away and I saw her breasts.

She was scared, but I kept one hand over her mouth and she couldn't get a word out. She kept clawing at me, pounding me with her fists. I was sweating bricks inside of that mask and that black leather jacket.

This was the real kick!

This was the most!

I started to move, back and forth, taking it slow and easy, enjoying it now. I watched her eyes. They looked wild, now that she was getting the message that she wasn't a virgin anymore, that somebody had rammed his way right into her body and was having a time with her.

Then something went wrong.

I don't know how it happened, but somehow she managed to twist her body to the side, breaking the contact between us. It threw me off balance and I tried to grab hold of her, and then all of a sudden she drew one foot up and rammed me hard in the guts. And I mean hard. My belly was touching my backbone when she kicked.

I grabbed my middle and she rolled out from under me and got to her feet, I was still wobbling around, sucking in my breath. Christ, if she had put that kick six inches lower she would have ruined me for life. She turned around, took a step, almost fell over, then gathered strength and streaked for the door. She threw it open and ran out into the hall.

I was sort of stunned for a moment. I was busy running through my fuddled brain the three thoughts that I had been pushed off her, that I had been kicked mule-hard in the belly, and that she had gotten away.

Then I started after her.

I reached the door. I looked out in the hall, through the slits in the mask, and saw her running wildly for the exit down to my left. Her blouse was hanging open and her bra, ripped, dangling loose, but that didn't bother her, I guess.

I ran after her. I was just in time to see her reach the exit and scoot through it. There was sort of a ramp there, and then you came out in a courtyard that opened onto the avenue. I didn't know what to do. I followed her halfway up the ramp. She was still running like crazy.

Then I stopped chasing her. She was out in the open, now. I couldn't follow her while I was still wearing this crazy mask, and I sure as hell couldn't follow her if I took the mask off. So I stopped dead in my tracks. I peeled off the mask and folded it up and jammed it into my pockets. I wiggled out of the leather jacket and draped it over my arm. I took my gloves off.

Then, slowly, I walked up the ramp.

And heard the loud screech of brakes.

And heard a quick half-scream, ending in the middle in a sort of gurgle.

Jesus Christ, I thought. I came up through the courtyard, ducked around to the side so it wouldn't seem like I was coming out of the same place the girl was coming out of, and went back around the corner to the avenue.

There was a big crowd. Maybe fifty people had collected already. There was a truck stopped right in the middle of the street, and a cop was holding the mob back, and the truck driver—who was a man built like an ape—was leaning against his truck and sort of crying hysterically.

I saw the blood in the street.

I saw Elaine. Or what was left of her. She was lying behind the truck. It had gone right over her. When a car hits you, it knocks you flying, but when a truck that big slams into you it steamrollers you. She had been drawn right under the wheels. Somebody came running out of the stores with a blanket, and they stretched it over the body. People were getting sick, other people were crying, And the crowd kept getting bigger and bigger.

I made my way into the middle of it.

"What happened?" I asked someone.

"Girl came running out from behind that hedge," a woman told me. "She just ran out into the middle of the street like she was out of her head. The truck driver didn't even have a chance to stop. Not a chance."

"The girl was half naked," somebody else said. "I saw her. Her blouse was all ripped open. Like maybe someone tried to rape her and she was running away."

"A pretty little girl," somebody else said.

"Her name was Elaine," put in somebody else. "She went to school with my daughter."

The cops were starting to shove the crowd back. I decided I had seen enough. I slipped back through the crowd and went around to the front of the house again. More people were pouring out of the houses and hanging out of the windows to see what had happened. I kept on walking. I felt very peculiar and all mixed up inside.

But there wasn't any big kick.

And I felt kind of sorry for the kid. Hell, I didn't mean for her to run in front of a truck. It wasn't like I was out to kill her. Just to bring her down off her high horse. Just to show her not to be so snooty.

There was one thing I wouldn't ever know, either. I wouldn't know if she had run in front of the truck because she was hysterical and didn't know what she was, doing, or because she had been raped and wanted to kill herself. Not that it made much difference.

I went back into the house. People were still streaming out to find out what all the fuss was about. I got into the elevator and rode upstairs.

Getting out on my floor, I went down to the incinerator room first and dumped the Halloween mask into the chute. Then I went in into the house. There was nobody there but Sis. She looked pretty pale.

"Where's Ma?" I asked.

"I told her about the accident. She went down to see if she could do anything for Mrs. Halperin."

"Look, Sis," I began. "I didn't know she was gonna get run over by—"

"Nobody said you knew."

"Did you see it?"

"No. I was coming upstairs when it happened. I got out and saw how she looked."

"She kicked me and ran away. I think she was out of her mind or something."

Sis shook her head. "I feel all rotten inside. Like I helped to murder her. Just for your lousy kicks."

"Stop it," I said. "Nobody told her to run into the street like that. I wasn't even chasing her."

"Okay, okay. But what do you want me to do now? What am I supposed to tell the cops?"

"Not a friggin' thing. Who knows that you were down in the washroom when I came in?"

"Nobody."

"But Ma knows you took the wash down?"

"Yeah. But she thinks I left the machine before you busted in."

"Okay, let it go at that. You were in the room with Elaine, and you went out, and you don't know what happened after that. That's the safest thing in case anybody asks you anything. But nobody's gonna ask. And you don't have to speak up till they come bothering you."

"Where are you going to go now?"

"Out," I said. "I want to get away from here. I don't want to hang around."

I left. There was still a mob in the street, discussing the tragedy, although by this time a police ambulance had come and taken the girl away, and the truck had gone, I guess to the police station to report the details of the accident. I wondered if they'd be able to tell from what was left of her that she had been raped. Or at least partly raped. I wondered.

I had to go somewhere now. Not to the candy store. I didn't want to be with the other Golden Dragons right now. I didn't want to be with anybody, What I wanted was a drink, first of all, and then maybe a place to lie down and calm myself a little.

That meant the clubhouse.

Now that I was a full-fledged member, I had my own clubhouse key. So I walked quickly over there. At this hour in the morning, the place would probably be empty. During the day the Dragons didn't hang out at the clubhouse, they stayed at the candy store. So I'd have the place to myself. Unless there were still a couple of guys sleeping off the party we had had the night before. I had left around midnight, and there were still some guys there.

I let myself in.

The clubhouse was deserted. It was a mess, too. The way we worked it, a different guy every day had to go over to the clubhouse sometime in the afternoon and get it tidied up from the night before. It was Monk's turn to do the job, but he hadn't been here yet. Chairs were turned over, there were empty beer cans everyplace, cigarette butts all over the floor. A real mess.

I went into the kitchen to see how the drink situation was. The guy assigned to cleanup detail is supposed to get money from the gang treasurer—Jimmy Nails—to pay for drinks for that night. So maybe there wouldn't be anything around.

I opened the refrigerator. There was a quart bottle of beer standing in there, with its top off and maybe three inches of beer left in the bottom. On the kitchen table, there was a quart jug of muscatel with maybe an inch left. And the bourbon bottle had just about a shot and a half left.

I found a glass, rinsed it out, poured the beer in. Then I added the bourbon and the muscatel. I stirred the whole mess around with a spoon.

It wasn't bad. I mean, the state I was in I needed any kind of drink. I wasn't particular. The taste didn't matter. The beer-bourbon-muscatel mixture tasted lousy, but it had alcohol in it, and that was all I was looking for. I drank it down in five big gulps. Then I realized there wasn't any more liquor in the place. I went inside and sat down on the couch to feel sorry for myself.

The only thing to do now, I figured, was to go out and buy some. Or else wait for Monk to show up with the fresh supply. One or the other.

But I didn't do either. I just sat there, going over and over in my mind the scene with the dead girl. Dragging her into the storage room, throwing her down, ripping off her blouse, her bra, her panties. And now there was nothing but bloody mush.

And I hadn't even raped her. My body ached, and so did my gut where she had kicked me. I hadn't had the pleasure from her. And now she was dead. A lousy shame. And nothing here left to drink. Another lousy shame.

I heard a key being fitted into the keyhole outside. I brightened up. It was Monk, I figured. With his arms full of beer and wine and whiskey. Just what I was waiting for, what I needed.

The door opened. Someone came in.

It wasn't Monk, though.

It was Lisa.

CHAPTER TEN

I don't know which one of us was the more surprised. We looked at each other across the whole length of the room. She was wearing a polo shirt and tight jeans, and her breasts stuck out sharp against the polo shirt, and I felt a quick jab of want when I saw her, all blonde and beautiful by the door.

"I didn't think there'd be anyone here," she said.

"Neither did I. I figured you were Monk, coming over to clean up the place."

"I lost a pin here last night. I didn't miss it till this morning. And I stopped off here to look for it before going over to the store. What brought you here?"

"Looking for a drink, mostly. And a chance to be alone a little."

"How come? You bugged about something?"

"Just felt like being alone," I said.

"I don't want to bother you, then," she said "Lemme just find the pin and I'll clear out."

"*You* aren't bothering me, none."

"I shouldn't be here, though. Alone with you. Maybe I better go now."

"Let's look for the pin, first. What was it like?"

"It was copper. Sort of shaped like a fish. With blue paint on it. I mighta dropped it near the couch."

I walked over, bent down, poked around under the couch for a moment. Lisa was crouching just ahead of me. Her back was to me, and I saw the way her jeans went tight over her buttocks when she crouched, and it sort of made my pulse go four times as fast.

My middle ached. I wanted to finish what I had begun with Elaine Halperin an hour before. And there was Lisa, right in front of me.

I reached down and touched metal. Lisa's pin. I picked it up and crawled across the floor till I was right behind her. Then I put my hand in front of her and on one of her breasts.

"Don't Danny."

"I want to."

"We mustn't. Even if we want to. I'm afraid."

"Of what?"

"Mike. What he'll do if he finds out."

"There's just the two of us here. Mike won't ever know."

"Suppose someone walks in?" she asked.

"The only guy likely to come in's Monk. And he won't be here for hours. He's got cleanup detail."

"It still ain't safe, Danny," Lisa rose to her feet in one graceful motion. I got up right along with her, keeping my hand on her breast. I flattened myself against her from behind, to let her know I was ready and able any time she gave in.

She put her hand over the one of mine that was squeezing her and started to lift it. In a quiet voice she said, "I better leave, Danny. Before we do something we hadn't ought to do?"

"What about your pin?"

"It don't matter."

"Yes, it does. Mike gave you that pin, didn't he?"

"What of it?"

"You want it back. You ought to stay and look for it."

"Not now. Not with just the two of us here. It's dangerous. I might lose control of myself. Let go of me, Danny. Let me leave."

"Suppose I find your pin?" I went on. "Will you give me a reward?"

"What kinda reward?"

"Turn around and I'll show you," I said.

She turned. I held out my closed hand and opened it slowly. "That the pin you lost?" I asked.

"Yeah, that's the one." She reached for it, but I closed my hand before she could get it.

"Not so fast," I said.

"Give it to me, Danny." She was smiling, but she had a worried look.

"First I want my reward."

"Stop playing games."

"I'm not. I want my reward."

"Like what?"

"Like a kiss," I said. "No kiss, no pin. Make up your mind."

"Give me the pin."

"Gimme a kiss."

She looked kind of exasperated. But then she shrugged and said, "Okay, silly. If you want to play games like a little boy. Come kiss me, and then let me have the pin so I can get out of here."

I grinned. I knew that once I had gotten her to give in to the kiss I could get the rest of what waited from her without any sweat. I planted my feet pretty far apart and drew her to me, with her up against me, and I put my lips to hers and we just sort of kissed like kids might, and I gave her half a second or so to heat up. Then I opened my mouth, snaked my tongue out, parted her lips with it. My tongue crept past her teeth, into her mouth.

She caught her breath and I knew I was getting to her, because she wriggled tighter up against my body. I held her snugly and slid my hands around back, under her sweater, up the warm smooth skin of her back. I found the catch of her bra and unhooked it. By now she was cooperating; she shrugged her shoulders and the bra fell away from her, and I brought my hands around front so that the big taut round bowls of her breasts were in my fingers. I held her tight, with each nipple caught between two fingers, and I moved my fingers to heat her up, and the nipples got stiff in a hurry and we were still kissing and she made a noise deep down in her throat.

Our lips parted, we came up for air, and she said in a foggy kind of voice, "No Danny, no. We mustn't. We mustn't—"

But she was just saying it. She didn't try to stop me. I held her braced between my legs as we stood, and I dragged down the zipper of her jeans and opened the button and pushed the jeans down, over her hips, and she let them drop the rest of the way and kicked them off. Then I took hold of the waistband of her panties and rolled the panties down, until they were at her knees, and she helped them the rest of the way. Sweater and unhooked bra came next, and she was naked.

She was something. All white and soft and slim and curved, with the lovely golden hair on her shoulders, and my hands running up and down her back.

She started to undress me, as we stood there. Then when we were both naked, we got down on the floor, and I felt her silky body underneath me. I braced myself on my hands against the floor as she began to arch her body away from the wood, and I kept moving, in and in and in until I was tingling all over and practically wanting to bust out crying. She let out a gasp and started to move fast and her body shook all over and I held her tight while she wriggled and moaned and shook.

That was the best medicine in the world. I felt great. All the sourness, all the wound-up tension that had been in me for the last hour vanished like it had never been. We lay sprawled out on the cold floor, and I fitted my hand over her breast and she smiled, and I stroked the silkiness of her and wondered how it had happened that just one girl had been allowed to be so beautiful, and how it had happened that I had been allowed to have her not once but twice.

I wanted her for keeps, now.

I couldn't bear the idea of letting anyone else have her, not even for a minute.

"Lisa—" I said hoarsely.

"What is it, lover?"

"Lisa, I want you to be my deb. You hear me? I got to have you."

"Don't talk that way, Danny."

"You think I'm kidding?"

"Mike will kill us both."

"I'm not afraid of him."

"I am," she said. "He'll go wild if I try to break up with him." She slipped her hand along my body. "Don't make trouble, Danny. You've got Vickey. You don't need me."

"Vickey's just a dame. You're special. You're out of this world."

"I belong to Mike Reilly."

"That can be fixed."

"What are you saying, Danny?"

"It's coming close to time this gang had a new Prez. Maybe I'll go out and get myself the job."

"Mike is dangerous, Danny. You've never seen him in a stand. I did. I saw him kill somebody. The other guy never had a chance. Never saw the blade coming."

"You ain't scaring me."

"Please," she said. "Listen to me. Believe me. Don't start trouble with Mike. Let things go along like they've been going. If you want me, you can have me a couple mornings a week, over here. Mike don't have to find out. But don't rock the boat. Don't buy trouble."

"Nah. I don't want to sneak behind anybody's back." I touched the tips of her breasts. She was lying on her side, facing me, and her breasts were like round apples shining in the sun. I ran my fingers around them. "I want you to be my deb, Lisa. I'm gonna get rid of Reilly. I'm gonna challenge him to a stand."

"He'll kill you."

"Maybe he will. But I'm not afraid of him. I'll cool him off. And then you'll belong to me. Okay?"

"Okay, Danny," she whispered. "But be careful. Why don't you wait? Maybe there'll be a rumble and he'll get killed, or something."

"That's the easy way out. I'll challenge him."

Her lips were an inch from mine. I moved mine the other inch. She had soft, moist lips. My tongue slipped into her mouth, and then all of a sudden I found that I wanted to do it again, and so did she, and our bodies moved together and this time it was even better than the last and then we came back down together and sort of dozed for a little while.

Then I opened my eyes. Lisa was napping, with a smile on her face. I bent down and kissed her and she woke up.

"We oughta get dressed," I said.

"Yeah. Somebody might show up."

"Here." I reached around behind me and found her panties. "And this too." I gave her the bra.

She grinned. "What are you gonna do about Mike?"

"I'll fix him. Gimme another week, maybe two weeks. Then there'll be no more Mike Reilly to worry about. Then there'll be just the two of us. That sound okay, baby? That the way you want it to be?"

"You're the most, Danny."

"More than Mike?"

"Absolutely the most."

I stood up, feeling pretty good about the world, and started to put my briefs on. I had one foot through them when there was a sound outside, and then the door was starting to open.

Too late to hide.

Too late to get dressed.

Too late to do anything except follow through with whatever happened.

It was Monk, showing up finally to get the clubhouse in order. He pushed the door open and came in, and stood there with a stupid smile on his face.

I was half into my briefs. Lisa was wearing a bra and nothing but a bra, and she was sitting on the floor about to get into her panties. Monk wasn't too smart, but it didn't take a hell of a lot of brains to figure out what we had been doing.

"Jesus Christ," Monk said slowly.

He was a guy about seventeen, short and stocky, with little eyes put close together and a flat nose. Monk wasn't a leader, he was a follower. Let everybody else be the generals, he just wanted to be told what to do and where to go. Right now he didn't know what the hell to do. He just stood there gaping, and practically drooling at the sight of Lisa's half naked body.

"Maybe I better get outa here," he said, and started to inch back out the door.

"Hold it!" I yelled. I pulled my pants on and grabbed the switchblade out of the pocket. "Come on back inside here, you goddamn ape!"

He came in. He looked at the unopened switchblade in my hand, then looked at Lisa's bare pink backside, then back at the blade.

I said to Lisa, "Hurry up and get dressed. This ninny can't think straight when you're waving your fanny around that way."

Lisa nervously got into her jeans and sweater. She was very pale. I knew she was scared witless.

I said to Monk, "Go on into the kitchen and put your beer away. Then come on out here."

He nodded and went away. Lisa said in a panicky voice, "I *told* you we shouldn't have done it! He'll spill it to Mike and there'll be hell to pay!"

"Don't worry. I'll fix him."

"Danny, you aren't gonna cut him up—!"

"Not unless I have to. Hey Monk! Step it up!"

He came out. His piggish little eyes were worried-looking. He said, "Jeez, Danny, I didn't mean to bust in, only I didn't know—"

"Shut up," I said. "Look, Monk, you know who Lisa here belongs to, don't you?"

"Yeah. Sure. She's Reilly's deb."

"Very good. You get a gold star for that. She's Reilly's deb, and I'm not Reilly. And obviously since we were undressed, we were just havin' a ball. And I got no business with Reilly's deb. You follow me?"

"Yeah. Sure." With a ninny like Monk, I wanted to make sure I spelled out everything.

"Okay," I said. "Now, if you go and tell anybody about what you saw just now, Reilly will find out, and Reilly will be very sore at me. Understand that?"

"Yeah, Danny."

"Reilly's likely to come at me with a knife. And I'd have to defend myself, Somebody would get hurt. I don't want anybody to get hurt, Monk. Do you want anybody to get hurt?"

"Me, Danny?"

"Well, then, you just keep your mouth shut about what you saw today. Don't say anything about it to anybody. Not to your deb and not to Coco and not to Zorro and not to Reilly and not to anybody. You know what I mean?" I moved very close to him, and suddenly I flicked out the blade of my switcher. Monk jumped. I kept my arm down near my hip, and held the blade right in front of Monk's stomach.

I said in a low voice, "You know what I'll do to you if you tell anyone what you saw? I'll make a eunuch outa you, Monk. You know what a eunuch is?"

"A younuck?"

"Eunuch. That's what they used to do in the olden days. They'd take a knife and cut everything off. That's what I'll do to you, Monk. Cut it all right off. You wouldn't like that. So keep shut."

"Jeez, yes, Danny." The dumb bastard was practically shivering. "I won't say a thing. Not a single goddamn thing, Danny."

"You better not. You better just get busy cleaning up everything that needs to be cleaned up around here, and forget what you saw." I looked at Lisa. "You all ready to clear out?"

"Just about."

"Come on, then."

I tossed one last reminder to Monk to keep his trap shut, and Lisa and I left the clubhouse. As we went through the courtyard, she said, "Do you think you scared him enough, Danny?"

"He won't say anything to anybody."

"Maybe he's too dumb to be scared."

I shrugged. "We got to take our chances. The worst that can happen is I'll have my stand with Mike a little sooner than I was figuring, is all." We came to the street. "You go out first," I said. "Walk to the left. I don't want anybody seeing us together."

"It's lousy, doing all this hiding and seeking."

"It won't be for much longer," I told her.

I leaned against the wall and watched her walk up the stairs and turn to the left. She had the neatest little backside I ever saw. And a neat hip-wiggle. I watched her till she was out of sight. All I had to do was think of her, and I went stiff. I wanted her real bad as my steady. Bad enough to kill, if I had to.

Vickey could be dumped easy enough. I hadn't known her long enough to give much of a damn about her. And then it would be me and Lisa, me and Lisa from here on. Danny Flaherty, Prez of the Golden Dragons!

I counted off fifteen seconds. Then I came out of the doorway and into the street. Lisa was around the corner and gone by then. I went down the other way, figuring I'd go slow around to the candy store. I didn't want to get there the same time Lisa did. I didn't want Mike Reilly to start suspecting anything till I was ready to handle him.

First I had to figure out which guys in the gang I could count on to support me when the showdown came. Unless I had support, I'd be putting my head into a noose.

Monk would be with me. He'd be too scared not to.

Jimmy Nails and Johnny Slash would probably go along with me, too. I could tell they were a little tired of being held down by Reilly. They were itching for action, for a rumble, and Reilly was making them sit tight.

Mack Brown? Hard to say. But I figured that he'd come down with Reilly if he had to make a choice. And that meant I could count out Mack's three sidekicks, Bishop, Sonny, and Charley.

I could count on Lookit, because of his interest in Sis. And most likely Demo too. Smokey would be against me, I figured; he hadn't liked me from the start. So that made five with me, five against. Counting me and Reilly, that left four guys undecided. Coco and Cannon would be more likely to stay with Reilly than support me. Zorro would be with me. And Vince, he was off in his horsehead world and couldn't be figured on either side.

So it boiled down to pretty close to an even split. Reilly could figure on seven supporters in the showdown, and I could count on six, Vince didn't matter. But of my six, Jimmy Nails and Johnny Slash counted double, and maybe their influence would turn a couple of the borderline waverers toward me. We'd see. The important thing was to take care of Mister Mike Reilly.

I headed for the candy store. I figured I'd saunter in and sit down maybe with Vickey and act like nothing out of the ordinary had happened this morning. Nothing like rape and a girl run over and then in hour loving it up with the Prez's deb.

Only I never got to the candy store.

I was halfway there, and walking along whistling to myself, when out of nowhere this police car comes cruising up the street in the opposite direction, going pretty slow. And all of a sudden the bastard makes a U-turn and comes up to the curb maybe four feet from where I was walking.

I didn't need to look inside to know that it was my old pal Sergeant Spinelli riding that buggy.

Stay cool, man, I told myself.

The car door opened. A cop got out, on the curb side. Spinelli. It was the first time I saw him out of his car. He was a big son of a bitch, six foot two. He said, "Get in the car, Flaherty."

"Again? Look, Officer Spinelli, you keep taking me for little rides, but I got things to do. I was just on my way to do some shopping for my mother—"

His face was like a slab of rock. I wondered whether he was picking me up on account of what had happened to the Halperin dame. Had there been an eye witness I didn't know about? Or had Sis squealed?

"Get in the car."

"But—"

"Goddamn it, *get in*."

CHAPTER ELEVEN

There wasn't anything friendly in his face right now. No big-brother buddy-buddy crap. Spinelli meant business and nothing but business right now. I didn't want to cross him. I got in the car. I was kinda uneasy, but I tried to stay cool.

He didn't want me in the back seat, neither. Not this time. Spinelli took me and pushed me into the front seat, right next to him. He closed the door and said, "Let's go," and the cop at the wheel drove off at a good clip.

I yelled, "Hey! Where are you taking me? What the hell is this—"

"We're taking you down to the station house, Flaherty," Spinelli snapped. "Because we wanta have a little talk with you. So shut up and take it easy."

"What kind of jazz is this, Sergeant? You can't just grab a guy off the streets like this! It ain't legal! It ain't—"

"Shut up and don't make noise, kid. I hate a kid who makes noise. Sometimes I get an uncontrollable impulse to ram his teeth down his throat, get me?"

I shut up fast.

I still couldn't figure what was going on. Had somebody squealed about the rape? Or did this have anything to do with the grocery store holdup, maybe? I concocted a whole big wild idea that maybe the Golden Dragons had conned me into making that heist and then had ratted to the fuzz so they could get rid of me the easy way. But I stopped to think and decided that that didn't make any sense.

We came to the precinct house, six blocks away and pulled up right in front.

"We get out here," Spinelli told me.

He and the other cop hustled me inside, up the main steps and past the desk and through a hallway and right back to the far end of the building, where there was a little room without any windows. The room was like an oversize closet. It was maybe ten feet on each side, and there was nothing in it but a wooden table and a backless stool and two or three armchairs, and there was a hot bare electric bulb dangling from a cord attached to the ceiling.

Spinelli and two other cops were in the room with me. One of them bent down and plugged a tape recorder into the wall. He pushed a button and the tape spools started turning, and the second I saw them going I said loudly, "I don't know what this is all about, but I want a lawyer."

"Shut your friggin' mouth!" Spinelli said. No big brother act now. He slapped me across the face. Then he told the other cop to shut the tape recorder off and turn it back to the beginning again. Before they switched it on, Spinelli said to me, "Get this straight, Flaherty. When the time for it comes, you can have fifty lawyers. Five hundred if you want. But right now we just wanta ask you some questions. You don't need no lawyers. You cooperate with us, we'll get through fast and maybe let you go. But if you start getting snotty, we'll make sure you feel sorry about it."

I looked at him. My lip felt puffy where he'd slapped me. I didn't say a thing.

Spinelli took his jacket off. It was maybe a hundred degrees in that little room, and no fan.

He said, "What were you doing on Tuesday night after eight o'clock, kid."

"How the hell should I remember?"

"You'd better remember. Start thinking."

Tuesday night was the night of the grocery store job. So that was what they were bugged about. I half closed my eyes and pretended to be counting the days back on my fingers, Friday night, Thursday, Wednesday. After a minute I said, "I went to the movies Tuesday night."

"Which theater?"

"The one on Tenth Street."

"What movies did you see?"

The tape recorder was going round and round. The light bulb above my head was starting to fry my brains. I was sweating cannonballs. I said "How the hell am I supposed to remember a thing like that?"

"It was only four days ago. You better remember those movies, Flaherty."

"Look, if you'd only tell me what you're after, Sarge. We were buddies the other day. What—"

"What movies did you see, Flaherty?"

I thought fast and hard. Sis had gone to the movies either Tuesday or Wednesday, I didn't remember which, but the show hadn't changed till Thursday anyhow. And she'd told me about the flicks she saw. I screwed up my lips and thought hard, and then I said, "One of them was about dragstrip racers and the other one had Jerry Lewis in it."

If he had quizzed me on the plots, I would have been sunk. But he didn't seem to want to push the question any further.

He said, "Who'd you go with?"

"Some girl from the neighborhood. A little blonde name of JoJo."

Spinelli frowned. "What's her real name?"

"I don't know."

"How can you date a girl and not know her name?"

"She said her name was JoJo. I didn't ask for her life history, Sarge."

That made him sore, and I thought he was going to belt me again. But he must have thought better of it. He just said, "Where does this JoJo live?"

"In the project."

"What building? What apartment?"

"I don't know, Sarge. I just walked her back to the main entrance. I didn't take her upstairs."

Spinelli looked annoyed. "You dated a girl and you don't know her name or where she lives. That don't sound very likely, Flaherty."

"It's the way it was, though."

"Where'd you meet her?"

"Sarge, what's the point of—"

"Where'd you meet her?"

"In front of the house. I was standing there and she came out and I said, You wanta go to the flicks?, and she said, Yeah, let's go, whoever you are, and I told her my name and she said she was Jojo and off we went." It was the kind of yarn that couldn't be proved—but Spinelli had no way of disproving it, either, unless he searched through the whole project looking for a JoJo and didn't find anybody who matched. Which would be a big job.

Spinelli sighed. Sweat was streaming down his face. "All right. What time did the movies break up?"

"Around midnight, I guess. Maybe quarter of."

"And what did you do then?"

"I took the girl over for a soda in the all-night luncheonette," I said. "Then we walked over to the project and sat on one of the benches for a while. We fooled around a little. You want the details?"

"Never mind. What time did you get back to your own apartment?"

"Around one-thirty."

"And you were with JoJo from midnight until half past one without a break?"

"That's right. Hey, look, Sarge, are you gonna tell me what this is all about?"

He wiped the sweat off his face with a dirty handkerchief. I was sopping wet, but nobody wiped me off. Spinelli said slowly, "Maybe you heard that on Tuesday night somebody robbed a grocery on 11th Street. You hear about that?"

"Yeah. It was in the paper."

"Well, it happened between quarter to twelve and one o'clock Tuesday night. The very time you say you were with this Jojo whose name you don't know."

"And you think I held the store up?"

"It ain't just a robbery charge, Flaherty. The old man got hit over the head with a big bottle. He was in a coma till this morning. Then he died. So it's a murder charge, Flaherty."

That rocked me, but I tried not to let it show. Now I knew I had to play it real cool.

"Jeez," I said. "The poor old guy. But what's this got to do with me, huh? You ain't trying to hang that rap on me, are you?"

"Just maybe you might have been mixed up in it, Flaherty. I say just maybe. You're new around here. You might pull something like that because you figured none of the shopkeepers would recognize you."

"Not me, Sarge. I play it straight, You look me up, you'll see I ain't got a record uptown. I tell you, you got the wrong lad."

"Maybe we do, maybe we don't."

I shook my head. I acted real innocent. Spinelli and his two pals hammered at my story for the next fifteen minutes, but I stuck to it. Sweat drenched me like I was up to my neck in the ocean, but I stuck to my story. After a while Spinelli and his buddies got tired of the innocent act. They moved in on me.

They gave me a workout.

The first thing I noticed was that they were shutting off the tape recorder. Wouldn't do to make a record of a suspect getting intimidated, now. Then Spinelli's hand went up and slapped me across the face. My head went spinning back. One of the other cops stepped in and jabbed me in the ribs, not hard enough to break anything but hard enough to hurt. I sucked in my breath and the next second had it knocked out of me when a fist landed in my gut.

They slapped me silly for maybe half an hour, stopping every couple of minutes to ask me questions.

"Where'd you go Tuesday night?"

"To the movies."

"Who with?"

"Girl name of JoJo."

Wham! Bang! Slap!

"How late were you with her?"

"Half past one."

"What films did you see?"

"Jerry Lewis. Dragstrip."

Pow!

"Cut it out, Sarge. I—didn't—do—it!"

"You're lying, Flaherty!"

"Lemme alone."

Bash!

A guy can take that only so long. I passed out. The heat got to me, and I sort of slumped over, and next thing I knew they were splashing cold water in my face and I was awake and glaring at them.

"Gimme a drink of that, Sarge."

"Later. Talk first."

"I told you the truth."

"You got a police record, Flaherty. You were lying to us. They got your name on the books."

"That ain't so."

A fist thudded into my chest.

"You're a punk, Flaherty. You skulled that poor old man and took his dough."

"No!"

A backhand swipe on the face.

"Where'd you hide the money, Flaherty?"

"I didn't take it."

"We know you did. Where is it?"

"Lemme alone."

Fingers digging into my shoulder. Squeezing. Hands grabbing me. Shaking.

"You're a murderer, Flaherty."

"No. Lemme outa here. Gimme a lawyer."

"Later. Confess first."

"Christ almighty, I told you half a million times if I told you once—"

Another slap.

Another.

Another.

I gotta say this for them. They were persistent. They kept it up till I ached all over, till blood and sweat was running down my face and into my mouth, till I was so dizzy I didn't know what was going on. And I figured any minute they'd start the real torture. Sticking splinters in my eyes. Pulling off my toenails. Holding cigarettes burning between my legs. Christ only knew what they might do to me to make me confess. I remembered things I had heard about in the Middle Ages. They could stretch me on the rack. They could put screws around my thumbs.

But I wasn't going to give them the satisfaction. I stuck to my story. I was so slaphappy I was actually starting to *believe* it, by now. In the back of my mind I remembered clobbering the old geek with the bottle, maybe half a million years ago on some other planet. The real me, the one that was sitting here getting the living crap beaten out of him, had gone to the movies that night with a chick name of Jojo. And afterward we had sat on a bench and I had put my hand up her front and felt her around. Sure. I remembered the whole thing now. How she said, "No, Danny," when I squeezed her and opened her bra. It was all so real to me, so goddamn real, and the robbery was just something distant and kind of faint and smoky.

I even remembered those movies I hadn't seen. Remembered the dragstrip kids with their crewcuts and their souped-up rods, and the teenage movie star with her platinum blonde hair and her pointy knockers sticking through her sweater. And Jerry Lewis clowning it up. Sure. I remembered.

After a while Spinelli and his goons got tired of using me as a punching bag. They slacked off and looked at each other like they felt a little foolish about what they were doing, considering as how three of them were banging one guy around and getting nowhere. They kept at the questions, just for the hell of it.

Then a fourth cop came into the room and called Spinelli over. There was a big conference that went on maybe five minutes. I didn't hear a word of it. I just stayed on that backless stool, holding tight to keep from falling off it, and waited for what was coming next.

Then Spinelli came back. "There's been sort of a mistake, Flaherty."

"Yeah?" I said without interest.

"We picked you up on account of there was a Flaherty in your neighborhood that the cops wanted. Only we just checked and it's Jack Flaherty. Not you. Somebody else."

"That's nice," I said.

I smiled, or tried to with my puffy lips. Sure, I know Jack Flaherty. He wasn't any relative of mine, just a guy who had been in the Shining Sinners for a while, maybe a year and a half older than me. He had been picked up by the cops a couple of times on petty charges, and last I had heard of him he had robbed a pile of dough from his uncle and was on his way to Chicago. But my police record was clean. That much of what I had been saying was true.

So Spinelli and company had decided out of the goodness of their hearts to let me go. They brought in a rag wet down with cold water, and wiped some of the sweat and blood off me. Then they gave me a Pepsi to freshen me up. Big hearted Spinelli with his Pepsi.

When I was fixed up some, Spinelli came over and turned on a smile, not the big brother smile but a kind of Dutch uncle smile, and said, "Let this be a lesson to you, Flaherty. Stay on the right side of the law. You may be innocent this time, but you're bound to catch it if you try to break the law and don't ever forget that."

"Goddamn oversize bastard. Picking on a guy who was minding his own business. Fill me up with buddy talk, then drag me in and slap me silly."

"Look, Flaherty, we gotta do our job. It was all a mistake, picking you up."

"Sure."

"It was," he said.

"I oughta sue you for false arrest," I muttered. It was a dumb thing to say. I should have picked up my marbles and cleared out without making threats. For half a second I thought Spinelli was going to haul me back inside and try working me over again.

Then he said, "Just don't try any crap like that, Flaherty. You hear me?"

"I didn't say I would. I said I ought to."

"Just don't make any trouble for us over this. You won't accomplish anything except making life very hard for yourself. You make any trouble for us and we'll clamp down on you so tight you won't even be able to get away with jaywalking, hear me?"

"Yeah."

"Now get out of here."

I got.

I was kind of dizzy, and I ached in half a million places. But at least I was outside the police station, and that was something. I had to laugh. Here they had the guy who had clonked the old man—and the guy who had raped Elaine Halperin, too—right in their mitts, and they hadn't been able to get a confession! They hadn't gotten a thing! They had worked me over and I had held tight!

The dumb bastards, I thought.

I went over to the park and sat there for a while. It was still the middle of the day, the sun bright and hot, and I sat on a bench and rested like I was ninety years old. I sat there till I got some of my strength back. And when I figured no fuzz was on my trail, I got up and started walking over to the candy store where the Dragons hung out.

I was boiling mad, let me tell you. My ribs were sore and my chest was sore and my guts ached and my face was puffy. But at least I hadn't given an inch. *They* had been the ones who had had to give up. Them and their goddamn bottle of Pepsi.

I went into the candy store.

None of the gang was there.

I walked over to the soda counter and sat down. The soda jerk grinned nervously at me.

He said, "Gosh, Danny, you look all messed up. You in a fight or something?"

"Never mind that. Where's everybody?"

"They were here till half an hour ago. Then they went away."

"Where to?"

He shrugged, "They didn't say. They just got up and the whole bunch of them went out."

"Okay. Gimme a chocolate malt." I didn't have the strength to go hunting them down, I took the malt over to a booth and sat down there by myself. When I had it inside me, I felt a lot better.

About ten minutes later, Vickey came into the store.

"I was looking all over for you," she said. "Where—hey, man, what happened to you?"

"The fuzz wanted to ask me some questions. Where is everybody?"

"Down in the park. There was sort of a fight going on there, and we all went to watch."

"What kind of fight?" I asked.

"Two Puerto Ricans. They had knives. One of them cut the other's face up." Vickey sat down next to me at the booth.

"You hurt bad, Danny?"

"I'll live."

She wanted to comfort me. She put her hand on my leg and started to play games. Any other time, I wouldn't have minded. But she was bothering me now. I had Lisa on my mind, and I didn't want Vickey fooling around with me. I took her hand off.

"No?" she said.

"Not now. Just lemme alone."

"Okay, okay. Don't bite my head off."

"The Puertos still fighting?"

"The cops came and got them. I guess the rest the gang will be coming up from the park any minute."

"Yeah. Too bad I missed the fun."

"You hear what else happened today?"

"What?"

"Girl from the housing project got run over by a truck. The way I heard it, somebody was raping her in the basement, and she came running out into the street with everything showing and ran right under the truck."

"Yeah?" I said. "Tough break."

"Killed her," Vickey said. "I knew her, too. Girl name of Elaine Halperin. Very bright girl. But sorta snobby, you know what I mean? Wouldn't have anything to do with me. She didn't approve of me."

I shrugged. "No loss, I guess. So the fuzz had a busy morning. Three of them beating me up, and a girl getting run over, and two spics fighting in the park—"

"Why were they beating you up, Danny?"

"They were trying to arrest me for murder." I looked up. A couple of guys had come into the candy store. Johnny Nails and Coco, followed by Cannon, Mack Brown, Lookit, and a handful of debs. They all came over to me. They started talking at once, started telling me about the girl who was run over, about the fight in the park. All the latest news and gossip.

I saw Monk.

Monk was looking at me, and he was sort of trembling. His stupid face was white as a sheet, and after a second he turned away from me like he was afraid to keep on looking at me. I felt kind of uneasy.

Monk looked guilty.

Like he had spilled the beans to Reilly, maybe?

I took a deep breath. I wasn't in any shape for a stand, now. It was all I could do to keep from falling over after the job Spinelli did to me. I didn't see Reilly, but he'd be getting here any minute, and then I'd know if Monk had told him or not.

There was Lisa, now. And Sis, and Zorro and Kemo. The whole gang was trooping into the store.

And there was Reilly, coming in last, all by himself. He had a funny look on his face. Like he was a million miles away. I just sat where I was. Lookit was telling me all about the fight in the park, but I wasn't listening. I was watching Reilly, trying to figure out if he knew that I had laid Lisa earlier today. I couldn't tell a thing from his face except that he had something on his mind.

He came over to me.

CHAPTER TWELVE

Reilly lowered himself into the booth, facing me and Vickey, and looked me over carefully. The buzz of talk suddenly died down.

"You missed some fun," he said.

"I was busy."

"Yeah. What the hell happened to you, anyway? You walk into a cement mixer or something on your way over here? You look roughed up."

"I *got* roughed up," I said. "It was the fuzz. Cop car stopped and they picked me up. Spinelli. Took me to the precinct house and locked me in a little room without windows and worked me over."

Reilly looked sympathetic. "Jeez, man. What did they want to do that for?"

"About Tuesday night."

"The grocery store?"

I nodded. "Seems the old geezer just died. Skull fracture, Spinelli said."

"Spinelli. He the big ape with the broken nose?" Reilly asked.

"Yeah. Know him?"

"Sure. He's the juvie patrol for this area. He keeps an eye on all of us around here." Reilly was talking very quiet-like. Something funny was going on. He said, "How come Spinelli picked on you, anyway? He don't even know you run with the gang."

I shrugged. "He mistook me for some other guy named Flaherty from uptown. A guy name of Jack Flaherty, with a police record. So they gave me the works for about an hour or so. Then somebody told them I was the wrong guy, so they turned me loose."

"You didn't tell them anything, huh?" Johnny Slash wanted to know.

I looked up and gave him the cold eye. "Use your head, geek. If I had told them anything, would they have let me walk outa the station?"

"Oh. Yeah. Yeah, you got me there," Johnny admitted with a little chuckle.

A couple of people laughed. But not Mike Reilly. There was an ugly look on the Dragon Prez's face. "So the old guy died, huh?"

"Yeah."

"And the cops picked you up and worked you over and let you go."

"Yeah."

He tapped the table with a fingertip. "So now you're in the clear, then?"

I shook my head. "I guess I am. Who knows about what the fuzz think?"

"You didn't lead them here?"

"Nah. I went over to the park and waited for a while before I came around."

Reilly moistened his lips. He looked like he was thinking something up. I was sure now that Monk had spilled the whole story to him about how he had caught me and Lisa with our pants down. And Reilly was thinking up some special way of getting even.

He was quiet for about half a minute, and everybody else stayed quiet too. Then just when I thought I'd go nuts from the silence, he said, "Then the fuzz won't rest until they've pinned that grocery job on somebody. Been a lot of action around here this week and they've got to make some arrests. Which means then that they'll be out to grab us next. Me, Johnny Slash, Zorro, anybody they can get hold of. They'll pull us in one by one and work us over hard until somebody admits knowing about the job. And then it means up the creek for you and me and Johnny. They'll fry us, Flaherty. They'll put us in the hot seat."

I shrugged. "How many guys are there who know who pulled the job?"

"The whole gang. And the debs. Somebody's bound to crack. They'll pick up a deb and she'll tell them. You think the fuzz won't do it?" Reilly folded his arms. "Hell with that. We'll have to take our chances. Tell me, Flaherty—what you figuring to do about getting even for what the cops did to you, man?"

"Getting even?" I blinked away my surprise. "Man, you don't *get even* with the fuzz! You just keep far away from them and hope they don't trouble you none again."

Reilly's soft voice had a hard edge on it now, "Around here we get even, Flaherty. If the fuzz beats us up, we fix them. That's the way we do things around here. So tell me. How you planning to fix Spinelli?"

"Man, you're funning me. It just don't make sense to make trouble with the fuzz."

"I'm talking straight. Spinelli's a troublemaker around here. He's bucking for Captain, and he figures the quickest way to get there is by putting the Golden Dragons behind bars. Or sending a couple of us up to the hot seat. We been looking for an excuse to finish him off for a long time. Now we got one, man. A damned good excuse."

I looked Reilly straight in the eye. "You telling me to go out and kill a cop?"

"I'm not telling you anything, man. I'm just letting you know how we feel about that cat Spinelli. We don't like him. And he put you down, didn't he? You can't go around letting the fuzz put you down. We'd be better off rid of him."

"Yeah," Jimmy Nails put in suddenly. "He maybe even gives tips to the Eagles on where we're gonna go. That man's a menace."

"That's right," Mack Brown said. "He got a cousin in the Eagles to be a spy, that's what people say."

Reilly shut them up, "Spinelli's trouble," he said. He came back to the main point, that I wanted to duck but couldn't. "And he did you wrong. He pulled you off the street and worked you over."

"Okay, he did. I ain't saying he didn't. And I hate him for that bit."

Reilly nodded. "But you're just gonna sit there on your butt and not do anything to him?"

"Killing a cop is a big thing," I said slowly. "The other fuzz try to hunt you down. They pass your picture around. They don't give you a break. And when they catch you, they kick your teeth in before they arrest you."

"A smart man can get away with it," Reilly said.

"Maybe."

"Been plenty of fuzz knocked off in this city by guys who got away with it."

"Maybe yes, maybe no. But it ain't a smart thing to go around doing."

Reilly looked me in the eye real hard. "You want to stay in the Golden Dragons, Flaherty?"

"What do you think?"

"Just answer."

"Sure I do."

"Okay then, man. You got voted in, but we can vote you out just as fast. We don't let no chickens into the Golden Dragons, hear?"

"I hear you."

"Are you chicken, Flaherty?"

Everybody was watching, now. There was a solid ring of Dragons and debs clustered around us, catching up every word of the quiet conversation Reilly and I were having.

I looked Reilly right in the eye. I saw the trap, now. Reilly had me boxed in. It was real neat. If I went after Spinelli and got cooled, that finished me as a rival for Reilly's power. If I cooled Spinelli and got picked up myself by the fuzz, that was even better, it got rid of two of Reilly's enemies at once. And if by some fluke I finished off Spinelli and walked away easy, well, then Reilly could figure out some other way of putting me down.

He knew I was hot for Lisa, though. And he was out to get me. I looked up, saw Lisa, her pretty face pale, her lips clamped in a tight line. She was worried. She knew what was going on. She was trying to encourage me, I thought.

"Well?" Reilly prodded. "You chicken man?"

"No," I said, still looking him in the eye. "I ain't chicken."

I realized that right then and there I was agreeing to go out and kill Spinelli.

Now that it was decided, some of the tension went out of the gathering in the candy store. I even relaxed some myself. Nobody said anything further about it. I would be allowed to pick the time myself. Tomorrow, the next day, even the day after. They wouldn't rush me. I was on my own, now, and it was up to me to prove that I wasn't chicken, that I was worthy of being a Golden Dragon.

I'd go cool off Spinelli, I told myself. Then I'd come back to the clubhouse and take care of two other little jobs. I'd get rid of Mike Reilly and I'd get rid of that lying scut Monk. And I'd be boss of the Golden Dragons.

And Lisa would be mine.

Right now, though, I had to be satisfied with Vickey. I nestled up against her, felt her a little. She would do for now.

Excitement makes you need a woman more. That night at the clubhouse, after I had had a couple of drinks, I said to Vickey, "Come on. Into the back room."

"Sure, Danny. Sure."

I took her by the hand and we went back there and I closed the door. Her eyes were half slitted, and she was already steamed up, her breasts going up and down. Not a bad piece at all. Only Lisa was ten times as much.

We stood together and her belly ground against me and my tongue drove into her mouth. Then we came up for air and she said, "Danny, why'd you let Mike talk you into going out to cool that cop?"

"He called me a chicken. I gotta show him I'm not."

"But cooling a cop—"

"Kill it, baby. I got other things on my mind besides what happened today."

"I'm worried about you, Danny. I don't want something to happen to you."

"I'll be okay."

"I'm real gone on you. You're the most, man. The most I ever had."

I felt a little sorry for her, because I knew that one way or other she was going to get the shaft. She'd lose me if I got killed by Spinelli or if I went to stir. And if I came out on top, I was going to drop her for Lisa.

Time for her to worry about that when it happened. There was still right now to think about.

I pulled her toward me. My hands went over her blouse, opening it, seeking the full breasts inside. I stripped off her clothes, grasped her breasts, held them tight, until she started to gasp. My hands went down her back, over her buttocks, everywhere. Then she peeled me, and when we were both naked she made me hit her the way she liked it. My hand slapped down again and again until the skin was red and sore-looking, and she turned around, wrapping her body around me, sliding over me, twining around me and I stood there holding her, leaning back a little to support the weight. When it was over, I backed up and sat down on the mattress, and we relaxed for a while, fooling around with each other.

After a while we got dressed and went outside. The party was going full blast. I saw Reilly on the couch with Lisa, and jealousy went through me. He was deliberately doing it in public. He had her sweater pulled up and her bra off, and he was holding her breasts. When she saw me come into the room she threw me a look and I knew what she meant. She was saying, *"I'm sorry, Danny, I got to play along because he's a dangerous guy and he wants it this way, but someday soon things will be a whole lot different."*

I went into the kitchen to get myself a cold beer. Vickey didn't tag along after me. But while I was opening the can, Sis came in. She looked kind of rumpled up.

We hadn't been alone since that morning—it seemed like a hundred thousand years ago—when we arranged to decoy Elaine Halperin.

Sis said, "You gonna go after that cop?"

"I gotta."

"It's risky, Danny."

"There ain't no two ways about it."

She shrugged. "Someday it'll catch up to you, Danny. First that grocer. Then the girl this morning. And now a cop. Your luck won't hold."

"Who are you to talk?"

"I ain't done nothing wrong."

"You been laying with Lookit and god knows how many others. What happens if you get knocked up?"

"Don't change the subject."

I looked at her for a long moment. Then I said, "Sis, I'm going after this cop because I *got* to do it. If something happens to me, okay. I'll take my chances. Only don't try to mess with me."

"Okay, Danny. Okay. But—"

Whatever she was going to say, it didn't get said, because Lookit came into the kitchen and grinned and put his hand on Sis' backside and suggested that she go into one of the bedrooms with him. He waved to me and off she went. I walked slowly back toward the living room.

The doorbell was ringing. Nobody answered it, but then I saw Vince the junkie scuttling across the room like the house was on fire.

Vince opened the door and went out into the hall. Just for the heck of it, I walked over.

The junkie was standing out there talking to a little pockmarked guy maybe fifty years old. The connection.

The minute the pockmarked guy saw me, he looked up suspicious-like and said, "Who's this?"

"That's Danny," Vince said. "One of the gang."

I looked down at the capsule in the pusher's hands. "You sell the stuff?"

"Maybe. You on it?"

"No," I said. "But I'm looking for a quick jolt."

"Smoke reefers," Vince said. "Don't go near H, Danny. I warn you—"

"Don't worry about me," I said. "I know when to lay off. I just need a quick blast." I looked at the connection, who was shifting his feet uneasily, "How much for half a cap, man?"

"Eight bucks."

"Make it five."

"Danny, don't," Vince said. He meant well, the poor bastard.

"Shut up," I said. "Five okay?"

"Seven."

"I ain't gonna give you a nickel more than five," I said.

The pusher chewed his lip. He probably figured me for a promising new customer, because after a moment he said, "Okay. Just this once, on account you're a friend of Vince's, five bucks. But after this it's eight bucks a half cap, you hear me?"

"Sure, man."

"You want to buy a spike too?"

I shook my head. "I'll use Vince's. That okay with you, Vince?"

"Anything you say, Danny."

I forked over the dough, five bucks, took the little capsule of white powder from the pusher. The moment the deal was complete, the pockmarked man vanished. Vince closed the door and we headed toward the bathroom together. A couple of guys looked after us.

I didn't feel like explaining what I was doing. I just wanted the kick, was all. I wasn't aiming to get myself hooked. One jolt every now and then doesn't hook you. I had promised I wouldn't ever take any more H, but this was a special situation, and I figured I could relax the promise just this once.

We closed the bathroom door.

Vince said, "You shouldn't oughta fool with H, Danny. You might get like me."

"Not a chance."

"I tell you—"

"Stop it. Just give me your spike. Help me get fixed. Once you take your fix, you won't be any good for helping me, man."

Vince had a hiding place under some loose tiles in the bathroom. He opened it up now and took out his equipment.

The hypodermic needle.

The spoon.

The length of rubber hose.

The book of matches.

"You ever had a fix, man?" he asked me.

"Yeah. Once. But you better show me what to do."

He nodded. He took my left hand and wrapped the rubber hose around the arm so the vein stuck out good and sharp. Then he opened the little cap of H and poured the white powder out onto the spoon. He struck a match and started to cook the H, to make it dissolve, and when he was satisfied with it he poked the tip of the hypodermic into the stuff in the spoon and filled the syringe up.

He handed it to me.

"Here, man. Give yourself the shot. I ain't gonna put it in your arm for you."

I took the needle from him. I held it a moment, hovering over the bulging vein.

"Come on," Vince said. "Hustle it up. I want to take my fix when you're through."

I nodded. No sense stalling. I jabbed the needle into my vein and shot the white liquid in. When the syringe was empty, I yanked it out of my arm.

Vince grabbed it from me. He got busy fixing his own. But I didn't pay any more attention to him. The stuff had me. It didn't send me way up and out, like M does. It just made me feel free and easy, nice and loose.

I walked into the other room, or maybe I floated, and I found an empty armchair and sat down. Vickey came over to me, but I didn't pay any attention to her. I felt relaxed like I hadn't been in a long time.

I could even see the future. I saw me taking a zip-gun and blowing a hole in Sergeant Spinelli's chest. I saw Spinelli grabbing himself and sagging, toppling, falling over dead. And I walked away from the scene.

Then I saw myself walking into the Dragons' clubhouse. *"Where's Reilly?"* I said in my hophead dream. And Reilly came out to see me, and I told him I had killed Spinelli, and then I pointed the zip-gun at him and said I was going to kill him too.

And Reilly got down on his hands and knees and licked my shoes and begged me not to kill him. But I said, get up, and when he got up I aimed the gun at him and grinned and said, *"T. S., Reilly,"* and I shot him in the belly.

Then I looked around the place and said, *"Now where's that lying skunk of a Monk?"* and Monk came forward, and he was shaking all over, and I asked him why he had squealed to Reilly about me and Lisa, and he didn't know why, just asked me not to shoot him, and he was so scared that he wet his pants, but I wasn't having any mercy. I loaded the gun and shot him in the groin. And he fell down and put his hands to himself and bled like a pig, and I let him scream in agony for half an hour and then finally I put him out of his misery by putting a bullet into one of his eyes.

Now all the Golden Dragons came clustering around and applauding and telling me I had to be Prez. So there I was, Prez of the gang.

And Lisa was mine.

She was in the back room waiting for me, they told me. So I went in back and there was Lisa, stark naked on the bed, and I got on her and she lying took me and we made it for an hour and it was the greatest ever.

Yeah. Okay.

Except it was all a dream, only a hophead dream. The evening ticked away and I came back to reality, and I hadn't killed Spinelli or Reilly or Monk, and I wasn't Prez of the Dragons, and I had a long way to go before I'd ever have Lisa again. I felt pretty lousy then. I was so sure everything I dreamed under the H was true, and it was like being cheated to find out it hadn't happened.

I got up and walked out.

I went home, walking alone through the hot quiet streets. It wasn't even midnight yet. Somewhere people were crying because their daughter was dead, and somewhere else an old grocer's widow was crying for him.

And somewhere else Sergeant Spinelli was having a good time. Maybe he was in bed with his big fat wife, if he had a wife, and he was telling her how he had a skinny Irish kid in the station house today and beat the crap out of him. Then he was reaching for his wife, giving her a good bang, making plenty more little Spinellis—

Crap.

Tomorrow I'd go after Spinelli.

I'd show him. I'd show Reilly.

I'd show the whole friggin' world!

CHAPTER THIRTEEN

When I woke up, I felt like hell. My mouth had a funny taste and my eyes didn't want to focus the right way. My arm was a little sore inside the left elbow, too, where I had stuck the needle. I wished I hadn't touched the H. First you go up, then you come way down.

I slouched out of bed and into the shower without bothering to see if anybody else was up and around. It was towards ten in the morning. I came out of the shower with a towel around my middle, feeling a lot better now that I had doused myself with cold water. But I was still a long way from feeling good.

Sis was there. She was wearing a housecoat that she hadn't bothered to tie too tight. It was flopping open in front and her breasts were half showing.

"Morning," she said.

"Fix your gown. Everything's hanging out."

She laughed.

"What's so goddamn funny?" I snapped.

"You," she said. "You're so mixed up. You don't give a damn what happens at the clubhouse, I can run around naked for all you care, but now you tell me to close up my front."

"You oughta be decent in your own house."

She grinned. "Yeah. If you say so, man." She pulled the gown tight in front. "How you feeling?"

"Not so hot."

"You were on H last night, weren't you?"

"Shh! Why don't you shout it?"

"Nobody else home," Sis said.

"Where are they?"

"Ray went down to the library to take out some books. Ma's doing the marketing."

I nodded. "You had breakfast yet?"

"No. I was just going in when I heard you taking a shower, and I figured I'd wait," We went toward the kitchen. Sis said, "You *were* shooting up with horse, huh?"

"It matter to you?"

"Just curious."

"Well, I *was* on H. What of it?"

"You studying to be a junkie?"

"I can take the stuff or leave it alone," I said. "I needed something to pep me up last night."

She nodded. "Yeah."

Sis poured coffee for me. "Danny," she said. "Maybe we ought to get the hell out of here."

"Huh?"

"You and me. We're just going to hell, both of is, going to hell in a handbasket. Dope and sex and robbery and now you're gonna kill a cop. Where's it gonna end?"

"Get off it, Sis."

"I'm worried. I know, the other night we were talking about kicks, how good it was to have your kicks, that you only live once. But—"

"Cool it, kid."

"No, Danny. I —"

"*Cool it, kid.* Stop bugging me!"

"Don't shut me up. Danny Hear me out. I—"

I boiled over. I reached out and slammed her across the face, hard. I had never hit her like that before. Oh, I had poked her plenty in fun, but this was the first time I had really belted her. She was leaning back on her chair when I hit her, and it sort of took her by surprise and her chair went over backwards. She landed on the floor and her gown went up around her hips. I looked down at her naked body for a second, and then she pulled the gown down. She was half crying, half looking daggers at me. I wanted to say I was sorry, that I hadn't meant to hit her that hard, that she was just bugging me too much.

But no words came. I just looked at her.

She got up slowly. She stood there with her eyes on me, and after a long moment she said, "Okay, Danny. Play it hard. Go kill that cop. Go kill the President, if it'll give you kicks. Do anything you goddamn please. I should care. The cops'll flay you alive, but I should care."

She turned and walked into her bedroom and slammed the door. I shook my head. Damn crazy kid, I thought. I lifted the coffee cup to my lips and gulped it down. Hot, black coffee. It made me feel better about things.

I finished up breakfast, got dressed, shaved, headed out of the house. There were some people in the elevator when I got in, and they were still buzzing about the death of Elaine Halperin.

"... terrible thing. A sweet little girl like that, the kind you'd be proud to have your son going out with."

"They say she was raped before she ran under the truck, too. Horrid."

"Dreadful what human beings can do. Why would someone rape a wonderful girl like that?"

"Probably some sex-starved monster, somebody so ugly he couldn't get a woman to look at him."

I kept in the corner of the elevator, my back to the two middle-aged women. I tried not to grin. What would they say if I turned around and told them that I was the one who had raped the girl, not because I was sex-starved but just for the sheer hell of it, just for the kicks? As it was, I bet they were looking me over suspiciously. Any teenager gets suspicious looks today. The older people, they figure we're the enemy. When we get into elevators with them, they look us over and they frown and wonder if we're *that* kind, the kind that stabs and beats and kicks and robs and rapes.

Well, we are. Some of us.

We are the enemy. But only because they've made us the enemy. With their laws. With their jails. With their club swinging cops. The older people try to grind us down, try to keep us in our place, try to deny us our kicks. So we fight back.

We're the enemy.

I chuckled to myself as these old hens rehashed the Halperin girl's death. Then I walked out, out into the street, and headed for the candy store.

Maybe half the gang was there already. A funny sort of silence fell over everything as I walked in.

I went over to Reilly and called him aside.

"I'm gonna cool off Spinelli," I said.

"When?"

"Today, maybe. Or tomorrow. No later than tomorrow for sure."

"Okay. Why announce it? Go and do it."

"I need a piece. You want me to strangle the bastard, maybe?"

"You've got a knife," Reilly said.

I shook my head. "I can't do it with a knife. I'm no miracle man, Reilly. I want a gun."

"So buy one," he said.

"Lend me one."

He was quiet for a minute, or so it seemed like. I watched his jaws clenching. Then he said, "Okay. I'll lend you a gun. Right now?"

"Right now," I said.

"Lisa keeps it for me. It's a zip."

"Zip's okay," I said.

Reilly called Lisa over. In a lot of gangs, a guy lets his deb keep his weapons. It's safer and smarter that way, because nobody ever thinks to check a girl for guns. Reilly said, "You got the zip?"

"Not on me."

"I didn't figure you had. I'm lending it to Flaherty for the job he wants to do. Get it."

"It's home," Lisa said. "Be back in five minutes."

"I'll walk you over to get it," I said.

"You stay here," Reilly snapped suddenly.

I gave him a long, slow look, and said. "I'll walk over with her. I feel like taking a stroll anyway."

His jaws worked, but he didn't come back at me with anything. I knew he was sore as hell about the way I had just shown him up. But he was most likely figuring that I'd be dead soon enough, or hunted by every cop in the city. So he could afford to shrug off any little show of defiance I might make.

When we were outside, Lisa said, "Danny, I'm awfully sorry about all this."

"Don't be. It'll work out."

"You shouldn't be mixed up in a cop killing. They'll hunt you down."

"They got to know who to hunt, first. I'll make out, don't worry about me. And then I'll change things around here. I'll get your boyfriend Reilly out of the picture. And that lousy squealer Monk."

"You figure he told!"

"Who else? Mike knows all about us, now."

"He hasn't said anything to me."

"He wouldn't. He wants to hang onto you after I'm out of the way. But he's in for some surprises."

We were walking south, toward the extreme lower border of Golden Dragon turf. It wasn't the housing project area anymore. This was slum territory.

We turned into a street that was all brownstones, right down the block on both sides. It was close to noon, and the street was empty. Lisa walked fast, like the long-legged girl she was. I was at her side, as close to her as I could get, though. I didn't put my arm around her.

"This one," she said, pointing to a dilapidated-looking three-story brownstone.

"Want me to come up?"

"Sure."

We went in. The stairs were dark and smelled of garbage. Up, up, up to the third floor. Lisa took out a key. I moistened my lips. Out here, in the dark, I wanted her furiously.

"Lisa?"

"Mmm?"

"Give me a kiss."

"Wait, silly. Let's go inside."

"Won't there be anyone home?"

"Not now." She unlocked the door and we went in. It was a small, shabby dump of a place. Old furniture, cracked walls, dirty windows. Couple of religious pictures hanging on the wall. Dingy.

"Who lives here?" I asked.

"Me and my grandmother," Lisa said. "My brother's in the army. He's twenty-two."

"What about your parents?"

"They got killed in a fire when I was three years old. I don't remember them. I've lived with my grandmother ever since."

"What does she do?"

"Works in a clothing factory. I'm sort of on my own all the time."

I looked at her. She was so beautiful it hurt. It was sort of like seeing a rose growing on a junkheap to see a girl that pretty coming out of a house like this. I took a couple of steps toward her.

"When—when are you going to go after the cop?"

"I'm gonna snoop around a little today. Maybe I won't actually do it till tomorrow."

"Will I see you again before you do it?"

"No."

She nodded. Then she came toward me until the tips of her breasts were pushing up against me. "Kiss me, Danny. Please kiss me."

I put my arms around her and pulled her tight against me. Her belly wriggled against mine. Her lips parted, her tongue slipped into my mouth, then after a moment retreated and I followed it back into hers. I got my hands between our bodies, put them on her breasts, felt the firm ripe roundness of them. Then I started to undress her. I peeled away blouse and bra, and there were her breasts, pale and big and good to touch. I played with the nipples. Then I pulled her jeans off, and her panties, and I squeezed her hard. She let out a little sigh. I ran my hands down her body, her satin-smooth body.

This might be the last time, I thought.

The last time I made it with Lisa.

The last time I made it with *anybody*.

I wanted it to be a good one. I wanted it to be as good as the one I had dreamed about the night before, the hophead lay that had gone on for hours.

This time it was the best I ever had. The weather was hot, and our bodies were lathered up with sweat, and we went back and forth on the bed for a long time. Half a dozen times *I* thought we were going to go over the top, but I held back in time and let Lisa tremble it out, and then she was ready to go again and I was still with her. We rolled over and over, my sweaty hands gripping her tight, hoisting her body high off the bed, practically standing up myself, and her eyes closed or else half-slitted, her lips moist and drooping, her blonde hair covering us both, her sweet smell in my lungs.

Then it ended. I felt the finish coming, and I gripped Lisa tight and gave her the signal, and we raced over the top together, gasping and shivering. When it was over, I put my head down in the double mountain of her breasts.

Lisa said, "Mike is gonna be sore."

"Let him be."

"He'll know what we did."

"To hell with him. I'll fix him soon as I'm through with Spinelli."

We came away from each other. I looked down at her as she lay on the bed. Her face was flushed, and the rosiness went down her throat as far as the upper halves of her breasts. She had a smile on her face, the satisfied smile of a woman who's been well loved. She lolled back, completely relaxed, her knees in the air and one leg crossed over the other to show me just a tiny bit of her delicious bottom.

"I better get going," I said.

"Stay some more."

"After I do the job. Get me the piece."

"Okay," she said. She rose, going past me naked to the dresser. I followed her, rubbing the flat of my hand against the softness of her rear cheeks. She opened the dresser's bottom drawer and crouched down to rummage under the blouses and bras and panties.

She pulled something out.

"Here," she said.

She handed me the zip-gun. It's a homemade kind of weapon, comes in pretty handy when you can't get yourself any other kind of gun. A piece of wood mounting a firing pin on it, maybe a door bolt or something like that, and hooked up with some good strong rubber bands. You use a car aerial cylinder for a barrel, and fire .22 caliber cartridges. You'd be surprised how those rubber bands can shoot a bullet out. At close range it's deadly.

The good thing about a zip-gun is you can make one in an afternoon, cost maybe a dime or a quarter. And if you want to use a real gun, it costs you anywhere from five bucks on up, depending on whether you use one of those little West German .22s that you can get in a lot of places, or a bigger job. I never had a gun. I always used a knife in the gang stuff. But now I needed it.

I put the gun away. "What about slugs?" I said.

"I just have a few, Danny." She gave them to me. I kissed her one last time. Then I straightened out my clothes and left.

"So long, Lisa."

"So long, Danny. Good luck."

"Yeah. Thanks."

I walked out into the hot street. There wasn't any turning back, now. I had the gun. I had my mind made up. Now I had to come across.

And I was alone in this, all alone.

I had to go through with it. If Reilly hadn't known that I was cutting him out with his deb, he knew it now. So I had to take care of Spinelli and then take care of the Dragon Prez. *Had* to. I could always chicken out and save my skin, but that wasn't the way I played it. I had never chickened before, and I wasn't going to start now.

I strolled down to the corner. Rubbing out the cop wasn't all that dangerous, I told myself. What was involved? Just a shot coming out of nowhere, the whine of a .22 going through the air and landing in a man's skull or in his chest, the man dead.

You couldn't trace that shot from anywhere. One flip of the trigger and Spinelli would be gone, and I would be a big man in the gang.

And then Reilly. And then I'd be the biggest man in the gang.

I didn't like the idea of killing somebody. But what the hell. It didn't bug me that much to think about eradicating Spinelli. The guy had beaten the living crap out of me, hadn't he? My face was still puffed up where he had hit me, wasn't it?

And it wasn't like I hadn't killed before. I had killed the old grocer, and him I hadn't even hated like I hated Spinelli. I guess you could say I killed the Halperin broad too. So I wasn't exactly a beginner. And I had to shoot Spinelli to prove to the gang that I wasn't chicken. In a way, it was the final step in my initiation.

This was it, now.

This was what would make me a Golden Dragon at last.

I started to figure out how I was going to go about doing it.

Spinelli was a motor cop, not a beat-marcher. That meant you could never tell where he was likely to be. He would just be cruising around the neighborhood all the time, looking for trouble. It wasn't as easy to get a motor cop as it might be to pick off a guy who was just walking his beat. That way, you could hide in an alley and spang him when he came by. But you couldn't trail a cop car and shoot into it. That was too risky. You missed and they'd run you down and go over you twenty times.

I'd figure out something, though.

First thing was lunch. I walked around the block and down to the next one. I was right at the southern end of the Dragon turf, now. There was a drugstore there, and I walked in and went to the lunch counter.

"Bacon and cheese sandwich on white," I said.

The counterman nodded and put a couple of strips of bacon in the pan. I watched them sizzling.

They reminded me of a guy sizzling in the hot seat. I looked away from them.

I ate lunch quickly, paid, and went out again. I looked around the street.

And I realized I had my setup.

It was simple and sweet. I didn't need to look any further than this block that I was on right now. I could set up my party for Officer Spinelli right here.

Easy. The street wasn't very busy. Like all the rest of the streets around here, it was sleepy, everybody inside the houses or else off at work. It wasn't like uptown, where millions of people sit around on their front stoops from morning to midnight.

There was this drugstore here, and a couple of other little stores on the corner, a laundry and a woman's hairdresser and maybe one or two others, but most of the middle of the block was just brownstone houses.

There was a big alleyway in the middle of the block. I walked up to it. It ran all the way through the block to the next street. For its whole length, the alleyway was fronted with all kinds of garages that I could duck into, if I had to hide. Or else I could just run all the way through the alley to the next block and manage to lose myself there.

Everything looked smooth enough. All I had to do was get Spinelli to come up the block and get out of his car. Then I could plug him from a hiding place and beat it up the alley. It would all happen in a hurry, before the other cop in his car knew what the hell was going on. And if I didn't like the way the situation was shaping up when Spinelli got out of the car, I could just hang back in the alley and do the job some other day.

I worked everything out real clear in my mind, and there weren't any holes in the idea. *Bang!* and scram. That was all.

I felt kind of puffed up about it. I'd show those Dragons once and for all that I wasn't chicken. They'd push Reilly out and make me Prez of the gang. And once I got in, I was going to make those bastards sit up and take notice. First thing I'd do would be to arrange a rumble with the Red Eagles and grab half their turf. Just by way of serving notice that I meant business.

And every night, Lisa....

Hell, I'd let the Mayor himself have it if it brought me closer to Lisa, Just the thought of her made me tingle all over.

She was going to be mine.

I walked down to the corner and headed north again. There was nothing more I could do today. It was getting late, maybe Spinelli was off duty already. I didn't want to go to the candy store or the clubhouse. I didn't want to see anybody in the gang until it was over. I hated the waiting. I hated their faces as they looked me over. I wanted to be able to walk in and say, "It's taken care of, I did it, the bastard is cooling off on a slab."

Not till then would I go back there.

I checked things over in my mind. I'd do the job tomorrow morning, I figured.

I went quickly home and spent the rest of the evening watching television.

CHAPTER FOURTEEN

I didn't sleep so good that night. First I had trouble falling asleep, and then after I did get to sleep there were dreams. I kept dreaming about the killing, over and over and over again. Seeing myself, hiding in the alley, waiting for Spinelli, taking aim, firing, watching the slug travel straight and true for Spinelli's middle, watching his big form crumple to the sidewalk—

Watching myself running like crazy.

The dream always ended there. I never found out whether I got away or not. I must have dreamed it half a million times that night, and it always ended with me running away up the alley.

There were other dreams, too. Dreams of Lisa, naked and waiting for me, her hands reaching for me, her breasts rising and falling. Dreams of Mike Reilly and me in a stand, sometimes my knife plunging into his gut, sometimes his into mine. Blood bubbling out, boiling into the open through the gash. His blood sometimes. And sometimes mine.

It took half a million years before morning came. I woke around eight, rolled over, went back to sleep and didn't get up until eleven.

The apartment was empty. Pa working, Ma down marketing or something, Sis probably with the gang, Ray doing I didn't know what, maybe back at the library for more books. I wasn't very hungry. I fixed myself some coffee and some toast, and that was all I had.

Today was the day.

Today I had the big kick.

I headed out, down the elevator, out into the hot street. The heat wave still hadn't broken. Scorching hot weather had hung over the city for maybe two weeks, and it still held. The sun looked like it filled half the sky. The streets were dry and dusty and baked-looking.

Block after block after block. Down to the street I had cased yesterday, the street where all the action was going to take place, a block from where Lisa lived. I thought about tonight, after all the fireworks was over, when I'd be able to make my next move and get Lisa all for my own. I shivered just to think of it.

I walked into the drugstore where I had eaten the sandwich yesterday. There were a row of phone booths in the back of the store. I went into an empty phone booth, dropped a dime in the slot, and dialed for the operator.

When she answered I said, "Operator, give me the police, fast."

"Just one moment, please." She sounded pretty goddamn cool about the whole thing. I heard some clicking going on in the receiver.

Then a bored voice said, "Police Department."

I said, "Listen, I'm calling from a phone booth in a drugstore on 8th Street just off Avenue B. There's a big bunch of juvenile delinquents in and outside the store, and I'm afraid there's going to be a fight. What I guess you'd call a rumble." I was trying to make my voice sound square and educated-like.

"A rumble? Who's this—?"

I didn't stop to pass the time of day. A lot of questions came sputtering out of the receiver, but I just hung it back on the hook and left the booth.

Casually, I walked out of the drugstore, made a right turn, headed for the alley. The street was as quiet as a cemetery. Far at the other end, a couple of kids were playing with big plastic hoops, but that was the only sign of life on the block. I didn't worry about them any. They weren't more than five or six years old, and they were half a block away and not looking at me.

The morning kept on getting hotter and hotter.

I ducked into the alley. Nobody saw me go in. There was a big pile of garbage cans standing at the mouth of the alley, and I ducked down behind them, crouching away so nobody coming from either direction could see me.

Now that the waiting was almost over, I felt cool and loose.

I figured that what the police would most likely do was notify the nearest cruising radio car to come over and investigate the reported rumble. The chances were pretty good that the car sent over would be Spinelli's car. I could have been wrong, of course. Maybe this was Spinelli's day off. Maybe he was in the precinct house questioning some poor bastard and beating him up. Maybe some other prowl car was closer to 8th Street than Spinelli,

I didn't know. But it didn't really matter much. I was in the catbird seat. If anybody but Spinelli showed up on the scene, I would just fade away into the alley, and try again some other time. Sooner or later I would get Spinelli. If not this time, then the next.

I waited.

A lot of things went through my mind. I kept seeing Lisa, and picturing how it would be when I was boss of the Golden Dragons. Lisa would be mine. And any guy in the gang who tried to touch her, or even put his hands on her, I'd cut him up. Mike Reilly had been a goddamn fool for risking Lisa in my initiation. He should have known that once I had had her, I could never settle for anything less. Vickey was okay, but Lisa was special, with her milk-white skin and her high round breasts, and the muscles rippling in her legs as she wrapped them around your body—

Soon, I thought.

Soon she'd be mine for keeps. I figured out all sorts of plans. Pretty soon that old grandmother of hers might kick off, and Lisa would be all alone. By that time I'd be old enough to quit high school. I'd move out on my folks and live with Lisa, and we'd come and go as we pleased and make it every night. I'd get a little job somewhere and maybe Lisa would bring in some money dancing in a nightclub. And we'd have a ball. We'd live it up. No cruddy half-buck-a-gallon wine for us then. We'd drink the best. And have a party every night. And after the party, we'd get into bed, and there she'd be warm against me.

Yeah, man!

That was the life!

And it would be mine soon. Soon.

Three or four minutes passed. They seemed like hours. And nothing was happening. I heard the kids with the hoops laughing down at the far end of the block. A dog barked somewhere. Overheard, an airplane droned.

Sweat dribbled down my back. Weren't the cops going to come at all? Had I goofed? Maybe they figured I was a crank, that it wasn't worth sending a police car over to investigate the rumble report.

And then the police arrived.

I peeped up over the garbage cans and looked out as far as I dared, and saw a cop car turn the corner and come cruising slowly up the street. The sun was on the windshield of the car, reflecting back at me, and I couldn't see who was inside. I could only hope it was Spinelli,

I took out the zip-gun that Lisa had given me. Carefully, I slipped a slug into place.

I waited.

The car stopped in front of the drugstore. For a moment nobody got out. The fuzz were sizing up the situation. Then the door opened on the curb side.

Spinelli got out.

I grinned when I saw him. *There you are, you big ugly bastard. And you're gonna get a surprise in another half a second. You won't even know what hit you. It's a little present from a guy you had some fun with the other day. I'm just the guy you were slamming around. Too bad you won't even know who nailed you.*

Spinelli was standing on the sidewalk, scratching his head, looking around for the rumble that was supposed to be going on. He had his back to me. I raised the zip-gun. His back gave me a big target. I decided not to wait for him to turn around. It was safer this way.

I let the slug fly!

But I wasn't used to aiming a zip-gun, or something. The slug went wild! Instead of plunking through his back and shredding up his heart and lungs, like it was supposed to do, it skimmed past the side of his neck.

I had hit him—blood was pouring out of his neck just below the ear—but it was only a light flesh wound. He was still on his feet, the lousy son of a bitch!

Of all the rotten stinking luck!

I tried to reload. My hands were shaking like I was an old man with palsy. The other cop would be coming out of the car any minute. I knew I couldn't crap around here much longer. Spinelli was standing kind of stunned, with his hand to the bloody place on his neck.

Suddenly he turned around.

He saw me. He started to run.

Not away from me

He ran straight toward me!

I backed up in a hurry as he came pounding into the alley. My hand was shaking, not because I was going chicken, but just because I was so tensed up, with every nerve twinging like a guitar string. I was sweating. Everything was getting all crapped up. I had to do something.

I was looking right into Spinelli's ugly face, now. I could see the blood streaming out of his neck where I had nicked him. He looked mean. He looked angry.

But he didn't stop!

He kept on coming into the alley!

I never saw a madman like that. I pointed the zip-gun at him, all loaded again. I took aim again. He saw me getting ready to shoot him, but he didn't stop, just came thundering onward like a charging buffalo.

I fired and this time I put the slug right into his belly. If you hit a man with a .45 shot at close range, you can knock him down, but this was only a .22 and he was a big man. Spinelli staggered, almost fell. But the bastard stayed on his feet. He was still running toward me, one hand clapped to his side, the other one fumbling for the gun at his hip.

"Damn you, Flaherty!" he called.

"I'm gonna kill you," I shouted back. "I'm gonna blow you apart, Spinelli!"

I cursed him wildly. I wanted him to drop where he was. I had hit him twice, hadn't I? I had shot him right in the gut. But he wouldn't drop. Like I mean, he just wasn't human. I kept backing up in the alley, and he followed me right along.

I tried to load the gun a third time as I moved. I wanted to stick one shot between his eyes and let him try to keep running. But now he had his own gun out. I didn't want to argue with a Police Special against a one-shot zip-gun. He was running in a kind of lopsided way, like he might drop any second, and I figured that wounded as he was his aim wouldn't be any good and he couldn't hit me. I decided to run. Maybe I could get away from him and slam another shot into him after he dropped. The other cop was coming into the alley now, but we were almost half a block away from him by this time. I put my head down and ran.

There was a loud noise, like a cannon going off next to my ear, and the same second the bullet came smashing into my shoulder. It felt like I had been hit with an axe. I had never known pain like that before. I took four crazy running steps, off balance, and fell down.

The concrete jumped up to meet me. I landed hard, but I rolled over. I tried to put the slug into the gun, tried to shoot him dead anyway while I still had the chance. My hand was shaking, and my whole left arm was gone numb. I fumbled the bullet, got it halfway into the mount.

Then I saw Spinelli standing above me, looking like he was about nine feet tall. His face was white and blood was pouring out of him, staining his shirt.

He fired again.

He hit me in the other shoulder. The gun fell out of my hands and I dropped back on the ground. For a minute I couldn't hear or see. And I couldn't move, either. My whole back was on fire.

And there was Spinelli—bloody, *smiling*. Like he was real pleased to have brought me down.

… They took me away. They put me here. I ain't never getting out of here, either. They put me up on trial for the grocery store man's murder, on account of I couldn't produce any kind of alibi for that night and they wanted to hang something else on me besides just assault on a cop. They didn't have any real case against me, no proof, nothing but the jury hated my guts from the start. So I got marked down as guilty of second-degree murder. I got life imprisonment for that, with a chance for parole after thirty years. Except that I also got a sentence of ten to fifteen years for shooting up Spinelli, and the judge arranged it so one sentence wouldn't take effect until the other one was finished. No matter how you slice it, I'm not going to get out of here. If I live long enough, I may be free when I'm sixty or seventy, only by then who gives a damn about going back outside? Christ, I won't be that old till the year two thousand and something!

So here I am. Plenty of time to think. Plenty of time to write all this down, just how it happened.

Plenty of time to miss Lisa.

I see her in my dreams. I reach out, and put my hands on her breasts and feel the little hard nipples, and she starts to move and I move and off we go to paradise. Only just before I get to the crucial moment, my eyes open, and there isn't any naked Lisa in my arms. There's just an empty cell and a stinking cot underneath me.

I'm but eighteen years old. And it looks like I ain't gonna ever have a woman again.

Christ, did I ever mess myself up!

I'm not going to forget the way that goddamn cop wouldn't give up, either. The way he followed me all the way into the alleyway to catch me, with blood dripping from him. Didn't matter that I had a gun. Didn't matter that I was aiming it at him. He just wanted to catch me.

Christ, I miss Lisa!

Christ, I miss the touch of her lips and the smell of her body.

I ain't never getting out of here. Let me tell it to you straight man: I ain't no chicken and never was.

But that Spinelli, he wasn't chicken either.

THE END

Running with the Barons

....

ROBERT SILVERBERG

CHAPTER ONE

Marty Capuano was in a new town and didn't like it much, but he tried to hide his feelings. He told himself that it didn't matter where he lived. He'd be top man soon enough. He'd grab off some action. There'd be plenty of nice pink boobs in his hands, ripe and jiggly, and the girls would open up for him just like they had when he was running the gang back in New York.

He'd be boss here soon, all right. And when he was, he'd make a different chick every night.

Marty took out his switchblade knife and lovingly fingered the thick, corrugated butt. The blade was always where he could reach it in a hurry. Just a flick of a finger, and out snapped the six inches of keen-honed metal. And there wasn't a bladesman in the world who could put one past Marty Capuano. He was a regular wizard with the shiv.

That was what they'd called him, back in New York, when he was running the Shining Barons—Wizard. Marty the Wizard—and he had earned it.

Marty scowled.

From downstairs he heard the noises of the moving men bringing the Capuano family furniture into this new house. It was old, cheap, beat-up furniture. The kind of used-up furniture that everybody had in his house, back on New York's Lower East Side. Furniture that had belonged to uncles and aunts and was handed down, and furniture bought at the Salvation Army warehouse—ten bucks for an armchair and twenty-five for an overstuffed sofa.

Marty had made a lot of girls on that sofa, too. Pull off their panties and sit them on your lap and spread their legs and give it to them, *voom!*

Marty listened to the sounds from below. His mother was down there, yelling to the moving men in her heavily accented English, supervising them as they put the stuff where it belonged. Marty's kid brother Frankie was down there too. Helping out, the fink! Marty made a face. They had asked him to help out, too, but he hadn't answered them. Instead he had gone straight upstairs to the empty rooms, where he could be away from them. He wasn't interested in helping out. Hell, they hadn't asked him if he wanted to move to this hick town they had picked!

Jenkinsville, Ohio. Population 85,000. That was the sign that was stuck up all over town. The Jenkinsville people probably thought that this was a pretty goddamn big important town, with its 85,000 measly people. A regular city, they thought.

Marty Capuano snorted contemptuously. 85,000 people! Hell, they had that many living on his block, back in New York! Or at least it seemed that way.

But the Capuano family had pulled up stakes and moved out to Jenkinsville. The deal was something about a better atmosphere for kids to grow up in, and a good job in the mill for Old Man Capuano, and a chance to buy a not-too-old house for not-too-much money. So the whole family had up and moved out of New York.

Marty hadn't wanted to come. It meant leaving behind a place where he was *king*. It meant leaving behind a lot of girls with soft, round, sweet backsides and hot, willing loins.

But his father had threatened to take a strap to him if he put up a fuss. And his father was the only man in the world who could say that sort of thing to Marty Capuano and come away with a whole gut. Anyone else, Marty would have sliced him; but he couldn't touch his father.

Marty looked out the unwashed upstairs window. Small, scruffy little boxes that were called tract houses stretched as far as he could see. Further back, there was a big mill whose belching smokestacks cast a smoky pall over everything. A river ran past one side of town—dark red-brown, with thick mud. The river looked foul and polluted. Marty scowled at the town. It was a stinking little burg.

Nowheresville, U.S.A. He hated it already, and he hadn't even been here two hours.

Marty was a small, ratty-looking kid of eighteen. He stood five-feet-three when he drew himself up to full height and with lead weights in his pockets he would have weighed just about one-twenty. His face was pale and acne-pocked, and his nose stuck out like a beak; but he had the sharpest eyes a human being could have, and his corded wrists were as strong as steel. And fast. And flexible. In less than nineteen years, Marty Capuano had carved up plenty more than his share—even killed a few when he had to.

The girls didn't mind his looks. He had something more important for them that they liked—something that didn't show, at least not while he had his pants on. He used it well, and that was much more important than how he looked.

He yanked out his knife and flicked the switch. Half a second later the blade was out, fixed and ready. Marty smiled. He feinted at his shadows on the bare wall, did a double-twist and an undercut, and came slashing sharply up through the air. It would have been a kill, he thought smugly.

The old touch was still there. Yeah. It was always going to be there.

But I gotta go look for some action, he thought. Find me a little fighting and a nice piece of tail. Otherwise this dumb town is gonna bug me to Endsville.

He went downstairs.

The moving men had just dumped all the furniture in the middle of the living room, and Marty's mother and his punk brother Frankie were moving it around and putting it in place. Marty's old man had reported to work already. He couldn't afford to miss even a day, not while there were others around who could do the unpacking.

As Marty passed through the big downstairs hall, his mother called out to him. She was a heavy woman, swollen by years of hard work and from a life of eating doughy pasta.

"Well, Marty? You have a look upstairs? You approve?"

"It's okay, Ma. I guess it'll do."

Frankie looked down at him with smoldering eyes. At the age of sixteen, Frankie was already four inches taller than Marty, and he hadn't even stopped growing, yet. Marty hated him for that. Frankie hadn't started drinking when he was twelve, or smoking at nine. That can cut a guy's size way down; Marty had found that out the hard way. But it was too late to do anything about it now. All he could do was hate his kid brother because Frankie was shooting up straight and tall; maybe he'd even become a six-footer before he was through.

Frankie said, "How about giving us a hand here, Marty? You haven't done a damn thing since we got here."

Marty looked up at the ceiling and whistled mockingly. "I'm gonna go out and look around a little."

"Gonna go out!" Frankie repeated acidly. "Go look for trouble, that's all you want to do! Or find some girl you can make! Why the hell don't you stay here and help Ma and me get the place fixed up? We want it to look nice when Pa gets home for supper."

Marty stared coldly at his kid brother, and his hands opened and closed a few times. Marty was smaller, all right, but he was a lot tougher. In a hand-to-hand fight, he could cripple Frankie, and both of them knew it.

Marty said, "Shove it, buster. You hear me? *Shove* it!"

"I'm just asking you to help out a little around here."

"If you want to work," Marty replied, "you can work till you bust your tail. I ain't stopping you. But I didn't ask to be dragged out to this nowhere place, and I tell you I ain't about to work up no sweat pushing furniture around. You hear all that?"

"Yeah, I hear it, tough man."

"Then keep your trap shut."

His mother began pleadingly, "Marty ..."

"Leave him alone, Ma," Frankie said quietly. "He's no good, and he's gonna stay no good. We're just wasting our breath trying to talk to him. Here, I'll give you a hand with the table."

"Yeah," Marty said, "drag the table around like a good kid. Remind me to hunt up a medal for you."

Frankie's eyes blazed. He went over to Marty and pulled himself up tall, making a big thing out of the four-inch difference in their heights. "Go on, you hood! Head out of here, if you're going! Don't stick around making wisecracks, because Ma and I are plenty busy. We can't waste time with you!"

Marty's hand went to his blade, lying ready in his pocket, but he didn't pull it out. He didn't like to show the steel in front of his mother. "Why, you runny-nosed fink, I ought to cut you from—"

"Marty!" Mrs. Capuano's great bulk came between them. "Don't talk that way! He's your brother! Your own brother!"

"He's a fink," Marty repeated.

He turned and sauntered out the front door, hands in his pockets. Someday that Frankie was going to need some wising up, Marty thought. Lousy, stinking punk. Better chop him down to size before he gets so big he thinks he can boss the whole damn family around.

Marty shrugged and forgot about his brother for the time being. He wondered where he could find some real action in this sleepy little burg.

It didn't take him long to make up his mind where to go.

When the Capuanos had gotten off the train from New York that morning, Marty had happened to notice a couple of boys in the familiar black leather jackets, hanging around a candy store across from the train depot. It was like a scene straight from home.

That seemed like as good a place as any to begin. Marty ambled over to a nearby bus stop, a little concrete alcove with a bench in it.

A girl was sitting on the bench. She was in her late teens, and had a sweet, open face and blondish-brown hair cut short, with bangs. She wore a pink sweater that was drawn tight against the thrusting hillocks of her breasts.

Marty felt his throat grow dry. He saw himself on top of her, thrusting away, hands gripping her cool buttocks and chest rammed against those hot-tipped boobs. Because of all the confusion involved in packing up and moving out of New York, he hadn't had a broad in the sack for over a week. Marty wasn't used to going without for so long. He'd lost his cherry when he was twelve and a half, and ever since he turned fifteen he'd always had a steady piece.

The sight of this pretty girl with the stacked front excited him, setting up a twisting in his loins. But she looked too pure. She had the sweet, virginal look of the "good girl," not like a gang deb at all. In New York, Marty knew, he could never get to first base with such a girl; but then, this wasn't New York.

He looked at her, and she smiled warmly at him. Out here in Ohio, he thought, everybody smiles at everybody else. In New York you don't smile at anybody unless you want to get something out of him.

Marty walked over and said, "Is this the place where I get the bus that goes down near the railroad depot?"

"That's right. It ought to be along any minute. It's the red and blue bus." She paused a moment. "You're new in Jenkinsville, aren't you?"

"Yeah. Just made this scene today."

She giggled. "You talk funny. So tough and hard. I bet you're from New York!"

Marty sat down next to her on the bench. He couldn't keep his eyes off those jutting breasts. He wanted to rip that pink sweater off her, tear away her bra, throw her down on the ground and take her on the spot. But he held himself in check.

"Yeah," he said. "I'm from New York. East Side."

"And your family just moved to Jenkinsville?"

"Yeah. My old man, he got a job in the mill."

"What's your name?"

"Marty. Marty Capuano."

She wrinkled up her brow a little at the Italian name. Probably hadn't ever known anybody with an Italian name before, Marty thought.

"I'm Jill Webster," she said. "Are you going to go to Jenkinsville High?"

"Me? Hell, no. I'm past eighteen. No more of that school jazz for me, thanks."

"Over eighteen? But you don't look that old!" She paused, as if realizing she had said the wrong thing. Her face went bright red.

I bet she's blushing right down to those big knockers of hers, Marty thought. Geez, I'd like to cop a feel of them!

She stammered, "I'm sorry ... I didn't mean ... well, you know ..."

"Sure. Forget it."

He moved closer to her on the bench. For the first time, she began to look a bit apprehensive.

Marty said, "I'm so new here I don't know the score. But I'm looking for a girl. I don't like to stag it, know what I mean? So tell me, you free tonight? I mean, maybe we could hit some of the high spots in town, if this burg's got any high spots."

She twisted uncomfortably. "I ... uh ... I'm sort of busy tonight."

"Well, what about tomorrow? Or the day after? There's lotsa time. But I want to get to know you better. A whole lot better."

"You don't understand," she said. "I guess we just don't move as fast out here as you New Yorkers do. Anyway, there's a fellow I've been dating. His name is Jim Cartwright. He's on the high school basketball team, and he's a real prince."

"Yeah, I bet. But me, I was a *king* where I came from. I could teach you lotsa things he don't even know about." He was trembling all over. He wanted to wrap his arms around her, squeeze those high breasts, thrust his tongue into her mouth, stick his hand between her thighs to feel the hot, eager moistness.

She moved away a little bit. "Well, I don't want to seem rude, but you're a stranger, and—oh, here comes the bus."

She seemed relieved. The bus pulled up; she got on it first, and the driver smiled at her and said, "Howdy, Jill."

"Hi," she said.

Just one big, lousy, happy family, Marty thought darkly. He got aboard the bus. The driver smiled at him, too. "Hello, there."

He ignored the greeting. "What's the fare?"

"Depends on how far you're going, friend."

"Hell of a system. In New York you pay your two dimes and you ride wherever you want to ride."

"This isn't New York, friend. Where do you want to go?"

"Down to the railroad depot."

"That'll be twenty-three cents."

Marty handed over a quarter. "It's cheaper in New York."

"All I can say, buddy, is that this isn't New York you're in now. Here's your change."

The bus pulled away. Marty looked around for the chick.

She had found a seat near the center of the bus, where the most passengers were. She was sitting next to a fat old lady, and there weren't any empty seats nearby. She didn't look at him, either.

Angry, Marty walked past her and took a seat in the back. She was giving him the frost treatment. Well, maybe she was scared of him. Maybe he had moved a little too fast for her.

He looked at her, and saw her breasts going up and down with every breath she took, and he felt desire like a hot knife plowing through his guts. He stripped her naked in his mind—white flesh, golden triangle, ruby nipples. Jill Webster, her name was; he filed that away in his memory.

Five to one she's still got her cherry. Looks like the pure type, but I'll take care of that, he thought. He made a solemn vow. Even if he had to take her at knifepoint, he was going to make that chick. She probably thought he was some kind of big city trash. Well, he'd show her, he swore. And that basketball-star boyfriend of hers wasn't going to stop him, either. A real prince, she'd called him. If he was a basketball player, he was probably tall. Six-three, six-four. Marty Capuano hated all tall people.

I'll chop him down to my size, he thought, and then I'll give it to his pure little sweetheart, right between the legs.

Jill got off the bus about ten stops further on. Marty watched her walk away, her head held high, her breasts thrust proudly outward. In his mind he pictured the smooth, firm curve of her buttocks, the whiteness of her thighs, the generous swells of her swaying breasts. She was quite a chick. And someday she was going to be in bed with him. He made that a to-the-death promise to himself.

Marty always kept that kind of promise.

CHAPTER TWO

Some time, later, the bus driver called out, "Railway depot!" Marty was the only passenger left in the bus by then. He swung out of his seat and slouched toward the door.

It was a warm mid-June day. The sun was high overhead, bathing everything in hot white light. Marty was fingering the butt of the blade in his pocket as he stepped off the bus. Moving slowly, he walked across the wide street to the row of stores on the other side, facing the depot. There was a butcher shop, a little laundry, and a grocery store, and right at the end of the block was a candy store.

Marty took a good look around.

A couple of leather-jacketed loungers were still standing around outside the store. Marty sized them up.

If things worked here like they did in New York, these guys were watchmen, maybe keeping an eye out for members of a rival gang. This was the turf of one gang; they had it staked out. No members of the other gang were allowed to cross the boundary line between the turfs. If anyone came across, it was cause for a rumble. At least, that was how it worked in New York, and most likely it was pretty much the same here.

Marty grinned to himself. It was going to be fun to see what happened when he came barging in on these little two-bit gangs.

The loungers were tall and freckle-faced and hickish-looking. They didn't have the quick, nervy, edgy look of native New Yorkers.

They studied Marty with care as he passed calmly between them and went into the store. Evidently they decided he was a stranger who ought to be watched, because out of the corner of his eye he saw them turn to stare after him.

People tended to underrate Marty because of his size. But they soon found out that a short man with a knife in his hand is a lot taller than a six-footer without one.

The inside of the store was dark and dingy. There were half a dozen marble-topped tables in back, the usual soda counter off to one side, and plastic pretzel boxes, bubblegum dispensers, a pinball machine, a magazine rack, a shelf of paperbacks, and all the other stuff you usually find in a candy store, no matter if it's on Delancy Street, New York, or Nowhere Street, Hickstown.

Marty flicked a quick glance all around the place, taking everything in. Some people were sitting at the farthest booth in back. Four of them—two guys, two girls. The guys had black leather jackets on, even though the temperature was around eighty. Finks, Marty thought. Gang finks.

The counterman was a tall stringbean with a bald head and a bulging Adam's apple. He looked like the kind of guy who wanted to try real hard to stay out of trouble.

Marty sat down at the counter and spun a quarter on the dirty, mottled stone. "Gimme a vanilla malt," he said.

The soda jerk peered at him out of sorrowful eyes. "Sure, fella."

He turned and fussed with his metal container and his mixing machine. Marty swiveled and eyed the four in that back booth. There was room for two more in the booth. It was the big kind, jutting halfway across the floor.

Marty could see one of the girls, the one facing the front of the store. She was a looker—from the neck down. Her face was thin and washed-out looking, with thin lips and stringy red hair. But she wore a tight yellow poor-boy shirt that strained across eye-opening boobs. The girl at the bus stop had had good knobs, but this chick was extra-special. Marty liked his women to have big, soft breasts, like wads of foam rubber, that you could pillow your head down into.

The guy sitting next to her looked fat and slow. Not much on the ball, Marty guessed. He felt excitement starting to boil up in him, the way it always did when he was on the brink of action. He'd show these hick finks a couple of things about fighting! Maybe this was a nowhere town, but it seemed to be full of girls with big knockers. And Marty was hungry to get one now, any chick, even a skinny one. He wasn't fussy about what she looked like or who she belonged to. He just wanted to make one, fast.

"Here's your malt," the soda jerk said, in his dumb-sounding voice.

Marty took the full glass and the half-full metal container, and nudged the quarter across the counter. "This enough?" he asked.

"Plenty. You get a nickel change."

He pocketed the nickel. Then he took the malt and causally walked toward the booths in back. He wasn't heading for the empty booths, either.

He walked over to the one with the four people in it, looked down them, and said in a quiet voice "There's room for one more here, ain't there?"

The fat fellow glared at him. "Plenty more booths in this place, pal."

"I want to sit in this one."

"But we're sitting here," said the thin one at the other side of the table. "And we don't know you. Take one of the empty booths, huh, and stop horning in on strangers."

"I want to sit here."

The soda jerk came over to see what was going on. He peered at Marty and said, "Look here, sonny, don't bother them people. You got no call disturbing them. This is their booth."

"But I want to sit with them."

"There's lots of other booths. Why can't you sit in one of the empty booths?"

"Because I want to sit with these birds," Marty answered coldly. "And if you're smart, you'll keep your long nose out of this, unless you want me to cut you up for bird meat."

"Tough man," the fat one jeered.

"Maybe I am." Marty glared sharply at him. "Maybe I'm plenty tough enough to make you let me sit down here with you!"

"Don't say things like that," the fat boy warned. "If you come around here looking for trouble, I tell you you're going to get what you're looking for. And more of it than you know how to handle, tough guy."

"I'll risk it." Marty shrugged. He sat down on the end of the booth, next to the big-boobed redhead in the tight yellow poor-boy. He knew how important it was to establish, right at the start, his ability to barge in and make people take notice of him.

Deliberately, he took a long sip of his malt. Then he said, "I'm Marty Capuano. Just got here today. I'm from New York."

All four of them looked grimly at him. The thin one on the other side of the table from him said in a low, ugly voice, "We don't give a damn if you just got here from Mars, buster. Get the hell out of our booth before we bounce you out, hear me?"

The two watchmen from out front had heard the rising voices of the argument, and they had come inside the store in case there was going to be trouble. They stood just inside the door, hands on hips, watching.

Marty said coolly, "Aren't you gonna introduce yourselves? I thought you hicks were supposed to be polite. It sorta ain't polite to just sit there like lumps. I told you my name. Now you tell me yours."

He grinned cockily at them. The two guys looked uneasy, the girls scared. Marty knew he had them buffaloed. They didn't know what to make of the pint-sized stranger. In this neck of the woods, nobody came around deliberately looking for trouble.

Marty turned to the girl next to him. He put his hand on her jutting left breast and gave it a good squeeze. Nice meat there. She turned bright red. He felt the ache in his loins. He could have rammed it into her right here.

"Let go of her!" fat one said.

"Make me."

"We don't allow any fighting in the store, Capuano. That's part of the agreement we have with the owner. If you want to come out back, you can get what you're asking for. Understand?"

Marty understood. Sure! That was what he wanted! Action! A fight—and then sex!

"A hand-to-hand stand?" he asked.

"Yeah," the fat fellow said. "I'll have a stand with you, you half-pint wop."

"What did you call me, blubber face?"

"I called you a half-pint wop. Because that's all you are, Capuano. And the faster we show you the way things work in Jenkinsville, the faster the air will start smelling fresh and clean again out here."

Marty was very pale, and his lower lip was trembling. He had been planning to slice this fat one up just a little, give him a few fancy slashes by way of demonstrating his ability with a blade. But now it was a lot more serious than that. Nobody had ever called Marty Capuano a half-pint wop and lived. Now it would have to be a fight to the death, Marty knew. He'd have to wipe out those words with blood. He'd have to drag his knife through the fat boy's guts.

"You shouldn't have said that to me," Marty murmured. "You shouldn't have called me a wop. I kill people who talk to me that way."

"Listen to the big man. Listen to the pint-sized dago."

Marty's jaw muscles knotted. He downed the rest of his malt, trying to keep himself under control, trying to keep from reaching across the table and slashing the life out of his tormenter right now. This had to be done right. A hand-to-hand stand, knife against knife.

"When do you want to hold the stand?" Marty asked.

"Right now. Outside. Or are you chicken?"

"Come on. Let's get this over with."

Marty stood up and stepped back to let the others lead the way. The stringbean soda jerk looked at them peculiarly as they filed out of the store, the two watchmen first, then the two girls, then the thin boy, after him the fat boy, and finally Marty.

They left the store and circled around the corner, back to a closed-in area that looked like a parking lot. The lot was empty, and Marty figured maybe it was never used. An alleyway connected it with the street, but it wasn't easy for anyone passing by outside to look in and see what was going on.

Marty noticed a few more kids in black leather jackets arriving. There were eight of them now, and the two girls. The way Marty felt, he could take on the whole bunch, two at a time, come out of the stand untouched, and bang both chicks afterward for a chaser.

They formed themselves into a loose, semi-circular group, facing him. Marty stood square, one hand on the butt of the knife in his pocket. The butt was warm from constant handling. Marty felt good touching the butt. It was like a part of himself.

He glared around. He was the shortest of the lot.

He said crisply, "Listen to me, you dumb hicks. My name is Marty Capuano. My home town's New York, but I live in this goddamn nowhere burg now. And before I'm through, this whole town's going to know my name."

"Sure, Capuano," said the fat fellow, who seemed to be in charge. "They'll know your name, okay. When they read it on the obituary column."

There was a chorus of derisive laughter. Someone called out, "You tell him, Charley! Tell the runty bastard off!"

"Who said that?" Marty snapped. "I'll take on the man who thinks I'm a runty bastard as soon as I'm through with Fatso, here."

Nobody said anything.

"Well?" Marty demanded. "Who said that?"

"It don't matter," said Charley. "This is my fight. You and me, little man. You and me."

"So who are you?"

"I'm Charley Beck, and I'm boss of the Jenkinsville Barons."

Marty grinned. "Barons, huh? My outfit in New York was called the Barons, too—the Shining Barons—and I ran the whole scene. Just the way I'll be running the Hicktown Barons pretty soon."

"First you got to get me out of the way," Beck said.

"That won't be any trick."

"We don't like snotty little wise punks bothering us in the store. Not even punks from New York, Capuano."

"You the only gang in town?"

"There's the Dragons, too. Just the two of us in this town, Barons and Dragons."

Marty grinned. "And you're the big cheese of the Barons, eh, Beck?"

"Yeah."

"You're a lump of lard. Pig blubber, to be exact."

Marty watched anger change the amiable fat face into a cold, ugly mask of hate. Marty was ringed by about ten of the Barons, now. Evidently word was spreading through the neighborhood that Charley Beck was having a stand with a loudmouthed stranger.

Marty sized Beck up with the eye of an expert. Beck looked like he was nineteen or twenty, and he was big. Not all of him was fat, either. He was jowly around the cheeks, and there was a rubber tire around his belly, but Marty knew there was plenty of real muscle behind the outer layer of fat. Enough muscle to drive a blade right through Marty and out the other side, if he got the chance.

But he wouldn't get the chance.

Kill him fast. Then grab the girl and take her off and let her have it. Strip down her panties, spread her legs, go to it! Hot, pulsing throbs of lust. Drive deep, churn around. Squeeze her breasts, her butt. Relief.

Beck was a six-footer, and he probably weighed close to 250. It would be a bad mistake to underestimate him. He was big and he was strong; otherwise he wouldn't be in charge. Weaklings didn't get to the top rung of a gang, not even in hick towns.

Marty slipped his hand into his knife pocket, and the switch practically leaped of its own accord into his palm. He grinned and pushed the button, and the blade came flicking out. It was razor-keen, diamond-bright. Marty took good care of his blade, so his blade would take good care of him.

The other Barons dropped back a pace or two at the sight of the gleaming blade. They hadn't figured on things happening that fast.

"Come on, Beck," Marty taunted mockingly. "This here thing is a shiv. You know anything about them out here in the sticks? You know how to use them, and all?"

"We know," Beck said quietly.

"Let's see how you do in a stand, then. If you're the big cheese of this gang, let's see how good you really are."

"Get back," Beck warned his pals. "Don't mix in this."

A second later there was a switch in his hand, with the blade out. The big guy looked pale but not scared. Hick or no hick, he looked like he knew how to use that knife.

Savage joy coursed through Marty's scrawny body. Next to making it with a broad, fighting was the greatest pleasure of his life. *This is it! This is action! This is what I'm alive for!*

He spat contemptuously and went into his killing crouch.

Beck stepped forward and they circled each other warily for a moment, in absolute silence, feeling each other out like two boxers going for the world championship. Only this was a lot more serious than a boxing match. This was for keeps.

The onlookers backed up, not wanting to get in the way and be carved up by a sudden lunge. Marty could tell by the way the other man moved that he was a lot faster than he looked, and also that he knew how to handle that knife. But Marty wasn't worried. He'd been up against crack knifemen before. It was always the other guy who came out of the stand with a split skin.

Marty hung poised, ready. He never liked to let the other guy get a jump on him. And he wanted to carve this fat boy up and carve him good. Nobody called Marty Capuano a half-pint wop and got away with it.

Marty waited for Beck to make the first move. And at last, his patience used up, Beck went into action. His opening thrust was a quick feint toward the heart, and an intended upcut that would have slashed across Marty's face and marked him for life. Marty darted to the left just in time, and as he stepped aside he brought his knife down in a quick swipe that nicked Beck's knife arm.

First blood.

First blood always told.

Beck came barreling in, worried by the ease with which Marty had cut him, anxious to make a quick cut himself. Marty went in under Beck's guard, then had to duck away as Beck pivoted with surprising speed. Marty was caught off balance. Beck's blade cut a lean, thin line behind Marty's left ear. It was just a scratch, but it stung.

It made him even meaner. Beck had outfaked him. Beck had cut him. Marty didn't like to get cut.

He went for Beck. He went in with the knife low and menacing, the way he had been taught to keep it. He had learned the art of knife-fighting practically from the cradle. He had learned it in the best school in the world, on the Lower East Side.

Beck slashed out, trying to parry. Marty felt the wetness of the blood dripping from the shallow wound on the back of his neck. He brought his blade up, switched directions with lightning speed. The blade ploughed through the soft part of Beck's right arm like so much butter.

It was the first serious wound of the encounter, and now Marty knew he'd have nothing further to worry about. He grinned, yanked the knife out, and planted it in Beck's shoulder. A spout of blood leaped forth.

Marty smiled up at the bigger man and saw Beck's pale face, nearly a foot above him, his lips clamped tight from the pain.

Beck was scared. He had been cut three times, and he knew that he was going to get killed on the next one. He hadn't figured that Marty would play for keeps.

Marty cruised in smoothly for the kill. He used his favorite trick, the most terrifying one. He shifted the knife from hand to hand, back and forth, as he drifted inward. There was no telling which hand the knife was going to be in when the blow came. And it didn't matter. From either hand, the blow would be deadly. Marty was ambidextrous. He had spent long months training his left hand until it was just as strong and quick and deadly as his right.

He finished it all off in a second. He passed the knife from left to right to left again, while Beck stood gazing stupidly as if hypnotized, with the blood dripping down his wounded arm. Marty clucked harshly and passed the knife twice more, back-forth-back-forth, just to put a little frosting on the cake. The blade ended up in his left hand and he brought it up sharply with a twisting motion on the end of it, all wrist action, deadly action.

The blade went into Beck's belly, and Marty's wrist dragged it up through layers of flesh and internal organs until it reached Beck's heart. The Baron leader blinked in surprise, not really believing that he was dead, and then his eyes glazed over. He crumpled and fell, and lay without moving in a spreading pool of blood.

It was suddenly very silent in the parking lot. "Geez!" someone whispered. "He cooled Charley!"

Marty turned around to face the whole lot of them. He felt tired and sweaty, and the cut on the back of his neck bothered him. But the thrill was the only important thing. He had killed again. It was a thrill second only to the pulsing thrill of sex.

He was in double figures now—Beck was his tenth kill in solo hand-to-hand stands.

"Okay," Marty said, breathing hard. "Who wants to be next?"

CHAPTER THREE

Nobody moved. Nobody said a word. Their faces were pale, unbelieving.

Marty pulled out his dirty handkerchief and mopped the blood off his neck. He looked down at the corpse of Charley Beck, then up at the row of uneasy Barons.

"I asked you, who's gonna be next?"

No answer.

"Nobody gonna be next? Hell, some tough gang you are! I just iced your president, and you stand there like a bunch of stupid finks!"

The thin fellow who had been in the booth when Marty sat down said haltingly, "There ain't nobody gonna take you on, man. You can be sure of that."

"You ain't human," said another in hushed tones. "Like, I mean, we never saw nobody do things like that with a knife."

Marty grinned. He liked to hear them talking like that. He knew they were scared spitless of him. He was still Marty the Wizard!

He looked them over. Ten of them, all sizes. And a couple of chicks, too. He could use a girl right now. It was always good when you had a girl right after you had a fight. Love-sweat mingled with kill-sweat.

Breaking the stony silence, Marty said, "It seems to me like the Jenkinsville Barons are in a bad way for need of a new pres. Okay. I nominate me. Anybody else want to nominate anybody?"

Nobody spoke.

Marty said contemptuously, "Ain't any of you gonna try to take it away from me? You just gonna sit tight and let a stranger walk in and take over your gang?"

"We want to go on living," the thin one said. "We ain't that dumb."

"Okay, then. I declare nominations closed. Anybody object?"

Nobody objected.

"Now we'll have the elections," Marty continued. "Democratic as all hell. Everybody in favor of me, just don't say nothing. All opposed, step up here one at a time with your knives out."

Marty waited in silence for about ten seconds. The Barons were put down. They weren't about to give him any opposition.

He said finally, "I guess the vote is unanimous, ain't it? That's nice. Suppose two of you guys dispose of the former president, and two more of you clean up the mess. Then I want to find out what the picture is in this town, before we try for a rumble with—what in the hell's the name of that other hick gang?"

"The Dragons," someone offered.

"Oh, yeah. The Dragons."

They hopped to it when Marty gave the word. He could see they were scared absolutely spitless of him. Maybe they thought they were real tough—and maybe they *were* real tough, as Jenkinsville kids went. But they were just bush leaguers when it came down to the final tally. Maybe this outfit had done a little bopping in its day, but Marty was willing to bet high that none of them had ever seen a man get cut up the way he had cut up the late Charley Beck.

They worked fast to clean up. One of them went out into the street and drove an old jalopy into the lot. It was a battered '38 Chevrolet that was owned jointly by a couple of the Barons. There was a plaid robe in the trunk, and they wrapped the late Charley Beck in the robe and dumped him in the back of the car.

"Where you figuring on taking the meat to get rid of it?" Marty asked.

One of the Barons said, "We're gonna weight it down and dump it in the river downstream, just below town. It'll be fish meat by tonight."

Marty chuckled harshly. "You know, the way you guys talk, you'd think there was a knifing in this town every day."

"We've put a couple of guys into the river already, Marty. We ain't as chickie-chicken as you think we are."

Marty smiled approvingly. This bunch had promise, he had to admit. They hadn't been brought up in a place like New York, where all the softness you had was burned out of you by the time you were six. But they had guts, all the same, in their smalltown way. Maybe he could shape this bunch up into something. It all depended on how tough that other gang, the Dragons, was. You needed tough opposition if you wanted to make things a little exciting.

The car, with Beck's body aboard, drove away. Marty knelt to examine the place on the ground where the bloodstains had been. The Barons had done a good job of covering up. You couldn't tell, now, that any blood had been spilled on the ground. Even the flies, attracted immediately when Beck fell, were circling in confused spirals now, wondering what had happened to all that nice, red, drinkable blood.

Marty looked around. "You guys have a clubhouse?"

"Sure, Marty."

"From here, how far?"

"We can walk it."

"Let's go over then. I want to see what sort of shack you've got."

They left the parking lot and headed for the clubhouse. And shack it turned out to be, in the strict sense of the word.

In New York, the clubhouse of the Shining Barons had been a basement apartment in a decaying tenement. For $30 a month they got four rooms, and the landlord didn't give a damn what went on in those rooms at any hour of the day or night.

But the Jenkinsville Barons' clubhouse was literally an old shack, two stories, with a crumbling, unpainted exterior. It was on the edge of town, overlooking the muddy river, about a mile upstream from where Charley Beck's body was being dumped.

Marty stood at the entrance, looking in. He could see four or five more Barons lounging around inside sipping beer, and a couple of other girls. He heard some muttering from inside as the news was spread about the gang's change in leadership, and one voice drifted back to him plain as day, saying, "Geez, no! You really mean he cooled Charley?"

Marty walked inside, grinning. He felt seven feet tall. He felt like Alexander the Great and Napoleon and Julius Caesar all rolled into one. He said, "Yeah. I cooled Charley. I'm in charge here, now."

They were looking at him closely, trying to size him up. He went on, "For the benefit of you others, my name is Marty Capuano, and I'm from New York. I used to be boss of the Shining Barons from the East Side. Now I'm living here, and I had a slight dispute with your man Beck about who ought to be boss here. Beck lost. Now, how about making with the names?"

He met them all, and as each one sang out his name, Marty fixed it in his memory. He had a good memory for certain things, things he thought were useful. Like, historical dates were worthless to him, but the names of living persons were important. If you remembered people's names, you could control them a little. People were always impressed by a guy who remembered names.

There were fifteen Barons altogether—plus the Baron Debs, the girls' auxiliary. The ages of the Barons ranged from fifteen to nineteen, just about, and they all looked pretty tough—but they were all scared of Marty, and it showed.

They were all bigger than he was, too, and that made him feel good. To think that fifteen big guys were scared of one little man with a knife. One damned good little man, who knew how to use that knife. Now for a nice, soft, busy, jiggling hunk of action, Marty thought.

He eyed the group of debs, feeling the hot throbbing in his loins that meant he had to have a woman right away. He looked them over. There was that lean one with the yellow knit shirt, the one with the thin face and the stringy red hair and the oversized bust. He'd felt those boobs in the candy store, and he'd liked the feel. She was the one that had been Beck's girl.

She didn't seem to be taking the killing too hard. Her face was serene, and she hadn't been crying or anything like that.

Marty walked over to where she stood, near the window. She was an inch taller than he was, and she was wearing flat shoes.

"You," he said. "You were in the candy store. You used to make it with Charley, huh?"

"Yeah."

Her big round outthrust breasts rose and fell evenly with each breath. They stuck out like basketballs. She wasn't afraid of him.

She didn't look like she was afraid of anything.

"What's your name?"

"Jojo."

Marty looked her over minutely from head to heels. There didn't seem to be much fat on her, except up front. All the softness had collected in her bosom. The sight of those swelling globes stretching the knit fabric made his throat go dry and his breath come a little faster. The palms of his hands itched. This girl was built. Built just the way he liked his women. He wanted to give it to her right now, right here. Push her down, fall on top of her, give her a shove.

The clubhouse was silent. Everybody was listening, but pretending not to notice.

Marty said, "You're in the habit of making it with the head of this outfit, Jojo. Okay. Suppose you stay in the habit."

She met his glance steadily. Her eyes were a clear green. Green eyes, red hair. Nice combination. She said huskily, "I'll stay in the habit, if that's what you want. I'm with you all the way, little man." Marty slapped her hard across the face, giving her the same sort of powerful wrist action he used in slitting open someone's belly with his blade. The force of the blow knocked her backward, into a chair. Her lower lip started to puff out. She didn't get up. Her green eyes were wide with fright and surprise, and she cowered, her hands fluttering before her face nervously in case Marty tried to hit her again.

But Marty didn't hit her. He said thinly. "Get up."

She got up and backed uneasily away from him. "What was that for? Why'd you hit me?"

"I don't like to be called *little man*," he said, loud enough so the message would get across to everybody in the room. "You hear that? You call me Marty or boss or pres, but you don't *ever* call me *little man!*"

"Sure, Marty. I got you."

He looked around. The Barons were watching him, the same nervous way they had watched him cut up Charley Beck.

"That goes for all the rest of you," he snapped. "Sure, I'm short. But I don't let nobody make any smart remarks about that to my face. You make any cracks about my height, and I'll carve my initials on your eyeballs. You all hear me?"

They nodded. They didn't give him any lip. Marty knew he had them hooked.

He smiled, breaking the sudden tension in the room. "Anything to drink around this place? I'm thirsty as all hell."

"We got some beer in the icebox, Marty."

"Okay. Trot it out."

One of the guys brought him a can of beer. It was a brand he had never heard of, some local beer. But it wasn't bad stuff, he decided. He downed half the can in one greedy guzzle before his thirst was slaked.

After thirst, you took care of hunger.

He pointed a finger at Jojo. "Do they have a bed upstairs?"

"Yeah."

"Good. Lemme finish my beer. Then you and me go upstairs and have some fun. The top man's deb has to be plenty good."

"Charley never complained."

"I'm not Charley, babe."

He finished the rest of his beer in three swallows and set the empty can down.

"Come on," he said to Jojo.

She led him up the rickety stairs to the second floor of the shack. He kept his eyes on her round, twitching buttocks. There were several rooms on the second floor. She pushed open one door.

"This is the president's room," she said. "It belongs to you now."

Marty nodded. There was a bed, of sorts—an old second-hand bed with no linen on it. The mattress was stained and worn. Some weapons were hanging on the wall, a baseball bat and a few tire chains and things like that. There was nothing else in the room.

There was a hook-and-eye kind of lock on the door, and he slipped the hook into the eye and jiggled it to make sure it wouldn't come loose. He didn't like to be disturbed while he was making out.

Jojo sat down on the bed, fully dressed. Her lip was puffing up where he had hit her. Her face was completely expressionless, showing neither anticipation nor revulsion. It was the face of a girl who had been won as a prize in war. She was about to go to bed with the conqueror, not because she wanted to, but because she had to.

Marty looked at her. "The way you look, you'd think I was gonna torture you."

"What am I supposed to do? Light firecrackers or something?"

"You ought to look a little more cheerful. It isn't every girl who gets the chance to climb into the sack with Marty Capuano." He grinned. "That sounds pretty swellheaded, don't it?"

She didn't answer.

"Go on," he said. "I won't hit you anymore. It's swellheaded to blow my own horn, ain't it? But you just wait. You'll see I ain't just making noise. I'm good. That's a fact, not just my opinion. You wait and see."

Her expression did not change. Marty shrugged. There were other ways to win her over besides talking to her.

"Take your shirt off, Jojo," he ordered brusquely.

Her hands went to her waist, tugged the shirt out from beneath the wide belt encircling her hips. She slipped it off over her head, then dropped it carelessly on the floor next to the bed. She was wearing a white, satiny bra that seemed about to burst under the outward pressure exerted by her breasts.

"Now the bra," Marty commanded.

She reached around back to undo the hooks. The fabric fell away, and her breasts—as if relieved at being confined no longer—tumbled forward excitingly. Marty caught his breath sharply. Her breasts were huge, size forty at least, but there was nothing unsightly about them. Firm chest muscles supporting them, keeping them from drooping. They rose proudly upward and outward, expanding with each breath she took—big, pale white globes streaked delicately with blue veins. Her nipples stood up like tiny turrets on the full hemispheres.

"You like?" Jojo asked.

"I like just fine. *Molto bene!*"

"I've got the biggest pair in the Baron Debs," she said proudly.

"Let's see the rest," Marty told her.

Jojo stood up, unbuckled her belt and unbuttoned her corduroy hip-huggers—they were men's-styled—unzipped the fly down the front, and pushed them down to her ankles. She slipped off her sandals, then rolled filmy blue panties down over her hips, and kicked them off along with the wide wale cords.

She had a peculiar body, Marty thought. It was as if those enormous boobs belonged to somebody else, and had somehow been grafted on. The rest of her was very thin. Her belly was flat, her hips were narrow and boyish, her buttocks lean and muscular. She had the agile, coltish look of a twelve-year-old—with the huge, eye-opening breasts of a showgirl.

40-21-33, Marty thought. One hell of a weird figure. But nice. Plenty nice.

He unbuttoned his shirt, wriggled out of it, dropped it on the floor, followed it a moment later with his shoes, pants and underclothes. Jojo was looking at the exposure of his maleness in a frankly appraising way. She hadn't seen many guys built like he was, Marty knew. He smiled, seeing the way her eyes brightened at the sight of his lean, hard body. Maybe he was short in stature, but he had other advantages. He had size where it really counted. Muscles ripped over every inch of his skin. He walked toward her, knowing he had made a big impression. Ol' blubbery Charley had never looked so good, he knew.

"Come here," Marty said, lying down on the mattress and pulling her down next to him. His hands cupped her mountainous breasts, and he found they were so big that his hands could not fully contain them. Their bodies pressed tight. She was warm, eager.

Marty didn't waste any time with preliminaries, the first round. It had been too long since he'd last had a woman—and the sight of the snowy mounds of her breasts and the reddish triangle at the base of her belly, and the feel of her soft flesh against his, inflamed him beyond control. Tightening against her, he pushed at her thighs and took her quickly. He heard her faint moan of mixed pleasure and pain as he lunged forward and drove himself deep.

It was all over in an instant. Marty lay still, heart pounding in gradual declaration as the tension ebbed away after the electrifying jolts of his climax. The tension of moving, of traveling, of meeting that girl Jill at the bus stop, of the death duel in the parking lot—all the strain of those things ebbed out of him in one long, gasping moment of relief, leaving him limp and relaxed.

"I needed that in a hurry," he murmured. "I was all strung up, you know? But the next one's gonna be all for you."

A few moments passed. He caressed her thighs, her buttocks, her belly. He felt his virility returning, the way it always did in a couple of minutes after the first round. One act of lust never put him out of commission for long. He turned to take Jojo again, his lips grazing her big, red, lust-stiffened nipples. He moved to her then, and their bodies began to grind rhythmically once again.

This time Marty went slowly, and gave Jojo a chance to perform. She knew what to do with her body, all right. Their passion gradually rose higher and higher, until her writhing body beneath him was slick and glossy with sweat, and from her drawn-back lips came little sighs of pleasure, then more tempestuous moans.

Suddenly she cried, "Now, Marty! Right now!"

He slammed his throbbing, rigid body hard against her, and their bodies clamped tight, her heels digging into his legs and his hands on her buttocks. The squeaking of the bedsprings formed an accompaniment to their ecstasy; and then, once again, it was all over and they were lying quiet, drained and exhausted and satisfied.

Marty rose from the bed.

Jojo lay there, sweaty, her limbs still sprawling. "How about some more?" she murmured.

"Some other time," he said. "We got plenty of days ahead of us for making it."

She smiled, her arms hugging her breasts in pleasure, her eyes closed. "You're the most, Marty! Like I mean, man, the *most!*"

"I bet old Charley Beck never loved you up that way."

"Nobody else was ever that good for me before, Marty. You're really the most."

Marty smiled. He felt good now. Things were working out okay. He dressed quickly, sensing a warm glow all around him. Jojo started getting dressed too. Sated as he was, he was still capable of feeling a twinge of desire as he watched her bend over to capture the jutting spheres of her breasts in the bra, and he almost decided to drag her down onto the bed for a third round. But twice was enough for now. He was hungry, anyway, and it was time to start heading for home. It had been a busy afternoon—a kill, a lay, everything.

The clubhouse was nearly empty when he went downstairs. A few couples still huddled in the corners of the room, necking, but most of the Barons had already checked out for their evening meal.

"You leaving, Marty?" asked one of the Barons, the thin fellow. His name was Nick Lorrey, Marty recalled.

"Yeah," Marty said. "I'm checkin' out for a while."

"Comin' back tonight?"

"Anything on? What happens around here in the evenings?"

"Not much, tonight. We got some beer, and we figured on a little party." Lorrey leered knowingly. "But you had your party already, huh? You and Jojo."

"I'm always ready for more," Marty said. "Maybe I will come back tonight. Maybe not. Just remember who's running this outfit now, whether I'm here or not."

"Sure, Marty. You're the boss. We ain't ever gonna forget that," Lorrey said flatteringly. "Not after the way you cooled ol' Charley this afternoon."

"You stick with me," Marty said. "We're all going places. We'll turn this town upside-down before we get through. We'll have the real kicks, like I mean, *real*."

He walked outside. It was six o'clock, and the sun was starting to drop out of sight behind the river. The clouds in the sky were sunset colors, purples and golds and pinks. Everything was peaceful and quiet as the evening calm settled over the town. The mill seemed abandoned and quiet—there was no night shift—and the traffic wasn't heavy enough to be making much noise.

In New York at this time of day, Marty thought, it's like a madhouse. Rush hour, with people running all over the place, and cars tooting and beeping, and noise and odors everywhere.

But this wasn't New York. This wasn't a bit like New York.

He made his way up the hill from the river to the bus stop, and a few minutes later one of the blue and red buses came along. It was the same one he'd been on before, now heading back on the outbound leg of his route.

Marty gave him some change, and managed to smile in return for the cheery "Hello, there," that the driver gave him. He took a seat near the middle exit door.

Being aboard the bus reminded him of the girl he had met earlier in the day, when he was on his way downtown.

Jill Webster, that was her name. The girl with the choir-girl face and the chorus-girl knockers.

Even though he had satisfied himself with Jojo, Marty suddenly felt a desire for the other girl so intense that it knotted up his stomach. He longed to strip her naked, lay bare her white flesh, and slake his throbbing lust for her.

Jojo was okay in the sack, more than okay, she was tremendous. And she could be had for the asking. That was good, in a way, but in another way it was no good. Jill was a challenge. Most likely she was pure, a virgin, even though she had a boyfriend. It would be a real accomplishment to make her. It wasn't any accomplishment to make Jojo; she'd probably lost her cherry when those watermelons on her chest were the size of green plums.

Marty needed a big project to keep from getting bored, and he made up his mind that Jill Webster would be his first big project. She was no doubt disgusted by him, he thought—disgusted because he was short and tough, and spoke with a Brooklynese accent, and had an Italian name. Well, he'd show her. He gave himself a short deadline for scoring with her. And if he didn't have any luck talking her into it nicely, there were other ways it could be done. Like having a bunch of the Barons grab her on a dark night and bring her to the clubhouse, where they gag her and spread-eagle her on the bed.

They had done that plenty of times in the Shining Barons. The debs didn't mind. They liked to see the holier-than-thou girls getting raped. So the Shining Barons would go out and comb the turf, searching for pure-looking girls or women.

Sitting back in the bus, Marty smiled at some of the memories.

There was the time they had waited outside a bank, after hours, and had grabbed one of the female tellers. She was a young woman in her middle twenties, with a homely face but built like a brick outhouse, and her hips and buttocks gave promise of sensuality going to waste.

"We'll put a flag over her face and do it for Old Glory," Marty suggested.

So they waited; and, moving like parts of a well-designed machine, they grabbed her and gagged her and carried her off, blindfolded, before she knew what was happening. In the clubhouse they had taken the gag off, and she had whimpered, "Please ... I'm a virgin ... don't touch me ..."

"How old are you, sister?"

"Twenty-seven."

"Twenty-seven, and you're still a virgin? We'll be doing you a big favor, then."

Then they had stripped off her clothes, revealing the lush feminine body that had been hidden beneath the shapeless outer garments. It was a sad trick that fate had played, sticking such a body with such a face. Her face was ugly as all sin—with pasty, unhealthy-looking skin, crooked teeth, sunken eyes, and dark hairs on her chin and upper lip. But below the neck she was a knockout, ripe and breasty and curvaceous.

As boss of the Shining Barons, Marty had been the first to have her. He soon found she had been telling the truth about being a virgin. Marty sprawled out on her and spread her legs and put himself against her and pushed, and she cried out in pain. When he lunged more forcefully, her scream almost deafened him. But before Marty was through with her, she was whimpering in pleasure; and when he rose from her trembling, naked body half an hour later, she tried to drag him back on her again. Each of the guys had taken a turn with her, and some of them had taken two turns, and by the time they were through balling her she was so sex-happy she didn't know which way was up. They gave her a drink and horsed around with her, pinching her boobs and patting her fanny. Finally they helped her get dressed, and she kind of staggered out of the clubhouse with starry eyes and a rosy glow.

The Shining Barons went wild with laughter. "We did that broad a helluva favor," Marty whooped. "What the devil was she saving herself for? A little bed fun was just what she needed."

And he was right. The next night they hung around the bank just to see what would happen, whether she would have a police guard or not. But she came out alone, and stood in front of the bank for a long time, looking around in all directions as if waiting for the gang to come grab her again.

That had been a real gas, Marty thought, chuckling over the memory of it. The expression on her face was almost pathetic with disappointment when she realized that the Shining Barons weren't coming to rape her again. It had been the first real thrill in her whole dull life, and she wanted more. But they weren't about to give her more, so finally she got on a bus and went home, back to her lonely bed.

Marty heard a few weeks later from one of the male tellers at the bank that she had suddenly become hot as a pistol. She had gone out on a date with one of the other male tellers, who had tried unsuccessfully in the past to seduce her a couple of times, and this time she practically raped him the minute they were alone. Then she went on to romp with several more tellers, too. She turned into a regular nympho. It was quite a personality switch. You could never tell what a little raping would do to an old maid, could you?

Maybe a little raping would be necessary for Jill Webster, too. Marty would have preferred to have her come around willingly, of course, but he figured it might be worth a few kicks to have to force her.

He was still thinking along those lines when the bus pulled up at the street corner nearest his new home. The Capuano house was in the center of a side street lined by nearly identical two-story wooden houses. Marty walked along the block until he reached it.

He knew which one it was even without looking for the address, because of the odors of Italian cooking emanating from it. Two to one it was lasagna, he thought. Ma loved to cook lasagna.

He pushed open the front door without bothering to knock, walked into the spacious living room, and from there into the kitchen. It looked like Ma and Frankie had done a pretty good job of fixing the place up.

They were all sitting at the kitchen table, Ma and Pa and Frankie, and they looked like they'd been waiting for him.

"There he is, Ma," Frankie said bitterly. "The king has finally deigned to return. Now we can eat, at last."

"You know you ought to get home by suppertime, Marty," his mother said.

Her voice was quiet, and there wasn't much anger in it; she had learned a long time ago that it was just a waste of energy to get angry with Marty. He would just stand there, listening to her shout and rant; then he would shrug his shoulders, and everything she had just said to him would roll off him like water off a duck's back. Then he'd go on about his business, as if she'd said nothing at all.

Marty took a seat at the table next to Frankie, and looked at his father. Angelo Capuano was a short, thickset man, rapidly losing what was left of his once-bushy thatch of dark hair. He was a bit taller than Marty, but not much. Right now the old man wasn't saying anything. He just sat there staring at his plate, looking tired, like a man who had little strength left at all.

Ma dished out the meal, carving thick chunks of lasagna out of the big Pyrex casserole dish she cooked it in. They all pitched in hungrily for their first family meal in Jenkinsville.

Marty ate greedily, without talking to anyone. He had used up a lot of energy today, and he had to replenish it with food. He burned energy fast.

Halfway through the meal, Ma looked up at him as if for the first time, and gave a little gasp of fright.

"Marty … your neck … you're bleeding!"

Marty quirked his lips. He had forgotten all about the wound he had received in the fight with Beck. He kicked himself mentally for not having fixed it up, knowing that Ma would certainly make a fuss over it.

"It's just a scratch," he said.

"It's a deep cut," she insisted. "Let me bandage it!"

"After supper, Ma. It'll keep till then. It don't bother me none."

His kid brother swiveled around to face him. Frankie didn't smile. "You musta had a close one today, huh, killer?"

"Shut up, you fink."

His father spoke, in his quiet, washed-out voice. "Have you been fighting again, Marty? Tell me … were you in a knife fight?"

Marty shrugged uncomfortably. He didn't like to lie to his father. He said, "Yeah, sort of. It was nothing, serious."

Nothing more serious than killing a man, he thought. Just icing off ol' Charley Beck.

"I told you not to fight no more, Marty," father said wearily. "We left New York and came out here so you wouldn't fight—so you could live right, like a human being, not like a jungle animal. And already the first day, you're in a fight. You didn't even wait one single day. It's gonna be just like it was in New York, with the fights and the stinking gangs. The very first day …"

He didn't go on. He couldn't. He just looked wearily down at his plate. Angelo was getting to be an old man fast, these days. He hardly ever seemed happy about anything, Marty thought. He felt sorry for his father.

The discussion ended. Nobody pushed Marty for details of the fight.

After dinner he let his mother wash the cut and bandage it. It wasn't too deep, as even she could see, and it had already started to form a scab.

When she was through, she sighed and said, "I wish you'd find some way of staying out of trouble, Marty. Trouble seems to hang around you like flies in a meat market."

Marty said nothing.

She went on, "A boy your age, finished with high school. You ought to get yourself a job. You can't just go on loafing around all the time, sponging off your papa and mama. How long you think that can go on, huh? You think we gonna work our fingers to the bone to feed you the rest of your life, Marty?"

"Jobs ain't always so easy to get, Ma. Employers don't like to give jobs to eighteen-year-old kids. They give the work to the older guys, married guys with families of their own, or single guys who've finished their military service."

"But you haven't even tried, here."

"It'll be the same old story."

"All right," she persisted. "Maybe you can't find work. You can join the Army, then. You gotta go sooner or later. Get it over with now, and you'll be twenty, twenty-one when you get out. Ready to settle down, have a family, get a decent job."

Marty listened to it all, and said, "Yeah, Ma," when she was finished. But it all went in one ear and right out tire other. Marty Capuano wasn't going to volunteer for any military service. And he didn't need a job, either. He could take care of himself okay. If he had to, he could support himself with his blade.

He felt warm and satisfied inside. One day in this no-place town, and he was boss of the Barons! He had notched a kill and he had a woman!

There was still Jill Webster to think about, but he wasn't going to sweat it. Hell, he thought, what more can you expect out of one single lousy day?

CHAPTER FOUR

Later on that evening, Frankie and Ma and Pa started to get back to the job of unpacking and setting up the house. There were still drapes to hang, closets to dust, and all that jazz. Marty decided to clear out before they started needling him to do some work.

He thought of going down to the Barons' clubhouse again, but changed his mind. No point fooling around down there for the rest of the evening whet he had something better to do.

There was no telephone in the house, yet—they wouldn't be putting one in until the middle of the week, probably—so Marty strolled up the street to a malt shop across the way from the bus stop. This place wasn't much like the candy store near the depot. It was cleaner and newer; and a different breed of kids hung out in it— the high school kids the good kids who liked to come in for Cokes and a buzz at the jukebox.

They all turned to look at Marty as he walked in. He knew what they were thinking. They were thinking that he was short and skinny and hard-looking, and they didn't know what such a ratty type was doing in their nice clean malt shop.

Marty didn't give a damn. He asked the counterman, "Where's the phone?"

"In the back," the guy told him.

There was a booth back there, and a stack of phone books, one for each neighboring town in the county. Marty picked up the Jenkinsville directory.

He had to laugh. It was as thin as a magazine. It wasn't even as heavy as the Staten Island phone book, let alone any of the really big New York directories.

He opened it to the "W" listings and started looking for the Websters. There were eleven of them. Pursing his lips, Marty checked the address. Five of them, he already knew, were on the far side of town. And Jill lived somewhere near here.

That left six numbers. What the hell, he thought. At worst it would cost him sixty cents. But then he'd know Jill's phone number and address.

He picked out one of the numbers. Webster, David, 711 Springvale Rd. 532-9234. After dropping a dime into the slot, Marty dialed and waited for three rings, and then a woman's voice said, "Hello?"

"Hello," Marty said, trying hard to keep the New York toughness out of his voice. "I'd like to talk to Jill."

"Jill? Oh, you've got the wrong number. Jill is my husband's niece. Her father is Lawrence Webster, on Stonybrook Terrrace."

"I see. Sorry to have bothered you, ma'am."

"Quite all right."

He hung up and checked the phone book again. Yes, there it was— Webster, Lawrence, 107 Stonybrook Terrace. 532-8761.

Marty dropped another dime in. And waited. And another female voice answered.

"Hello?"

This one sounded young. "Jill?" Marty risked. "No, this is Evelyn. Who's calling please?"

"I'm a friend of Jill's. I'd like to talk to her."

"Any friend of Jill's must be a friend of mine What did you say your name is?"

"I'm new in town," Marty replied. "I met Jill this afternoon, and I … uh … wanted to ask something. My name is Marty Capuano."

"Capuano?" she repeated skeptically. "All right. Hold on a moment, and I'll see if Jill's here."

"Thanks."

There was a pause of perhaps half a minute. Marty was sure he heard voices, muffled by a hand being placed over the receiver. Then another girl's voice said, "Hello?"

Marty said, "Jill? Look, I'm sorry if I'm disturbing you. I'm the fellow you met at the bus stop this afternoon."

"Oh, yes. I remember." Her voice suddenly sounded icy. "Why did you call?"

"I was just wondering … you see, I'm so new in town, and being all alone and everything … sort of wanted to know if I could make a date you. Like, maybe, if you were free tonight…."

"I think I told you this afternoon that I already have a date for tonight," she said primly.

"Well, I thought maybe you were just saying that to discourage me."

"As a matter of fact, I happen to have a habit of telling the truth, and I was in the process of getting dressed for that date when you called. Now, before you start asking me for other nights, I might as well tell you that I'm just about going steady."

"With the basketball player?"

"Yes. So you're wasting your time trying to make a date with me."

"You mean there isn't even an outside chance, huh?"

"I'm afraid not."

Sweating profusely now, Marty clenched his free fist until his nails bit deep into his palm. He wanted her so much he could taste it.

Jill went on, "And now, if you'll excuse me, I'd like to finish getting ready to go out. Jim is due to pick me up in a few minutes, and I'm going to be late as it is. Please don't bother to call again, as I'll have to tell my sister to hang up on you."

"But …"

Click!

Marty scowled at the dead phone after she had hung up. He had a sudden picture of her at the other end of the line—half-dressed, wearing only panties and garter belt and stockings, ripe breasts bare and creamy and red-nippled and swaying, buttocks and hips and golden triangle only half-hidden under the gauzy material of her panties. A bright lance of lust went through him. So she'd had the nerve to hang up on him! Marty didn't like girls to be rude to him. He didn't like to get turned down cold, either.

He smiled mirthlessly as he left the phone booth. This Jill wanted to play hard to get? Okay. He had other ways he could get to her. They weren't pretty ways, but they were effective. She'd regret what she'd said. In his mind's eye he saw her naked, terrified, legs spread wide, begging for mercy.

He walked out of the store, ignoring the curious stares of the regulars. Jill had a sister too, he recalled. Evelyn. Most likely an older sister, from the way she sounded on the phone. That might prove interesting, too. First give Jill the business, then investigate the older one.

He still didn't feel like going down to the clubhouse, but it was too early yet to go home. He decided he wanted a drink. He looked around for a bar.

There were none in the immediate neighborhood. It was primarily a residential district, and evidently the zoning laws prohibited bars in this section. Se Marty started to walk, heading in the direction of the railroad depot, and after he had gone eleven or twelve blocks he caught sight of a swinging neon sign announcing: BEER.

He entered the barroom. The place was full of old slobs, weather-beaten mill hands in their fifties and sixties, watching television. Marty walked up to the bar. The barkeep, fat and bald, looked down at him in surprise.

"Let's have a beer," Marty said.

"First you better show me your ID card, sonny."

Marty's lips thinned. He hated being called "sonny," and he hated being challenged on his age.

"I'm old enough," he said.

"You'll have to prove that, or else you'll have to go somewhere else for your beer."

Fuming, Marty pulled out his wallet and fumbled for his draft card. Up till the time he'd turned eighteen, he'd carried a phony card that a buddy had given him, but now he had his own. He produced it triumphantly.

"There you go, buster."

The bartender picked it up and squinted near-sightedly at it. Then he shook his head and handed it back.

"This don't get you any drinks in here, son. Who'd you think you were kidding?"

"What the hell do you mean?" Marty demanded hotly. "There's nothing wrong with that card!"

"I didn't say there was. But according to this you're only a little past eighteen."

"So?"

"Don't you know, son? You've got to be twenty-one to drink in this state."

Marty felt about two inches high. He was aware that all of the older men in the bar were looking at him in amusement.

Sure, the draft card was good in any bar in the state of New York. But New York was more liberal in its liquor laws than most other states. Marty had clean forgotten that. The card was no good here.

"You can't even sell me a beer?"

"Not for a couple more years, kid. Now, why don't you go find some place to buy a nice, cold root beer?"

Cheeks burning, Marty made his way out of the bar. He heard the old farts guffawing behind him. They thought it was a good joke to see a wise-mouthed kid get tripped up that way.

"Keep laughing, you bastards," Marty muttered under his breath, as he looked back from outside. "Just keep on laughing. But someday I'll make you laugh out of the other side of your heads."

He checked the bar's name. THOMPSON'S, the sign said—on Hillside Drive, near Flagler Street. He made a careful note of that.

Nobody was going to make a monkey out of him without paying for it. That was another project for him, now. Come by here late some night with the other Barons, and smash the place up. He shook his fist at the bartender through the dirty glass window and walked away, muttering curses. He wanted a drink more than ever, now.

It was still early—quarter to nine or so.

Disgusted, he got on a bus and rode down to the clubhouse. Five or six couples were in the place when Marty walked in. They were necking, but they snapped to attention as soon as they saw him. Rock-out music was playing on the cheap phonograph.

"Jojo here?" he asked.

"She was," a boy named Stan told him. "But you weren't around, so she left."

"She coming back?"

"Maybe. She don't live far away. Just up the hill a bit."

"Go get her," Marty said. "Tell her I'm here and I want her."

Stan glanced at his girl. She had her blouse unbuttoned and her bra unhooked. The rosy tip of one full white breast peeped out. It was obvious that she didn't want him running any errands for Marty just now. But the memory of what had happened to Charley Beck that afternoon was still horribly clear in everyone's mind. Stan got up and ambled toward the door.

"Make it fast," Marty called after him. "I ain't got all night."

He wandered on into the kitchen. There was an old, dilapidated icebox in there. Marty opened it up and saw a dozen cans of beer. He took one out, popped the top, and started to guzzle.

He was on his second can of beer when Stan returned, Jojo with him. She was wearing skin-tight capri pants and a sweater that exhibited her boobs delightfully, Marty thought.

"So you showed up after all," she said.

"You see me standing here, don't you?"

"I waited around for a while, earlier, but you didn't show so I figured you'd had enough this afternoon. My old man is always yelling for me to spend an evening at home, anyway. So tonight I almost did."

"I never get enough," Marty said. "I was busy at home, that's all. From now on I'll be here every night."

"Well, so will I," said Jojo.

Marty finished his beer and put it down on top of the icebox. "Come on," he said. "Let's go upstairs for a little session, huh?"

"Suits me just fine, Marty." She winked. "You're the most, man. Really the most."

They went upstairs, into the room that was reserved for the president of the Barons. Within a couple of seconds, Jojo was out of the stretch capris. The sweater followed in an instant, then her bra and panties. And then she was naked, with her large, hard-tipped breasts bobbing like grapefruits.

Marty advanced toward her, slipping out of his clothes on the way, and they tumbled down onto the mattress together. Her body was warm and alive, responsive to his touch. He caressed her, and found her hot and moist and ready. She opened for him. He took her, swiftly and deeply.

They moved in silence, breaking the stillness only with occasional gasps or grunts of excitement. Their feverish fervor rose to a dizzy pitch; then her hands tightened convulsively on his shoulders, her hips thrashed wildly, and she cried out, "This is it, man! This is the real thing!"

When it was over, she looked up at him, smiling the kittenish smile of the truly satisfied woman.

"You're a wonder, Marty. You're real dynamite."

"I'm better than Charley Beck, huh?"

"He wasn't even in your league."

Marty slipped his hand under her breasts. They were heavy, warm, throbbing with life.

"How old are you, Jojo?"

"Me? I just turned eighteen."

"How long you been a Baron Deb?"

"Going on four years."

"You started young, huh?" Marty said. "Were you Charley Beck's girl right from the start?"

"Uh-uh. Beck was making time with an old bag named Nancy, back then. And I was going with a fellow name of Jack Reinhart."

"What happened to them?"

Jojo shrugged. "Nancy got knocked up. Last I heard, she married some fink and moved to Cleveland. The fink thinks the kid's his own."

"And Reinhart?"

"He got cooled off two years ago. Ambushed by the Dragons. That's when Marty took me over as his steady deb."

"You were a little past fourteen when you first became a deb, right? Were you built like you are now?"

She nodded. "Just about. I developed early. Started sprouting knockers when I was ten and a half. They were bigger than most grown women's by the time I was thirteen, and they been this size since I was fifteen. The doctor said it was something glandular—said it like it was no good."

"It's plenty good," Marty murmured, holding her big warm breasts. They filled his hands and overflowed.

"It always was strange, though. I mean, a skinny girl like me with a pair this big."

"I don't mind. That's the way I like 'em. I like a girl with big boobs, but I hate a fat pig with flab all over. And most of the time you don't get one without the other."

"You musta had lots of girls, huh, Marty?"

"My share," he said. He pillowed his head down against the swelling bulk of her breasts. "How old were you when you first made it with a guy?" he asked.

"I'll never tell. But I will say this: I was pretty damn young. You ain't heard the worst, either," she said. "The guy was my own uncle."

Marty sat up and stared at her. "You're kidding! Your uncle?"

"Wish I was kidding. He was my mother's brother."

"What kinda crazy uncle would boff his sister's kid? Did he rape you?"

"Well, not exactly. I mean, he didn't have to use force, 'cause I was too ignorant then to know what he wanted, and I didn't try to stop him. He was only nineteen, twenty. He was out of work, and came to live with us. There was this hot night in the middle of the summer … my folks were out visiting friends. I took a shower and came out of the john with nothing on. I didn't figure anyone was home, see, and anyway, I never was very prudish about covering up my body in my own house—at least, not until after that night."

"Yeah? Go on."

"So I was walking to my room in my birthday suit, and along comes this crazy uncle. Seems he'd been out on a date and tried to make the girl and got put down, and he'd come home all hot. I saw him looking at me real funny-like; his eyes about popped out when he discovered how big my boobs actually were, because I never wore tight sweaters or anything to show 'em off at that age.

"And he says, 'C'mere,' and I start to blush because I'm naked. So he grabs me and takes my knobs in his hands, and says he's gonna show me a nice new trick, lots of fun. He drags me into his room and pushes me down on the bed; and then he takes his pants off, and now it's my turn to do the bulgy-eyed bit! Well, the next thing

I know he's on top of me, and we're making it. It hurt like hell, and I started crying. And when he finished, he started crying too, and told me he was sorry he'd hurt me but he just couldn't stop himself, he needed me so bad. He begged me not to tell my folks."

"And did you?"

"Nah. I felt sorta sorry for him. Anyway, we were scared my old man would have shot him and me both if he'd ever found out, so I had to keep quiet. After that he was real nice to me, and he petted and kissed me a lot when we were alone in the house. Finally I got so hot one time that I asked him to bang me again, and that time I liked it."

"Where is he now?"

"Got killed crossing a street when he was drunk," she said. "My mother cried her eyes out at the funeral, and so did I, but for a different reason. After all, he was my first lover, my only one so far, and we'd been making it pretty often. I was pretty shook up over losing him. I didn't want another guy for a long time after that, not till long after I started hanging around with the Barons." She coughed. "I been doing a lot of talking. Let's go down and get some beer."

"Later," Marty said, and pulled her toward him. His lust had been aroused by her story, and she soon became eager to satisfy him.

During the next couple days, Marty spent most of his time at the Baron's clubhouse—getting to know the gang members better, finding out things about the town and about the rival gang, and eyeing the other debs. Far the time being, Jojo was all he needed to satisfy his lusts, but Marty got tired of a girl fast, no matter how hot she was. Two or three months, and he discarded any woman. Jojo didn't know that. But she'd find out. Marty had never kept a steady deb for longer than ten or twelve weeks.

He was itching to try his luck with a couple of other Baron Debs. Right now they were both going steady with other members of the gang, but that didn't worry Marty any. He was boss in this outfit, and they all knew it. Any guy who said otherwise was a candidate for cooling. But Marty didn't plan to switch chicks for a while. He didn't want to give up Jojo until he was completely bored with her, and he knew it was more important right at the start of his leadership of the Barons to cement their loyalty through friendship, not through fear alone, so he kept his distance from their girls.

As he got to know the Barons better, during the first week, he saw that they weren't bad as fighters, but most of them didn't have the natural killer instinct. Maybe it was the small-town atmosphere, or something, that did it. Anyway, they didn't seethe with kill-lust the way New York gang kids did. They didn't have the boiling drive to go out and stomp and smash and hurt. These guys just wanted to cut up a little, that's all. They didn't have the fighting spirit, and that was why they rolled over and played dead whenever a real tough man like Marty Capuano told them to.

But a couple Barons had real potential. After a few days of close watching, Marty was able to sort the naturally tough ones out from the phonies. He paid close attention to these two.

One was called Jolly Roger, and the other was known as Big Henry.

Jolly Roger was tall and spindly, maybe six-feet-three, with the longest arms Marty had ever seen, and great big hands the size of dinner plates. He was almost addicted to playing basketball. There was a basket rigged up out back of the Barons' clubhouse, and it was safe to figure that most of the time Jolly Roger would be out there pumping one-handers through the rusty hoop, scrambling to retrieve the ball, and shooting it through again.

Big Henry wasn't big in height—just in circumference. He was a barrel of a guy, no more than five-feet-six, but weighing close to three hundred pounds. It was all muscle, too. He was built like a little round boulder. And he could pick up a table by one leg and hold it in the air as long as he wanted to.

Marty picked Jolly Roger and Big Henry as his lieutenants. He had three big projects in mind for this summer. He wanted to get hold of Jill Webster, he wanted to smash up Thompson's Bar on Hillside Drive, and he wanted to stage a big rumble with the Dragons. Three projects. Three demonstrations of Marty Capuano's power in Jenkinsville.

He told them about the rumble, first. He called them aside on the third day, when the death of Charley Beck was beginning to be forgotten, and Marty was starting to be accepted not only out of fear of his knife, but also in recognition of his talents as a leader.

He said to Jolly Roger and Big Henry, "Listen, I've been lookin' this bunch over, and I figure you two are the best men in it. I've got plans for you. Big plans."

"Such as?"

Marty said, "I want to have a rumble with the Dragons. I want to show them that they're the Number Two outfit in this town."

Jolly Roger looked down at Marty. Quite a ways down. The top of his head was about a foot closer to the stratosphere than Marty's. "A rumble, huh?"

"You bet. How long has it been since you had a real rumble with the Dragons?"

"A long time," Big Henry said. "A year, maybe. We been keeping things pretty peaceful."

"Well, enough of this peace jazz. We'll grab a couple blocks of their turf and dare 'em to push us off."

Jolly Roger looked doubtful. "They're a pretty tough bunch, Marty."

"So are we. We're tougher. And before I get through training you guys, we're going to be *ten times* tougher. You with me?"

"We're with you," Big Henry said.

"Yeah," chimed in Jolly Roger.

Plans for the rumble were circulated to all of the Barons. Nobody objected. There were some sour faces, but if anybody disliked the idea of the rumble they kept their gripes to themselves.

The next day, Marty started in on sharpening the Barons up on knife-play. He concentrated on drilling Jolly Roger and Big Henry. He taught them all he could teach, and that was plenty. They were good blade men to start with, but by the time Marty had given them a few days of instructions, they were exceptional—and lethal. Jolly Roger—with those big; long, snakelike arms of his—could wrap a knife into a guy's back when he thought it was coming in the front way; and Big Henry was so squat and solid that you just couldn't get through his guard for beans, when he was blocking with the blade.

They were both good, damned good. Marty knew he was still better than either of them, because he was the best knifeman there was. But they were both good all the same. There was no taking that away from them.

There was a third member of the Jenkinsville Barons who was pretty good with a blade, too. Marty didn't want to put in any time helping this guy get any better.

His name was Tom Brewster, and he didn't go by any gang nickname. He was a good-looking six-footer who had been in the gang for three years, which made him one of the veteran members. He was nineteen, a little older than Marty. Brewster was a good knifeman; but the only trouble with him, as far as Marty was concerned, was that Marty had his eye on Brewster's girl.

Brewster made it with a chick named Mary Anne—a girl with golden-blonde hair and blue eyes, cute breasts and bedroom thighs, and a look of soft, languorous sexiness about her. Marty was greatly interested in her. From each day to the next he got a little more tired of Jojo, as he began to get used to the way she kissed and the way she groaned in passion and the way she moved her body, and he was thinking of switching over to Mary Anne in a few more weeks. Mary Anne and Brewster were a pretty solid pair right now. There'd be trouble in the works when Marty tried to take her away from him; and someday soon, Marty knew, he was going to have to stand down and fight Brewster. So it made no sense to waste time training him now—there was no use making him any tougher than he already was.

But he'd deal with Brewster later. The rumble was getting organized. It was time for Marty to get moving on another of his projects—the rape of Jill Webster.

CHAPTER FIVE

The weather was getting hot now, real hot, up in the 90s—T-shirt weather, not black-leather-jacket weather. Most of the Barons had part-time summer jobs that left them free to goof around in the afternoons and evenings, and gave them some pocket cash.

Marty didn't need a job, because he still had $500 left from money he had piled up in New York, money he had gotten in muggings and robberies. Nobody in his family knew that he had the money. But at least he never asked his parents for cash, and they were grateful for that. When he used up his hoard, he knew he could always get more the same way.

One night in the middle of his second week in Jenkinsville, Marty decided it was time to get going on the Jill Webster project. He beckoned to his lieutenants, Jolly Roger and Big Henry, and he also added a third Baron, Nick Lorrey. They went upstairs to Marty's private room, and he locked the door.

"What's up?" Big Henry asked. "Real mysterious, huh?"

"Must be about the rumble," Jolly Roger guessed.

"Nah," Marty said, "I got something else in mind. Any of you guys know a girl name of Jill Webster, lives over on Stonybrook Terrace?"

Big Henry shrugged. "Never heard of her."

"Nick? Roger?"

Jenkinsville wasn't the biggest city in the world, but still, in a town of 85,000 people, everybody didn't necessarily know everybody else.

"I think I know her," Nick said. "She's got nice face, darkish blonde hair, fills a sweater real good ..."

"Yeah, that's the one," said Marty.

"She goes to Jenkinsville High. Dates one of the basketball players," Jolly Rogers contributed. "I know the guy, Jim Cartwright. Pretty good man under the basket."

"Okay," Marty said. "So you know her. How would you guys like a roll in the hay with her?"

"*Her?*" Nick asked incredulously. "You got her wrong, Marty. She ain't the kind of girl who puts out. She can't be had."

"Don't you think I know that?" Marty said sharply. "I didn't mean *have* her. I meant *take* her. All four of us."

"What you getting at, Marty?" Big Henry wanted to know.

Marty leaned forward and lowered his voice. "I got the hots for this Webster chick. But I called her up to try to make a date, and she was pretty goddamn snotty to me. She even hung up on me. Get that—she hung up on *me*."

"She's the kind of girl who's saving it for her husband," Jolly Roger said. "Real clean-cut type, you know?"

"Yeah, I know. Well, I plan to change all that. I figure to grab her some night and take her down by the river, where nobody'll bother us."

"You mean, rape her?" Nick asked.

"You catch on fast."

"But—"

"You chicken?" Marty demanded immediately. "I picked you out because I thought you belonged on this job. If you wanta chicken out, just say the word, Torrey."

"No, I'm not gonna turn chicken."

"Okay, then." Marty quickly flicked a glance at each of them, sizing them up, seeing how they stood. They looked uncertain. He said, "It'll be plenty of fun for all of us. The others don't need to know. Or the debs. We grab this pure chick, take her down to the river, work her body. Girls like that are always too stunned to identify their attackers afterward."

"You mean you done this before, Marty?"

He laughed. "Lots of times. Dozens, like. On the East Side, we used to do it for kicks when we had nothing else to do." Briefly, he told them the story of the spinster bank teller who had turned into a passionate whirlwind after the Shining Barons had worked her over, and they all laughed.

"When we gonna do this, Marty?" Jolly Roger asked.

"Next week's the best time. I checked the paper today, and there ain't gonna be no moon next week. A nice dark night is just what we need for this."

Their eyes were bright with anticipation now. Only Nick seemed skeptical. He said, "Don't get me wrong, Marty, I'm with you all the way on this. But you can ruin a girl's whole life this way."

"A little lovin' up never ruined nobody, Nick. It'll probably do her some good."

Lorrey shrugged. "What the hell. At least we get some kicks."

"Did any of you guys ever pull off a rape before?"

"Uh-uh," Big Henry said. "Mugging, yes. But we never forced a girl to put out."

"Well, there's always a first time," Marty said, "And this time is going to be it. I want to show that lousy snot-nosed broad that she can't hang up a phone on Marty Capuano!"

They talked for half an hour more, getting everything set up. Marty figured they had three or four possible nights to do it in. After that, the moon would be too bright to make it safe, and they would have to wait till next month.

The following Monday night, they set out for Stonybrook Terrace to get Jill Webster. As the newspaper had predicted, it was an absolutely moonless night, pitch black. And Jenkinsville didn't have street lamps every couple of dozen yards, the way New York City did. The streets were pretty dark.

Jolly Roger, Big Henry, Nick and Marty told their debs they were going off on an important scouting trip and wouldn't be back till late. Nobody questioned that.

They used the beat-up old car, the '38 Chevy that was owned jointly by Jolly Roger and Nick. Nick drove, with Marty sitting next to him, and Jolly Roger and Big Henry sat in the back. Nick took side streets and back roads, just to avoid any undue attention.

Stonybrook Terrace was only a few blocks from the section where the Capuanos lived, but the houses there were a lot fancier. They weren't wood frame dwellings; they were made of expensive brick or stone. Nick pulled the car up quietly and parked it in the 200 block on Stonybrook Terrace. Jill lived at 107, across the street and half a block down. It was a big house, three stories high, with a flagstone walk and a well-kept garden in front.

It was quarter past eight. Marty hoped they weren't too late.

"Put your masks on," he ordered.

Each of them produced a mask from his pocket. They were grotesque, rubber Halloween masks that Big Henry had quietly borrowed from his kid brother. With the masks on, they looked like four ghouls from some nightmare world.

They waited. Lights were on in the Webster house. Fifteen minutes went by.

"Maybe she's gonna stay home and watch TV tonight," Jolly Roger suggested, his voice made hollow and mysterious by the mask.

Marty shrugged. "We'll wait till ten. If she don't show by then, we'll try again tomorrow night. And we'll keep trying till we get her."

"You must have it in for that broad real hard," Big Henry said.

"I do," Marty muttered. "Real hard."

They waited some more.

"Remember," Marty warned them. "If she comes out with the

boyfriend, you club him, Roger. Big Henry and I will grab the girl. Nick, you stay at the wheel, and keep the motor running. The minute she's inside the car, haul tail. And remember, nobody say anybody's name—not unless you want your last kick to be a few million jolts as a guest of the state. You all clear on that?"

"Sure," they answered.

"Right."

"We're with you."

"And be careful not to let her see the license number of the car, either. Keep her eyes covered a long as you can."

They waited. Now it was almost nine. They started to fidget.

"I guess she's staying home tonight," Big Henry said.

"We'll give her another hour, like I said before."

"Sure, Marty."

They kept on waiting—and finally, around nine-fifteen, the front door of the Webster house opened, and Jill came out.

"She's alone!" Big Henry whispered.

"Looks like she's going to mail a letter!" Nick chimed in.

"Okay," Marty cautioned. "Get ready. She must be coming up to the mailbox on the corner here. That means she has to walk right past the car."

She was coming toward them, on the other side of the street, with a letter in her hand. She was barefoot, wearing plaid shorts and a knit shirt, and was obvious that she had just come out to mail the letter and then planned to go right back into her house.

As she started to cross the street toward their car and the mailbox, Marty whispered harshly, "Now!"

Nick turned the key in the ignition and got the car started. Marty, Big Henry, and Jolly Roger slipped silently out the far side of the car, and crouched down until Jill was only a few feet from them.

The girl did not see them leap out, did not hear them until they were right upon her. Then her eyes went wide at the sight of the three grotesque masked figures that loomed up out of nowhere to surround her.

"What—?"

Jolly Roger snaked one enormous hand over her mouth, silencing her. With his other hand he gripped her wrists.

Big Henry stooped and grabbed her by her ankles. Marty caught her under the arms, his hands locking around her chest. He could feel the fullness of her firm young breasts and the frightened pounding of her heart.

They whisked her into the waiting car.

It all happened in a matter of seconds. One moment the girl had been approaching the mailbox, envelope in hand. The next, she was lying on the floor in the back of the old car, with one handkerchief thrust in her mouth and another knotted behind her head. Big Henry knelt over her, holding tight to her arms and keeping her down out of sight. Marty and Jolly Roger sat above her, ready to lend a hand if she somehow broke loose. In the front seat, Nick drove serenely, never looking back.

They did little talking. The less they spoke, the less chance there was that Jill might recognize somebody's voice. Marty studied her through the eye-slits of the mask, looking down at her terrified face, the eyes wide with pleading and bewilderment. He felt no pity. She was a representative of that part of society that he despised. The good people, the clean people, the polite people. The rich goodie-goodies who looked down on him, as if he were dirt. He was striking back at them out of the slums. He was getting even for all those East Side years when they'd kept his family in near-poverty.

The car glided through dark, silent streets toward the river. It came to a halt about a hundred yards from the river's edge, about a quarter-mile downstream from the clubhouse. It was dark and lonely here, where the river was bordered by a little clump of thick woods. No one would see or hear anything around here.

They carried her from the car to the woods, and came to a halt in a clearing. They propped Jill in a sitting position. She was kicking and whimpering.

"The top first," Marty said, keeping his voice muffled so she wouldn't recognize it.

He watched as Jolly Roger grabbed her polo shirt and pulled it upward. Big Henry gripped her legs in his unbreakable grasp, and Nick held her arms over her head while Roger got the shirt off. There was no light here, but Marty's eyes were accustomed to the dark—cat eyes, they were—and he could see the pale, soft flesh of her shoulders.

"The bra," he said.

Jolly Roger unhooked it … Marty stood over her, looking down hungrily. The bra dropped away. She jerked convulsively, trying futilely to cover her bare breasts, but Nick held her arms steady and pushed her over backward. Lying on her back as she was, now her breasts tended to flatten out a little. But they were good to look at, all the same. Young, tender, quivering breasts, breasts that had probably never been handled. The nipples were small and pink, looking up like little eyes.

"Nice," Marty murmured. "Real nice." His breath was starting to come in gasps. He eyed those soft, trembling, satiny globes of nude flesh, and he smiled.

"Take the rest off," he ordered.

Big Henry reached up and unzipped the plaid shorts, and started to drag them down over her hips. She pressed her buttocks desperately against the ground, trying to make it impossible for him to get the shorts off her, but Big Henry lifted her backside up easily and yanked the shorts off. All she wore now was a pair of nearly transparent green panties, through which Marty could see navel and triangle and everything else. His palms felt sweaty. He gave the signal, and Big Henry drew the panties off too. Jill's nude body seemed to gleam palely in the faint starlight. Her hips were soft and rounded, her navel just a dot in the tender flesh of her belly. Her breasts were rising and falling rapidly in her panic.

"The rope," Marty ordered. "Tie her hands together, so she don't scratch our eyes out."

Jolly Roger pushed her up to a sitting position again. Her breasts were fuller this way, more exciting,

Nick handed Marty a rope, which he deftly knotted around her wrists, tying her hands together behind her back. Blindfolded, gagged, her hands tied, her breasts shaking with each motion, she was utterly helpless. She quivered uncontrollably—a naked, pathetic, terrified creature.

"Okay," Marty said. "I'll go first. You guys stand guard."

They nodded. Nobody questioned his right to be first with this girl.

Marty stepped forward, unzipping his trousers. He was aroused and ready. Jill couldn't see him, but she realized what the unzipping sound meant, and she quivered with new terror. Marty gestured to Big Henry and Nick, and they released her. He knelt above her, grabbing her by the shoulders and pressing her down.

His hands sought her breasts. Only a few short weeks ago she had snubbed him, had refused to even talk to him. And now she lay here, stark naked, at his mercy. Her breasts felt cold to his touch. He tightened his grip, cupping them in his callused hands, savoring their softness and their firmness.

Her legs were locked together, the ankles desperately entwined. Marty looked at his companions.

"The legs," he said.

Big Henry nodded and grabbed her feet. With his bull-like strength, which few women could have resisted for long, he pried her legs apart. She kicked and bucked, but Marty held her tight, forcing his way between her thighs, ignoring her writhing attempts to thwart his intentions.

He remained there, unmoving for a moment, thinking about what he was going to do, remembering all the other girls he had done this to, what thrills he'd had. Then, suddenly, he thrust himself savagely forward.

Jill screamed—as loud as the gag would let her—but it came out as a muffled yelp. She felt nothing but fiery pain.

Laughing, Marty thrust again and again, his pleasure increasing in proportion to the girl's agony.

Marty stayed on her for five minutes … ten … gliding up and down slowly, delaying his satisfaction so he could watch her tormented face. At last he decided he had wrung enough pleasure from her tortured body. With one final flurry of motion, he slaked his desire.

He lay still a few moments, then rose to his feet and zipped up his pants.

Jill lay on the ground, making no attempt now to struggle, her nude body shaken by deep, convulsive sobs. She looked crushed, soiled, defeated. Which she was.

Marty scooped up three twigs, stuffed them into his fist, held them out.

"Shortest twig gets next round," he said.

They drew, and Jolly Roger got the shortest twig. He fell on the girl and satisfied himself quickly; he was followed by Nick and finally Big Henry. By the time they all were through with her, the girl was unconscious.

Marty stared down at her nakedness. Now that he had violated her, he had no further interest in Jill Webster. He never went back to a girl he had forced. He had demonstrated his power, and that was all he had set out to do.

"Looks like she's done a fadeout." Big Henry observed.

"That's what happens to most of them," Marty said. "Come on, let's split."

"Just leave her here?"

"What you gonna do?" Marty asked. "Drop her off at the police station?"

After taking one last backward glance at the nude, piteously crumpled form lying in the clearing, Marty led them back to the car. Big Henry had removed the gag, the blindfold, and the rope from her, just to keep the cops from finding anything that might turn out to be a useful clue.

Nick gunned the motor and the car started moving.

"Where to?" he asked. "Back to the clubhouse?"

"Uh-uh," Marty said. "Over to the bowling alley. That's our alibi."

About half the Barons had gone bowling that night. The manager of the alley would never be sure which members of the gang had been at his place and which hadn't.

They said little as they drove over to the alley. Marty knew that the other three were a bit shocked at what they had done. What the hell, he thought. This was the best way to toughen them up, make real stompers out of them. Maybe just for the hell of it they'd go after Jill's big sister next month, to see how the high-and-mighty Websters took to a steady diet of raping.

The alley was pretty full, and nobody noticed them come in, especially since they entered one at a time. Marty bowled for about an hour, and he bowled fast, so there were four games on his score sheet when he turned it in at the desk. It looked as though he'd been bowling for most of the evening—in case anyone asked—and just to drive the point home, he engaged the proprietor in a conversation before he left.

It was a little before midnight when he got home. The house was dark, but a light was on in the living room. As Marty walked past, he saw his father sitting in an armchair. Just sitting there, wide awake, staring off into space.

"Evening, Pa. Where's everybody?"

"Your mother and your brother went to sleep early. They said they were tired."

"So how come you're up?"

"I wasn't sleepy. I just wanted to sit here and think."

Marty shrugged. You could never figure old people out. They would just sit and think and stare out at nothing.

His father asked, "Where did you go tonight? What did you do?"

"I went bowling, Pa. With some of my friends."

"Your new friends. The tough boys of the town, I bet."

"They're okay."

"All you did was go bowling? You didn't get into no trouble? You didn't fight with nobody?"

"No, Pa. Just bowling."

"I wish I could believe you." The old man spoke in a thin, tired voice. "You're always fighting, always hurting other people. Why are you so cruel, Marty? Why did you grow up this way?"

"Look, Pa ..."

"Why can't you be a nice boy like your brother Frank? Why must you hurt people? Why must you hurt your Ma and me so much? We didn't want you to grow up to be a hoodlum. We ..." He paused. "You aren't listening to me, are you?"

"You're tired, Pa. Why don't you go to sleep?"

"You go to sleep, Marty. And think about your sins a little. Maybe God will still change you. You aren't too old to be saved."

"You got to go to sleep too, Pa. You got to work tomorrow."

"Don't worry about me. Good night, Marty."

"Good night, Pa."

CHAPTER SIX

Marty moved off, up the dark stairs, leaving his father still sitting and sighing in the dimness. Marty hated it when the old man talked like that. It was bad enough when Ma shouted, or Frankie got sarcastic. But the old man sounded so worn-out and tired. It was like listening to a ghost wailing in the wind, to hear him. Marty remembered when his father had been sturdy and strong, not too many years ago.

Somewhere around the time Marty had been arrested for stealing some old bitch's handbag, he thought, that was when Pa had started to get old. Marty was only twelve then. It was the only time in his life he had ever been caught. He got off with a suspended sentence on a promise of good behavior, but from that day on Angelo Capuano was sure that his oldest son was going to turn out bad, and the family would be disgraced.

Marty reached his room. This new house was big enough so Marty and his brother could each have their own private rooms. It hadn't been that way in New York; they'd had to share one little room. And at the place before last, when Marty's older sister Louisa had still been living with them, all three had been squeezed into a single room—Marty and Frankie sharing one bed, Louisa sleeping in the other.

Marty grinned, remembering those days. Louisa was five years older than he was. He remembered how it had been when he was thirteen and Louisa eighteen, and Frankie eleven.

At night, little Frankie would be fast asleep, but Marty would wait up, just feigning sleep, until Louisa came home from her dates. She would turn on the little lamp and get undressed, and Marty would watch her. He waited for her underwear to come off, so he could see her plump buttocks and her high, big breasts and the curly tuft of reddish hair at the base of her belly. He had been watching her undress for years, ever since he was old enough to know that there was a difference. He had watched Louisa ripen from a skinny little girl into a voluptuous, full breasted young woman, and he had watched her at her mirror, with her hands supporting her bulky breasts, examining herself.

Toward the end, after he had made out with a few girls himself, he was beginning to wonder what it would be like to boff his own sister. He knew guys who had done it, guys like Whitey Scambollio, who had a twin sister. They slept together all the time. And other guys, too. When you lived where six or seven people were crammed into one or two rooms, you weren't fussy about who you slept with.

But before Marty had ever got up enough guts to try crawling into his sister's bed, Louisa had gone and gotten married. Now, at twenty-three, she lived in Jersey City and had three kids and a fourth one on the way, and she had lost her figure and looked like a fat, sloppy pig. But Marty remembered the days when he had peeked at her body out of half-closed eyes, and her body had excited him to a frenzy.

He dropped off to sleep thinking of the girl he had just raped, wondering if there would be any suspicion cast his way. Probably she would be too shell-shocked to dare accuse anybody.

Marty slept soundly, and when he finally woke up the following morning the house was empty. His father had long since left for the mill; Frankie was out too, probably looking around town for a job that would help contribute to the skimpy family finances. And his mother was not in the house either. She usually went marketing at this time of day.

Marty made breakfast for himself, left the dirty dishes in the sink, and went out of the house, figuring to go down to the clubhouse and spend the day there. He wondered about Jill Webster, whether she had managed to find her way out of the woods and get help.

He didn't have to wonder long.

As he stood at the bus stop, a truck pulled up and a man got out to stuff some newspapers into the vending tray at the corner. Jenkinsville had one newspaper, the *Daily Record*, a cheesy-looking little rag that came out every day around eleven, and was sold on the honor system from newsstands at every other street corner.

Marty took a paper from the tray without bothering to pay for it, and the big black headline leaped up out of the page at him:

BODY OF LOCAL GIRL FOUND IN RIVER

The story was smeared all over the front page. Marty read it avidly. It said:

> The body of Jill Webster, 17, daughter of Mr. and Mrs. Lawrence Webster of 107 Stonybrook Terrace, was found floating in the river near shore about a half-mile below Jenkinsville, shortly after dawn this morning.
>
> Leonard Hickens, 64, a fisherman from Tompkins Falls, made the discovery. He said the body of the attractive

teenager, and honor student at Jenkinsville High, was entirely nude, floating face down.

Miss Webster had been missing from her home since about nine o'clock last night, when she left the house to mail a letter, according to her sister, Evelyn Webster, 19.

A preliminary report from Jenkinsville Coroner Dr. W. F. Samson indicates that cause of death was drowning. The coroner added that the dead girl had definitely been violated sexually, apparently several times, within the twelve hours prior to her death.

Police investigators reported having found several articles of clothing in the river-edge woods several hundred yards upstream from the site where the body was found, and the Webster family has definitely identified the clothing as having belonged to the deceased.

Police Chief John Nathanson speculates that the girl had been abducted and was raped in the woods, then was abandoned by her attackers.

"It's quite possible," Chief Nathanson ventured, "that in the darkness and in her state of shock and confusion, she wandered into the river and drowned. There was no indication that she had been murdered as a direct result of the sexual assault."

The police chief added that, in view of the still-unexplained disappearance of 19-year-old Charles Beck several weeks ago, a new wave of teenage violence may be descending on Jenkinsville. "Jenkinsville's smoldering gang feuds have been dormant for many months," he said, "but we feel this may be an indication that the young hoodlums are ready for new activity."

Investigation of the Webster girl's death will continue until the case is solved, the police thief stated. He added ...

The bus arrived. Marty folded the paper, put it under his arm, and got aboard.

This morning there was no cheery greeting from the driver. He looked solemn, as did everybody else aboard the bus. The Webster case had no doubt upset the whole town.

Marty took a seat in the back and opened his paper. He heard the other passengers buzzing about the crime. "So terrible ... such a beautiful girl ... intelligent, too ... kidnaped right in front of her own home ... a person just isn't safe after dark anymore! ..."

He forced himself not to smile. He felt the big kick spreading through his body, the surge of adrenalin that signified his power.

He was *somebody*. He was *big*. He had done something that had set the whole town talking. He, Marty Capuano!

And he was one hundred percent safe. He hadn't counted on the girl going into a daze and falling into the drink, but it was just as well that she had. There was no one left to place the blame or him, now. Only four people in the world were in or the secret, and none of them were going to go spouting off about it.

Everything was working out just fine, Marty thought. First, that snotty bitch was taken care of. Next, they would do the job on Thompson's Bar. After that, they'd stage the big rumble that would establish the Barons as the boss gang in Jenkinsville.

And after that? No plans, yet. But Marty knew he was sure to think up something. He knew how to find action when he wanted it.

At the clubhouse, the rape was naturally the big topic of conversation. Marty sensed it the moment he walked in.

None of the Barons or their debs had actually been a friend of the dead girl, since Jill had come from Jenkinsville's higher social strata, and the gang kids were from the lower-income levels. But most of them had at least known of her, had seen her around at Jenkinsville High School. Marty heard them talking about the circumstances of her death, whispering the details to each other.

He spotted Jolly Roger and called the tall boy into the kitchen.

As soon as they were alone, Roger said, "Geez, Marty, I didn't think she was gonna go and fall in the river!"

"To hell with that! Have you told anybody who did it?"

"You nuts? I been playing it cool, Marty!"

"How about Big Henry and Nick?"

"They ain't gonna say nothing either, Marty. We ain't none of us looking to get sent up for life, you know."

Marty nodded. "Just make sure you three keep your mouths shut about this. Don't go bragging around. We can't even tell the others in there."

"Sure, Marty."

"Because if we tell them, and they start blabbing outside the gang, we've had it. *Had it*, you understand? And I'll personally cut your liver out if you get loose at the mouth, Roger."

The tall boy laughed nervously. "Don't worry ne about me, Marty."

Later in the day, when he was upstairs in his room with Jojo, she started talking about the rape. It was after they had made love, and they lay sprawled out naked on the bed, with the hot afternoon sunlight streaming in the open window. Marty was sitting with his head propped up on his fist, watching the glistening little beadlets of sweat trickle down through the valley between Jojo's incredible breasts.

She said, "That was a hell of a thing, about that girl getting raped and drowned."

"Yeah."

"I bet she was a virgin before last night, and she purposely crawled into the river because she thought she was disgraced."

"Maybe." Marty put his hand on her lean, flat belly and started to move it downward toward the zone of warmth.

"You did it, didn't you, Marty? You and Jolly Roger and Big Henry and Nick."

"*What?*" Marty sat bolt upright, and grabbed Jojo by her shoulders. He shook her violently, making her huge breasts bobble. "Who the hell told you that?"

"Why … nobody …"

He slapped her breasts hard. "Answer me! Who's been talkin' about me?"

White-faced, pale, she said in a frightened voice, "Ain't nobody been telling tales about you, Marty. I just guessed."

"Like hell! You a detective or something?"

"Well … I just figured that since the four of you went off somewhere together last night … and while you were away somebody grabbed that girl … and it's the kind of thing you might just do for kicks …"

"Well, I didn't do it, hear? Don't be so smart next time."

"Okay, Marty. I was just doing a little guessing."

"Don't guess so much. I didn't have a thing to do with what happened to that girl last night. I was in the bowling alley all evening, in case anyone asks you. Hear?"

"S-sure, Marty."

He knew that she didn't fully believe him, that she was still fairly certain he was guilty of masterminding the rape. But she was too much afraid of him to mention that again, to him or anyone else.

His hands were still on her shoulders. She caught his wrists and dragged his fingers down until they were on her breasts. She began to writhe hungrily, rubbing her body against him.

Her thighs opened for him.

He slid between them.

Roughly, almost brutally, he took her in a single swift thrust, and flesh slammed against flesh as they violently celebrated the rite of lust.

A week later, Marty decided it was time for the Barons to take care of Thompson's Bar.

The sensation created by the rape-and-drowning case had mostly died down by now. The funeral was over, the dead girl's parents had gone out of town to recuperate from the shock, and the police search had just about come to a dead end. In official circles, it was now thought that the rape had been the work of a band of wandering tramps, as hoboes habitually roamed through this area all summer, camping in the woods and moving on. It would be impossible to trace the activities of all of them. The crime would undoubtedly go down in the books as unsolved.

Now it was time for the second act of vengeance—revenge against the jeering bartender who had mocked him and made him the butt of laughter.

This time Marty called the entire Baron gang in on the job. He explained the project one night at the clubhouse.

"We're gonna pull a job at this bar on Hillside Drive, just across Flagler Street. I want to really wreck the place."

"How come, Marty?" Tom Brewster asked.

"Don't sweat the details. Just take my word for it, the bartender is a bastard, and I want to teach him a lesson. And it'll be a gas for all of us."

He outlined his plans. The bar opened at nine o'clock in the morning each day. They decided to handle the job between the hours of five and six in the morning, when the bar was closed and nobody would be around.

The next night, Marty borrowed the extra alarm clock and set it for four-thirty in the morning. When it went off, he listened to its insistent buzzing for half a minute, then came fully awake and punched in the button.

He was dressed and out of the house by quarter to five. By five o'clock, he was on the corner of Hillside and Flagler. The sun had not yet risen; the sky was gray, with a few pink pre-dawn clouds. The neighborhood was utterly silent, not a car or truck or bus in motion anywhere. There was a row of stores facing Hillside Drive, with the bar set in the middle of them and an alleyway running the length of the block behind the stores.

The Barons gathered. Twelve of them were there; the others couldn't manage to get out of their houses so early without arousing the suspicions of their families. None of the girls had come.

They clustered around the outside of the bar to hear Marty's final instructions.

"Remember, above all, you gotta be quiet. If we wake the whole neighborhood up, we're finished. We move fast, but we move careful and silent-like. Also, we don't stop to drink none of the booze. Any guy I catch drinking the stuff, I'm gonna let him have it, but good!"

He looked around. "Okay. Three of you stay on watch here—one at each end of the block, one right out in front. The rest of you come on around back with me."

The back door of the bar, which gave outward onto the alleyway, was easily forced. They pried it off its hinges, Big Henry providing most of the strength. There was a screen door behind it, but a quick slash of the shears one of the guys had brought along took care of that.

They entered the bar.

The work of destruction was methodical. They had brought crowbars, knives, and shears; and they had rehearsed their parts to perfection.

Jolly Roger moved along behind the bar, uncorking one after another of the dozens of liquor bottles stored there, and pouring their contents into the back-bar sink.

Big Henry went up and down the booths along the back wall, digging his knife into the upholstery and ripping it up.

Marty supervised the removal of the mirror behind the bar. He tugged at its sides, with one foot planted in the middle, and shattered it.

Nick Lorrey yanked out the pump lines that supplied beer to the taps, and turned them into crumpled wreckage.

Two of the others went down into the basement, where the beer barrels and liquor reserves were stored. They opened the bungholes of the beer barrels, letting the beer flow out until it was ankle deep in the basement. They smashed case after case of bottles by lifting them and dropping them to the floor.

Tom Brewster defaced the woodwork in the bar with his knife.

For nearly half an hour they worked the bar over, making little noise and wreaking utter destruction. Short of setting fire to the place, they couldn't have ruined it more thoroughly. Marty looked around, surveying the damage. It was a remarkably complete job. He remembered the times in New York when they had done this— his old gang, the Shining Barons. There was supreme joy in breaking into a place in the early hours of the morning and destroying it.

They had smashed up a butcher shop that way, he remembered, breaking into the refrigeration room and trampling on the cuts of meat. They had gone into a public school, ripping up books, hammering the blackboards to bits, shattering desks. They had pillaged a synagogue—and, the next week, just to show they weren't prejudiced—they had done the same to a Catholic church.

And now these new Barons of his were feeling the same joy he did. The joy of smashing, of ruining, of striking out against the smug faces of society. *Supreme Joy*.

"Okay," Marty said, "that's about it. Let's split this scene now."

As silently as they had come, they trooped out the back way, went around the side, and emerged in front of the bar.

Big Henry nudged Marty. "How about a brick through the front windows, just to finish the job off right?"

Marty scowled. "You want to wake up the whole neighborhood, you lumphead? We did plenty inside. Let's leave well enough alone."

Big Henry shrugged, looking crestfallen. "Okay, okay. Just making a suggestion, Marty. Just making a suggestion."

"Well, it's a lousy one. Let's get out of here."

They scattered, all going in different directions.

The sun was just coming up when Marty reached his house.

He tiptoed in and went upstairs to his room, trying to be careful not to awaken anyone. He had been gone about an hour. He hoped nobody had discovered that he was missing.

Quickly, he undressed and got back into his pajamas. Just as he got into bed, his brother Frankie appeared at the door of his room.

Marty glared at him. "Walkin' in your sleep?"

"Just came to see. I heard you moving around in here."

"So? I wanted a drink of water, punk. Get back to bed and pound your pillow some more."

Frankie returned to his bedroom. Marty let out a long, slow sigh of relief, and pulled the covers up over him.

That had been a close one. If Frankie had seen him fully dressed, there would have been all kinds of questions about where he had been, why he was up at this hour. And then later, when the news broke that Thompson's had been smashed up during the night, Frankie would certainly have put two and two together and come up with the right answer about why Marty had been dressed.

Would Frankie have turned his own brother in to the fuzz? Marty wondered about that. Many times Frankie had said in disgust, "I wish to hell the cops would catch up with you some time for some of the things you do, and lock you up for the rest of your life. At least then Ma and Pa could stop eating their hearts out, wondering what you'll be up to next!"

He said that, sure. But Marty didn't know if Frankie would actually report him. Still, it didn't hurt to play it safe, to avoid giving Frankie any information he might decide to use.

Marty closed his eyes. He dreamed of girls, nude and hot and full-breasted, with soft buttocks and jiggling boobs, dancing around his bed. One by one they slipped between the covers with him and lowered their voluptuous bodies, straddling him, and he gratified their desires and they his, and when he'd had them all, each one came around for a second turn. Briefly, he woke up.

I'm getting horny, he thought sleepily.

He knew that when he started getting hot dreams, it was time to find a new woman. Jojo had lost her fascination, as far as he was concerned. He made up his mind that right after the rumble with the Dragons, he'd give Jojo the boot and start making it with Tom Brewster's girl, Mary Anne.

There was no one in the house but his mother when Marty awoke again at half past nine. She was busy with the ironing. Frankie had a job, now, running errands at the Jenkinsville National Bank.

"Morning, Ma."

"High time you got up."

"What's for breakfast?"

"Fix your own. I'm busy."

They had the same conversation every morning. She went on with her ironing, taking no notice of him, and he helped himself to orange juice, toast, and coffee.

"Got a cigarette, Ma?" he asked, when he was through eating.

She looked up, her face heavy with sorrow. "You know I don't like you to smoke so much, Marty. All that smoking, that's why you're so small. You should do like me, if you have to smoke at all, and keep it to a half a pack a day."

"I didn't, ask for no sermons, Ma. I'm all out of butts, and I want to bum one off you, that's all."

She shrugged. "Take, then." Arguing would do no good.

He fumbled a cigarette out of her pack, lit up, and left.

"I'll be back in time for supper, like usual," he called to her as he passed through the front door. She didn't answer.

When the Jenkinsville *Daily Record* came out, a little later that morning, Marty grabbed it up eagerly. Most of the paper was made-up and printed the night before each edition came out, but the front page was always held open until the last minute in case some big news came in during the night.

And there was news, big by Jenkinsville standards. It was labeled a press-time bulletin, just as the Webster rape had been, and the ink was hardly dry.

The headline said:

VANDALS SMASH THOMPSON'S BAR

Marty grinned as he read the article, and felt certain pride of accomplishment.

> Thompson's Bar, 1321 Hillside Drive, was illegally entered and wrecked by vandals early this morning.
>
> According to Dan McDermott, the day bartender, who

discovered the damage when he arrived to open for business at 9 a.m. today, the interior of the bar was "completely smashed."

Michael Thompson, of 432 Donovan Lane, proprietor of the establishment, was summoned to the scene. He estimated that the damage amounted to at least $10,000. He added that insurance would probably not cover the full extent of the loss. He was unable to give any possible explanation for the attack.

The bar had closed at 3:30 a.m., its usual closing time. Residents of the area reported hearing no unusual sounds during the night.

At press time it was impossible to reach Police Chief John Nathanson for comment, but ...

Marty grinned broadly. Before he was through, he would show this town what the word excitement meant. Rape, vandalism, and now a rumble coming up. Jenkinsville would rock from the impact. As soon as all the talk about the Thompson business died down, he thought, he'd get the rumble going.

CHAPTER SEVEN

Jenkinsville was divided in half by the railroad tracks.

On the east side of the tracks was the turf of the Barons, running from the depot all the way over to the mill. The west side was Dragon turf, running right to the edge of town, where it trickled out and became farmland.

The way things worked out, the two halves of Jenkinsville were just about equal in all ways. Most Westsiders worked in the big machine factory, and Eastsiders generally worked in the mill; and as a rule people from the West Side didn't mingle much with the people from the East. East Side kids went to Jenkinsville High School, Westsiders to Roosevelt Memorial High. But there was no such thing as "the other side of the tracks" in Jenkinsville. There were slum areas on both sides of town, and there were some fine homes and wealthy people on both sides, too.

The only major difference, in the eyes of the teenage gangs, was that there was an extra movie house on the Dragons' side of the tracks—and that was very important.

The East Side had only one motion picture theater, the Baronet— from which the Barons had adopted their name. But over on the West, there were two movie houses. One of them was the Beverley—

where, like the Baronet, the usual fare consisted of "B" movies and second-runs of older films. The other was the Orpheum, a plushly appointed movie palace where the big hit films usually played. The trouble stemmed from the fact that the Orpheum was located deep in Dragon territory. The Dragons didn't like the Barons coming across town to see movies there, and they let it be known. The result was that any Baron who wanted to take in a show at the Orpheum ran the risk of coming home with ventilated skin if he crossed paths with any of the Dragon scouts.

Among the Barons, it was considered a mark of distinction to sneak across the railroad tracks with a deb, see the double feature at the Orpheum, and come back in one piece. Ticket stubs from the Orpheum box office were Scotch-taped to the walls in the Barons' clubhouse like battle trophies.

Marty Capuano intended to put an end to all that kind of jazz, by winning the rumble. He was aiming for a decisive showdown that would break the hold of the Dragons over the Orpheum, and make the route to and from the theater free territory for the Barons.

It wasn't going to be easy to force the Dragons to create a neutral corridor through their turf. It was going to take a lot of cutting and bopping. But Marty was glad of that—he was itching for some more real action, and the rumble was just what he could use the most right now.

So it was all set up.

He had been in Jenkinsville for several months now, and he knew the town inside out. And he was having things his own way. The body of Charley Beck had never been found, and so far as the local cops were concerned, it was simply a disappearance. The Jill Webster rape and drowning was on the books as "unsolved." The attack on Thompson's bar had been forgotten by everybody but Thompson.

Marty had found out by now that the Jenkinsville police force just wasn't up to par. The town had been governed by the same administration for the last twenty years, and nobody gave much of a damn about anything. In a recent economy move, the police department's budget had been cut back sharply, so most of the cops on the force were pot-bellied old guys whose chief aim in life was to hang on until they were eligible for their state pensions. The police force wasn't attracting any new blood. Young guys who wanted to become cops moved off to Cleveland or Columbus or Cincinnati.

The result was that almost anybody could get away with anything. The police would investigate, and Police Chief John Nathanson, who had held his present position since 1941, would issue a statement that investigation was proceeding—and, usually, that would be where the matter ended.

So Marty wanted to see how the local fuzz would deal with an outbreak of teenage violence. He didn't think they'd do a thing.

He picked out the night for the rumble a week in advance. It was a Saturday night at the end of July. The weather had been good all week, more like spring than like summer, with none of the crushing humidity you get in New York in July and August.

That week, the town carried big advertisements about the new feature at the Orpheum. It was some smash hit spectacular, starring Elizabeth Taylor and Richard Burton and Rock Hudson and Doris Day, and it was having its first run right now in all the big cities. It was the biggest publicity push for any Orpheum film all season. Marty decided that this was as good a time as any to test the power of the Dragons.

It wasn't that he gave a damn about what was playing. Marty never watched the screen anyway, not when he had a girl with him. He was always too busy with the girl to watch the movie. One hand up her skirt to grab the hot spot, the other one inside her bra to squeeze the boobs.

But it was the principle of the thing that mattered. Marty didn't want any damn bunch of punks telling him he couldn't go to the Orpheum whenever he liked. It was bad enough that he'd had to put up with parents and schoolteachers and cops and all sorts of other adults telling him what to do most of his life. He wasn't about to put up with that crap from any other gang.

Marty let the word get around town that he'd ordered a rumble. There was no use sneaking up on the Dragons; this had to be face-to-face contest, with the strongest outfit coming out on top, or it wouldn't prove a thing. So Marty fixed it so the word was spread. Not to the cops, of course. Just to other kids. The Barons told their outside teenage friends that all the Barons and their debs were going to attend the 8:30 Saturday night showing of the new film at the Orpheum. Marty knew that word would spread across the tracks to the Dragons, and they'd be ready to defend their turf with all they had. If the Dragons got put down in an open stand, it would smash their confidence a lot more effectively than if the Barons ambushed them.

The Friday night before the rumble, Marty made it with Jojo in his room upstairs at the clubhouse. The redhead was hotter than a firecracker that night. When they went upstairs, she shucked her shorts and halter the moment Marty locked the door, and she lay down on the mattress, naked—she hadn't been wearing any underwear—and looked up appealingly at him, opening her thighs to welcome him.

"Hurry up, Marty. I want you. I want you real bad."

He eyed her without much interest. He had reached that nowhere point in his relations with her, and she didn't arouse him at all. Her big breasts were just so much excess flesh to him now. And he was more aware than ever of the thinness of the rest of her body, the sharpness of her hip bones as he clung to her, the leanness of her flanks. It was time to get hooked up with a curvier chick, he thought. Like that Mary Anne. Mary Anne didn't have knockers to match Jojo's—nobody else in the world had a pair like that—but she was plenty well-stacked. She had the hips and thighs and juicy rear to go with the breasts.

It was time for a change, Marty thought. This was Jojo's last night with him. Tomorrow, after the rumble, he'd make the switch from Jojo to Mary Anne.

He realized Jojo was looking at him strangely.

"Something wrong, Marty?"

"Nothing."

"You're just standing there."

"I'm thinking."

"This is no time for thinking," she said. She stretched, extending her legs, arching her back, thrusting her big breasts upward and out. "I'm waiting for you, Marty. Why don't you come to me? Come here, Marty."

He walked slowly toward the bed, unbuckling his belt. He could use her now, the way he could use any woman at any time of the day. That was something ordinary, like blowing his nose when it was clogged. But he wanted more out of sex than nose-blowing. He wanted it to light him up and make him tingle, and he had to keep changing women if he wanted to get the real kicks.

Jojo grabbed him and tugged him down on top of her. He lay there calmly, trying to work up some excitement over her.

"You're more interested in that rumble than you are in me," she pouted.

"I got a lot to think about, babe. That rumble needs planning."

"You can plan it tomorrow. Right now let's get with it, huh?"

She took his unwilling hands and formed them into cups over her breasts. Marty allowed her to lead him, but he felt detached, bored with her. Her body writhed below his. Finally she put her hand on him and guided him to the hot, lathered well of her body. She gasped as they entered into the act, as with a sudden thrust he took possession of her. But the contact with her body failed to send a tingle through him. When things went right, it was like grabbing a live power line. But there was no voltage coming through now.

"Love me, Marty," she moaned. "Love me real good, man."

Propped on his elbows, Marty stared down at her. She had her eyes closed, her moist lips were hanging open, her breath was coming fast. Her face was a study in passion—but it just looked silly to him. He thought, there's nothing sillier than the way a girl's face looks when she's all hot, if a guy just sits and watches it without letting himself share what she's feeling.

He started moving up and down, and eventually she cried out that she couldn't hold on any more, and Marty pulled out all the stops and brought everything to a climax. But he kept his eyes open at the biggest moment, watching the expressions on Jojo's face. And at that moment he knew he was finished with her, that he could never bring himself to climb into the sack with her again.

When she opened her eyes, she smiled and said, "That was good, Marty."

"Mmmmn."

"I'm okay, huh? I'm a hot one in the hay, ain't I?"

"You're okay."

"You been acting funny lately, Marty. You been sorta distant, like."

"Have I?"

"Yeah," she said. "Like you're getting tired of me. *Are* you getting tired of me, Marty? I want you to tell me."

"When I'm tired of you, I'll tell you," he said shortly. "Don't give me no more lip now, huh?"

"But I don't want you to get tired of me," she said. "I want you all the time."

Abruptly, he pulled his body away from hers. He stood up, zipping up his pants and tucking his shirt in, looking down at her. Suddenly he was totally disgusted with her, lying there naked with her hair a mess and her legs spread and her big breasts rising and falling with her breathing.

"Nobody has Marty Capuano all the time, babe, you hear me? There were girls before you, and there's gonna be girls after you."

"No, Marty."

"Don't tell *me* no! We ain't married, Jojo, and we ain't gonna be. You're just my current shack-job, and when I'm through with you I'll let you know."

"You talk like you're through with me now."

"Maybe I am."

"No, Marty! You're the greatest—I gotta have you!"

"Cut it, Jojo. I got a rumble to think about. I can't do no worrying about you and what you gotta have."

"Is it somebody else in the Baron Debs?" she asked. "I'll scratch her eyes out. I'll rip her boobs off, you just watch me, Marty!"

He narrowed his eyes. "You listen to me, Jojo, and listen good," he said in a flat, level voice. "I ain't sayin' a thing about what I'm gonna do. But if I do decide to get myself a new deb, and you lay a hand on her, I'm gonna make you sorry you ever thought of it!" He sat down next to her and grasped her shoulders. "I'm gonna strip you down, and tie you up, and have every man in the Barons work you over two or three times. And when that's done, I'll take my knife and saw all this blubber offa you." To illustrate, he seized her breasts and made a mock-sawing gesture. She quivered, half from fright, half from the pleasurable torment of having her breasts handled.

He let go of her. "Just remember what I say, Jojo. When your time is up with me, you step down, and you don't make a fuss about it, hear?"

Her lips were trembling. "Marty ... you wouldn't really do that to me ..."

"If you ask for it, you'll get it."

"Am I through, Marty?"

"I told you not to bug me about it now."

"Will you love me once more now? Let's make it again, huh? Show me you want me."

She put her lips to him. Her head moved and her tongue did sly things, and he couldn't help but respond right away. But he didn't let her keep at him for long. He moved her head away. He didn't want her, not anymore, but he didn't feel like having a hassle with her till after the rumble.

"Some other time," he said. "I gotta worry about the rumble now."

Tears of disappointment glistened in her eyes. She started to say something, checked herself, then rose from the bed.

"Okay. Later," she said.

Marty watched with boredom as she pulled her halter tight around the swelling mounds of her breasts, and drew her shorts up over her thighs and buttocks. Shrugging, he turned away and went downstairs. It had to be pretty bad, he thought, when he quit after only one round. Time for a change, sure enough.

He spent the rest of that evening working out rumble strategy with his two lieutenants, Jolly Roger and Big Henry. The next day, Saturday, it was more of the same. The Barons were a well-drilled outfit by this time. They knew how they were supposed to handle themselves during the rumble. Marty had given them the full benefit of his eighteen years in the jungles of Manhattan.

At quarter to eight Saturday evening, the Barons set out from their clubhouse. There were fourteen guys in the group, plus their debs—two of the Barons were sick, or so they said. "Chicken fever," Marty figured. Oh, well, he wouldn't miss them. They weren't worth a damn with blades, anyhow.

It was a good night, warm but not hot, with a cooling breeze blowing crosswise from the river.

Some of the Barons had wanted to bring the tire chains and brass knucks and other such weapons from the clubhouse collection. But Marty had iced that idea.

"A knife is all you need for this rumble," he told them. "A knife talks big, and it does the job. All that other crap is strictly for the kiddies, let me tell you."

So they were armed with knives. The fast-action rumble party crossed the tracks, passed the stationhouse, and entered Dragon territory. It was the first time that Marty himself had actually been on the turf of the enemy, though he had made sure to send out plenty of scouts in the past couple of weeks. Big Henry and Nick Lorrey had cased the area pretty well, and knew where to make tracks in case the fuzz showed.

But Marty wasn't worried much about interference from the Jenkinsville police force. That bunch of old farts, more worried about their pensions than in keeping the law, would stay far away—at least until the rumble was in its last stages. Those cops weren't going to bust in and get themselves cut up—oh, no, not them!

The Barons sauntered along the quiet, summery streets. Marty led the way, and Jojo was walking by his side. She was wearing a thin velour-like blouse at least two sizes too small. Her breasts protruded from the soft fabric like twin cannonballs, the nipples cleanly in view. She wanted to show what she had, all right. She wanted the Dragons to notice, and probably she wanted Marty to notice too. But it was no news to him that she had big knobs. He was tired of Jojo's frontage. Tom Brewster's girl, Mary Anne, looked like she had big enough boobs to keep anybody happy, and Marty was anxious to find out whether the stuff that filled up Mary Anne's blouse was really all her own or not.

Well, he thought, *tonight I'll find out. After he rumble, in the confusion of the victory party, I'll just take her over.*

He made up his mind that this was definitely the night.

If Jojo gave him a bad time, he'd slap her teeth down her throat. He didn't like any woman to think she owned him. Mary Anne wouldn't dare say anything—she was pretty stuck on Brewster, sure, but she wouldn't pass up a chance to make some time with the boss of the Barons, Marty told himself confidently.

The only one likely to make trouble was Tom. He'd probably put up a squawk. Marty shrugged; he wasn't afraid of Brewster; but maybe Brewster would get cooled tonight anyway, in the rumble, and save him the trouble. That would make things a lot simpler.

At eight o'clock the Barons crossed Pine Street and entered the real heart of the Dragon turf. Flanking Marty and Jojo as they walked were Jolly Roger and Big Henry, each of them with their own girls. The rest of the Barons followed behind, with Lorrey and Brewster stationed at the rear. They were both good knifemen, and it was important to have a strong back wall, in case you were japped from behind.

According to Jolly Roger, who had lived on this side of the tracks for a while and knew the neighborhood pretty well, they would have to cross a big vacant lot three blocks from Pine Street on the route to the Orpheum. Marty figured that the Dragons would be lying in wait there. It was the best place around here for a rumble. Marty wondered if the bastards would use zip-guns. Marty liked it clean, nothing but switchblades. Zip-guns loused things up. Any fairy could pick a good man off with a zip gun from a distance. It was no good when strength and skill didn't count for anything.

As he walked along he kept quiet, feeling the gradually spreading tingle of battle anticipation. He remembered his other rumbles. The first big one he'd been in was when he was fourteen, and still a junior member of the Shining Barons. They'd had a set-to with the Scarlet Sinners in Donohue Park. The Scarlet Sinners were mostly Negroes and Puerto Ricans; the Shining Barons were mainly Irish and Italian. So each side had its own little scores to settle. It had been a bloody fight, lasting more than an hour. Three of the Sinners were chopped up, and two of the Barons died. Marty hadn't made any of the kills himself, but he had drawn Sinner blood.

After that there had been plenty of other rumbles. Marty had been elected War Leader of the Shining Barons when he was fifteen and the year after that he'd pushed Danny Petrucelli out of the top spot in the gang. Petrucelli had needed a little cutting up before he was willing to resign. And after that Marty had led the Shining Barons on the rumbles, just the way he was leading these Barons now.

The New York cops had been funny about the rumbles, Marty remembered. Sometimes, especially when they had been tipped off in advance, the fuzz showed up in squad cars to break up the rumbles before the fighting ever got started. Other times, though, they just seemed to sit back and let the rumbles take place; like they figured that if they let the gang kids kill each other off, they wouldn't make any more trouble for the decent, tax-paying citizens.

Marty smiled to himself, remembering the good old rough days in New York.

Then he looked ahead. They were a block away from the vacant lot. It was dark now, but the moon was full, brightening the place up. Marty could see that the Dragons were waiting for them at the lot, all right.

"You see them?" Jolly Roger asked.

"Yeah," Marty said. "Lots of them, too."

"More than we got," Jolly Roger observed.

Marty squinted, trying to count all the dark figures that he could see in the lot. His lips moved as he counted. "Eighteen, nineteen, maybe twenty," he said aloud. "Just Dragons, none of their debs."

"That's a lot," Big Henry murmured. "Twenty against fourteen."

"Fourteen Barons against twenty cheese-bellies," Marty said. "We could handle twenty dozen of them, if we had to."

He looked ahead. Twenty Dragons, spoiling for a fight. Marty quivered with the joy of battle:

We'll see how tough you hick kids really are, he thought. *Now we find out if you've got guts or not.*

He stopped and turned around. In a quiet voice, he said, "Okay. The Dragons are waiting for us. You debs stay back here till it's all over, you hear me? Don't try to mix in, unless you see some Dragon Debs show up and try to get into it. Otherwise, you just stay out of our way."

He grinned and licked his lips. "Let's move, now."

Fourteen Barons went forward to see what they could do with twenty Dragons.

CHAPTER EIGHT

When the Baron group was about fifty yards from the edge of the lot, the Dragons started to come to life. Marty saw them milling around, shifting uneasily.

Marty kept walking. A moment later, a tall kid in a black leather jacket detached himself from the shadowy group of Dragons and came strolling forward nonchalantly, then stopped when he was about fifteen feet in front of his gangmates.

"Who's that?" Marty asked.

Big Henry whispered. "That guy's Mack Lardner. He's their president."

Lardner was big, maybe six-feet-one, with broad shoulders and brown hair that fell over his eyes. He looked relaxed. He was tall and good-looking. Marty hated him just for that.

The street was very quiet.

Marty walked steadily onward until he was no more than a dozen feet away from Lardner, close enough for the opening challenge to be thrown. Lardner's unsmiling face was grimly set. His arms were folded. When he thought Marty had come close enough, he said in a quiet, mellow voice, "Where do you guys think you're going?"

"We're going to the movies, pal." Marty said. "It's a nice night to see a flick."

Lardner did not smile. "Which flick?"

"Why, we thought we'd just bop on over to the Orpheum," Marty said casually. "I hear they got a good show tonight."

Lardner shook his head slowly. "You're mistaken, buddy."

"What do you mean, mistaken?"

"You aren't going to any movie at the Orpheum tonight."

"No?" Marty asked. All this was ritualistic, a formal prelude to the combat that was about to come.

"No," Lardner said. "You don't want to go to the Orpheum, son. You're mistaken about that. What you want to do is turn your tails around the other way and get the hell over to your own lousy little Baronet. That is, if you want to see any flicks tonight, son."

"You talk pretty big, daddy-o. Who says that's what we're gonna do?"

"We say," Lardner replied evenly.

"And who the hell are you, daddy-o?"

"The Dragons," Lardner said calmly. "You're trespassing on our turf. We don't allow no trespassing by none of you Barons. So you got about five seconds to swing around and head yourselves back the way you came."

"And suppose we don't," Marty said. "Then what, big daddy?"

"Well, then, we'll have to convince you."

Marty nodded. The preliminaries were over. The glove had been thrown down, the challenge made and accepted. There was no need for further talk. It was up to the Dragons now to defend their turf against the invaders.

The Dragons were getting into formation behind Lardner. A couple of them were wielding tire chains A couple more of them brandished big lead-filled billy clubs. Marty smiled. Billy clubs and tire chains could do plenty of damage in a fight, but all a man really needed to defend himself was a knife. Just a knife. With quick eyes and fast enough wrists, and just the right twists of luck, a man with a knife would always come out ahead.

Marty sensed Jolly Roger and Big Henry at his sides, and the rest of the Barons fanning out in a big circle, the way they had planned it out at the clubhouse.

Marty brought out his knife. In the dead silence, the click of the emerging blade sounded loud and clear. Marty glared up challengingly at Lardner, who still faced him without having moved.

Lardner had a switch too. He pulled it out and thumbed the button that released the blade. It came out with a little whickering sound, sharp and thin.

Lardner said, "Come on, shrimp. I'll cut you down even shorter than you are already, you pint-sized bastard."

For a second, Marty saw nothing but blood red before his eyes. He checked himself, clamping his teeth together. By needling him about his size, Lardner had—knowingly or not—struck Marty in his most tender spot. But Marty didn't want to go into battle so filled with anger that he was blind. He waited a moment, until the sting of Lardner's taunts had died away, then he moved in, circling and dodging, and behind him came the rest of the Barons.

The rumble was on.

Marty had to move slightly uphill to get to Lardner. He breasted the rise and leaped forward; Lardner presented his blade, but Marty took advantage of the near-darkness to perform a quick double shift. He penetrated the taller boy's guard with deceptive ease; his blade licked out and ripped open Lardner's leather jacket just below the chest pocket. The jarring slash had deliberately been harmless. But Marty followed, lightning fast, with a second thrust that slipped over the bewildered Lardner's guard and drew blood from his forearm.

Marty grinned, and called out to his opponent, "You don't fight as big as you talk eh, daddy-o? I'm gonna cut you up into hamburger meat. I'm gonna feed you to the fish."

Eyes blazing with anger and fear, Lardner feinted forward at Marty. But it was a maneuver Marty had learned to deal with long before he was old enough to shave. He slipped sidewise, laughing in Lardner's face as the blade passed through the empty air where Marty had been a moment before.

Then a tire chain came whirling through the air, whistling past Marty's head. Only his catlike reflexes kept him from being put out of commission right at the start of the rumble. He angled his head to the left, hearing the fierce sound of the metal as it shot just an inch past his ear; then he danced around to deal with this unexpected new attacker.

But there was no need for him to act.

"I got him, Marty," Big Henry grunted, as he laid the wielder of the tire chain open with a savage thrust of his blade.

"Good one," Marty said.

An instant later, a short, chunky Dragon came angling in from the other side to come to the defense of his wounded comrade. But Jolly Roger's long arm descended swiftly to plant the knife in the newcomer's side.

Flesh-wounds, all of them. But the kill-lust was starting to sweep over the Barons. They were better drilled, better prepared, better led. The fact that they were outnumbered didn't seem to make any difference. Already they had drawn first blood, and in a moment, as the heat of battle rose in them, they would be starting to stab to kill.

The Dragon leader, Lardner, had dropped back at the moment of the tire-chain attack. But now he came forward again in a frenzied assault aimed at Marty.

"I'm gonna cut your guts out, you stinking little punk," Lardner muttered.

"Come on," Marty said, beckoning with his free hand. He knew Big Henry was covering him on his right flank. Teamwork, that's what did it. "Come on, you bigmouth. I'm waiting for you. I wanna see you slash me. I just wanna see it."

Lardner advanced. Marty stood his ground coolly, watching not only the point of Lardner's blade but the taller boy's body as well, judging by some subconscious skill the placement of Lardner's weight, measuring the way his muscles would have to move to drive him forward. Lardner lunged. Marty let the blade head straight for his belly, sidestepping only at the very last moment. Executing a pirouette that would have done credit to a ballet dancer, Marty swung around just as Lardner stumbled forward on the follow-through of his thrust.

Marty held his knife outstretched. He flicked his wrist casually, and Lardner ran right into the blade, uttering a soft, surprised little moan as the keen steel sliced through layers of skin and flesh and muscle, driven by the inexorable pressure of Marty's wrist. Marty buried the blade in Lardner's chest right up to its hilt, wrenched toward the heart, then yanked it out.

Lardner tottered, and blood bubbled from his mouth. He still didn't believe what had happened to him. He tried to say something, but all that came out of his mouth was a crimson flow of warm blood. He sagged, toppled, and fell face forward to the ground.

Marty didn't bother to check on whether or not he was still alive. He knew. Nobody stayed alive with a hole that big in his heart.

One down, Marty thought.

"Lardner's dead," he called. "I cooled off the Dragons' boss man."

He turned to survey the lot. Little groups of twos and threes were fighting in scattered clumps all over. Marty saw Tom Brewster kneeling over one of the Dragons, enthusiastically pounding his head against a rock. Somewhere else, Jolly Roger was licking his hand and screwing up his face with pain; he had just been nipped by a swinging chain, and his attacker was coming back for another try. Marty moved in swiftly and traced a bloody red line up the chain man's arm. A swift plunge, and Jolly Roger's attacker was out of commission for good.

"Hurt?" Marty asked.

"It stings, but I'll live."

"I cooled Lardner."

The news that the top Dragon was dead was spreading over the lot. It had a dampening effect on Dragon morale. The Barons pressed forward, and the enemy gave ground, dazed and helpless before the attackers. Marty heard the distant, shrill yelling from the sidelines.

Marty was all over the lot, spurring his men on, hurling taunts at the routed Dragons. Around, down, up, everywhere—Marty cut and slashed, raging like a demon. He dragged his knife through the soft throat of a plump, surprised Dragon. He ripped down into an unguarded back. Blood poured over him, but none of the blood that stained him was his own.

The Dragons were giving ground rapidly. They were forced back almost to the edge of the lot, and they had clustered together for protection, swinging their chains and billy clubs in a purely defensive attempt to keep the flashing knives of the Barons away.

Big Henry came by, exulting. "We used them up, Marty!"

"Yeah, man. We really wasted them."

"Like I mean, they're scared cats," Big Henry boomed. "Them and their big talk."

"I bet those guys never saw so much slashing," Marty said. He pointed across the lot. Nick Lorrey was dueling with a short, muscular Dragon. The Dragon was backing up steadily as Nick advanced, knife held high.

Then, suddenly, Marty heard a police whistle ring out clear and high over the lot. He froze in his tracks. Automatically, he clicked in the blade of his switch, and stowed the knife away in his pocket. The action was a reflex left over from his New York days. In New York, if the cops caught you with a knife in your hand during a rumble, they were liable to kick your teeth in, or maybe even wing you to make sure you wouldn't attack them. So at the first sound of sirens, all blades went into hiding.

Now Marty saw the fuzz—three of them, paunchy and slow-moving, coming toward the lot from the north. They were still half a block away, and they weren't in much of a hurry. It seemed like they wanted to give the gang kids a chance to disperse before they got there.

The surviving Dragons were vanishing in every direction, melting away into the night without stopping to worry about their fallen brothers. The Baron Debs were screaming in panic, "The cops! The cops!"

Marty stood in the middle of the field, looking around, taking a quick count of the bodies. Dragons were slumped here and there—three, four, five of them, dead. Two more Dragons were badly cut but were sitting up, trying to get up the strength to run away.

Marty smiled triumphantly. The rumble had been a rout.

"Come on, Marty!" Jolly Roger yelled.

Big Henry ran up to him and tugged impatiently at his arm. "It's the fuzz, Marty! You wanta get caught?"

"We cooled five of them," Marty said.

"Yeah, yeah. But don't just stand here, Marty. We gotta haul outta here, man!"

Marty nodded, snapping out of his daze of power. "Okay," he said. "Let's go."

They took off. Looking back, Marty saw the cops come up over the rise in the field and look around at the scene, dumbfounded. They weren't making any attempt to chase the fleeing Barons. "Split up!" Marty called. "Meet at the clubhouse later!"

The Barons separated going off every which way. As Marty ran, he felt the thunder of pride in his brain. He had come to Jenkinsville knowing he was destined to establish his power here, and he had established it. Jill Webster, Thompson's Bar, the Barons, the Dragons—all had fallen before him. And tonight Mary Anne, too, would be his.

He ran on toward the clubhouse.

He got back to the clubhouse a little after nine o'clock having taken the back streets and side alleys. His long run had left him only slightly winded. He slipped into the clubhouse. Three or four of the Barons had already returned, and two more arrived a few minutes after Marty got there.

Marty went upstairs to the washroom and cleaned himself up. He had blood on his blade, blood on his hands and his jacket. He wiped the leather clean of the bloodstains, and lovingly cleaned off the knife.

There was no thought of going back to the movie after a rumble like that. The Barons hadn't really given a damn about seeing that flick; it had only been a pretext for the rumble. And now on, the Dragons would think twice before they tried to interfere with the right of the Barons to cross the tracks and see movies at the Orpheum.

Within ten minutes, everyone had returned. There was beer in the icebox, and there was stronger stuff as well. Jolly Roger, who was so tall that no one who didn't know him questioned his age, had driven into the next town and bought a few bottles of whiskey for the victory celebration. But Marty preferred beer. The hard stuff was okay for those who liked it, but it was lousy for the reflexes, and Marty lived by his reflexes.

He looked around. No Baron had been seriously wounded. Four of them, including Big Henry, had minor cuts. Three more had lumps and bruises. Jolly Roger's hand was puffing up where the tire chain had struck it. But all of them would survive. There hadn't been a single major casualty among the Barons.

Marty grinned. "That was okay, huh? We iced five of them. Five Dragons dead, and not one of us hurt bad!"

But somehow there didn't seem to be the right spirit in the place, Marty thought. They should have been exhilarated. After a rumble like that, they should have been soaring way up to the stratosphere with kicks. Instead, everybody seemed quiet, sort of stunned.

"Hey! What's the matter with you guys?" Marty demanded. "This a funeral or something? A rumble like that, and you ain't satisfied? You're sitting around here like you're in church!"

Nobody answered. Marty remembered how they had looked when the rumble was at its hottest. They had been grinning, alive with the joy of cutting and slashing. But something had gone out of them on the way home from Dragon turf. Each man had gone his own way, and they had cooled down when left alone to think.

They all looked beat. Scared. Worn out. Pale. Worried.

"Let's live it up!" Marty yelled. "We got whiskey, beer, girls ..."

Big Henry shook his head, He seemed to be speaking for all of them as he said, "We overdid it, Marty. We shouldn't have cooled them like that. We shoulda just cut 'em up, not killed. The cops are sure to come around and make trouble for us now. We can't get away with it."

"To hell with the cops," Marty snapped. "If they come around here, we'll cool them, too. We're the Barons, remember?"

"But we shouldn't have killed so many," Big Henry protested quietly.

Marty glared at him, then at all the rest. "Listen to me, you lousy punks! You guys didn't kill nobody, hear? I killed them! Me! Marty Capuano! I iced every one of those five guys! I saw you lousy, chicken bastards—cutting up arms, legs, making cheesy little scratches! Why the hell didn't you go for the gut? For the throat? I didn't teach you to noodle around!"

"The rumble's all over, Marty," said Jolly Roger, in a quiet voice. "Ease off, man. Let's just cool it a while, now."

Scowling, Marty turned away, went into the kitchen, got himself a beer.

"Okay," he said when he came back. "We calm down, if that's what you want. I'm gonna do my quieting down upstairs with a nice, juicy broad."

Marty looked around. They still had that sheepish look. The victory party was getting off to a lousy start.

The bloodlust still raged through Marty. He was angry, mad through and through at these lousy, chicken-livered punks who went out to a rumble and then came home sick to their yellow guts because they had drawn enemy blood. Marty was still high as a kite on kill-kicks; way up there, and looking for trouble.

He hadn't figured this would happen. But he saw now he should have expected it. This wasn't New York. These kids were the toughest that Jenkinsville had, but they hadn't been raised in the Manhattan jungle. They weren't killers, and Marty couldn't make them killers.

They were soft at the core. They talked big, but they went chicken when it counted.

Marty spat. Jojo was in the corner, waiting for him to take her upstairs and toss her around a little. But he didn't want to ball Jojo now. There was nothing new and exciting about Jojo any more. He knew her all over, every single inch of her flesh, and the kick was gone.

She seemed to be reading his mind, because she got up and came across the room toward him. The party was starting to liven up. The whiskey and beer began to flow, and the Barons started to drown their memories of the violence they had participated in earlier that evening.

Jojo stood very close to Marty, so close that the huge globes of her breasts grazed the front of his shirt. She was breathing hard. She had hot pants, Marty knew. But she was going to have to find somebody else to cool her off, tonight. He was planning to plow other pastures.

Breasts rising and falling excitedly, Jojo said, "The rumble was great. You're the greatest, Marty. I got all hot inside when I saw you cooling those Dragons off. I wanted to rip my clothes off and grab you and get with it right there in all that blood, right out in the open."

"Yeah?" Marty asked without interest.

"You're really the most, man. And this is gonna be the greatest night we ever had, you and your Jojo."

"That so?"

She didn't seem to hear. "Let's go upstairs, Marty. You and me. We'll wail all night. We'll do it a dozen times. I want you to take me, flatten me, do whatever you want with me, Marty."

She was practically foaming at the mouth. She was so close to him that he could feel her hard nipples pressing against him, and behind them the firm bulk of her breasts. But he wasn't hungry for Jojo's boobs tonight.

"Well?" she asked. "Come on, let's go upstairs."

"No."

"No, what? You mean, later? Yeah, okay ... you want to enjoy the party some first. Okay, I understand that, Marty ..."

"No, you don't understand, babe. I mean not now, and not later, either."

"Not now and not later? But ... when, Marty?"

"Never."

"Never?" Her lip trembled. "You ... you're through with me?"

Marty nodded calmly. "It's all over, Jojo. I told you last night, I'd let you know when I got tired of you. Well, I'm telling you now, I've had it."

"But I been waiting all night for you! Watching you ice those Dragons, waiting to go upstairs with you and ..."

"Tough."

"Marty!" she wailed.

Others in the room were looking at them now, trying to hear what they were saying. Marty took a step backward. Jojo looked pale and bewildered.

"You dumping me, Marty?"

"You figured it right."

"I won't let you! I need you, Marty! I gotta have you! You can't dump me! You ..."

"*Shut up!*" he said.

His left hand shot out, caught her by the shoulder, held her fast. His other hand darted out and slapped her, not across the face but across the tender, thrusting mounds of her breasts. His palm cracked sharply, stingingly, against the delicate nipples, and he laughed as he hit her.

Stunned by the pain, Jojo recoiled, clutching her breasts. Marty chuckled. It was always more effective, slapping those oversized knobs, than hitting her in the face.

He turned away from her and looked across the room at Mary Anne.

She was sitting on the rickety old couch, next to Tom Brewster. Brewster had his arm around her, clipping one of her breasts. She was wearing a skintight silk jersey-blouse that revealed the contours of her breasts and even her nipples, and her skirt was hiked midway up her thighs. Her eyes were half-closed. Marty smiled. Brewster was getting her good and hot, but he didn't know that he was heating her up not for himself but for Marty Capuano. Her lips were parted and her golden-blonde hair was tousled and windblown, and the hand tight on her breast was sending tingling shafts of desire through her—desire which Marty soon would be quenching.

He smiled. In front of all of them—the whole Baron outfit, including Jojo and Brewster—Marty said, "You there. Mary Anne. Let's go upstairs and wail together for a while, just you and me, huh?"

All of a sudden, there was a big loud silence in the clubroom. Jojo, standing flat against the door, was white-faced; her lips trembled, tears stood out in her eyes. What Marty was doing now was hurting her a lot more than those slaps across her boobs had.

As for Mary Anne, she opened her eyes fast when she heard her name called out. She looked surprised, startled, but she was too smart to open her mouth. She knew the gang code. This was between Marty and Tom, and she'd belong to the winner.

Brewster slowly straightened up, taking his time about withdrawing his hand from Mary Anne's breast.

He said in a soft voice, "You got your own girl Capuano. You got no cause to mess around with mine. You keep away from Mary Anne, hear?"

"You gonna stop me?"

"If I have to, I will," Brewster said. "You may be boss of this gang, but you ain't gonna tell me how to run my life. Go give Jojo a toot if you feel horny."

"I've had it with Jojo. You can take her for yourself. I want Mary Anne now."

"I can't buy that, Marty." Brewster looked tense, worried. "I warn you ..."

"Yeah. Go on. Warn me."

"Keep ... away ... from Mary Anne!"

Marty shrugged. He looked at Mary Anne. She sat motionless. Marty jerked his thumb toward the stairs. "Let's go, Mary Anne. Let's go upstairs and have some fun."

"Don't listen to him," Brewster told the girl.

The room was silent. Big Henry, Jolly Roger, Nick Lorrey, all the Barons and their debs were watching to see what was going to happen, whether or not Brewster would be able to get away with defying Marty.

Brewster stood up slowly, and broke the silence. He said, "Capuano, don't try to give me a bad time. You're a big man, and you killed a bunch of guys tonight, but don't think you own the whole world, 'cause you don't."

"I take what I want. So far, nobody's been able to stop me. You wanta try?"

"You ain't laying your filthy paws on Mary Anne, that's for sure!" Brewster shot back at him, bunching his fists threateningly.

"Try and stop me," said Marty, his voice cold and menacing.

He crossed the room in three quick bounds, and reached out for the girl's arm to pull her off the couch. He grabbed her and got one hand on a full, ripe breast. Nice stuff, there. But a second later, Brewster sidestepped to force his way between Marty and the girl.

Brewster's hand went into his pocket and came out holding a switchblade. He nudged the button. There was the click of an emerging blade. The point of the knife was no more than six inches from Marty's throat.

Big Henry came toward the two of them, muttering hoarsely, "Geez, Tom, put that sticker away! This is the clubhouse, man. Don't fight in here!"

Brewster shook his head. "I don't give a damn where we are. Capuano's not gonna touch my woman. Not without arguing with my knife first. You hear me, Capuano?"

"I hear you," Marty said.

He smiled, the smile rippling slowly across his face from one corner of his mouth to the other. This showdown had been a long time in the making, a long time building up. Marty was glad the time had finally come.

He stepped back to put some distance between his neck and Brewster's blade, and flipped out his own knife—the knife that no more than an hour before had been red with the blood of vanquished Dragons.

Jolly Roger broke the shocked pall. "Marty, for the love of—"

"Shut up!"

"Don't do it; Marty. Don't make a stand in the clubhouse!"

Marty glared witheringly at Jolly Roger. "Who the hell you think you're telling how to run his business, big man? You want to stand up here with your knife when I'm done with Brewster?"

"Look, Marty ..."

"Shut up! Shut your stinking, blubber-lipped mouth, you hear?"

Roger's eyes gleamed angrily for a moment, but the gleam died away. He muttered something inaudible.

Everyone backed away from the couch, giving Marty and Brewster the whole center of the room to themselves.

Brewster was pale, waxy-looking, and little beads of sweat were rolling down out of his rumpled hair and along the sides of his cheeks. He gripped the butt of his blade so tightly that his hand shook.

"I'm gonna shred you up like so much cabbage, man," Marty said mockingly, grinning up at the taller boy. "And then I'm gonna take that pretty deb of yours upstairs, and I'm gonna give her the balling of her life."

"You talk a lot, Capuano."

"I mean what I say."

Round and round they circled each other, warily, balancing lithely on their heels, until three full circuits of the room had been completed. Then Marty decided it was time to make his move. He laughed—the rattle of a snake about to strike—and shot out his arm.

It was a lightning-like inward dart, blindingly fast. Brewster never had a chance. He never even saw what happened. Marty's knife licked out like a flickering metal tongue, and a ribbon of blood sprouted along Brewster's bare right arm from the elbow halfway to the wrist. Brewster howled as the pain cut like fire into him, but he held onto his knife.

"That was just the first one," Marty said. "There's lots more coming."

Confident, as he had been from the start, Marty circled him. Brewster, Marty knew instinctively, was helpless now; the cut that had been inflicted was only a flesh wound, but it had injected the poison of fear into Brewster, and he would be unable now to defend himself from Marty's thrusts. From here on out, it would be just a game of cat-and-mouse.

A second time, Marty feinted and slipped his blade inside Brewster's guard, aiming upward to draw a bloody line across the taller boy's cheek, just below his right eye.

"Next one goes *into* that eye instead of *under* it, Tommy-boy."

Brewster backed up warily. Blood streamed from his face and arm, making him seem a lot more seriously wounded than he really was. He held his knife up, making a pretense of defending himself, but it was like trying to defend against a bolt of lightning, and he knew it.

Marty weaved into the death-dance now, as he had done so many times before, shifting the knife dazzlingly from hand to hand, grinning cheerfully up at the panicky Brewster, and whistling softly to himself. Marty glanced meaningfully at Brewster's eyes, as if taking aim, while he cruised around the room readying for the final stroke, the death blow.

Then Brewster cracked.

He tossed his knife down on the rug and covered his face with his hands, then dropped to the floor, huddling himself up and sobbing wildly, uncontrollably.

"He ain't human! He'll kill me with that goddamn knife! He'll kill us all, one at a time! Make him leave me alone!"

Marty looked down scornfully. "Get up and pick up your knife, Brewster."

Brewster shivered. "Leave me alone, Marty. I don't want to die."

"Are *you* chicken, Brewster?" Marty contemptuously nudged the cowering, huddled shape with his toe. "Chick-chick? You chick-chick, big man?"

"Yeah," Brewster moaned hollowly. "I'm chicken. That's what you want me to say, isn't it? Now, get away from me! Leave me alone, Capuano!"

"I thought you were gonna put me in my place, Brewster. What happened? You blew your cool huh?"

Brewster didn't answer, nor even look up at Marty.

Marty laughed. "Get out of here, you chicken! We got no room for chickie-chicks in the Barons. Get out, and stay out!"

CHAPTER NINE

Marty folded his arms and waited. After a moment, Brewster uncertainly got to his feet, wobbling a little. He stared at Marty with eyes like blank glass beads, then turned to peer at the silent, watching Barons.

Mary Anne met his glance without interest. Most of the others looked away when Brewster's eyes came to rest on theirs.

Brewster looked like a dead man. He swayed for a moment, glanced down at the knife where it lay on the rug, and sobbed something deep and unintelligible in his throat. Then he turned suddenly and dashed out the clubhouse door.

Marty's harsh, derisive laughter followed him out. "Chicken-baby! Run home fast, chickie-chick!"

He closed the door and turned to face the others. Jojo was staring at him with cold, thin-lipped hatred. To hell with Jojo, he thought. Jojo had had it.

Marty said, "Anybody mind if I make a little switch? I'm breaking up with Jojo. Anybody who wants her can have her. From now on I'm making it with Mary Anne."

There were no objections from the Barons. Somehow, Marty hadn't expected any.

He grabbed Mary Anne's wrist.

"Let's go upstairs," he said.

She rose from the couch like an obedient puppet, and, without releasing his grip on her wrist, Marty led her up the stairs, down the hall, into his private fun room.

He locked the door. She stood by the bed, arms dangling limply.

"Ever been in here before?" he asked her.

"No, Marty."

"Are you glad you're in here now? Glad you'll be making it with the boss of this outfit?"

"Yeah, Marty."

He nodded. The girl was pale, and she was afraid of him, but she didn't seem to resent what he had done to Brewster—or else she was hiding it pretty well.

Marty said, "How long were you Brewster's deb?"

"A year and a half."

"Who'd you belong to before that?"

"Nobody before that," she said quietly. "Tommy was the one who brought me into the Barons."

"Is he the one who busted your cherry, too?"

A blush crept up her pale, delicate face. "No. There was one guy before him."

"Who?"

"He doesn't matter."

"Who was it, anyway?"

"His name was Freddy. We used to play together. One day we went swimming in the river ... without swimsuits."

"You went swimming B. A. Okay. And what did your pal Freddy do?"

"When we came out of the water he was all ... excited. I'd never seen a boy that way before. So big, and all. And then he said he wanted to show me something. We were still both naked. He said it would be fun. So I went over to him, and he made me lie down, and he got on top of me. I thought he wanted to wrestle, so I started to grab him, and he grabbed me, and he pushed my legs apart, and all of a sudden ..." Mary Anne shrugged. "All of a sudden he had me. Just like that."

"Hurt?"

"Like blazes. But he wouldn't let me up till he was through. He kept on and on. I was sore afterward, and mad as hell at him for hurting me. But a couple days later he got to me again, and it was more fun that time. After that we did it a lot—all that summer— until one day, Freddy's father caught us."

Marty whistled. He enjoyed hearing these stories from his women. "What happened then? Fireworks, I bet."

"He pulled us apart—both stark naked—and started hitting me. Hitting *me*, not Freddy; slapping my behind, my knockers, everything. And then he made me get dressed, and he took me home and told my parents what we'd been doing. So my father pulled up my dress and pulled down my panties and strapped my bare behind in front of my whole family, in front of my brothers and everything. I didn't see Freddy anymore after that. I wasn't allowed to. But the next year I met Tommy, and he told me about the Baron Debs, and I came around and joined."

Her story interested him. It was the old one of the girl who starts playing around too young, who catches hell from her parents for it, and who reacts by playing around even more. Most likely, Mary Anne would never have joined the Baron Debs if she hadn't been whipped for making out with Freddy. Parents are so dumb, Marty thought.

But he figured there had been just about enough talking for now. "We can shoot the breeze some more later," Marty said. "Strip."

He slipped out of his leather jacket and parked his knife on the edge of the dresser. He watched her. She was a couple of inches taller than he was, but he didn't mind that too much in a girl, anyway.

She peeled off the skin-tight blouse. She wasn't wearing anything underneath. Her breasts were ripe, full, standing out by themselves without need of any kind of support. They weren't big cow-boobs like Jojo had, but all the same they were far from skinny. Because Mary Anne was a natural blonde, her skin was milk-white, almost incredibly transparent. The rosy circles of her nipples stood out in stark contrast to the whiteness of her breasts.

She paused, half-naked, uncertain and uneasy. Embarrassment flooded through her, causing a delicate reddening of the entire upper half of her body.

I'll be only the third guy she's ever balled, Marty thought. *She's practically a virgin, compared to most of them.*

He grinned appreciatively. "That's nice to look at, what you got sticking out there. Go on, kid, take the rest of it off. Then we can have some fun, you and me. I'll show you some tricks old Brewster never heard of."

Her hands went to the button of her skirt. Marty waited, feeling the excitement thunder up inside him, the way it always did as he waited for his first look at a new girl's nude body. Sure, they all looked alike in the dark—but there was something about the first stunning revelation of thighs and hips and buttocks and breasts that never failed to send a welcome tingle through Marty's loins.

She unzipped the skirt, pushed it down over her hips, and started to step out of it. Marty was thinking that this kid would do just fine as a replacement for Jojo for a while—say, seven or eight weeks. And when he got tired of Mary Anne, he could always move on and make a play for one of the other debs—that kid Sally with the big rear end, maybe, or that tough-looking, lean little Maybelle. He'd work his way right through the whole damn bunch of them, discarding each one as soon as he lost interest in her. No one in the gang would dare say no, after the way he'd fixed Brewster.

Mary Anne draped her skirt over the back of a chair and rolled her panties down over her hips. Her sandals followed, and then she was completely nude.

She stood tensely, obviously ill at ease and embarrassed, as Marty looked her over.

"You're okay," he said.

Her pale body was beautifully fashioned—and probably still had greater beauty to come, since she was still in her teens. Her shoulders were wide, above her full breasts; and from there her body tapered to a breathtakingly small waist, then flared out again at the full, fleshy hips, then tapered again along the alabaster columns of her legs. She was softly rounded, with no projecting ribs or hip bones as Jojo had. The light golden triangle where her legs joined her body glimmered.

"You're okay," he said again. "Very much okay."

"You like?"

"Sure, I like. Come here."

She went to him, moving nervously. He said, "There's nothing to be scared of, kid."

"I'm still a little shook up about … about Tom."

"Don't be. Forget him. You saw the way he chickened out. He wasn't worth a doll like you, Mary Anne."

He guided her fingers to the buttons on his shirt. She helped him off with it; then, of her own accord, she started to unbuckle his belt and unzip his pants.

They sank down naked onto the mattress together. Her skin was incredibly smooth, and her soft golden hair smelled like fresh-cut grass. His hand roamed up her body, pausing for a moment at her hip, then sweeping up the sleek white skin to gather in the gently quivering swell of her young bosom.

She was stiff, tense. But Marty stroked her body tenderly, easing all the fear and nervousness out of her.

"It's funny," she whispered.

"What is?"

"The way you can be so mean and harsh when you've got a knife in your hand, and then be so nice and gentle now."

"I play a different game with a knife than with a woman," he said.

His hands parted her cool thighs and found the source of her passion. She shivered at his caress. "Sorry about Tommy?" he asked.

"Don't talk about him."

"But you like it, making it with the boss of the Barons?"

"I don't know … yeah, sure … only I'm afraid of you, Marty."

"Don't be."

"But what happens when you get tired of me, the way you got tired of Jojo?"

"I'm not tired of you, baby. I haven't even got to know you yet."

"But when …"

"Let's not worry about that, for a long time to come."

"Sure, Marty." Her voice deepened as the increasing throbs of desire went coursing through her body, the hormones doing things in her bloodstream, speeding up her heart, dilating her eyes, heating up her loins.

"Think you're ready?" he asked.

"Ready as I'm ever going to be."

She grasped his waist and pulled him over on top of her, and the next moment their bodies met and joined, and they clung together. Marty could feel her stiff little nipples jabbing into his skin, and he sensed the steadily mounting tempo of her pounding heart. He grinned confidently, knowing he could handle a woman as flawlessly as he handled a knife. They speeded up, reaching a climactic frenzy; her lips parted, and a hoarse cry of requited lust came forth. She lifted her head, sank her teeth lightly into his shoulder, and then suddenly she fell back—limp, fulfilled.

When it was over, Marty pillowed his head on her high-peaked breasts.

She said softly, dreamily, distantly, "I never felt quite like that before."

"You never made it with me before, that's all," he said.

"It's the greatest!"

"Wait a little while, and we'll do it again," Marty said. "And again and again and again."

"Did I hurt you with my teeth?"

"Uh-uh."

"I was afraid I might; but I just had to bite down on something, I got so turned on. You know how it is, Marty?"

"Yeah. Sure, I know how it is."

She was silent a moment. Then she said, "You must have made it with a lot of girls before me, huh, Marty?"

"You think I was a virgin?"

"No, I mean, like there must have been so many. How many girls you think you've made it with, Marty?"

"How the hell should I know?"

"Can't you guess?"

"Fifty, sixty, a hundred, maybe." He closed his eyes, remembering.

It was about six years since he'd had his first piece, and there'd been all kinds since then. Gang girls, good girls, white girls, Negro girls, even a few Orientals. Girls whose families were Puerto Rican, Irish, Italian, German, Polish, Mexican; Catholic, Jewish, Protestant and Atheist. Willing girls and unwilling girls. Tall ones and short ones. Girls who just barely had any boobs at all, and girls who weren't really girls anymore, but mature women.

Marty remembered the first one best of all. He wasn't even five feet tall yet, but his voice had changed, and he was a wiry little tough guy who didn't take any garbage from anyone.

He wasn't even a Junior Shining Baron then, just a neighborhood kid. And one of the other kids, Joey Michelucci, came running up to him one afternoon and said, "Hey, Marty, you wanna have some fun?"

It seemed that a bunch of the Shining Barons—the old bunch, now all in their twenties—had got this girl in the clubhouse, and she was putting out for everybody. So when the Barons had enough, they started inviting all the younger kids in the neighborhood to come grab themselves a piece while it was available. She wasn't a whore, exactly—just a girl who wasn't quite right in the head. She had a good body, but she didn't care who did what to her. Crazy Sarah, they called her in the neighborhood. She was around twenty.

So Marty and Joey Michelucci went into the Baron's clubhouse, and there were twenty or thirty guys standing around, and Crazy Sarah was lying naked on the bed with her legs apart. She had her eyes closed, and a kind of goofy smile on her face, and her big breasts were going up and down real fast.

Marty stood there listening to the older boys talking—his heroes, the Shining Barons, who were in their late teens then. Carmine Rinuccio, Ned Flaherty, Sean Ryan, Sal Santiliquido. Most of them were dead or in jail now, except for a few who were married or in Viet Nam—Marty didn't know which were worst off.

He heard the story. Crazy Sarah had been in the clubhouse all day. She'd already been had forty or fifty times. Some of the guys had been with her as many as three rounds.

When Marty walked in, nobody was making it with her, and Crazy Sarah called out without opening her eyes, "Who's next, huh? It's cold here without no clothes on."

Charlie Vengilano stepped forward and opened his pants. While he was giving it to her, Sal Santiliquido saw Marty, and yelled out, "Hey, here's little Marty Capuano. Let's let him have next turn!"

"He's cherry," somebody else said scornfully.

Marty reddened. "There's always a first time," he retorted. "All you guys were cherry once too, you know."

There was applause and cheerings at that, and it was decided that Marty would get next turn with Crazy Sarah. In a few minutes Charlie Vengilano got up from the bed with a satisfied look on his face, and Marty moved forward. He was scared, but he didn't let it show. He had never done this before, but he had a pretty good idea of what he was supposed to do.

He unzipped his trousers and got down between Crazy Sarah's big, meaty thighs. And he started. It all went okay. He was with Crazy Sarah more than ten minutes, while she moaned with delight, and the older Barons went wild with admiration over little Marty's performance. Finally he finished and got up from her and straightened his pants.

Everyone crowded around to shake his hand and congratulate him, and that was the way Marty embarked on manhood. He had Crazy Sarah twice more before nightfall, and then she got sick and had to go home, and the party was over.

As he lay next to Mary Anne remembering this, she said, "How come you're so quiet, Marty?"

"Thinking."

"About me?"

"About the first broad I ever had."

"Think about me, instead."

"Sure," he said.

He reached out and grabbed her breasts and pulled her to him. Her legs opened and he took her, and they began the ritual of lust again.

CHAPTER TEN

It was long after midnight when Marty decided he'd had enough of Mary Anne for one night. She was still hot and hungry for more, but Marty wasn't. He had his limits, and a man's limits are generally reached before a woman's, if the woman is eager for loving. Marty was willing to bet that in a couple of hours in the sack, he had completely blotted out all her memories of Tom Brewster.

They dressed and went downstairs. The place was practically empty. Only Big Henry was left; sitting in the corner nursing a tall can of beer.

Marty frowned. "Everyone gone?"

"Pretty near. Nick and Maureen are in one of the rooms upstairs.

Outside of them, the place is dead."

Standing by the door, Mary Anne said, "Are you going to walk me home, Marty?"

"Let her go by herself," Big Henry said. "I gotta talk to you."

Marty shrugged. "The man says he's gotta talk to me, Mary Anne. You better go on by yourself."

"Okay, Marty. Good night. And sweet dreams, lover-man."

"Yeah. Sweet dreams."

He nodded to her, and she blew a kiss and left. Marty turned to Big Henry. Big Henry said unsmilingly, "Sounds like you made a big impression on her up there."

"We had a pretty hot time upstairs, yeah," Marty agreed, sitting down with his legs straddling a turned-around chair. "That kid has a lot of talent she didn't even know she had. What you want to talk to me about, Henry?"

"What happened tonight."

"What about it?"

"It was no good, Marty."

"You gonna start giving me that crap again, man? Listen, you wanna be a preacher, you go sign up at the nearest church, hear? Don't bug me anymore, man. The rumble too much for you?"

"Not only the rumble. What you did to Brewster, too."

"What you talking about?"

"You took his girl away, and you made a fool of him, right in front of all of us," Big Henry said. "I'm giving it to you straight from the shoulder, Marty. That's no way to do things."

Anger blazed in Marty's eyes. "You looking for a fight?"

"Think with your brains instead of your knife, just this once," Big Henry said. "I know you can cut me to pieces, and I don't want you to try to prove it. But have you ever figured that Brewster might go to the cops? Tell them all about the rumble, and maybe about the Thompson job and Charley Beck, too?"

"He was in the rumble himself," Marty muttered. "He wouldn't talk."

"State's evidence never gets it very hard in a J. D. prosecution. He could sing and sing and sing. You were a fool to let him walk out of here, Marty."

"He won't talk."

Big Henry shrugged. "Maybe, maybe not. But you're taking a chance. Anyway, I want to say something else to you."

"Say it, then. I want to get home."

"You're a wizard with that knife, Marty. But you aren't making many friends."

"What are you driving at?"

"Charley Beck was pretty damned popular in the Barons. You iced him. Tom Brewster was a good guy too, and you just broke him apart."

"You tellin' me how to run things?"

"I'm tellin' you that you might be in for trouble if you keep on—taking other guys' debs whenever you take a liking to 'em, throwing 'em away when you get tired of 'em. That rumble, too. Hell, most of us didn't figure we'd do so much bopping. We weren't figuring on killing five guys!"

"Get to the point, man."

"The point is … that some of the Barons don't like you, Marty."

"Who?"

"I don't mean anybody in particular. I mean deep down, underneath. And one of these days they might start showing it. Just a word of warning, man. Why not slow the pace down a little? Me and Roger, we're with you. We think you're the greatest, you know? But we gotta warn you to ease up a little. We still ain't used to the New York way of doing things, see?"

Marty nodded slowly. "Okay, okay. I get what you mean."

"And you agree?"

"I'll think about it. Meantime, I got a job for you."

"Yeah?"

"Tomorrow, sometime. You and Nick and Lew pay a visit to Brewster, quiet-like. Don't rough him up too much. Just pass him the word that if he keeps quiet and forgets all about us, he'll stay healthy; but if he squeals, he'll land in the river."

Big Henry frowned. "Rough him up? But—"

"We'll all get busted if he talks," Marty said. "You and me and Roger, especially."

"Yeah, Marty."

"So take care of him, hear?"

"Yeah, Marty."

"Okay, then. Don't lose your cool, Henry. I'll see you around."

Marty got home around quarter to two. There was a light on upstairs, in his brother's room. Marty went up the staircase and into his own room without bothering about Frankie.

Marty started to undress. While he was hanging up his shirt, the door opened and Frankie came in, naked except for his underpants.

Marty looked up. "You're staying up kinda late tonight, huh, kid?"

"I had a date. I just got back about fifteen minutes ago."

"Date, huh? With who?"

"Girl named Janet. I met her last Friday."

"Does she put out?" Marty asked. "How are her knockers?"

"I didn't investigate," Frankie said scornfully. "She isn't that kind of girl."

"Somehow none of the girls you go out with seem to be *that kind of girl*," Marty said. "Ain't it time you went out and got yourself one who'll put out for you? What the hell, you gonna save it till you get married?"

"I didn't come in here to talk about my sex life, Marty."

"Oh?"

"I came in because I heard there was a rumble in town tonight."

"Do tell! Where'd you pick up that choice morsel of gossip?"

"It's all over town. I heard it when I came out of the movie tonight. Two gangs had a rumble on an empty lot. Five kids got killed, and some more went to the hospital."

Marty started to get into his pajamas. "I think that's shocking," he said. "Terrible. It proves that mob violence isn't just limited to New York, though, don't it?"

"I know you were mixed up in that fight, Marty. You probably killed those five guys yourself."

"You *know*, huh? Did you see me there?"

"I don't have any definite proof. But I know that if there was a rumble tonight, you were in it."

"What the hell business is it of yours?"

Frankie scowled. "This isn't just a little thing like vandalism, like busting up a bar, Marty. *Five guys got killed tonight.* In a town like this that's a regular massacre. There's bound to be a big investigation."

"So?"

"So you'll be questioned. And maybe you'll get sent to jail, or even executed."

"Wouldn't you just love that?"

"I sure would. But I don't want to see it happen, because it would kill Ma and Pa." Frankie shook his head. "Listen, Marty, I got a proposition for you."

"What kind of proposition?"

"I got a hundred bucks saved. You can have it all, on condition that you take off."

"Take off? You mean, like, blow town?"

"Yeah. Just pack up and leave, right now. You can write a note saying you're tired of the life you've been leading here, and you've gone off to enlist in the Army. You don't have to really enlist. You don't have to do a goddamn thing. All I want you to do is vanish and stay vanished, to spare Ma and Pa all the heartache of worrying about you."

"Ain't that sweet! I should go be a tramp so they won't worry!"

"It's better than making them nervous wrecks, waiting for you to come home every night, and all the time wondering if maybe you're already in jail, or all cut up, or even lying dead on a street somewhere."

"Keep your lousy hundred bucks. I'm not going anywhere."

"But—"

"You hear me? I said it's no deal. Now get out of here, baby brother, and let me sleep."

After one more attempt to persuade him, Frankie left. Marty got into bed and switched off the lamp.

He felt pretty good about making out so well with Mary Anne, and he thought the rumble had gone off perfectly. He wondered whether a not Brewster would spill. There would be big trouble if he did.

Marty woke about eleven the next morning. It was Sunday, and the house was quiet.

He went downstairs and saw that the others had already had breakfast. They ignored him, as though he had some kind of plague.

Then he saw the town paper, spread out on the table—and the headline, big and black and conspicuous:

FIVE DEAD IN TEEN GANG WAR

Marty sat down and looked at the story. It read:

A pitched battle between two teenage gangs left five dead and two seriously wounded last night. The encounter took place in a vacant lot at Marshall and Harrison Streets, about 8:30 p.m.

When police officers arrived on the scene, all participants who were still on their feet dispersed, and none were apprehended.

THE DEAD INCLUDED:

Mack C. Lardner, 19, son of Mr. and Mrs. Noah B. Lardner of 302 Aldiss Place.

Jerome D. Thomas, 17, son of Mrs. Bessie L. Thomas of 1779 Midland Avenue.

Roy J. Billinson, 17, son of Mr. and Mrs. Thomas S. Billinson of 4111 Fortnam Road.

Charles E. Lee, 16, son of Mr. and Mrs. David K. Lee of 1663 Hooker Street.

Michael T. Riddle, 18, son of Mrs. Martin B. Riddle of 2170 Chelsey Street.

Taken to St. Joseph's Hospital in critical condition were

Brian J. Lees, 17, of 1968 Patterson St., and Paul R. Kelsey, 18, of 2002 Patterson Street.

This latest outbreak of violence brought the following comment from Police Chief John Nathanson: "We will do everything in our power to apprehend the culprits and restore law and order in Jenkinsville. We ..."

Marty put the paper down. It was the same old jazz, the police making big promises and then failing to do anything.

Mrs. Capuano came into the room. She said, "There's some coffee on the stove, Marty. You slept too late to have breakfast with the family."

"You could have waited."

"Don't talk back to me, Marty!"

"Sorry, Ma," he mumbled.

The telephone rang. For a moment nobody spoke or moved. The Capuano family hardly ever got telephone calls.

"I'll get it," Frankie said.

As Frankie hastened to the telephone alcove near the front door, Marty remained rooted to the spot, thinking: It's the fuzz. They're calling up to tell me they want to ask me some questions about the rumble last night. That punk Brewster must have spilled everything.

Then Marty relaxed. Even in a jerkwater town like Jenkinsville, the cops wouldn't be dumb enough to phone up and make an appointment for an arrest. They'd just come around and pick him up, if they suspected him of being involved in a fracas that left five corpses.

Frankie returned from the phone. "It's for you, Marty."

"For me?"

"That's what I said. You getting deaf?"

"Just that I don't hardly get many phone calls," Marty said. "Who is it?"

"Didn't say."

Shrugging, Marty walked to the telephone alcove and picked up the receiver.

"Hello?"

"Marty?"

"Yeah. Who's that?"

"Big Henry."

Marty was relieved. "What is it, man?"

"It's about Brewster."

Marty tensed again. "What about him? He squealed?"

"Nah, nothing like that. It's just that me and Nick and Lew went over to his place this morning, like you told us to."

"You warn him about squealing?"

"Nope. He wasn't there. I talked to his folks, though. Seems he up and split sometime in the middle of the night. Left a note saying he was tired of Jenkinsville, and he was going to Cleveland to enlist in the Marine Corps."

"You're kidding!"

"So help me, that's what they told me. I made out we was just coming around for a social-type visit, you know. His old lady was all shook up about it. Said she couldn't understand why he'd run off like that. I didn't give her no hints, neither."

"So he's gone," Marty said. He felt his heart give a happy thump. There was no need to worry now that Brewster would squeal. Marty led a charmed life. "I guess he couldn't hack the idea of facing life in Jenkinsville after what happened to him last night."

"Guess not," Big Henry agreed. "You see the paper this morning?"

"Yeah."

"Big fuss, hey?"

"Sure is."

"We better cool it for a while, Marty, till the heat's off. It's a good idea to stay away from the clubhouse, and keep away from each other for a while, until Nathanson and his goons forget all about the rumble."

"Good idea. Spread the word around, okay?"

"Will do."

"Any other news?"

"The cops have been roaming around all over town this morning," Big Henry said, "but they don't know where to begin picking guys up, Brewster might have been a big help to them."

"Too bad he isn't around to give them a few leads," Marty said. "There anything else?"

"Nope."

"See you around, then."

"Yeah. See you around."

Marty hung up and walked back into the other room. His family was looking at him with interest. They were dying to know who he had been talking to, but they were all too afraid of getting him angry to ask.

"Friend of mine," Marty said noncommittally, and went into the kitchen to fix himself some breakfast.

The heat died down, as Big Henry had predicted, later in the week. The newspapers still carried stories about the massacre, but the articles got smaller and smaller. A few teenagers were picked up by the police and questioned, but they claimed they knew nothing about the gang rumble. The two boys in the hospital were questioned too, but they refused to give the police any pertinent information. They knew only too well what would happen if they sang, either about their own gang or about the Barons. Gang kids didn't sing to the cops. They protected their own kind, even if they were protecting deadly enemies.

After a couple of days, it was safe for the Barons to start using their clubhouse again. If anyone asked, they were a social and athletic club, like any one of a dozen other teenage clubs in town. That was harmless enough. On the surface, you couldn't tell a club from a gang, unless you happened to know that the Barons were not exactly social-and-athletic-minded.

Marty continued to make out—plenty—with Mary Anne.

Jojo seemed to be resigned to her fate, because in the middle of the week she showed up with a new fellow named Ted Dombrow, announced that he was shacking with her and that he wanted to become a probationary member of the Barons. He was admitted at the end of the week, taking the place that Brewster had vacated. Membership in the Barons was strictly limited to sixteen, and the only way anyone new could get in was to take the place of one of the old members who resigned.

Sex-wise Mary Anne worked out beautifully for Marty. She couldn't get enough of him. She did everything he asked her to do, even some of the specialties. And she was eager to learn.

Maybe it was her very eagerness that made Marty start to get tired of her after only two weeks. She was always available, always willing. Any time Marty wanted her, she opened up for him without complaining. Sometimes Marty preferred to have to coax a girl. But Mary Anne didn't need any coaxing,

He had her upstairs, and he had her downstairs.

One afternoon they made it right in the middle of the main clubroom, just for the hell of it. There were a dozen Barons around them, but Mary Anne was sitting on Marty's lap, and she was wearing a pleated skirt and no panties. He reached under her skirt and felt her warm, white buttocks. He simply arranged her skirt to cover both of them, and opened his pants, and slipped up on her from below. They kept right on talking while they were doing it. And afterward, Marty laughed and said to everyone, "I just made it with Mary Anne while we were sitting here." It was a real kick doing it that way, right in front of everyone, and nobody knowing what was going on.

They made it outdoors behind the clubhouse, and they made it in Mary Anne's living room one night when he took her home and there was nobody around. And one day they went swimming in the river, with Jolly Roger and a couple of the other Barons and their debs. Marty slipped her bikini bottom off, then slid around behind her and grabbed her boobs, and *bam!* They made it right under water. It was one of the greatest.

Mary Anne couldn't get enough. It was amazing, how passionate the dewy-eyed blonde had suddenly become.

But Marty started to get bored with her after a couple of weeks. He started to look around for his next steady piece.

He didn't give Mary Anne any hint of course. He didn't want to do that. But he looked closely at one Baron deb after another, trying to decide which one would be the most likely to please him after Mary Anne.

There were three or four possibilities. But the one he was most interested in was the girl who was going with Big Henry. Laura, her name was. She was a big, solidly built girl, with glistening jet-black hair that swirled down to her shoulders, and breasts that stood out like twin nose cones. Aside from Mary Anne, she was the most attractive girl in the gang. And she was strong and muscular, the kind of girl that could give a guy a real tussle in the hay.

But Marty was a little hesitant about monkeying around with her. She belonged to Big Henry, and Big Henry was one of the top men in the Barons. Not that Marty was afraid of the stocky guy—he knew there was no man alive who could put him down in a man-to-man knife-stand. But Big Henry had always admired and respected Marty, and had been loyal to him. It might not be so smart to kick a loyal lieutenant in the teeth by grabbing his broad.

Still, Marty was tempted. He didn't know what to do. He decided to let things ride along, to hang onto Mary Anne until the occasion presented itself to make a pass at Laura.

The summer moved along. It was late August now, and there was a nip in the night air that told of approaching autumn.

Marty had taken Big Henry's advice about lying low. The Barons had engaged in no new violence since the rumble. The town was just too small for any one group of teenagers to carry on a steady campaign of lawlessness and get away with it indefinitely; sooner or later, the culprits would be identified.

So the Barons played it cool for a while, mostly sticking to their clubhouse and sexing it up and boozing and having some horseplay with each other. There were no stompings, no muggings, no burglaries. Marty was biding his time, waiting for a good moment to assert his power in Jenkinsville once again.

There was no sign of renewed hostility from the Dragons. The bloody rumble had shattered their strength completely. Now it was possible for the Barons to go to movies in Dragon turf any time, without having to face any opposition. Still, they traveled in groups of five or six when they went to the Orpheum, just in case the Dragons got the idea of japping them from an ambush. It didn't play to be overconfident.

One night toward the end of August, Marty went home from the clubhouse early, around nine o'clock. The place had been dead, and he figured there wasn't much percentage sticking around, especially since Mary Anne was down with a summer cold and didn't feel much like making it.

So Marty went home and sat on his front porch for a while. It was a nice night, too nice to stay indoors. Frankie was away at his girlfriend Janet's place, and Ma and Pa were in the living room, watching television.

While Marty sat there, a tall boy he had never seen before came strolling up the street and paused in front of the house.

He looked at Marty. "This is the Capuano house, isn't it?"

"Yeah."

"Are you Marty Capuano?"

"That's right."

The boy came toward him. "Mind if I talk to you a while? My name's Jim Cartwright."

CHAPTER ELEVEN

The name struck a familiar chord in Marty's memory. He frowned, trying to place it, and then he remembered. Jim Cartwright had been Jill Webster's boyfriend—the basketball player, the one she was practically going steady with.

A cold icicle of fear pressed at the back of Marty's neck. He saw again that nude white body, the spread legs, the motionless breasts, the blood-flecked thighs. He leaned forward knotting his hands together tightly. He hadn't expected any visits from Jim Cartwright. Cartwright meant trouble, big trouble—and Marty had figured that the Jill Webster business was ancient history by now.

"Yeah?" Marty said. "Anything I can do for you?"

"I just want to talk," Cartwright said, climbing the porch steps.

He took a seat on the porch railing, facing Marty. Marty sized him up. Cartwright was big and rugged-looking, well over six feet tall, with a frank, open kind of face. He looked like he was about eighteen.

Marty played it as cool as he could, "What do you want to talk about, man?"

"First of all, I guess I ought to tell you who I am. Does the name Jill Webster happen to mean anything to you?"

"Sure, I heard of her." Marty kept his voice steady. "She was that girl who got drowned a while back in the river. Right after I moved into Jenkinsville."

Cartwright nodded. "That's right. She was the girl who was gang-raped over in the woods near the river, and then fell or was pushed into the river, and was found dead. Naked and raped and dead."

"What's your connection?"

"I was very close to Jill. We dated each other casually for years, but during the past year it got serious. We were planning to get engaged when I went away to college in the fall, to Ohio State."

"Oh. Sorry to hear that."

"It damn near tore me apart when I found out what had happened to her," Cartwright said.

"Sure. But why come tell *me* about all this? I didn't know the girl."

"She said you did."

"Huh? You crazy?"

Cartwright shook his head solemnly. "A couple of days before she died, she told me about a guy who'd been bothering her. A guy with an Italian-sounding name, she said. This fellow had just moved into town from New York City, and he'd met her at a bus stop one afternoon and tried to make a date with her. And then, a couple nights later, he phoned her up and tried again to make a date with her, even though she'd already told him she wasn't interested."

Marty shrugged. "I don't know what the hell you're talking about."

"I think you do. You see, Jill told me that this fellow with the Italian-sounding name was quite insistent. I didn't worry about it much, because I knew she'd put him down. Then, when she died, I was so broken up I forgot about him. But lately I've been checking around, and I've asked a lot of questions. There aren't many people in Jenkinsville who have Italian-sounding names, and of all the people who do, only one such family moved into town from New York City this June. Yours,"

Fidgeting, Marty said, "So you been playing detective. What are you trying to prove, anyway?"

"Jill was a virgin till the night she died. I know, because she wanted me to sleep with her, and when I found out for sure she was a virgin, I turned her down. I told her it would be a lot smarter and a lot better all around if we waited till we were married."

"That was damn noble of you," Marty said sarcastically.

"I thought so too," said Cartwright seriously. "I have some pretty strong ideas about the importance of marriage, and all. But then some bastards came along and hauled her out to the woods and pulled her clothes off and forced her. They didn't give a damn that she was a virgin, that they were taking something they had no right to take. You know, if I could find the guys who raped her, I think I'd twist their necks with my own hands until their eyes bugged out."

Marty moistened his lips and took a deep breath to indicate his impatience. "Listen, buddy, I know it was a lousy break for you to have your girlfriend hurt, to lose her like that. But what the hell does all this have to do with me?"

"You tried to date her just before she was raped."

"How do you know that for sure?"

"You've got an Italian name. You moved in at the right time of year."

"I've got a brother. Maybe he was the guy who tried to date your girl."

Cartwright shook his head. "I can't buy that, I checked on him, too. Your brother's name is Frankie, and he's a good bit taller than you. Jill said that the guy who was bugging her was *very* short. So it could only have been you, Marty."

"You've been doing a lot of detective work, haven't you?"

"I guess I have."

Marty took another deep breath. Cartwright had obviously done some careful checking, and it wouldn't be so easy to fool him. He decided to try a different tactic.

"Okay," he said. "Let's knock off all this beating around the bush. I'll admit it. The day I moved to Jenkinsville, I met your girl Jill at a bus stop. She was a looker, and I was brand new in town and wanted to find some company. So I asked her for a date. She said no. Couple days later, I was still feeling lonely. I figured maybe she'd change her mind, so I invested a dime and phoned her. The answer was no again. That was where the matter ended, as far as I was concerned. The next thing I know, they find her floating in the river, and holler rape."

Cartwright looked very pale. He gripped the porch rail tightly, saying nothing.

Marty went on, "There ain't no law against asking a girl for a date, and there ain't no law against phoning her up. I didn't molest her any. All I did was ask. So why'd you come here and bug me about it? You gonna tell me next that it was me who raped her? The police chief decided it must've been some tramps coming through town ..."

"I know what the police chief decided," Cartwright said. "I also know he only said that because he didn't know what else to say."

"And what else should he have said?"

Cartwright ignored that question. "Since the beginning of June,

Capuano, there's been all kinds of trouble in Jenkinsville. We've always had a little crime here, and we've got a lot of tough kids who like to make trouble. But never like this. Aside from Jill, there was a tough kid who mysteriously disappeared, a bar smashed, a lot of muggings and stuff like that, and a big gang fight with several guys killed. The whole town is scared. And it so happens that the beginning of the Jenkinsville crime wave turns out to coincide pretty closely with the date you moved here from New York. And we all know what sort of stuff goes on in New York."

Marty stood up and hung poised on the balls of his feet, staring hard at Cartwright.

"Lemme get this straight. Are you saying that I'm mixed up in all this crap?"

Cartwright shrugged, "Gang kids in New York are famous for raping innocent girls. And it's possible that some guy from New York, who got turned down by a beautiful girl like Jill, might just be sore enough to take her out to the woods and ..."

"Yeah? And what?"

"I don't need to spell it out, Capuano."

Marty's hand slipped into his knife pocket. He was very jumpy now.

"You gonna take all this to the police?" Marty asked. "They'll laugh you right outa the station. You can't prove a damn thing."

"Where were you the night Jill was raped, then?"

"None of your damn business."

"Afraid to tell me?"

"I was bowling," Marty said. "I was bowling all night at McCarthy's."

"That's what you say!"

Marty folded his arms. "Okay, Sherlock. So you figured out all by yourself that I'm the guy who busted your girlfriend's cherry. I say you're full of crap."

"Deny it all you want, Capuano. I *know* you did it. And it's a lucky thing for you I'm not your kind of person."

"What do you mean by that crack?"

"I mean that if I was, I'd kill you myself. But I don't believe in taking the law into my own hands. I'll just let the wheels of justice run you down."

Marty stepped close to Cartwright. It would be so easy to whick out the blade and stuff it in his throat as he sat here perched on the porch rail. But it would also be a stupid move, out here in front of Marty's own house with Ma and Pa right inside.

Marty said, "I think I've had about enough jazz from you, Cartwright. The answer is no, I didn't touch your precious cherry-pie, and I don't like to be accused of crimes I didn't commit. So suppose you get the hell off my front porch, before I throw you off."

"I'm leaving," Cartwright said, standing up. He was almost a foot taller than Marty. "I won't clutter up your exclusive porch more than another half a minute. But I want to give you a warning before I go."

"Which is?"

"Thing'll go a lot easier for you if you turn yourself in. If you go to the police voluntarily, you might be able to get away with just a heavy jail sentence … instead of the electric chair."

Marty laughed.

"Laugh all you like. I'll give you three days, Capuano. Tomorrow, Thursday, and Friday. If you haven't turned yourself in by Friday night, I'm going to call Chief Nathanson and tell him I suspect you of organizing all the gang trouble that Jenkinsville has had lately … as well as having raped Jill. They'll pick you up on suspicion and grill you good, and you better have some pretty neat alibis."

"Get out of here," Marty said. "Man, you're crazy! You're all screwed up!"

"You're the crazy one, Capuano. You're a mad dog. But I'm giving you a break you don't deserve. Turn yourself in by midnight Friday … or I'll report you myself."

Without another word, Cartwright turned, and left. Marty watched the broad back retreating up the street, and had to fight back a compelling urge to run after Cartwright and plunge the knife deep between his shoulder blades.

That would be foolish. There were half a dozen witnesses sitting on porches across the street. It would be a sure ticket to the electric chair.

But there were other ways of getting rid of Cartwright.

Marty turned and went back into the house. As he passed the living room, his mother looked up and said, "Who was that boy you were talking with on the porch, Marty?"

"Nobody important. Just a guy I know."

"It sounded from in here like you were arguing with him."

"We were just kidding around, Ma."

Marty went up to his room and got some change to make a pay phone call. It wasn't safe to call from inside the house, where his folks might overhear. He wondered how much of the conversation with Cartwright his mother had been able to comprehend over the din of the TV set. Not much, he hoped. Not enough to give the show away.

He walked up the street to the malt shop, and without looking at anybody he went straight to the phone booths in back. He checked all the booths first, making sure there was no one in an adjoining booth who might overhear his end of the conversation he was about to have. At this stage, it was risky to talk too much. If Jim Cartwright had got so wise, others could too.

Marty dropped a dime in the slot and dialed Big Henry's number. Big Henry was home tonight, because his father was sick, or something like that. In his own peculiar way, Big Henry was a very loyal son—sometimes.

The phone rang four times before someone picked it up. A woman answered, sounding faint and distracted.

"Yeah?"

"Is Henry home?"

"Yeah. Just a minute."

The phone clattered down hard on a table in Big Henry's house, and Marty heard the woman hollering, "Henry! Henry, phone call!"

Half a minute later, Big Henry's voice said, "Yeah?"

"This is Marty."

"Oh. What's happening?"

"Listen, I just got a visit from Jim Cartwright a little while ago."

"Who the hell is he?" Big Henry asked.

"The basketball star, remember? The one that was going with Jill Webster."

"Oh," Big Henry said. "Yeah, now I remember. What the hell did he want?"

"He's wise, Henry."

"Whaddya mean, wise?"

"He's been snooping around town since his broad got the treatment. And he knows who did it."

"All of us?"

"No, just me. He knows I was the ringleader. He just came around my place to tell me so. And you know what else he told me? He told me he'll give me three days to go to the cops and turn myself in. If I don't go in by Friday night, he's going to tip 'em off to pick me up."

Big Henry was silent for a moment. Then he said, "You ain't gonna turn yourself in, are you, Marty?"

"You crazy?"

"Well, I don't know. If he's got the stuff on you ..."

"Listen, use your head," Marty said fiercely, gripping the receiver. "There was another guy who had the goods on us too. Not about the Webster chick, but the other stuff. You know what happened to him?"

"You mean Brewster? Sure. He ran out of town."

"Okay, Cartwright isn't any tougher than Brewster. We gotta get him out of town too."

"You mean, rough him up?"

"Cartwright's gotta go," Marty said, "Otherwise he'll rat to the cops, and they'll pick me up, and next thing you know they'll be picking you guys up too. So we gotta do something about this guy Cartwright, and we gotta do it before Friday."

"We gotta get him, huh?" Big Henry asked. There didn't seem to be much enthusiasm in his voice.

"Yeah, listen," Marty said. "You and me and Roger and Nick—the same guys who were in on the deal about the girl, none of the others. We'll go get Cartwright tomorrow night, after it gets dark, and we'll drive him out of town. And then we'll stomp on him. We'll bust him up good."

"I don't like it, Marty. We've done plenty already."

"Sure we have. And we'll fry for it, too, unless we take care of Cartwright. He's all hopped up on account of what happened to his girl. He was giving me some crap about how she was saving her body for when he married her."

"I dunno, Marty ..."

"To hell with what you dunno! There ain't no room for argument. Tomorrow night we get Cartwright and take him out of town and work him over. Maybe we cool him off completely. That way we can be absolutely safe. He's the only one so far who's put two and two together about me."

"Kill him?"

"You sound chicken."

"I'm worried."

"What for? You can only fry once. And you got enough going against you to get fried right now. The girl died as a result of the rape. A jury'll recommend the maximum for that. So you can't get any worse by doing something else." Marty paused, "You're in this as much as me, Henry. So don't go chicken on me now."

"Okay," Big Henry said reluctantly. "Tomorrow night we take care of Cartwright."

"Yeah. At the clubhouse, that's where we'll meet. Pass the word along to Roger and Nick. Just us four, hear, none of the others."

"Yeah, Marty."

"See you tomorrow."

"Yeah, Marty."

CHAPTER TWELVE

Marty was jumpy all the next day. He kept thinking about Jim Cartwright. The big basketball player was certain to go through with his threat of informing the cops, if he wasn't stopped.

Cartwright had no definite proof of anything, Marty knew. All he could do would be to give the fuzz his word that the dead girl had told him that Marty had been bugging her. Marty knew they couldn't pin a rape charge on him for that.

But once the cops got their hands on him, he was afraid they might be able to squeeze things out of him. He would be asked to explain where he'd been during the various times that trouble had cropped up in Jenkinsville. Sooner or later the cops would become positive that Marty really was the instigator of all the violence, and after that they would turn on the pressure to make him confess.

Cops were basically the same everywhere, Marty figured. They weren't heroes, but they'd work hard to make a suspect confess. And the potbellied creeps that passed for cops in Jenkinsville would be teed off at him because he'd been making monkeys out of them all summer. They'd work him over good, in hopes of restoring their prestige by producing the "master criminal."

Marty had heard about some of the things the New York cops did when they had a juvie who was hard to crack. They denied all charges of brutality, of course, but Marty knew they sometimes employed it, all the same. Stuff with rubber hoses, and hot matches, and workouts with bare fists, and fancier things, too, when necessary. They could fix a guy so he couldn't bang a girl for a month. Marty had heard stories that curled his hair. Of course, the fuzz always took care that there would be no marks on the suspect when he came to trial. But they got their confessions, when they really set out to get them.

These Jenkinsville cops didn't look that tough, but that was all the more reason to fear them. They looked comical on the streets, so they would want to appear big and bold when they had him helpless in the stationhouse. They would show no mercy, because he wasn't a long-time local resident but a despised outsider, an interloper from the jungles of New York.

So Jim Cartwright had to go. No matter how reluctant Big Henry and the others were to get involved in yet another act of violence, it was absolutely necessary to take care of the basketball player before he sang.

Suppose he had left a note somewhere, to be opened in the event of his death or disappearance? They would have to chance it. If they didn't get rid of him, they were sure to fry. If they did, at least they stood a fair chance of getting out with a whole skin. Even one chance out of ten was better than no chance at all.

Marty fidgeted. He didn't like the idea of a sword dangling over his head. He wished it was evening, so they could take off after Cartwright and end this damned uncertainty.

He kidded around at the clubhouse all day, grabbing a boob here, a butt there, sticking his hands up the skirts of a couple of girls and getting a good feel. He hid his anxiety behind a mask of playfulness. But he was worried, worried down deep.

After going home for supper, he returned to the clubhouse around seven. Hardly anyone was there yet. But they started trooping in, one at a time, as the evening wore on. Marty eyed them, watching them, sizing them up. He knew now that he still hadn't won their friendship. They went along with him because they were scared of him, not because they liked him personally.

To hell with them, he thought. The chicken bastards.

They had fought well at the rumble, but they had lost their courage right afterward. Chicken livers, all of them. And even now, Big Henry was scared stiff of eliminating the one guy who could put them all behind bars.

Marty fidgeted. Nick showed up, and Jolly Roger. No sign of Big Henry.

"Got the car outside?" Marty asked.

"Yeah," Jolly Roger said. He looked very grim. "It's all ready."

"And a full tank of gas? We may need to go a long way."

"Don't sweat it, Marty. We got enough gas in the tank."

Marty paced around. His nerves were hopping. He couldn't remember ever having been this jumpy before. But it was lousy, knowing there was somebody walking around in this town who could turn him in any time he wanted.

"Where's Big Henry?" Marty asked. "We can't start till he gets here."

"He'll be along soon," Jolly Roger said.

"Yeah," Nick chimed in. "He'll be here soon. His old man is sick, you know."

"Who gives a damn about his old man? We're gonna be in a big mess if we can't find that guy Cartwright."

"Don't sweat it," Jolly Roger said again. "Big Henry's gonna be here soon. And then we're gonna fix everything up just right."

Nick walked over to him. "You're all keyed up, Marty. It's no good, you being this jumpy. I never seen you like this before."

"You won't again, either."

"You gotta play it cool, man," Nick said, "Why don't you go upstairs and relax a little? We got plenty of time. Grab yourself a piece while you're waiting. It'll calm you down, Marty."

Marty considered that. "Yeah," he said, "Maybe you're right. It's still early. We got plenty of time."

He looked around the room. Laura, Big Henry's broad, was sitting there waiting for Big Henry to come in. She was curled up with her long legs showing, and her big breasts tight against her sweater.

Marty scowled. He had hot pants for that Laura chick. But tonight wasn't the right night to begin fooling around. He couldn't risk getting Big Henry teed off.

Tomorrow, he thought. After Cartwright had been taken care of, after things settled down again, he would arrange a little switch. Big Henry could have Mary Anne, and Marty would take over Laura. Marty didn't think Big Henry would make too much of a fuss over it. Deep down, Big Henry was chicken, like all the rest of these Barons. He would yield to Marty's wishes.

The door opened and Mary Anne walked in, as if on cue.

Nick whispered, "There she is. Go on, have some fun with her until Big Henry gets here, Marty."

"Okay, okay."

He glanced at Mary Anne. She looked good. She was wearing tight blue denim stretch pants that outlined every lush detail of buttocks and loins, and she had on a low-cut jersey-blouse that showed the meaty tops of her breasts. Marty felt the quivering thrust of desire shooting through him.

"Mary Anne," he said.

"Hi there, Marty."

"I been waitin' for you."

"Yeah?"

"How you feeling today?" he asked. "You all better?"

"Sure I am. You want to go upstairs with me, Marty?"

"Answer that one for yourself."

"Let's go," she said.

Marty grinned, "You musta read my mind." He walked over to her and fondly clapped his hands to her buttocks. He could feel the taut, exciting flesh beneath the blue denims.

He said to Nick and Jolly Roger, "I'm going upstairs for a while. If Big Henry comes, tell him not to come after me. I'll be down in about a half hour or so."

"Sure, Marty. We'll tell him."

Marty winked at them and put his arm around Mary Anne's shoulders. They went up the stairs together, and into his room— the room that was the exclusive property of Marty Capuano, boss of the Jenkinsville Barons.

He locked the door.

"It's been a long time," Marty said. "Almost a week."

"Yeah, Marty."

"I get fidgety as hell when I've gotta go without a woman for that long, Mary Anne. Another day, and I woulda been reaching out for somebody else."

"I wouldn't want you to do that, Marty."

"I didn't think you would," he said. He leaned against the door. "Suppose you let me get a look at the merchandise. I wanta make sure it's still all there."

She grinned, parting her moist, full lips, and in one lithe gesture she stripped off the jersey. She was wearing a half-bra underneath it, just a strip of cloth that supported her breasts up to the nipples. She took a deep breath, swelling her bosom, and unhooked the bra.

Marty's mouth began to water. Some of the tension that had gripped him all day began to ease at the sight of those pale-white, ruby-tipped breasts.

"Geez, you look good," he said.

"How about a kiss?"

"Take the rest of the stuff off first."

"First the kiss."

"Have it your own way," Marty said.

She glided across the room to him and pressed up against him. He slid his hands between their bodies and cupped her breasts, holding them tight, but not so tight that it would hurt her, gripping the nipples gently between his fingers. She panted a little, and glued her lips up against his, and suddenly her tongue was in his mouth, darting around like a live fish.

They stayed that way for a couple minutes, tongue against tongue. Then she broke away from him, and he saw the little beads of lust-sweat that were starting to pop out on the rounded globes of her breasts, and he saw the way her nipples were standing up, stiff and straight, inviting him to come satisfy her.

Her hands went around her back, and she unzipped her denims and stepped out of them. He helped her off with the panties. Naked, she wrapped herself around him from behind and started to unbutton his shirt, and after she got it off, she took off his trousers.

They went to the bed together and lay down side by side, intertwining their legs. Marty was in no hurry to finish things off. Big Henry could wait, Jim Cartwright could wait, the Jenkinsville police force could wait, the whole goddamn world could wait, for all he cared. All that mattered was that he was here on a bed with a naked blonde next to him, a naked blonde with bedroom eyes and bedroom thighs and everything else.

His hands stroked her body.

"Kiss me," she murmured.

He kissed her.

"Kiss me all over."

He showered her breasts, her belly with kisses. "Keep going."

He knew what she wanted. He kissed her there, and she sobbed in pleasure.

Then it was her turn to do the kissing, and Marty lay back, feeling the softness of her lips traveling over his body, thinking that this was the greatest, that maybe he would postpone making a play for Laura for a while. He hadn't gotten too tired of Mary Anne yet, after all, he decided. His hands roamed over her silky skin, toyed with the golden sleekness of her hair.

Suddenly she pressed herself up against him tight, body quivering ecstatically. Her thighs gripped his in a powerful embrace. Eyes shut, her hips began to move.

"Take me, Marty. Now!"

He started to obey. But suddenly there was a loud knock on the door—three booming thumps.

"Oh, no! What the hell ...?" Marty muttered.

The knocking had shattered the mood as effectively as a bomb, They separated. Marty felt himself shivering from the impact of the interrupted lovemaking. There was a fierce pain in his groin. Somebody's going to pay for this, he told himself.

"Who the hell's out there?" he demanded in an ugly voice.

"That you, Marty?"

"Yeah, it's me, Marty. That you, Henry?"

"Yeah, it's me."

"You dumb bastard, couldn't you wait till I got through in here?"

"Listen, man, this is important."

"I'm about to bang Mary Anne, and you got to come bang on the door. I could cut your guts out for that, you silly savage!"

"But this is real important, Marty."

"I told Nick to tell you to wait till I was through," Marty snapped, There's plenty of time to do the job tonight."

His loins ached. He started to turn back to Mary Anne, feeling the exquisite torture of having had his lovemaking interrupted just at the very moment he had been about to begin to slake his pent-up lust. Now everything was fouled up, but he could still satisfy himself before he went downstairs to deal with Big Henry.

But as he started to grip the nude girl, Big Henry called through the door, "I gotta talk to you right now, Marty. Open up, will ya?"

Marty scowled, "Listen, damn it! I ain't about to open that

goddamn door till I finish what I started in here. Just tell me what the hell's happening that's so special."

"It's your brother Frankie. He's downstairs here."

Marty sat up suddenly, his eyes wide open. This was unexpected. "Frankie? What the hell's that little fink doing here?"

"He wants to see you right away, Marty. He says some of the Dragons broke into your house a little while ago, and gave your folks a working over. He's waiting for you downstairs."

An explosive howl of anger burst from Marty's lungs. He sprang up from the bed and ran to the door, throwing it open, ignoring the fact of his own nakedness and of Mary Anne's. The girl huddled on the bare mattress, having nothing handy to cover herself with. She flushed bright red all over as Big Henry looked sharply at her. She flung one arm across her chest to cover the peaks of her breasts, and fanned her other hand out over the golden triangle of her loins.

Marty grabbed Big Henry's shoulder and yelled, "You better not be kiddin' me about this!"

"I wouldn't kid around when it's this serious," Big Henry said.

Marty cut loose a string of violent curses. Suddenly he wanted to kill again. Kill *all* the Dragons. Kill the whole damn bunch of them this time, not just five!

He thought of his Ma and Pa getting beat up in their own house. He clenched his fists.

From the bed, Mary Anne called, "Marty, you gonna leave?"

"I gotta. We'll finish what we started some other time."

She reached out for her clothing. Her rosebud-tipped breasts swayed. Big Henry was still looking at her.

"Ain't you ever seen a naked broad before?" Marty asked sharply.

"I never seen Mary Anne that way," Big Henry said. "Her skin's so pink ... such nice boobs ..."

"Leave her be. Did Frankie say my folks were hurt bad?"

"He didn't say. All he said was you better come in a hurry. That's why I came up here and banged on the door. I didn't want to bug you, but I figured you ought to know ..."

"Yeah, yeah."

"You ain't sore, Marty?"

"Sure I'm sore. Sore as all hell. But not at you. You did the right thing."

Marty was pulling on his trousers and his shirt as he talked. Mary Anne had snatched up her clothes and was using them to cover her nakedness until Big Henry left. The broad had a funny streak of modesty in her, Marty thought.

He zipped up his pants, shrugged into his jacket, and put his switchblade where it belonged, in his pocket.

He glanced at the huddled Mary Anne and took a quick grab of one firm buttock. "You better get your clothes on, kid."

"But Marty, I want you now! I'm all heated up ..."

"Well, cool off. And if you fool with anyone else while I'm gone, I'll kill you."

"Marty—"

"You just wait," he snapped at her.

"You all set, Marty?" Big Henry asked. "You got your blade and everything?"

"Yeah." He patted his knife pocket. "It's right here. Come on, let's go."

Big Henry opened the door. Marty went past him and started down the stairs, his face grim, his mind in a turmoil. He was in physical pain because of the interrupted lovemaking, and he was still jumpy about the Jim Cartwright threat. But this was the only thing he could really think about, now. His Ma and Pa, attacked by the Dragons! His blood was boiling!

If they hurt my folks, he thought furiously, I'll cut their lousy hearts out, every one of them. I'll kill them all. Every last lousy stinking Dragon bastard.

He ran into the middle of the downstairs room, already busily plotting the revenge he would wreak on the punks who had dared to bring the gang feud into his own home.

He stopped short, looking around for his brother, "Frankie? Where the hell are you?"

But there was no sign of Frankie anywhere. Marty's face went blank with puzzlement. What he saw, in place of his kid brother, was the complete membership of the Jenkinsville Barons. They were standing in a semi-circle, from one side of the room to the other. Their faces were set tight and hard.

Big Henry was standing behind him on the staircase. Marty looked around and said, "I thought my brother was down here. Where'd he go?"

"Your brother ain't here," Jolly Roger said.

"He ain't? Then where the hell is he? Why'd he leave so fast?"

"The truth is that your brother ain't never been here, Marty," Jolly Roger said.

Marty frowned, mystified. The place was very silent, and he didn't like the peculiar way all the Barons were standing facing him. And the debs were sitting way off to one side, as if there was going to be trouble and they wanted to be away from it when it happened.

"Look," Marty said, "Henry told me my brother was here, and that the Dragons had busted into my folks' place. Now—"

Suddenly arms shot around him from behind. Thick arms, strong as iron. The gorilla-like arms of Big Henry.

Marty writhed and struggled.

"Hey! Hey, what's going on here?" he yelled. "Let go of me, you big stupid bastard! You hear me? *Let go!*"

Marty squirmed, but Big Henry wasn't about to let go—and Big Henry's grasp was unbreakable when he didn't want to let go. Marty kicked, lashing out against Big Henry's shins with his heels, but Big Henry didn't seem to feel it. He kept both of Marty's arms pinned. Marty strained to get his arms free so he could go for his knife, but he couldn't manage it.

"Where's he got the blade?" Jolly Roger asked.

"In his right hip pocket," said Big Henry.

"Keep your cotton-pickin' hands away from my pockets!" Marty yelled hoarsely.

"You talking to me, little man?" Jolly Roger asked. He reached down into Marty's knife pocket and pulled out the switchblade.

Without his blade, Marty felt naked. The only time he was without his knife was when he was in bed or in the shower, and even then he always kept the knife close enough so he could reach it. Now he couldn't reach it.

An icy whirlpool of panic went racing round inside his stomach.

"What the hell's going on here?" he demanded, his voice rising shrilly. "What kind of gag you guys trying to pull?"

Jolly Roger said slowly. "No gag, Marty. We figured it was time we told you a few things, but we had to get your knife away first. You won't listen to nobody when you got that knife. Only now you gotta listen, man, because you can't shut your ears off."

"We been doing a lot of thinking about you," Nick said. "We been talking over the way you been running this gang, and we decided we don't like it."

"You don't, huh?" Marty started to relax a little. Maybe they weren't going to rough him up.

"We didn't like what you did to Tom Brewster," Jolly Roger said. "He was one of us, and we liked him. But you took his girl away, and you cut him up, and you made him turn chicken."

"Charley Beck was one of us too," Big Henry said from behind him, "We grew up with him. You cooled him off because he was in your way."

"Yeah," Lew Beekman said. "You killed poor ol' Charley cold, so you could take over the gang."

"Sure I killed him," Marty jeered. "And I killed five Dragons, too. I killed them all in fair stands. But you chicken bastards wouldn't understand that. Let go of me, damn you, Henry!"

"He'll let go of you when we're through talking to you," Jolly Roger said. "Now, about that girl, Jill Webster."

"Shut up about her!"

"No need to, now. Everybody here already knows how you made us grab her so you could rape her, and then she fell into the river and drowned."

"You were right there too, you lousy bastard. You banged her too!"

"Sure I did. Because you would have called me chicken if I hadn't. But that was a rotten thing to do, Marty."

"We're afraid of you, Marty," Nick Lorrey said. "You're too good with that knife. You're a wizard with that switchblade, man."

Marty couldn't help grinning as he was reminded of his old nickname, Marty the Wizard.

"Sure I'm good!" he shouted. "And I taught you guys! I drilled you, didn't I? Showed you everything I knew!" Suddenly he realized he might be pleading for his life. He was outnumbered by better than a dozen to one, and for once he had no blade to talk for him. "I helped you put the Dragons down. You couldn't go to the Orpheum before I took over. Now you can. Look, guys, cut this crap out."

"You took Brewster's deb away, and you cut him up," Big Henry said. "Next, you'll be wanting all the other debs too. I seen the way you been looking at Laura."

"And this Cartwright guy," Jolly Roger said. "You raped his girlfriend, and now you want to kill him. You're too much, Marty, too much of a menace!"

"You guys flipped or something? Look, we gotta move fast, or Cartwright will sing to the cops. We gotta take care of him."

"We ain't going nowhere, Marty," Jolly Roger said calmly.

"But if he squeals, you'll get fried too!"

"No, we won't, Marty," Big Henry said. "He don't know *we* were involved. Only *you*. He don't know who was with you."

"But *I* know. You think I'm gonna fry alone? I ain't gonna keep quiet!" Marty screamed.

"You ain't gonna tell nobody nothing," Big Henry said.

Nick Lorrey took up the accusations. "You treat us like you own us, like slaves, Marty. Killing and cutting, and there isn't a man of us who can stop you—alone. There isn't a man in the world who can beat you with a knife, Marty. You're *too* good. Like Brewster said—you just ain't human! It's the truth."

Marty felt the sweat cascading down his body. His loins still throbbed with desire. He thought of Mary Anne's breasts, with their ruby tips, and wished he was up there nestling between them right now.

"Let go of him," Jolly Roger said to Big Henry.

Big Henry's crushing grip eased.

Marty stood all alone in the middle of the floor. He was the shortest man in the room, and he felt even shorter without his knife. And suddenly he knew he was never going to get back upstairs to Mary Anne and spread her legs and glide into that hot, moist valley of delight. Not with her, not with any chick, ever again. He knew he wasn't going to get out of this room alive.

His heart raced. They couldn't do this to him! He was a big man, a wizard with the knife!

He quickly thought back over his career. The girls, the rumbles, the stands. He saw heaving breasts, glittering knives, fountains of blood.

"Gimme my knife back!" he jabbered. "Gimme the knife, and I'll show all you lousy bastards! I'll cut you all up!"

Jolly Roger laughed. "Sure you will. Maybe you'll kill us all. So we ain't giving you any knife to use, Marty. You're too dangerous when you got a blade in your hand."

"You gotta go," Big Henry said. "If we don't get rid of you, you'll keep on pushing us—right into more hot water than we're in already. This way, we get rid of you and let things calm down, and maybe we'll make it all right without any hassle from the cops."

Marty started to back away, toward the door, but the semi-circle closed and formed a solid ring of humanity around him. They each took one step forward, cutting down the space. Marty ran around the ring, looking for a weak man, looking for a way out.

There was no way out.

He tried to push at one of them, tried to break chain, but he got hurled back by stronger arms than his own.

Sweat drenched him. For the first time in his life he knew real fear—cold, green fear. He felt like puking.

"You can't do this to *me!*" he screamed. "I'm your pres! I'm Marty Capuano, the best bladesman there is!"

"That's just it, Marty," said Big Henry. "We been talking about that for a long time. And when you gave the word that you wanted to carve up Jim Cartwright, the gang met, and we decided we'd had it with you. You got to go. You're a menace to society."

"Who gives a damn about society? I showed you how to get good kicks, didn't I? You're just bugging me a little, ain't you? Seeing if you can make me lose my cool? It's all a joke. Say it's a joke!"

They didn't answer with words. Suddenly, fifteen switch blades clicked into position in fifteen hands. They took another step closer to him.

"Don't do it!" Marty whined. "I'll leave your debs alone! I'll do anything you want! Only don't cut me!"

A blade glistened high above him.

He heard Jolly Roger saying, "You were too sharp for your own good, Marty. You're too dangerous to live."

Marty tried to hang onto the last moment. His head whirled as he tried to remember what it was like to feel the softness of a naked girl, what it was like to wield power with his knife, what it was like just to be alive.

"Big man … I was a *big man*," he mumbled.

Jolly Roger lunged forward. Marty felt the cold metal like a hot icicle slicing through his flesh. Then a dozen knives descended at once, and Marty Capuano screamed and screamed—until he couldn't scream anymore.

THE END

THE EROTIC NOVELS OF ROBERT SILVERBERG

As by Loren Beauchamp
Love Nest (Midwood, 1958)
Another Night, Another Love (Midwood, 1959)
Connie (Midwood, 1959)
Unwilling Sinner (Midwood, 1959)
Meg (Midwood, 1960; reprinted as *All the Best Beds* as by Don Elliott, 1967)
Nurse Carolyn (Midwood, 1960; reprinted as *Registered Nympho* as by Don Elliott, 1967)
And When She Was Bad (Midwood, 1961)
Sin on Wheels (Midwood, 1961; reprinted as *Orgy on Wheels* as by Don Elliott, 1967)
The Fires Within (Midwood, 1961)
Campus Sex Club (Midwood, 1962)
Sin a la Carte (Midwood, 1962)
Strange Delights (Midwood, 1962)
Wayward Widow (Midwood, 1962; reprinted as *Free Sample*, 1968)
The Wife Traders (Boudoir, 1963)

As by Dr. Walter C. Brown
The Single Girl (Monarch, 1961)

As by David Challon
Campus Love Club (Bedside, 1959; reprinted as *Campus Sex Club* as by Loren Beauchamp, 1962)
French Sin Port (Bedside, 1959; reprinted as *Rouge of the Riviera* as by Don Elliott, 1967)
Suburban Sin Club (Bedside, 1959; abridged & reprinted as *The Wife Traders* as by Loren Beauchamp, 1963)
Thirst for Love (Bedside, 1959; reprinted as *Wayward Widow* as by Loren Beauchamp, 1962)
Man Mad (Chariot, 1960)
Suburban Affair (Bedside, 1960)

Campus Hellcat and Other Stories (Bedside, 1960)

As by John Dexter
Stripper! (Nightstand, 1960; reprinted as *One Bed Too Many* by Jeremy Dunn)
Sex Thieves (Nightstand, 1961; reprinted as *Wife in Name Only* by Jeremy Dunn, 1974)
Sin Festival (Nightstand, 1961; reprinted as *The Goddess Makers* by Jeremy Dunn, 1974)
The Bra Peddlers (Nightstand, 1961; reprinted as *The Venus Affair* by Jeremy Dunn, 1974)
The Lust Plotters (Nightstand, 1962)
Passion Bum (Nightstand, 1962)

As Walter Drummond
Philosopher of Evil: The Life & Works of the Marquis de Sade (nf; Regency, 1962)
How to Spend Money (nf; Regency, 1963)

As by Dan Eliot
Dial O-R-G-Y (Ember, 1963)
Flesh Flames (Ember, 1963)
Lust Lover (Pillar, 1963)
Nympho (Ember, 1963)
Sin Doll (Ember, 1963)
Sin Hellion (Ember, 1963)
Sin Mates (Pillar, 1963)

Don Elliott (all published by Greenleaf under various imprints)
Love Addict (1959)
Gang Girl (1959)
Naked Holiday (1960)
The Flesh Peddlers (1960; reprinted as *The Flesh Merchants*, 1973)
The Lecher (1960)
Mistress of Sin (1960; reprinted as *Depravity Town*, 1973)

Party Girl (1960)
  Sin on Wheels (1960; reprinted as
  The Instructor, 1973)
Passion Trap (1960; reprinted as
  Carnal Cage, 1973)
Sex Jungle (1960; reprinted as
  Jungle Street, 1973)
Convention Girl (1960; reprinted as
  The Man Collector, 1973)
Summertime Affair (1960)
Woman Chaser (1960)
Backstreet Sinner (1961; reprinted
  as *The Bed and the Beautiful*,
  1973)
Expense Account Sinners (1961;
  reprinted as *Keep the Clients
  Happy*, 1973)
Lust Goddess (1961; reprinted as
  The Temptress, 1973)
Lust Queen (1961; reprinted as *The
  Decadent*, 1974)
The Lust Seekers (1961; reprinted as
  Till Love Do Us Part, 1974)
Sin Club (1961; reprinted as *The
  Lady from Soho*, 1974)
Sin Cruise (1961; reprinted as
  Fifteen Nights of Love, 1973)
The Sinful Ones (1961; reprinted as
  Every Night in Rome, 1974)
Wild Divorcee (1961; reprinted as
  Nowhere Girl, 1973)
Streets of Sin (1961; reprinted as
  The Untamed, 1974)
Hotrod Sinners (1962)
Kept Man (1962)
Lust Captive (1962; reprinted as *The
  Game Susan Played*, 1974)
Lust Cat (1962)
Lust Cult (1962; reprinted as *None
  But the Wicked*, 1974)
Lust for Two (1962)
Lust Lord (1962)
Lust Market (1962)
No Lust Tonight (1962)
The Orgy Boys (1962)
Passion Thieves (1962)
Roadhouse Girl (1962; reprinted as
  No Pleasure So Painful, 1974)

Sex Fury (1962)
Sexteen (1962)
Shame House (1962)
Sin Bait (1962)
Sin Kin (1962)
Sin Quest (1962)
Sin Sick (1962)
Three Sinners (1962; reprinted as *A
  Change for the Bedder*, 1974)
Wild Flesh (1962)
Lust Crew (1963)
Passion Patsy (1963)
Sex Bait (1963)
Sex Bum (1963)
Sin Crazed (1963)
Sin Made (1963)
Sin Servant (1963)
Beatnik Wanton (1964)
Black Market Shame (1964)
Flesh Bride (1964)
Flesh Lesson (1964)
Flesh Melody (1964)
Flesh Pawns (1964)
Flesh Prize (1964)
The Flesh Seekers (1964)
Flesh Taker (1964)
Gutter Road (1964)
Lust Burns (1964)
Lust League (1964)
Lust Set (1964)
Lust Spree (1964)
Orgy Isle (1964)
Orgy Maid (1964)
Passion Pair (1964)
Passion Partners (1964)
Passion Trio (1964)
Pickup (1964)
Shameless (1964)
Sin Bin (1964)
Sin Circuit (1964)
Sin Partners (1964)
Sin Service (1964)
Sin Sold (1964)
Switch Trap (1964)
Wanton Web (1964)
Alternate Wife (1965)
Carnal Carnival (1965)
Escape to Sindom (1965)

Flesh Bigamist (1965)
Flesh Boarder (1965)
Flesh Cry (1965)
Flesh Man (1965)
Good Girl, Bad Girl (1965)
Lust Doomed (1965)
Lust Finale (1965)
Naked She Died (1965)
The Nite Lusters (1965)
Nudie Packet (1965)
Of Shame Reborn (1965)
Only the Depraved (1965)
Orgy Slaves (1965)
Passion Killer (1965)
Passion Peeper (1965)
Passion Pusher (1965; cover listed as
   by Don Holliday)
The Shame Protector (1965)
Shame Scheme (1965)
Sin for Solace (1965)
Sin Kill (1965)
Sin Spin (1965)
The Sin Switch (1965)
Sin Warped (1965)
The Sins of Seena (1965)
Teaser (1965)
Would-Be Sinner (1965)
The Young Wantons (1965)
All on Sunday (1966)
Big Blast (1966)
Campus Traders (1966)
Cousin Lover (1966)
Diary of Desire (1966)
Every Bed Her Own (1966)
The Gay Girls (1966)
Initiates (1966)
Lust Demon (1966)
One Night Stand (1966)
Pain Lusters (1966)
The Passion Barons (1966; reprint of
   Streets of Sin by Mark Ryan, 1959)
Take My Wife (1966)
The Virtuous Ones (1966)
All the Best Beds (1967)
Carnal Counselor (1967; ghost-
   written, author unknown)
Diary of a Dyke (1967)
Flesh Fever (1967)

Flesh Tryst (1967)
Orgy on Wheels (1967)
Registered Nympho (1967)
Rogue of the Riviera (1967)
Those Who Lust (1967)
The Wanton West (1967)

As by Marlene Longman
Sin Girls (Nightstand, 1960;
   reprinted as *The Tormented*, 1973)

As by Dan Malcolm
The Mystery of the Judge's Mistress
   (*Guilty*, March 1962)

As by Ray McKenzie
The Wild Party (Chariot, 1960)

As by Gordon Mitchell
Immoral Wife (Midwood, 1959;
   reprinted as *Henry's Wife*, 1961)

As by Mark Ryan
Company Girl (Bedside, 1959)
Streets of Sin (Bedside, 1959;
   reprinted as *The Passion Barons*
   as by Don Elliott, 1966)
Twisted Love, (Bedside, 1959;
   reprinted as *Strange Delights* as
   by Loren Beauchamp, 1962)
Savage Love (Bedside, 1960)
Illicit Affair and Other Stories
   (Bedside, 1961)

As by Stan Vincent
The Hot Beat (Magnet, 1960)

As by L. H. Walker
The Lascivious Abbott (Greenleaf,
   1967; introduction by L. T.
   Woodward)

As by L. T. Woodward, M. D.
Sex Fiend (Monarch, 1961)
Sex and Hypnosis (Monarch, 1961)
Sex in Our Schools (Monarch, 1962)
Virgin Wives (Monarch, 1962)
The Deceivers (Beacon, 1962)

90% of What You Know About Sex is Wrong (Parliament, 1962)

Sex and the Armed Forces (Monarch, 1963)

The History of Surgery (Monarch, 1963)

You and Your Sex Life (Monarch, 1963)

Twilight Women (Lancer, 1963)

Masochism (Monarch, 1964)

Sex and the Divorced Woman (Lancer, 1964)

Sophisticated Sex Techniques in Marriage (Lancer, 1967)

I Am a Nymphomaniac (Belmont, 1967)

THE SCIENCE FICTION WORKS OF ROBERT SILVERBERG

Novels

Revolt on Alpha C (Thomas Crowell, 1955; Scholastic, 1959)

The 13th Immortal (Ace, 1956)

Master of Life and Death (Ace, 1957)

The Shrouded Planet (with Randall Garrett, as Robert Randall; Gnome. 1957; Dell. 1963)

Invaders from Earth (Ace, 1958)

Lest We Forget Thee, Earth (as Calvin M. Knox; Ace, 1958)

Stepsons of Terra (Ace, 1958)

Aliens from Space (as David Osborne; Avalon, 1958)

Invisible Barriers (as David Osborne; Avalon, 1958)

Starhaven (as Ivar Jorgenson; Avalon, 1958; Ace, 1959)

Starman's Quest (Gnome, 1958)

The Plot Against Earth (as Calvin M. Knox; Ace, 1959)

The Dawning Light (with Randall Garrett, as Robert Randall; Gnome, 1959; Dell, 1963)

The Planet Killers (Ace, 1959)

Lost Race of Mars (Scholastic, 1960)

Collision Course (Avalon, 1961; Ace, 1961)

The Seed of Earth (Ace, 1962)

Recalled to Life (Lancer, 1962; revised version, Doubleday, 1972)

Blood on the Mink (written in 1959, first published in 1962 as "Too Much Blood on the Mink" in Trapped magazine, re-published by Hard Case Crime, 2012)

The Silent Invaders (Ace, 1963)

Time of the Great Freeze (Holt, Rinehart and Winston, 1964; Dell, 1966)

Regan's Planet (Pyramid, 1964)

One of Our Asteroids is Missing (as Calvin M. Knox; Ace, 1964)

Conquerors from the Darkness (Holt, Rinehart and Winston, 1965; Dell, 1968)

The Gate of Worlds (Holt, Rinehart and Winston, 1967; Magnum, 1980)

Planet of Death (Holt, Rinehart and Winston, 1967)

Thorns (Ballantine, 1967)

Those Who Watch (Signet, 1967)

The Time Hoppers (Doubleday, 1967; Avon, 1968)

To Open the Sky (Ballantine, 1967)

World's Fair 1992 (Follett, 1970; Ace, 1982)

The Man in the Maze (Avon, 1968)

Hawksbill Station (Doubleday, 1968; Avon, 1970)

The Masks of Time (Ballantine, 1968)

Nightwings (Avon, 1969)

Downward to the Earth (serialized in Galaxy, 1970; Signet, 1971)

Across a Billion Years (Dial, 1969; Magnum, 1979)

Three Survived (Holt, Rinehart and Winston, 1969)

To Live Again (Doubleday, 1969; Dell, 1971)

Up the Line (Ballantine, 1969)

Tower of Glass (serialized in Galaxy,

1970; Charles Scribner's Sons, 1970; Bantam, 1971)

Son of Man (Ballantine, 1971)

The Second Trip (Signet, 1971)

The World Inside (Doubleday, 1971; Signet, 1972)

A Time of Changes (serialized in *Galaxy*, 1971; Signet, 1971)

The Book of Skulls (Charles Scribner's Sons, 1971; Signet, 1972)

Dying Inside (serialized in *Galaxy*, 1972; Charles Scribner's Sons, 1972; Ballantine, 1972)

The Stochastic Man (Harper & Row, 1975; Fawcett, 1976)

Shadrach in the Furnace (Bobbs-Merrill, 1976; Pocket, 1978)

Homefaring (Phantasia, 1983)

Lord of Darkness (Arbor House, 1983; Bantam, 1984)

Gilgamesh the King (Arbor House, 1984; Bantam, 1985)

Sailing to Byzantium (Underwood-Miller, 1985; Tor, 1989)

Tom O'Bedlam (Donald I. Fine, 1985; Warner, 1986)

Star of Gypsies (Donald I. Fine, 1986; Popular Questar, 1988)

At Winter's End (Warner, 1988; Warner, 1989)

Project Pendulum (Walker, 1989; Bantam, 1989)

Letters From Atlantis (Atheneum, 1990; Popular Questar, 1992)

The New Springtime (Warner, 1990; Warner, 1991)

To the Land of the Living (Gollancz, 1989; Warner, 1990)

Nightfall (expansion of the 1941 novelette "Nightfall" by Isaac Asimov; Doubleday; 1990; Bantam, 1991)

Thebes of the Hundred Gates (Axolotl/Pulphouse, 1991; Bantam, 1992)

The Face of the Waters (Bantam, 1991; Bantam, 1992)

Child of Time (expansion and revision of the 1958 novelette "Lastborn" by Isaac Asimov; Gollancz, 1991; US edition, The Ugly Little Boy, Doubleday, 1992)

Kingdoms of the Wall (HarperCollins, 1992; Bantam, 1993)

The Positronic Man (based on the 1976 novelette The Bicentennial Man by Isaac Asimov; Gollancz, 1992)

Hot Sky at Midnight (Bantam, 1994; HarperCollins, 1994)

Starborne (Bantam, 1996; Voyager, 1996)

The Alien Years (HarperCollins, 1998; Harper Voyager, 1999)

The Longest Way Home (Gollancz, 2002; Harper Voyager, 2003)

Roma Eterna (Eos, 2003; Harper Voyager, 2004)

The Last Song of Orpheus (Subterranean, 2010)

Majipoor Chronicles

Lord Valentine's Castle (Harper & Row, 1980; Bantam, 1981)

Majipoor Chronicles (Arbor House, 1982; Bantam, 1983)

Valentine Pontifex (Arbor House, 1983; Bantam, 1984)

The Mountains of Majipoor (Bantam, 1995; Bantam, 1996)

Sorcerers of Majipoor (Macmillan UK, 1997; HarperPrism, 1997)

Lord Prestimion (Harper, 1999; Eos, 2000)

King of Dreams (Voyager, 2001; Eos, 2001)

Tales of Majipoor (Gollancz, 2013; Roc, 2013)

Short story collections

Next Stop, the Stars (Ace, 1962)
Godling, Go Home (Belmont, 1964)
Needle in a Timestack (Ballantine, 1966)
The Calibrated Alligator (Holt, Rinehart and Winston, 1969)
Dimension Thirteen (Ballantine, 1969)
The Cube Root of Uncertainty (Macmillan, 1970; Collier, 1971)
Parsecs and Parables (Doubleday, 1973)
Moonferns & Starsongs (Ballantine, 1971)
The Reality Trip and Other Implausibilities (Ballantine, 1972)
Valley Beyond Time (Dell, 1973)
Earth's Other Shadow (Signet, 1973)
Unfamiliar Territory (Charles Scribner's Sons, 1973; Berkley, 1978)
The Feast of St. Dionysus: Five Science Fiction Stories (Charles Scribner's Sons, 1975; Berkley, 1979)
Sunrise on Mercury (Thomas Nelson, 1975; Pan, 1986)
Capricorn Games (Random House, 1976; Starblaze, 1979)
The Best of Robert Silverberg (Pocket, 1976)
The Shores of Tomorrow (Thomas Nelson, 1976)
World of a Thousand Colors (Arbor House, 1982; Bantam, 1984)
The Conglomeroid Cocktail Party (Arbor House, 1984; Bantam, 1985)
Beyond the Safe Zone (Donald I. Fine, 1986; Warner, 1987)
The Collected Stories of Robert Silverberg Volume 1: Secret Sharers (Bantam, 1992)
Pluto in the Morning Light: The Collected Stories Volume 1 (Grafton, 1992)
The Secret Sharer: The Collected Stories Volume 2 (Grafton, 1993)
Beyond the Safe Zone: The Collected Stories Volume 3 (Grafton, 1994)
The Road to Nightfall: The Collected Stories Volume 4 (Grafton, 1996)
Ringing the Changes: The Collected Stories Volume 5 (Grafton, 1997)
Lion Time in Timbuctoo: The Collected Stories Volume 6 (Grafton, 2000)
Phases of the Moon (Subterranean Press, 2004),
In the Beginning: Tales from the Pulp Era (Subterranean Press, 2006)
To Be Continued: The Collected Stories Volume 1 (Subterranean Press, 2006)
To the Dark Star: The Collected Stories Volume 2 (Subterranean Press, 2007)
A Little Intelligence (with Randall Garrett; Crippen & Landru, 2009)
Something Wild Is Loose: The Collected Stories Volume 3 (Subterranean Press, 2008)
Trips: The Collected Stories Volume 4 (Subterranean Press, 2009)
The Palace at Midnight: The Collected Stories Volume 5 (Subterranean Press, 2010)
Multiples: The Collected Stories Volume 6 (Subterranean Press, 2011)
We Are for the Dark: The Collected Stories Volume 7 (Subterranean Press, 2012)
Hot Times in Magma City: The Collected Stories Volume 8 (Subterranean Press, 2013)
The Millennium Express: The Collected Stories Volume 9 (Subterranean Press, 2014)

NON-FICTION

Treasures Beneath the Sea
(Whitman, 1960)
Sir Winston Churchill (as by Edgar
Black; Monarch, 1961)
First American Into Space (Monarch
Books, 1961)
Lost Cities and Vanished
Civilizations (Chilton, 1962)
The Fabulous Rockefellers (1963)
Sunken History: The Story of
Underwater Archaeology (1963)
How to spend money (as by Walter
Drummond; 1963)
Fifteen Battles That Changed the
World (1963)
Empires in the Dust: Ancient
Civilizations Brought to Light
(1963)
Home of the Red Man: Indian North
America Before Columbus (1963)
The History of Surgery (1963, as L.
T. Woodward)
The Great Doctors (1964)
Man Before Adam: The Story of Man
in Search of His Origins (1964)
Akhnaten: The Rebel Pharaoh
(1964)
1066 (1964, as Franklin Hamilton)
The Loneliest Continent: The Story
of Antarctic Discovery (1964, as
Walker Chapman)
The Man Who Found Nineveh: The
Story of Austen Henry Layard
(1964)
Great Adventures in Archaeology
(1964)
Socrates (1965)
Scientists And Scoundrels: A Book of
Hoaxes (1965)
Men Who Mastered the Atom (1965)
Niels Bohr: The Man Who Mapped
the Atom (1965)
The Old Ones: Indians of the
American Southwest (1965)
The Great Wall of China (1965)
The World of Coral (1965)

The Crusades (1965, as Franklin
Hamilton)
Antarctic Conquest: The Great
Explorers in Their Own Words
(1966, as Walker Chapman)
The Long Rampart: The Story of the
Great Wall of China (1966)
Rivers: A Book to Begin On (1966, as
Lee Sebastian)
Forgotten by Time: A Book of Living
Fossils (1966)
Frontiers in Archeology (1966)
Kublai Khan: Lord of Xanadu (1966,
as Walker Chapman)
Leaders Of Labor (1966, as Roy
Cook)
Bridges (1966)
To the Rock of Darius: The Story of
Henry Rawlinson (1966)
The Hopefuls: Ten Presidential
Campaigns (1966, as Lloyd
Robinson)
The Morning of Mankind:
Prehistoric Man in Europe (1967)
The Golden Dream: Seekers of El
Dorado (1967, as Walker
Chapman)
The Auk, the Dodo and the Oryx
(1967)
The World of the Rain Forests (1967)
The Dawn of Medicine (1967)
The Adventures of Nat Palmer
(1967)
Challenge for a Throne: The Wars of
the Roses (1967, as Franklin
Hamilton)
Men Against Time: Salvage
Archeology in the United States
(1967)
Light for the World: Edison and the
Power Industry (1967)
The Search for Eldorado (1967, as
Walker Chapman)
Sophisticated Sex Techniques in
Marriage (1967, as L. T.
Woodward)

Mound Builders of Ancient America: The Archeology of a Myth (New York Graphic Society, 1968); reprint (Ohio University Press, 1986) - Silverberg's fourth-most widely held work in WorldCat libraries

The World of the Ocean Depths (1968)

The Stolen Election: Hayes vs. Tilden, 1876 (1968, as Lloyd Robinson)

Four Men Who Changed the Universe (1968)

Sam Houston (1968, as Paul Hollander)

The South Pole: A Book to Begin On (1968, as Lee Sebastian)

Stormy Voyager (1968)

Ghost Towns of the American West (1968)

Vanishing Giants: The Story of the Sequoias (1969)

Wonders of Ancient Chinese Science (1969)

The Challenge of Climate: Man and His Environment (1969)

Bruce of the Blue Nile (1969)

The World of Space (1969)

If I Forget Thee, O Jerusalem (1970)

The Seven Wonders of the Ancient World (1970)

Mammoths, Mastodons and Man (1970)

The Mound Builders (1970)

The Pueblo Revolt (1970)

Clocks for the Ages: How Scientists Date the Past (1971)

To The Western Shore: Growth of the United States 1776-1853 (1971)

Before The Sphinx: Early Egypt (1971)

Into Space: A Young Person's Guide to Space (1971, with Arthur C. Clarke)

The Realm of Prester John (1972)

The Longest Voyage: Circumnavigation in the Age Of Discovery (1972)

John Muir, Prophet Among the Glaciers (1972)

The World Within the Ocean Wave (1972)

The World Within the Tide Pool (1972)

Drug Themes in Science Fiction (1974)

Reflections and Refractions: Thoughts on Science Fiction, Science and Other Matters (1997)

Musings and Meditations (2011)